A Different Kind of Blues

This Large Print Book carries the
Seal of Approval of N.A.V.H.

A Different Kind of Blues

Gwynne Forster

THORNDIKE PRESS
A part of Gale, Cengage Learning

Farmington Hills, Mich • San Francisco • New York • Waterville, Maine
Meriden, Conn • Mason, Ohio • Chicago

This is a work of fiction. Names, characters, places, and incidents either are the product of the author's imagination or are used fictitiously, and any resemblance to actual persons, living or dead, business establishments, events, or locales is entirely coincidental.
Thorndike Press® Large Print African-American.
The text of this Large Print edition is unabridged.
Other aspects of the book may vary from the original edition.
Set in 16 pt. Plantin.

LIBRARY OF CONGRESS CATALOGING-IN-PUBLICATION DATA

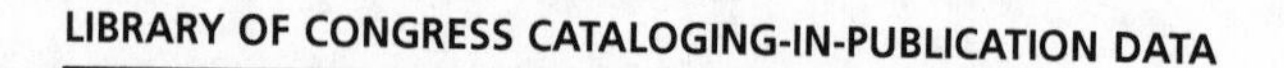

Names: Forster, Gwynne.
Title: A different kind of blues / Gwynne Forster.
Description: Large print edition. | Waterville, Maine : Thorndike Press, 2016. | ©2008 | Series: Thorndike Press large print African-American
Identifiers: LCCN 2015039330 | ISBN 9781410485052 (hardback) | ISBN 1410485056 (hardcover)
Subjects: LCSH: African American women—Fiction. | Large type books. | BISAC: FICTION / African American / General.
Classification: LCC PS3556.O742 D54 2016 | DDC 813/.54—dc23
LC record available at http://lccn.loc.gov/2015039330

Published in 2016 by arrangement with Dafina Books, an imprint of Kensington Publishing Corp.

Printed in Mexico
1 2 3 4 5 6 7 20 19 18 17 16

ACKNOWLEDGMENTS

My thanks to Carol Joy Smith, who I first saw sitting on a high stool in the office of our university dean and who has been a true friend ever since. Through my personal triumphs and times of happiness and at the transition of each member of my paternal family, Carol has been there for me. My thanks also to my husband, who is ever my solid rock.

Chapter One

Petra Fields sat on her back porch that early June evening, fanning the unseasonable Ellicott City, Maryland, heat, drinking sweetened ice tea, and playing cutthroat pinochle with her two friends, Lurlene Bruce and Twylah Hill. In her thirty-six years, she didn't remember experiencing such unbearable heat.

"Girl, I sure am glad you left your cigarettes home," Petra said to Lurlene. "Smoke gives me a headache."

"Everything gives you a headache," Lurlene said and threw out the ace of spades, trumping Twylah's ace of hearts. "You didn't used to complain so much."

"I don't complain unless you're smoking. Everybody with any sense has quit."

Lurlene raked in a winning sixty-four points, folded her cards, and stacked them in front of her, an indication that she didn't intend to play any longer. "Now you get off my case, girl. I'm trying to quit, and the least you can do is help by not mentioning the word 'smoke.' I wish you'd go see a doctor about those headaches. It's probably that job of yours stressing you out."

"Yeah, my boss is to die for," Petra said, looking skyward and pretending to swoon. "I ache just thinking about him, and I have to watch his idiot secretary crawling all over him, hugging him, and doing everything but you know what. The man's married, but does that tart care? Lord, forgive me."

"What you need to do is pray," Lurlene said. "You're in church every time the door opens, but you're as big a sinner as I am."

Petra looked toward the ceiling and rolled her eyes. "I'm not sinning when I tell the truth. That girl is a tart."

"Now don't y'all start dragging that poor girl's name through the mud," Twylah said. "For all you know, she ain't doing a thing more than you see."

"I gotta be going," Lurlene said. "It's hot, and I wanna get out of these clothes. One of these days after I get rich, I'm gonna have everything I own air-conditioned, starting with my brassiere."

"Me too," Twylah said, "not to mention a few other garments. Y'all want to play after work tomorrow?"

"I can't," Petra said. "Right after work, I have an appointment to get my annual checkup. Dr. Barnes is so self-important that he makes you pay if you miss an appointment. We can play day after tomorrow. Okay?"

Lurlene pulled air through her front teeth. "Barnes makes me sick with his prissy self. If he was practicing in Baltimore or Washington, he wouldn't make a living. See y'all day after tomorrow."

Twylah released a guffaw. "My daddy says Barnes is in cahoots with Ken Woods, the undertaker over on Pratt Avenue. He said Woods ought to give Barnes a percentage of what he takes in."

Petra didn't care for those sentiments. "Everybody knows Barnes isn't a genius," she said in a voice suggesting boredom with the topic, "but he's the only black doctor in this part of town, and we have to support our own."

Minutes after Petra arrived at work the following morning, Jack Watkins, her boss and head of Watkins Real Estate Agency, called her to his office. "Have a seat, Petra. This will only take a couple of minutes," he said in what appeared to her as cold and unfeeling tones.

Petra sat down, but she didn't lean back in the chair; indeed, she sat ramrod straight, pressed her elbows to her sides, and waited for the ax to fall. "Yes, sir."

When he raised an eyebrow, she remembered that she hadn't addressed him as "sir" in at least seven years. "I'm promoting you from receptionist to office manager as of today, and you'll get an additional fifty a week. That means you have your own office."

She closed her mouth, thanked him, and managed to get out of his office without dancing like a wild woman. Then, she cleaned out her desk and moved into her new office. Petra remembered to telephone her mother with the news that she'd just gotten a two hundred dollar a month raise, and her chest seemed to swell to twice its size. Oh, how she enjoyed telling that to her mother, the woman who said she'd never amount to much, that she had sacrificed a good life for a few minutes of sex with a man she thought so little of that she didn't even tell him she was pregnant with his child. Forty-two thousand dollars a year was at least proof that she wasn't a failure.

"You deserve every bit of it," her mother said. "You're a hard worker, and I'm proud of you."

Petra caught Jack and his secretary holding hands in the coffee-room pantry. Knowing that he wouldn't object because he was vulnerable, she asked him if she could leave half an hour early to keep her doctor's appointment.

"Sure," he said. "For half an hour, you don't have to ask. Just let me know ahead of time."

She left work at four o'clock, stopped at Orchid Nails, got a manicure, and arrived at the doctor's office promptly at five-fifteen. After a lengthy exam and several tests, she looked at her watch. Seven o'clock. He still hadn't told her to get dressed. At a quarter of eight, he came into the little cubicle, where she lay freezing in a thin white gown, treated her to his patented smile and said, "That's all for today. I expect you're exhausted from these tests. Drop by tomorrow after work, and I'll give you the test results."

Didn't he care that she'd been freezing in that over-air-conditioned office for nearly three hours? With chattering teeth, she tried to smile. "I'm more tired and hungry than exhausted. I'll see you tomorrow." She dressed and left, wondering how doctors managed to diagnose a patient's illness before they had access to high-powered

MRI and CAT scan testing machines.

As soon as she left the doctor's office, she called Lurlene and Twylah and canceled their date for the next afternoon. Apart from some annoying headaches, nothing was wrong with her; she was only thirty-six years old and hadn't taken a day of sick leave from work in at least four years. She wished Reginald Barnes didn't have to seem so important, but at least she only had to see him once a year. Recently, she'd been tempted to switch to Dr. Meredith, the white doctor who some of her acquaintances used, but she believed in supporting her people when she could.

Buoyed by her promotion and the additional two hundred dollars a month income, she decided to eat dinner at The Trolley Stop Restaurant on Oella Avenue, a few blocks from the Benjamin Banneker Museum. Her daughter, Krista, was at her grandmother's, so she didn't have to cook if she didn't want to. After a steak dinner, she passed a movie theatre on her way home and, on an impulse, decided to see the movie. At last, she could afford to splurge occasionally. Life was good, and she'd been waiting a long time to say that. Then she went home, kicked off her shoes, and turned on the television. With Krista away, she didn't have to watch the BET channel with its tasteless messages. Steve Harvey's jokes were more to her taste.

The next morning, Petra decided to go to her doctor's office on her lunch hour instead of after work so that she could meet with her girlfriends, provided they hadn't made other plans. "Hadn't expected you till later today," the doctor's receptionist said when Petra walked in. "Have a seat, and I'll get your test results."

Petra sat down, picked up a copy of *The Maryland Journal* from the table beside her, and began to read.

"Come in, Ms. Fields, and have a seat."

She looked up and saw Dr. Barnes standing just inside the door of his private office. "How are you feeling?"

"I'm fine," she said, sat down and crossed her knees.

"Any pains in your head?"

Petra stared at him. Why would he ask her about headaches now? She hadn't mentioned her headaches to him, because he hadn't previously asked. "Uh . . . yes. Sometimes, they're very unpleasant."

"Hmm. I can imagine." He pulled up a chair, sat with his knees almost touching hers, and took her hand. "I'm afraid the news isn't good."

She lunged toward him. "What do you mean? There's nothing wrong with me," she said, her voice rising. *"Is there?"*

He nodded his head up and down. "I'm sorry to tell you that you have a brain tumor, and it's inoperable. You've got four to six months left."

"What?" she screamed. He repeated it.

Petra jerked her hand out of his and jumped up. "You're lying. You don't know a damned thing about medicine. You're making this up to sound important. I knew I should have gone to another doctor."

"Petra, please. I know this is difficult for you. It's hard for me to have to tell you this, and I'd give anything if I didn't have to do it."

"I don't believe you. You don't know what you're talking about." She tried to control her trembling lips and to ignore the tears that cascaded from her eyes and dripped down her dress. He reached out to console her, and her fists pounded his chest. "Leave me alone. Just get away from me," she hissed as anger furled up in her. Anger at the doctor, at Providence, and at life. Helplessly, she sank into the chair, devastated.

"Miss Parks," Barnes said to his receptionist, "please get Ms. Fields some water." He turned back to Petra. "At least you know," he said, "and you can put your affairs in order. I'd do that right away."

Petra gazed at the man who had just taken away her hope for the future. "Put my affairs in order? Is that what you say I should do? I don't have any affairs, Doctor. I don't owe anybody a cent. I pay my bills at the end of the month, and I never buy more than I have money to pay for."

Barnes cleared his throat. "Well, there're final arrangements to be made, and you can spare your mother and Krista the need to take care of all that."

"Final arrangements. What do I care about final arrangements? If they want to dress me up and put me on display, that's their business. I want no part of it. Thanks for nothing." She stared at the astonished man. "And you be sure you don't leave here before I do. All you doctors know is how to stick your hands out for money. You're as greedy as a hookworm in a large intestine and just as useful."

She walked out of the office without looking back. Never mind his hard-and-fast rule that bills should be paid when service was rendered, or that her home was not within walking distance. She struck out down Oella Street with tears obscuring her vision, not considering the direction or the distance, unaware even that she walked. Her cell phone rang, but she didn't connect the sound to the gadget in her pocketbook. It rang continuously and, irritated by the noise, she looked around for a way in which to quell it and realized that the sound came from her phone and that she had walked all the way to the Patapsco River. She sat on a bench several yards from the river's grassy edge and answered the phone.

"Petra, this is Jack. Where the hell are you? My two agents have closings, and I have to check out a store that's just been put up for sale. Get the hell back here."

Simultaneous with Jack's demand, a sharp pain settled in the top of her head, not worse than any other she'd had, but sufficient to remind her of what she faced. She took a deep breath, closed the cell phone, and put it back into her purse.

Drops of rain soon escalated into a shower, and she put on the plastic rain hat that she always carried in her pocketbook and scampered through the wet grass to the old B&O Railroad Station. She stood on the ancient platform waiting for the rain to ease up and through her mind flashed the things she had dreamed of doing, the places she had always wanted to go, the experiences she'd never had.

"Why me?"

"What did you say, miss?" a man who stood nearby asked her.

She shook her head. "Nothing. I was talking to myself." Petra didn't know the man and didn't want to talk with him or with anyone else, so she ran across Maryland Avenue to the drugstore and phoned for Well Tried Taxi. Half an hour later, she walked into her house.

"Where've you been in this rain, Mom?" her daughter Krista asked, greeting her with a kiss as she usually did. "You're soaking wet."

She had to decide whether to tell her mother and Krista about the doctor's diagnosis; but looking at seventeen-year-old Krista, whose eyes sparkled with hope and dreams, she couldn't do it. For nearly eighteen years, it had been her and Krista. After Krista's birth, Petra moved out of her mama's home as soon as she could save enough money for a down payment on a house of her own. It hadn't been easy raising a child alone, especially not one as precocious as Krista, but her daughter was the joy of her life.

The sound of rain against the window

brought her back to the present. "I didn't have an umbrella," Petra said, stating the obvious.

"You're snowing me, Mom."

Petra hugged her daughter, now developed into a beautiful young woman. "Am not," she said, fighting back tears. "You're home from school early. Feel like making some chili con carne? Nobody makes it like you do."

"Okay, I'll put it on, but can you look after it and cook the rice? I have a lot of homework. By the way, Reverend Collins called to ask if you'd do the church bulletin this week. He said something's wrong with his computer."

"Something was wrong with his computer last week. If he wants me to be responsible for the bulletin, he should say so."

"It's not much, Mom, and he knows he can depend on you."

"All right. I'll go down there and get his copy." She didn't feel like eating or preparing that bulletin or pretending that life went on as usual. It didn't. At least not for her. In six months, she wouldn't be there. And she didn't much feel like hearing any of the reverend's pious words. What meaning did they have for her?

After changing into dry clothing, she

walked four blocks to the parsonage of the Disciples Church and knocked on the door. "I didn't expect you so soon," the Reverend Jasper Collins said to Petra. "Come in while I . . . What's the matter?" For a man in his eighth decade of life, his youthful looks buttressed by thick hair not fully gray, and Jasper Collins didn't look a day over sixty. He peered at her over his wire-rimmed glasses. "Something's wrong with you, Petra. You look like you lost your best friend. Minnie, could you bring us a pot of tea, please," Collins called to his wife. To Petra, he said, "I'm not prying, but it may help to talk about it. Nothing you say will go any farther than my ears. Is it a man?"

Petra shook her head. "I wish it was, Reverend. You don't know how badly I wish it was a man. I could deal with that."

He bowed his head. "Let us pray." She bowed her head, but his words didn't soothe her as they did in the weekly Wednesday prayer services when she left the meetings spiritually renewed.

After the prayer, he said, "Now tell me what the problem is."

Minnie placed before them a tray containing a tea service for two and several slices of coconut cake, smiled at Petra, and left the room. Petra poured a cup of tea, added sugar, and took a small sip. How could she make herself utter the words? If she said them, she would believe them, and she couldn't do that. But the preacher, being a man of God, might be able to help her. The TV preachers healed people. Maybe he could, too.

She leaned back in the chair. "Yesterday, my boss gave me a fantastic raise, and I didn't even have to ask for it." Her voice broke at the same time that he smiled and said, "Wonderful. I'm glad to hear that. So what —"

She interrupted him. "Today, less than twenty-four hours later, when I thought I had the world by the tail, Dr. Barnes told me that I have less than six months to live."

"He what?!"

"You heard me correctly. He advised me to get my affairs in order and to do it soon."

The reverend's lower lip sagged. He rubbed his hands together and shook his head from side to side. "My Lord!"

"I don't know what to do. I'm not going to tell people and have them feeling sorry for me."

"No, I guess you wouldn't want that. Are you sure that's what Reggie Barnes said?"

"Yes, sir. That's what he said, and he'd just read the results of my tests."

"Hmm. I see. Well, sister, it's a bitter pill, but in some ways you're being blessed." She glared at him and stood, prepared to leave his house in a huff. "Now, now. Sit back down. No point in getting angry. You have a chance to get your life in order and put yourself right with your Maker. Not many people have this chance. If you want to be forgiven for your sins, you have to forgive everybody who's wronged you and ask forgiveness of everybody you've wronged."

She didn't like the sound of that, but she knew that, like many holiness preachers, Pastor Collins meant what he said. "I don't remember all the times I wronged someone," she told him. "So what will I do?"

"Make a list." He left the living room, returned a few minutes later with the material for the bulletin, and handed it to her.

"I feel like doing all the things I always wanted to do, seeing places I wanted to see."

"Go ahead and do that, so long as it's nothing bad," he said. "But first, seek forgiveness from those you've wronged and forgive the ones who've wronged you. Mark my word. You can't afford not to do this."

"Yes, sir."

He walked with her to the door. "I'll be praying for you, child."

Petra looked up at the tall, distinguished

man and suddenly envied him his great age. "You can tell the Lord about this, since I guess he can keep a secret, but not anybody else, please," she said. "I'm not even going to tell my family."

He raised an eyebrow. "We'll discuss that another time."

At home, Petra walked into her kitchen and looked around. Nothing had changed. The uncluttered countertops sparkled; the stainless steel sink shone as if it had just been polished; and the eleven-year-old stove looked as if it had never been used. She shook her head and sat down on a stool beside the window. For eighteen years, her life had been like her kitchen. But to what end, and did it matter?

She got up, measured one and three quarters of a cup of water for a cup of rice, put it on to cook and sat down to list the names of people she thought she had wronged, beginning with incidents in her childhood. She soon tired of it, mainly because the exercise led her to realize that she shouldn't think herself superior to some people who she regarded as her inferiors. Petra did not and never had enjoyed self-examination, though she had many commendable habits. But she had some bad traits, too, knew it, and did nothing to change them.

She stirred the chili, put the list aside, and chopped tomatoes and green peppers to make salsa. Who would take care of Krista? Her mother — Krista's grandmother — was a licensed practical nurse, and although she could take care of herself easily, she didn't earn enough to do that and send Krista to college.

"If only I had been more frugal," Petra said to herself. But how much more could she have pinched and stinted? She'd worn the same pair of shoes daily for nearly a year and had had them repaired twice, and she only owned one coat.

"Is the chili ready, Mom? I have to finish this report tonight, and I intend to get an A. Top grades mean college scholarships. Right, Mom?"

"They sure do, honey, and if any student gets one, I know you will. I'm chopping vegetables for salsa, and as soon as this is ready, we'll eat. Hmmm. This chili smells good."

Petra set the table, called Krista, and sat down to eat. She didn't feel like eating, but she couldn't afford to alarm her daughter. She'd been blessed with a wonderful child, respectful and obedient, for which she was grateful, and she wanted their relationship to remain warm for as long as she lived. But when she thought of what she had to tell her daughter, goose pimples popped out on her flesh. She resisted a sudden urge to get up from the table and hug her only child, for that would alarm Krista.

"You're not eating, Mom, and this is the best chili I've made in ages," Krista said.

"I know, but I ate cake down at Reverend Collins's house, and you know how Miss Minnie insists you eat."

"Tell me about it. You should have brought me a piece. It wouldn't curtail my appetite."

"No. You could eat two cakes and not gain an ounce." She looked at her lovely daughter, seventeen years old, beautiful hair and complexion, her father's bedroom eyes, and a near-perfect size ten body. "Well, I'd better put this bulletin together. You know how nervous Reverend Collins is about his church bulletin. But you go finish your homework. I'll clean the kitchen."

"You sure you don't mind?" Krista asked her, for she considered it her job to clean the kitchen after meals and never left the chore to Petra.

" 'Course not. You take care of your studies."

Petra cleaned the kitchen, typed out the bulletin, and looked around for something else to do. She was in trouble at work, but she didn't care. Only yesterday, it promised her so much, but now. . . . Nothing. She went back to the kitchen and got her list. She had to tell her daughter the truth and ask her forgiveness, and she doubted anything else would cost her so dearly. But she couldn't do it until after Krista turned in her term papers and took her final exams. That meant she had to be a consummate actress at least for the next two weeks. And she had to make up an excuse for Jack.

I know what I'll do. I'll go on the church's annual retreat to Ocean City next week. Mama will be glad to stay with Krista, and, once I get to Ocean City, I won't have to talk to a soul or do anything else that doesn't suit me.

"You got some explaining to do," Jack said when she walked into the office the following morning. "What the hell happened to you?"

Might as well put her cards on the table. "While I was out to lunch, I got some bad news. I freaked out."

"It had to be awful for you to act like that. Not only did you walk out and leave your computer on and your desk unlocked, but you hung up on me."

"I did *what*? When did you call me?"

Jack threw up his hands. "All right. I hope you get it straightened out. One day I give you a nice raise, and the next day you do something you never did before. I put some stuff on your desk, and I need it before you leave today."

"I'll get right to it." She thought for a second. Might as well ask him now. "Jack, I need next week off. I know it's a month earlier than I usually take vacation, and I'm not giving you much notice for this, but I can't help it, Jack. I don't have a choice."

He stared at her until she thought she would wither from the heat of his gaze. "I suppose this is connected with the problems you got yesterday." She nodded. "All right, but leave your desk clean."

"Thanks. I can't tell you how much I appreciate it."

"Get yourself straightened out." He said it in a gruff tone, but she knew he cared. If only she *could* straighten it out.

"How long is the retreat, Mom?" Krista asked Petra as her mother closed her suitcase and got ready to leave.

"Ten days. That means I'll be back for your graduation. I know you always like it when Grandma stays with you. You can call me if you have any problems, but I'm sure you and Mama can handle everything. It's good Mama will be here, because she's making your dress for the graduation gala." Nervous chatter, and she realized Krista knew it.

"Oh, she's finished with that. You have a good time, and don't come back with that long face you've been carrying around here for the last couple of days." Krista paused. "You sure you're okay?"

Petra's eyebrows shot up. To her knowledge, Krista was not a worrier. "Sure I am. You and Mama have a good time eating catfish, collards, and cornbread. I'll call you."

Petra hugged her daughter, and when Krista stepped back and looked at her quizzically, she knew she had communicated to Krista her sense of desperation. Quickly, she pasted a smile on her face and said, "I've never been to one of these retreats, and I haven't the slightest idea what I'm getting into."

Krista's relief was evident in the slow deep breath that she took before returning Petra's hug. "Get outta here, Mom, before you miss that bus."

Petra took the single seat opposite the bus driver, closed her eyes, and went to sleep, the first time she'd slept soundly since learning of her illness. She did not want to spend three hours making small talk with someone with whom she had nothing in common except membership in the same church.

The bus arrived at the hotel in Ocean City shortly after noon, and she got out, gazed at her surroundings, and thought how much she would have enjoyed being there in different circumstances. She registered, went to her room and looked out at the enormous stretch of water and the numerous sailboats that it accommodated and decided that she would enjoy herself. Everybody had to die; most people just didn't know when. She put on her bikini bathing suit and a pair of dark glasses, put a book and a towel in a tote bag, grabbed her beach umbrella, and headed for the beach.

With the sun still high, a cool breeze drifted in from the ocean. She was about to relax when she remembered that she hadn't told Lurlene and Twylah that she'd be away for a few days. What else had she screwed up in the last couple of days? They began meeting at her house and playing cards to encourage Lurlene in her attempt to quit smoking. To Lurlene's way of thinking, Petra had probably committed a crime, for her friend counted on their card-playing sessions — when she wasn't allowed to smoke — to ease her withdrawal from cigarettes.

She took out her cell phone and dialed Twylah's number. "Girl, where are you? Your mama said you went off on some church retreat. I can't imagine you doing such a thing. Who's on this retreat other than you and the preacher?"

"About thirty other sisters and brothers. The preacher must be eighty if he's a day, so don't worry about Reverend Collins. I forgot to let you and Lurlene know. My boss gave me permission Friday, and I had to hustle to get ready to leave Saturday. Mama's staying with Krista."

"I know that, Petra. I called there and talked with your mama. She said you hadn't been acting right. And don't let that preacher's age fool you; my mama was born when my granddaddy was seventy-eight."

"I don't know what Mama could mean by that. Till she came over to my house this morning, I hadn't seen her in a little over a week. And another thing: I wouldn't care if Reverend Collins was born ready to go; he's too holy for my taste."

Twylah's whistle irritated Petra's ear. "You ain't in a good mood," her friend said.

"Never mind that, Twylah. You keep up

with Lurlene; I'd hate it if she went back to smoking."

"Yeah. Me, too. See you when you get back."

Petra's lower jaw dropped when the Reverend Collins sat down beside her. "Mind if I share your umbrella for a few minutes?"

She told him that she didn't.

"Are you at this retreat to escape, or are you seeking spiritual renewal?"

Lying was not a sin that she could afford, so she told him the truth. "I'm trying to get my act together, escaping, you might say."

"Have you begun asking forgiveness of people you've wronged? You have to do it."

"I know. I want to talk to my daughter first, but I have to wait till after her exams and graduation. It wouldn't be right to upset her now when she's trying to graduate."

"That's right. So ask the next person on your list. You did make out a list, didn't you?"

"Yes, sir, and it's a long one."

"Then I'd say the sooner you start, the better. If you need help, come see me."

"Yes, sir. I think I've had enough of this sun. Maybe it's better early mornings."

"Yes, it is. Why don't you take a trip on

one of those big cruisers? You might enjoy it."

Until he joined her, she had managed to think of something other than her illness. She jumped up and gathered her things, glad to get away from the man. "Thanks. I will," she said.

Several hours later, she found herself on the big cruise ship, *Tanga.*

She wasn't much of a gambler, but she spent half an hour at a slot machine and managed to lose only three dollars. Of course, she'd had about eighty dollars in winnings at one time and gambled it away. No more of that for her. She went to the buffet restaurant, paid the required twenty-five dollars, and spent the next hour eating.

"I don't care if I get fat," she said to herself and made up her mind to find a good homemade caramel cake and eat every bit of it. At worst, it would make her sick, and she didn't care about that, either. She wandered to the upper deck, watched the line dancers, and decided to move on.

"Come on," a male voice said. "It's fun, and you look as if you could use some." When the disc jockey played "Boot Scootin' Boogey," the revelers filled the dance floor. She danced beside the man until the end of the piece. Then, he asked her if she'd like to go down to a lower deck and see a movie with him.

"How old are you?" she asked after giving him the once-over.

"I'm twenty-four. Why?"

" 'Cause I've nursed my last baby. My daughter will be eighteen in a few weeks," she said, waved at him, and walked on. Days earlier, she would have been flattered that a man twelve years her junior found her interesting; but on that day, the idea bored her. *I don't have time for that kind of frivolity. I've got too many serious things facing me.*

Although she didn't take another trip on the cruiser, she whiled away the ten days on the beach, in the shops, at the hairdresser, and browsing in a local gallery, always careful to avoid the Reverend Collins. When the bus returned to the church to discard its passengers, Petra got out first; but when she would have rushed away, she heard the preacher call her name and walked back to him.

Tall, handsome, and distinguished looking in spite of his eighty years, he stood ramrod straight as she approached him. "You've had plenty of time to think about what's right, Petra. Now, you start doing what you know you have to do. I know you don't like thinking about it, but you've been given this time to get yourself right with your Maker. I'm here if you need me."

"Thank you, sir. It isn't going to be easy, but I guess I have to." She walked away without waiting for his reply.

Several days later, tears rolled down Petra's cheeks when the principal handed Krista her diploma. At least she'd been alive to see her daughter graduate. In spite of her unhappiness about her situation, she couldn't help being grateful for that. She wanted Krista to go to college and to have opportunities that, because of her own stupidity, she'd been denied. But unless her daughter got one of the scholarships for which she had applied, it wouldn't happen.

The following evening, after they finished dinner, Petra took a deep breath and looked at Krista. "Let's sit in the living room. I have to talk with you."

Krista's gaze swept over Petra. "Are you all right?"

"Oh, yes. I'm fine," she said. "I have to correct something, and it's not easy for me to do this. All of your life, I've held you close to me, treating you as if you were mine alone, although you aren't, and I've lied to you about your father. He isn't dead, at least not as far as I know."

A frown covered Krista's face. She narrowed her left eye and bounced forward. "What are you saying?"

"All he ever talked about was his dream of finishing college and that nothing was going to prevent him from getting his degree at Howard University. He would have been the first person on either side of his family to get a degree, and a lot of his relatives pitched in to pay for his education. I'd just finished high school, and he was entering his junior year at Howard. It was my fault I got pregnant; he asked if I was on the pill, and because I wanted to sound sophisticated to this college man, I lied and said I was protected. I never told him I got pregnant, and he spent his junior year at a university overseas."

Petra thought the silence would deafen her. It seemed that many minutes passed, and Krista sat facing her and looking her in the eye, but not saying one word. But she saw her daughter's jaw working and knew she was angry.

"How on earth could you dare do such a thing," Krista said at last. "How could you do this to me? What's his name, and where is he?"

"His name is Goodman Prout, but I don't know where he is. I do know that wherever he is, he's probably teaching music."

"He's a musician? Are you serious?"

"Yes, he was getting a degree in music with a major in piano and a minor in strings. I don't think you should contact him and upset his life. He's probably married, and —"

Krista interrupted her. "I don't care if he is married. And don't give me any advice about him. I don't want to hear a thing you've got to say."

Her daughter had never spoken to her disrespectfully, and the words cut her like scissors shredding her insides. "Krista, I was a child, the same age as you are now. What would you have done?"

Krista sucked her teeth. "I wouldn't be stupid enough to get pregnant. You take care of the kitchen. I'm going to start looking for Goodman Prout."

Petra knew that there was no point in trying to dissuade her. "Will you at least try to forgive me?"

"That'll take a lot of doing."

Krista went to her room, closed the door, slumped against it, and released a heavy sigh. Her heart beat so fast that it frightened her, and she groped her way to the bed and fell across it. She had a father, a living, breathing father who she'd never seen and who didn't know she existed. What would her life have been like if he had been a part of it? Would she have walked to school on those cold days, or would he have driven her in his car? Would he have gone to her school plays, the debating team activities, and other things that she participated in, and would he have been proud of her? Would her life have been more pleasant? Would she have loved him, or would he have been a drunken slob like Jaynell Cook's father? Was her mom ashamed of her? How could her mom do such a thing to her?

Fury boiled up in her. She sat up and kicked the chair that stood beside her bed. She had a right to know her father, and she intended to find him, no matter who it hurt. And her mom had a lot to account for. She hadn't told her only a lie, but a hideous one.

"If she thinks I'll forgive her for it . . . Well, she'll wait a long time."

Petra didn't know if she had ever before seen that door closed all the way. "If I start crying now, I'll flood the place," she said aloud. She dragged herself into the kitchen and began the after-supper cleaning, something Krista had done from the time she was twelve. "I guess this is not the first change I'll see, but I sure hope nothing else will be this painful. At least I'm not going to sit still and wait for the devil to get his due."

She telephoned Lurlene. "It's just seven o'clock. You and Twylah want to come over and play some cutthroat?"

"Don't mind if I do. Twylah just left here, but I'll call her and tell her to meet me over at your place. I'll bring some chips and a big bottle of soda."

Half an hour later, Petra's two friends arrived and sat down at the kitchen table. "Open a window," Twylah said. "I ain't got no use for the heat, and I thought you didn't till you took off to Ocean City. Why would anybody as dark as you want to sit on a beach and bake in the sun? Girl, you were born with a suntan."

"She wasn't after no suntan," Lurlene said. "I bet she's after one of those church brothers. Nobody's gonna make me believe she trying to get her soul saved. Wednesday night prayer meeting at church with her mama is one thing, but a ten-day religious retreat is another kettle of fish."

"Get off my case, you two. All you think about is men."

Lurlene dealt the cards. "I suppose you know of something better than a good man? I sure don't."

"She don't neither," Twylah said, "and if I

find something better, I'm gon' box it and sell it. Where's Krista?"

"Krista's in her room," Petra said.

"In her room? Now that she got her diploma, she don't greet nobody?"

"Maybe she's upset about something," Lurlene said. "Leave her alone. That's a good girl. Never heard one thing against her moral character." She threw out a joker, named it an ace, and won that round.

Petra soon tired of the game and of the company. One part of her mind was on her daughter, and the other fought with her doctor's diagnosis. "I'm beat," she said after they played for a little more than an hour. "This has been a rough day."

Twylah folded her cards and looked hard at Petra. "I'd think that since you saw your only child graduate from high school yesterday, you be ready to kick up your heels half the night." She heaved her 240-pound body up from the straight-back chair and raised her arms in a refreshing yawn. "If anybody wants to go on one of the ghost tours, let me know. They won't be no more of 'em till Halloween, and it would do you good, Petra, to see something silly like a ghost show. Let's go, Lurlene."

For a long time, Petra sat in her living

room, the darkness alleviated only by the street light.

"He's a musician, so I'll begin with the Internet. He must have a Web page," Petra said to herself a couple of evenings later, as she sat in the public library wasting time, avoiding the unpleasantness of her daughter's barely controlled anger. If she remembered Goodman Prout's talent and ego, he would have succeeded handsomely in the nineteen years since she last saw him, and he'd make sure that a wide circle of people knew it. She couldn't find his Web site, but she didn't doubt that he had one. She called a friend whose daughter graduated from Howard.

"Louise, does your daughter have any alumni bulletins or directories? I need to locate somebody. His name is Goodman Prout. There couldn't be two of those."

"She has a couple of them. Hold on."

Petra tried not to think of what she'd do next if Louise's daughter didn't have a directory.

After four or five minutes, Louise returned to the phone. "There's a Goodman Prout in Catonsville, and he has a music school or works in one." She read out the address. "That's about five miles or so from here.

You think he's the one?"

"We'll see," Petra said, though she didn't doubt that that Goodman Prout was her daughter's father. She thanked her friend, hung up, and got the telephone number from the Baltimore operator.

Although Krista hadn't spoken to her since she told her that her father was alive, they'd eaten together twice daily, at breakfast and again at supper. That night after the evening meal, Petra told Krista, "You wanted to know where your father is, and I did some research and located him, but until you speak to me and treat me with respect, I refuse to give you the information." She knew what the Reverend Collins would say to that, but she was tired of her daughter's rudeness.

Krista looked at her mother and then lowered her gaze. "Did you know him well?"

Petra's lower lip dropped. "Of course I knew him well. We'd been dating for over a year. I'm going to call him and tell him that he can expect to hear from you."

Her daughter's hopeful expression saddened Petra. "Thanks. I guess he wouldn't believe me if I just called him and laid this trip on him. Is he nice?"

"He was, but remember how long it's

been since I saw him. I'll call him tomorrow."

"You gonna let me know what he says?"

"Of course."

"Thanks. I . . . uh . . . I'll straighten up the kitchen."

Petra's gaze followed Krista as she carried dishes into the kitchen. Only Heaven knew what was in store for Krista.

Goodman Prout hopped onto the deck of his suburban home, a sleek, modern brick house between Baltimore and Ellicott City, Maryland, the place of his birth. He'd done well, making a good living for himself, his wife, and his two children, doing what he loved best, playing and teaching music. His sons possessed considerable musical talent, and his attraction to Carla, his wife, began when he first heard her beautiful soprano voice. His life focused on and revolved around music. He attributed his peaceful, happy home life to the love of music that he and his wife shared with their fifteen- and sixteen-year-old sons.

"One of my students has a recital Saturday," he said to Carla as he stepped into the kitchen, "so I may stay a little late today to give him extra practice time."

"No problem," she said, after drinking the

glass of orange juice. "School's out, so it won't matter if the boys eat a little late." She kissed him on the cheek. "See you this evening."

He could take the bus or the commuter train, but he preferred to drive his Lexus, and not only as a status symbol, but because he had at last been able to give his family the recognition they deserved, and the Lexus was a part of his achievement. He strolled into Goodman Music Studios, turned on the air conditioners, made coffee, and sat down to review his schedule for the day. He had four piano students, and his assistant's schedule included three violinists, a cellist, and a guitarist. What he needed was another soundproof room for a voice teacher, but his present studio couldn't accommodate it, and he hated looking for another building and then soundproofing each room. He sipped his coffee and leaned back in his desk chair. Life was good, and he didn't plan to allow greed to burst his bubble.

The phone rang, and he lifted the wireless from its base. "Goodman Prout speaking. What can I do for you?" The silence annoyed him, but he didn't react; it could be someone who wanted to begin music lessons and was shy about doing it. "You've reached Goodman Music Studios. Do you have the wrong number?"

"Goodman, are you on a secure line?"

He leaned forward, his antenna alert. That voice sounded familiar, but be couldn't place it. "Yes. What do you want?"

"This is Petra. Petra Fields. I hope you're all right. I have something to tell you, and I'd rather speak with you in person, if possible."

What on earth could she have to say to him after almost twenty years? "Well, Petra, this is a surprise, and you sound as if what you have to say is urgent. Where are you?"

"I still live in Ellicott City."

"Can you meet me at The Crab Shanty at five-thirty? I can't stay long."

"Thanks. I'll be there."

If he hadn't expected Petra, he would not have recognized her. About five feet six, taller than he remembered, her hair had lengthened to below her shoulders, her dark-hazel eyes still had that slumberous look, but along with her thick lashes, they gave the impression that she cared for no man. Her body was not that of a girl, but of a beautifully proportioned and voluptuous woman.

He stood when Petra entered the cozy

restaurant and walked to meet her. "You are one lovely woman, Petra. I almost didn't recognize you. Let's sit over here." He walked with her to the table he'd already chosen, called the waiter, and looked at her. "Hot, hard, or soft?"

"Lemonade or sweetened ice tea. It's pretty hot out there."

Goodman ordered lemonade for her and a gin and tonic for himself. "What's on your mind, Petra? You sounded . . . well, I wouldn't say frantic, but at the least, distressed. What's up?"

"I've been remiss about something that's terribly important, and now, I'm having to pay for it. I have a child for you, Goodman, and I —"

He bolted upright. "*What?* You're . . . you're out of your mind! You can't be serious." He slumped in the chair. "I guess you are." He drained the glass of gin and tonic, signaled the waiter, and ordered another one. "I saw you just before I went to Europe that summer, and you didn't look right to me, but I consoled myself with the thought that you'd have told me if you were pregnant." He'd taken the coward's way out, and he knew it at the time.

"I didn't want to know," he went on. "I had my life planned, and marriage definitely didn't figure into it. I had a scholarship to spend my junior year at The Royal College of Music in London, and I wouldn't have let your pregnancy or anything else get in the way. I know it sounds awful, considering how close we'd been, but . . . It's funny you didn't tell me."

"Because I knew you'd go through hell or high water to get that degree and that you wouldn't marry me and ruin your chances."

The waiter brought the second drink, and he drank half of it at once. *What a bomb!* "You're right," he said. "I don't think I would have. What do you want from me now?"

"Nothing for myself, but our daughter wants to meet her father. I let her believe you were dead, and I finally had to tell her the truth."

"You told her *what*? Good Lord! How'd she take it when you told her I wasn't dead?"

"How would you take learning that your mother lied to you about something that important and let you believe it for the first eighteen years of your life? She'll be eighteen soon and, for the first time ever, she treated me rudely. She's furious with me. I told her I'd speak with you, and I promised to tell her how this conversation with you went.

She's going to call you, and she's very nervous about doing it."

"What's she like?"

"She's an inch taller than I, looks like you, graduated from high school with honors last week and hopes to go to college this fall. She makes good grades, and she's neat and well-mannered. I'm proud of her."

"Well, I'll be damned. I know I should have asked you if you were pregnant, because I thought you were. This is going to be awkward, Petra, because I have a wife and two sons, aged fifteen and sixteen. This happened before I met Carla, but there's no telling how she's going to take it. I don't see how I can avoid telling her. Does . . . What's her name?"

"Krista."

"That's a nice name. Tell her to call me at the studio. By the way, she wouldn't happen to like music, would she?"

"Indeed, she does. The house is never quiet when she's at home. Blues, jazz, classical, country, she doesn't care as long as she's listening to music. She has a decent singing voice, too, but I haven't had the money to give her music or voice lessons."

She glanced at her watch. "Time really flies. We've been here an hour," she said. "Thanks for coming."

"Of course I came. I hadn't heard from you for nearly two decades, and I knew it must have been important."

She lowered her gaze for a minute and then, with what seemed to him a resolute, albeit sorrowful expression, she looked him in the eye and said, "Goodman, I hope you'll forgive me for not telling you I was carrying your child. If you want her to take a DNA test, I don't think she'll object."

"No. No. . . . At least not now. You said she looks like me. Tell her to call. And Petra, there's nothing to forgive. If I'd known, I might not even have finished college, and I'd probably be far worse off than I am today."

"Thank you, Goodman."

She left him sitting at the table, and he realized that she hadn't given him her address. Krista. He had an eighteen-year-old daughter named Krista Fields. Sometimes, life could be a real bitch. Feeling as if he'd been stomped by an elephant, he downed the remainder of his drink, paid the bill, and left. He hated uncertainty, and he was enveloped in it.

Petra walked home, unmindful of the heat or the distance. What a load off her shoulders! Goodman had been surprised, but he hadn't been angry or uncooperative. That ordeal was behind her, and she'd gotten off far more easily than she thought she deserved. She didn't fool herself about Krista's subdued behavior, though. She knew her daughter could nurse a grudge indefinitely.

However, the odor of food cooking that greeted her when she opened her front door relieved her anxiety about the mood in which she would find her daughter when she reached home. She dropped her pocketbook on the living room sofa and headed to the kitchen.

"What did he say, Mama? Did he say I could call him?"

Not even a greeting? What had she expected? "Your father said you may call him at his office. Here's the phone number."

Chapter Two

As she prepared to leave for work, Petra passed her daughter's closed bedroom door, turned back, and knocked. From birth, Krista had been the joy of her life, the reason why she had worked at demeaning jobs and struggled to attend night school while working days, the reason she had willingly allowed the best years of her youth to pass . . . never having enjoyed it. Their strained relations pained her, and she didn't know how to repair them. The door opened, and Krista stood there in her pajamas, her entire demeanor declaring her obstinacy. Did an eighteen-year-old high school graduate plan to spend the day lolling in bed rather than looking for a job? And did she dare broach that subject? It was best to cut to the chase.

"Did you call your father?"

"No."

"Why not?"

"I'm scared."

"You can be certain," Petra said, "that he's more afraid than you are. There's no point in thinking you can punish him by making him wait; he has a family, and he's happy with his wife and two sons. I hate to say it, but you're the outsider, so try to be considerate. While you're hanging out here in your room, your classmates are getting the few available summer jobs. I'll see you this evening." She no longer expected Krista's childlike kiss on the cheek, nor her happy hug when something especially pleased her. She walked out, locked the door, and headed for work.

You should tell Jack that you'll be leaving, her conscience nagged, and you should give him a chance to hire your replacement so that you can teach her the job. What you're doing isn't right.

But what was she supposed to do, sit at home and wait for the inevitable? She punched her card, went to her office, and sat down to work. "I don't feel as if anything's wrong with me," she said to herself, "but I know there's something, because these headaches are getting to me." She went to the cooler to get a cup of water so that she could take a pill for her headache.

"There you are," Jack said. "I . . . uh . . .

I'll be away at a conference over the July Fourth weekend, and . . . uh . . . Jennifer is taking leave, so you'll have to run the ship for the next six days." He patted her on the shoulder. "But I know you can do it. That's why I promoted you."

"I'll do my best. Don't forget to brief me on anything that's pending."

She shook her head in wonder. Jack had a beautiful wife, and three bright and intelligent children yet he'd risk that by going on a tryst with his secretary. Maybe being single wasn't such a bad idea. She'd prefer it to life with a faithless husband, provided someone would invent an automatic libido control mechanism.

"Who am I to talk? I'm not perfect, and I still have to deal with all these wrongs I've done to innocent people," she admonished herself. She shouldn't have told Jack what everyone in the office other than he knew, that Sally and Gail were lovers. She'd told him as a joke when she caught him cataloguing Gail's assets, but he'd roared out of control, and it was then that she remembered Jack's homophobia and his intolerance of people with physical defects or who spoke with any kind of accent.

Properly chastened, thanks to that incident, she no longer engaged in the office gossip, something that she had once relished. She'd never cared much for Sally Kendall, and since Jack fired Gail, Sally had become unbearable. Still. . . . Though she didn't usually procrastinate, she decided not to speak with Sally until Jack went to the conference and she would be in charge of the office. She reasoned that, if she were boss, however temporary, Sally would be less likely to make her the recipient of angry venom.

On the morning of Jack's first day away, Petra telephoned Sally in her office. "Hi, Sally. This is Petra. How about lunch today. I have something I want to tell you."

"Me? You want to tell *me* something? Oh, all right. Meet you in the lobby at twelve-thirty?"

"Perfect," Petra said and immediately wished she had just walked into Sally's office and had the conversation there. Now, she had to eat with the woman, and anybody who saw them could assume that they were an item. "Don't be an idiot, girl," she said to herself. "Just do what you know is right." *Scratch that. It's what Reverend Collins said was right.*

"You're a bag of surprises," Sally said when they met. "You never waste time talking to me. What's up?"

"I'll tell you at lunch."

Sally raised both eyebrows, pushed the revolving door, and walked out of the building ahead of her. Petra tried to figure out whether Sally's move reflected arrogance, refusal to acknowledge status, or something else. She shrugged and admitted the possibility that that may have been Sally's way of opening the door for her. *Lord, am I becoming paranoid?*

"If it's important, maybe you'd better wait till after I eat," Sally said. "How do you like being office manager? I always thought it involved doing whatever Jack didn't feel like doing."

"In a way," Petra said, though she knew that comment wasn't meant to be complimentary. "But I have fixed duties as well."

"In any case, the place runs a lot smoother than it did when Jennifer messed in everybody's business. Are they spending the weekend together some place? I don't know of any conference on real estate anywhere in the good old US of A this weekend. Do you?"

"Gosh, I haven't checked," Petra said, mindful that it was because of her gossip that she had to ask Sally's forgiveness. She could hardly swallow her hamburger and French fries, so great was her dread of the task she faced. However, Sally ate her lunch heartily, and after consuming a hamburger and French fries, ordered apple pie à la mode and ate that.

"It's time to get back to the office," Sally said after a glance at her watch. "Forty-five minutes is not long enough for lunch. Why don't you use your clout and get us an hour?"

"You can imagine what Jack's reaction would be," Petra said, feeling a chain beginning to knot in her belly.

"So what's this all about?" Sally asked. "If I was getting a raise, you'd have told me in the office."

"Right." They passed a coffee bar, and on an impulse, she grabbed Sally's sleeve and urged her into the bar. "Look, Sally, this is killing me. I did something awful, and I have to tell you and ask your forgiveness. I caught Jack checking out Gail, and I jokingly told him to forget it, that Gail was your bird, and he went berserk. How'd I know he'd —"

"You what?" Sally screamed and grabbed Petra by the collar. "You're the one who told Jack that and got Gail fired? You did that? Damn you. I ought to wipe up this floor with you."

Petra knew that all heads had turned in

their direction, and she broke loose from Sally's grip, stepped out onto the street, and headed back to work. She should have told her in the office, but that might not have worked out either. As she entered the elevator, Sally stepped in with her.

"How could you be so foolish?" Sally hissed. "You don't know what your loose tongue did to me. Jack won't give Gail a reference; she can't get a job, and I hardly make enough to take care of myself, much less her as well. I never planned to shack up with Gail, but since I have a job and she can't get one, I feel responsible for her. Besides all that, it's now public gossip, because Jack's not only a bigot; he also has a big mouth."

"I can't tell you how sorry I am, Sally. I was just teasing Jack, because he tomcats at every good-looking woman he sees. I didn't know he'd act the fool. Please forgive me."

Sally glared at her. "Forgive you? Why don't you ask me to stab myself? That would be a hell of a lot easier."

Petra dragged herself to her office and dropped into a chair. She had tried to do what was right, but had incurred the anger and distrust of first her daughter and now her colleague. She had no stomach for the work facing her. If only she could go down to the river and enjoy its quiet and the peace she always found there. Maybe if she told her minister that she had tried to set things right with her daughter, her daughter's father, and her colleague, he would tell her that her heart was in the right place and she could skip the other people on her list.

"Oh, no, sister," he said when she expressed her wish not to make any more confessions.

"What else is there?" she asked him.

With his finger wagging in her face, he said, "Some of those are the most egregious offenses. No. You have to ask forgiveness of all of them."

"But —"

"I can't give you absolution until you do it," he said. "And considering what you're facing, you'd better finish this soon."

Petra went home and checked her list. Josh Martin. She hadn't thought of him in years. She didn't hear any music and knocked on Krista's door; still no sound. She glanced inside her daughter's room, saw that she was alone in the house, and set about cooking dinner. Four weeks had passed, and except for the occasional headaches, she felt as she always had. Waiting for other changes in her health had begun to wear on her. She cleaned a roasting hen, stuffed it with herbs, bread, and sausage, and put it into the oven to roast. After cooking rice and preparing vegetables to cook in the microwave oven, she got the Ellicott City and Baltimore telephone books and looked for Josh Martin's phone number.

"Oh, that was so long ago. Maybe he's already forgotten about it. Why remind him?" she asked herself. On an impulse, she phoned Reverend Collins. "Maybe I'm just making these people miserable, Reverend Collins. Sally was mad enough with me to kill me. Why should I call somebody I haven't seen since high school graduation and tell him I did something nasty to him?"

"What kind of reaction did you expect from Sally Kendall?" the minister asked Petra. "Did you think she was going to open her arms with a smile and thank you for wrecking her life? Yes, she should forgive you, but whether she does is not your problem; that's between her and her Maker. You asked me for help, and that's what I've tried to give you. Do what is right, and take your medicine."

"Yes, sir," she said in a voice so subdued that she hardly recognized it as her own. It seemed silly to bring it up now, but the incident *had* nearly prevented Josh from graduating. After determining that he still lived in Ellicott City, she telephoned Josh.

"Josh, I'm sure you won't remember me, but I'm Petra Fields, and I need to talk with you about something important. Could you . . . uh . . . meet me for lunch or dinner one day soon?"

"Petra Fields? Get outta here, girl. It's been . . . I don't know how many years. Are you here in Ellicott City?" She told him that she was. "Hmmm. I won't ask why we've never run into each other. I suppose it's easy to miss a person in a city of sixty thousand people. Lunch is best for me. I don't dine out at night without my wife. Where would you like us to meet?"

"I live on the west side of the Patapsco," she said.

"So do I. Is Harper's near enough to you?"

She told him that it was, and they agreed to meet for lunch the next day. She hung up and went outside to sit on her back porch and perhaps get some breeze. The moon seemed to be traveling at great speed in and out of the clouds, darting among the stars, cold and oblivious to the summer heat. It stayed a little longer behind the clouds, longer and longer each time it disappeared until, at last, it didn't return. The wind's velocity increased, and she heard someone's garage door bang shut. A dog howled, and in the distance, an ambulance wailed. At the sound of faraway thunder, she folded the porch chairs and went inside. Storms both petrified and fascinated her, and she lingered at the closed window to watch the lightning dance across the sky.

"What will all this be like years from now when I am no longer here?" It was a thought that hadn't previously entered her mind, and she savored it for some minutes. How many grandchildren would she have, and what kind of people would they grow up to be? One month already gone. What good would it do to tell her mother and Krista? They would only worry and plague her with their questions and their concern. No. It was best this way.

Dressed in a rose-colored blouse and a wide skirt of gray and rose voile, she walked into Harper's restaurant at precisely twelve-thirty. She expected Josh to have the appearance of a successful man, for if he hadn't been, he would not have suggested Harper's restaurant.

"Well. Well," he said, striding to meet her, his face wreathed in smiles. "You're lovelier than when you were eighteen." He grasped her right hand and kissed her on each cheek. "It's wonderful to see you again, Petra."

She blinked several times. The man was a steamroller, and a gorgeous one at that. "Thanks, Josh. You look both well and prosperous. I hope life's good for you."

A smile creased his face. "Indeed, it is, Petra. What about you?"

She forced a smile, relaxed, and let it come naturally. She was, after all, genuinely glad to see Josh. "I'm doing very well, Josh. I —"

"Let's place our orders," he said, noting that their waiter stood at the table. "I don't know how much time you have." They gave their orders to the waiter. "Would you like red or white wine?" Josh asked her, and, with that question, told her more about himself than she saw in his appearance.

"So. What do you want to tell me?" he asked, and this time he didn't smile.

"This has been worrying me, Josh, so I'm glad to see that things are going well with you."

He sat forward, rubbing his chin with his left hand. "What do you mean?" he asked, and his tone carried an urgency that told her she might have caused him some distress by walking back into his life after eighteen years.

"You see, Josh, I'm the one who told our chemistry teacher that you were cheating on the final exam, and I shouldn't have done it, because it was none of my business. I know it got you into trouble, and I'm sorry. I hope you can forgive me." She fortified herself with the courage to weather his outrage.

"Run that past me again. You've been worried about *that*? I cheated, and I got what was coming to me. I also learned a valuable lesson, Petra, so that was the best thing you could have done for me. I had cheated all the way through school, and the harsh punishment the principal laid on me for cribbing on that exam was exactly what I needed. I haven't done it since.

"I learned that I was smart enough that I didn't have to cheat, and I graduated from State University with honors. Now, I'm head of a thriving computer software company. You did me a genuine favor. There's nothing to forgive. I should thank you."

"I'm so glad to hear this, Josh. I'm learning not to be so self-righteous. You mentioned your wife. Do you have children?"

His smile returned in full flower. "You bet. I've got the most fantastic little girl. She's the light of my life." He took a picture from his billfold and handed it to Petra. "I hate every minute that I'm away from her. What about you? Any children?"

"My daughter just finished high school, and she's hoping to go to Howard or the University of Maryland — whichever offers the best scholarship — in the fall."

They spoke of old times, of classmates that they still knew or hadn't seen since graduation. "I'm so relieved, Josh, that I didn't cause you any problems, and I'm happy that you're having a good life. I have to get back to work now."

He stood and extended his hand. "I'm glad we met, Petra. Lunch is on me." He leaned down and kissed her cheek. "Have a good one."

Little did he know.

She stopped by the post office and mailed her mortgage payment. In a few months, she'd be able to buy a car. Her mama had preached against buying what you couldn't afford, and that was one lesson she'd learned well. It would be wonderful not to have to walk or wait on buses that never ran on time. She couldn't wait to . . . What on earth was she thinking. She had forgotten, and for a few minutes . . .

I'm not going to get morbid, and I refuse to spend my time crying and feeling sorry for myself. At least I'm not lying in bed, wasting away. I'm walking around, working, going to the hairdresser, and doing what I always did. Maybe I'll go to sleep one night and not wake up. That would be wonderful.

Encouraged by her pleasant meeting with Josh and the realization that her tattling hadn't hurt him and may even have helped him, she prepared herself for her next encounter with someone she believed she had wronged.

Meanwhile, Krista had decided to exclude her mother from her personal problems, including those she encountered job hunting. "I'm not going to be a nursemaid to anybody's kids," Krista promised herself, walked into the personnel office of a department store and said, "Good afternoon, I'm looking for a job."

"We have an opening in the packaging department as a package wrapper," the woman said. "You seem intelligent."

Krista stared at the woman. "How much intelligence does a person need in order to wrap packages? Anyhow, I haven't had experience doing that."

"We can teach you, and we have an equal opportunity policy, so you needn't worry. We'll give you plenty of time in which to learn."

"In that case, why don't you teach me how to be a sales clerk? I can handle a computer; I'm very good at math; and I can smile at the drop of a hat."

"You've got an attitude, too."

Krista let herself laugh. She was looking at the sixth person that week who had offered her menial work when clerical positions were available. "Miss, I've had several offers of jobs working in back rooms doing backbreaking work, but I know I'm capable of something better. After you get a few dozen doors slammed in your face, you get attitude. I don't want to work in a package room with a bunch of men who use all kinds of language."

"Excuse me a minute." The woman answered the phone. "What do you mean, he walked out again? I'm fed up with his antics. Pay him for the rest of the month, and tell him not to come back." She looked at Krista for a long time, saying nothing. "All right, miss. You've got a job selling table linens and accessories on the fifth floor, and I want you to start right now. Come with me."

The woman stayed with her for an hour and a half, showing her how to use the store's computers, where to find stock, and briefing her on aspects of the store's policies. At the end of the working day, she returned to Krista's station. "I understand you've done well. Be sure and wear low-heel shoes tomorrow, and be here at a quarter of nine."

"Thank you, ma'am," Krista said. It wasn't brain surgery, but it made her proud that she had handled the linens section on her first day at work and hadn't made a single error. She got home before her mother, and was glad of it. She went into her room, closed the door, and took out her cellular phone. If she used that rather than the house phone, her mother wouldn't know who she called.

"May I please speak with Goodman Prout."

"This is Goodman Prout. With whom am I speaking?"

She had proved she could get a decent job, so she had a right to talk to Goodman Prout woman to man, if not daughter to father. "This is Krista Fields, Mr. Prout. My mother has just told me that you are my father."

After a long, disconcerting pause, he said, "Yes. That's what she told me, too, so you are not to address me as Mr. Prout. Your mother told me that you have good manners. I want to see some evidence of it."

Stunned by his response, and well aware

that she deserved her comeuppance, she said, "I'm sorry, sir. I haven't had any practice at this. Do you mind if I come to see you?"

"Of course I don't mind. I suppose she told you that I have a wife and two sons. I haven't told them about you yet, and I don't plan to until after you and I meet. Can you come to my office tomorrow? I'm in Catonsville. The city bus should bring you here in half an hour or so."

"I'm working tomorrow. I just got the job today. I get off at a quarter of five."

He gave her instructions as to how to reach his office. "I hope to see you tomorrow between five-fifteen and five-thirty. Please be on time."

"I will. I hate to wait for people."

As agreed, she took the bus to Hilliard Street, walked two blocks to the address her father gave her, looked up, and saw a sign that said Goodman Music Studios. "Wow! I wonder if he teaches music." Immediately her excitement abated. What if she was making a mistake, and she should have left him alone as her mother at first suggested. Maybe she wouldn't like him. The elevator door opened, and, immediately, she backed away from it, allowing the door to close. She let the wall take her weight. Suppose he didn't like her and didn't want her.

She struggled to control her quivering lips. It had always been her and her mom and, as mad as she was at her mom, she knew that, if necessary, Petra Fields would give her life for her daughter. But this man . . . He already had children, so he probably wouldn't want any more. Maybe she should go home. She blew her nose and told herself that she was a big girl. How did a person talk to a father?

The elevator door opened again, and she took a deep breath and forced herself to enter it. She remembered her mom saying that he was probably more scared than she. Oh, what the heck! It wasn't her problem. He was the one responsible for her being alive, and he was the one who had to deal with it. One thing for sure, she was not going to beg him for attention or anything else.

"He's not gonna be any more important to me than I am to him," she said to herself. "I'm playing it cool."

Still feeling as if her heart had plunged to the pit of her stomach, she stepped out of the elevator, laid back her shoulders, and, with shaking fingers, rang the bell below the sign that read Goodman Music Studios.

Goodman stood at the window wondering

how his life was about to change, for it would indeed never again be the same. An eighteen-year-old daughter that he hadn't nurtured. The doorbell rang, and he swung around and stared at the door as if he expected to see her walk in.

"What the heck's come over me?" He rushed to the door, opened it, and stared at the tall, handsome young woman who bore a look of expectancy, and who had a striking resemblance to his sons. She was his, all right, from her feet to her proud head. "Come in, Krista. I'm Goodman Prout, your father."

She stepped in and focused her gaze on him. Then, she looked around and said, "Hi. Nice place."

So she meant to orchestrate their relationship, did she? He was having none of it. He was the parent, and if he was to have a relationship with her, it had to be as he directed.

"Have a seat, Krista. I want to look at you for a minute. This takes some readjusting."

She sat down, crossed her knees, and swung her leg. "Like what?"

He was raising two sons who respected and adored him, and neither was a smart ass. He leaned back in his chair. "Not many fathers and daughters have experienced what you and I are going through right now, Krista, and thank God for that. Both of us are victims, though you actually suffered the greater loss. So let's not begin by hurting each other. I can't make up for the nearly eighteen years I didn't know you existed, and I am not going to try. I want to be a father to you now in every way that I can, but that depends on your willingness to behave as my daughter. Do you understand?"

"Yes, sir. I'm surprised that I look so much like you," she said.

"Since you have my genes, you wouldn't expect to look like Louis XV, would you?"

Her eyes twinkled, and she, too, leaned back in her chair. "Never can tell. I have a friend with one blue eye and one brown one. Whose genes does he have?"

Goodman couldn't help laughing. "Sounds like the devil's been there. I understand you're furious with your mother."

"Wouldn't you be?"

"I don't know. You see, I had a hunch she was pregnant, but I didn't ask her because I didn't want to know. I had plans that didn't include marriage, and she knew that, so she let me off the hook by not mentioning it. If she'd told me, I wouldn't have any of this." He gestured with his hand. "And I wouldn't have completed my education.

"Understand that my poor family and relatives near and far pitched in to help pay for my education. I'm the first person on either side of my family to go to college, not to speak of graduate school, and I was not going to let them down. Petra knew that. I owe her plenty."

"That's deep. You went to graduate school?" she asked him.

"I got an undergraduate degree at Howard University and a graduate degree at The Royal College of Music in London."

Her eyes sparkled and a smile settled on her face, betraying an eagerness that only the youth possess. "Mom said you went to London in your junior year. You went back again? Gee. What do you play? I mean do you teach?"

"I play the piano and the guitar well, and I teach piano, guitar, and violin."

"Can you teach me piano? I always wanted to learn to play the piano, but I never told Mom because I didn't think we had enough money."

"I'll enjoy teaching you. Your mother told me that you love music, and she said you have a good voice."

"I do love music, but I don't know about my voice." She sang a few bars of George

Harrison's "Something" and looked at him. "What do you think?"

"It's a beautiful instrument. Your mother's right. When would you like to begin piano lessons?"

"Like I said, I just got a job, and the store is open six days a week. As soon as I know which day I have off, I'll let you know." Her face clouded in a frown.

"What's the matter?" he asked her.

"Uh . . . Am I . . . I mean, are you going to let me meet your children?"

"You mean my *other* children? Your brothers. I hope to as soon as I shock them with news of your existence. I have to go home now, but first, I want your cell phone number. I notice you didn't call me from your home phone." Her eyes widened, and her bottom lip dropped. "Right," he said. "You didn't want your mother to know you called me. That doesn't make sense, but it's up to you. I have to leave now, and I'll drive you home."

She laid back her shoulders and gave him a stern look. "I hadn't planned to go home from here."

So she didn't want to obey him. He'd see about that. "Really? Krista, playing games won't help. Don't forget; it was you who initiated this relationship. I'm taking you home."

"Yes, sir."

Petra hadn't given him her address, and he didn't trust Krista to do it, for her use of a cell phone to contact him was sufficient evidence of her capacity for deviousness. He drove up to Petra's house, put the car in park, but didn't unlock the front passenger door until he walked around and used his key. He opened the door for Krista, and after she got out, he kissed her cheek. That she seemed speechless did not surprise him.

"Thank you for coming to me. We'll begin your music lessons as soon as you give me a day. My regards to Petra."

He waited until she was inside the house before he drove off to what awaited him at home when he told his family about Krista.

Petra heard Krista come into the house and said to her mother, "I have to hang up now, Mama. Krista's home, and I have to put supper on the table. Twylah and Lurlene are coming over later to play pinochle, and I want to finish cleaning the kitchen before they get here."

"Can't Krista do that?"

"Sometimes she does, but here lately, since I told her about Goodman, she's less cooperative, and she's morose."

"She'll grow out of that. What you having for supper?"

"Fried catfish, string beans, baked cornbread, and sliced tomatoes. I made a coconut pie."

"Sounds good to me. Give my regards to the girls, and tell Krista I want to see her."

"Yes, ma'am. I sure will."

Petra and Krista sat down to eat supper, and after Petra said grace, Krista didn't start eating as she usually did at the moment Petra said amen.

"I got a job at Dwill's today, Mom. I'm the sales clerk in the table linens department. Me. All by myself."

Petra hardly believed what her ears heard. "Are you serious?"

"Yes, ma'am, and I'm going to work right up to when school starts. That way, I'll have money for school, and I get a discount at the store, so I can buy all of my school clothes for thirty percent less than sale prices. Can we make a list of the things I'll need so I can buy some each week?"

Since she hadn't received an acceptance from her favorite schools, she shouldn't be overly optimistic, Petra reasoned, but she didn't want to discourage her. At least, she had managed to find a good job.

"All right. We can work on that this weekend. It'll be interesting."

"Sure will. What do you know, Mom? I just left my father. He drove me here from his studios."

Petra's fork clattered on her plate, and she wished she'd had the presence of mind to hide her surprise. "Wh . . . When did that happen? I mean, when did you call him?"

"Yesterday."

"How'd you get along?" Petra asked her.

"All right. I don't know how I feel about him. I have a feeling that he's bossy and very strict, and he hasn't told his wife and kids about me. Said he was waiting until after he met me. You think he'll tell them?"

"If he said he will. Goodman was always very straight, but I don't know how he is now. When he tells his family, it's going to cause some problems, because they won't understand, and they won't want a stranger intruding in their happy home. He's going to have a hard time."

Krista's face twisted in anger. "Why, for Pete's sake? I have as much right there as they do."

"That may be true, but human beings are not always reasonable." Petra's words were those that her grandfather had frequently used when counseling her.

"Humph," Krista snorted. "A lot I care. He's gonna teach me to play the piano, so they can go simmer themselves. I don't have to love him or them; all I want is free piano lessons."

Petra didn't like the sound of that. "Krista, don't be self-centered. You're almost eighteen years old, and, by law, in a few weeks your father won't be required to do anything for you. If he gives you piano lessons, be grateful."

"Yes, ma'am. He's real good-looking, Mom. You should've hooked him."

"I could have, but by now, he'd hate me, and I wouldn't know what country he lived in."

"Yeah, I guess you're right. He said he was dead set on getting a degree. I wonder what his kids look like. If Aunt Twylah and Aunt Lurlene are coming over, I'll clean the kitchen. Are you gonna cut that pie before they come?" She drifted into her room, humming as she went.

"At least she's speaking to me, though I know that doesn't necessarily mean she's forgiven me," Petra said to herself. She heard the doorbell and went to open the door.

"Hi. Come on in," she said to her two friends.

"Hey, girl," Twylah said. "When you going to the hairdresser? Either straighten that stuff or shave it off. Wool belongs on sheep."

"Oh, get off of Petra's back," Lurlene said. "What girlfriend needs is somebody to primp and preen for."

"Y'all get off my mom's case," Krista said, walking over to hug her mother's friends.

"Lurlene's thoughts begin and end with the word 'man,' " Petra said.

"Trust me, it's not just my thoughts that gets a bang out of men," Lurlene said, "but I'm not going there right now."

"No, and it's just as well," Twylah said. "I'd swear that last one you had tagging along behind you checking out your back action must've had some kind of psychosis. Never saw such a jerk."

"Y'all leave poor Harry alone," Lurlene said with a grin. "The brother thought his money would buy anything he wanted. I let him look, but he got nothing here."

"Hmmm," Petra said. "That must be why he asked me if there was a Viagra for women. Deal, Twylah."

"Oh yeah? How come he expected you to have the answer to that?" Lurlene asked Petra.

Petra looked at her run in spades, her two aces, and a marriage and bid two hundred and forty points. "I thought we agreed that poor Harry wasn't rowing with both oars." She played her run in spades first.

"I see where this game's going," Twylah said. "Girlfriend's showing off. I ain't got nothing in my hand but skin."

"Y'all want some coconut pie?" Krista asked as she walked into the room carrying a tray. "I made some coffee, but you can have some ice tea, if you want it. I gotta get up early. Good night."

"Girl, you blessed to have such a nice daughter, so refined, and all," Lurlene said. "Half the time, I don't know where mine is. You don't know how lucky you are."

Don't let your mind go there, Petra admonished herself. She had decided not to tell them, so she had to put up with occasional conversation that disturbed her. That was a small price to pay for the pleasure of having them treat her as they always had.

Lurlene ate a piece of the pie and rolled her eyes skyward. "This pie sure is good. Is there anything you can't do, Petra? I tell you, when I grow up, I wanna be just like you."

Petra tasted the pie and admitted to herself that she'd never done a better job of it. "To be like me, Lurlene, you have to grow a few inches, and lose some of that top."

"You go way from here. These boobs is my personality."

"Oh yeah," Twylah said. "Seems to me you too old to have a bouncing personality. You'd better prop 'em up, 'less you want 'em to be hitting your knees a few years down the road."

"This sure was a good game," Lurlene said. "We better get going, Twylah, 'cause you know I gotta punch the clock at eight tomorrow morning."

"Me, too," Twylah said, "and I'll be standing on my poor feet down at the post office. Every time I get a raise, they promote me to something else that I have to stand up in order to do. The way I look at it, happiness is sitting on my fanny." Petra walked to the door with her friends, told them good night, closed, and locked the door.

She hadn't had time to savor the good that had happened that day. Krista had a good job, and formed a relationship with her father. Calmness stole over her, as it dawned on her that Krista would not have to depend on her grandmother alone, because Goodman would be there for her when she needed him. When Krista said that Goodman was bossy and probably very strict, Petra knew he meant to be a father to his daughter. She poured a glass of ice tea, sipped it, and gave thanks. One enormous load was off her shoulders.

Petra finished her ablutions and as she was about to get in bed, her glance fell upon the yellow pad on her night table and the list of names with which she had to deal. She stared at the name Jada Hankins. Maybe she didn't have to contact Jada, since she didn't know the woman. In this case, it wasn't what she did, but what she didn't do. She'd been a coward. She turned the radio on for company and lowered the volume. She hadn't felt guilty about Jada at the time, because her trial revealed that she had a shady past. Her name wasn't Jada Hankins, but Rose Jackson; she'd changed it in order to make herself more glamorous. And she wasn't a registered nurse, either, although she worked as one. It seemed that she'd been without work for two months, added RN to her name, and went to work as a private-duty nurse the very next day. What did she owe a woman who had that kind of history? To her mind, nothing.

However, as she walked to work the next morning, the Reverend Collins fell in step with her. "Good morning, Petra. How are you feeling this morning?"

"The same, sir. How are you?"

"For a man my age, I'm feeling exceptionally well. How're you coming with your list? Have you finished it yet? From what you told me, you should work on it a bit more diligently. You don't want to get before the throne and have to bow your head."

"If I get that far, I'll gladly bow my head."

He stopped walking. "Mind your words, young lady. And get on with what you have to do. I don't preach no sinner's funeral."

As he crossed the street, she said beneath her breath, "Who gave you the right to decide who's a sinner and who isn't?" She used her lunch hour to find Jada Hankins's address and phone number, and discovered that the woman lived on the other side of the Patapsco. She went back to her office, closed the door, and made the dreaded call on her cell phone.

"Miss Hankins, I'm Petra Fields. We haven't met, but we do have something in common, and I'd like to meet with you for a few minutes after I get off from work. I have something to tell you, and it won't take me but a few minutes." At the long silence, she continued. "Don't worry, miss Hankins, it isn't anything bad. Could we meet some place for coffee?"

"I'd say no way, but you got my curiosity up. How about the sushi bar on Hoyt

Street? It's right next door to the police station, so I don't expect you'd try anything stupid there."

Petra inhaled deeply and let the air out slowly. "You definitely don't have to worry about that. I can be there at five-thirty."

"Fine. I'm wearing a white skirt and a green T-shirt."

She told the woman good-bye, hung up, and heard a knock on her door. "Come in."

"I see you close your door these days," Sally said as she sauntered in. "I'm sorry I acted out with you the other day, but I was mad enough to eat nails. I hope you don't report me to Jack for insubordination. I can' afford to lose this job."

"I'm not out to hurt anybody, Sally, so you can relax. I don't blame you for getting angry, but it wouldn't hurt you to find a more reasonable way to express it."

Sally's expression was one of disbelief. "You mean you're not going to tell him."

"No, I'm not. Now, would you please let me finish this ad?"

As if she'd just been saved from an executioner, Sally's face creased into a smile. "Sure. And if you need any help, let me know."

Petra finished the ad, put it on Jack's desk, and called it a day. She had barely half an hour to get to the sushi bar, and she had a premonition that this meeting with Jada Hankins wouldn't be the last one. Her grandfather had always said that premonitions were the Lord's way of warning you to be careful. She'd be careful. But, these days, nothing frightened her, because whatever it was, it couldn't last long.

Petra took a seat near the back of the little restaurant so that she could watch the woman as she walked in and could gauge her personality. Within a few minutes, Jada Hankins strode in, tall, neat, and self-confident.

"Hmmm. She's going to be a problem. This is one proud woman." Petra stood and smiled. "Thanks for coming, Miss Hankins. I'm Petra Fields."

Jada's smile barely made it to her face. "Hello," she murmured.

My, my, Petra thought. If her grandfather's sayings had any merit, the woman's handshake indicated weak character. "Would you like coffee or something else?" Petra asked her.

"No, thanks. I take care of my shape. What did you want to tell me?"

This woman was not going to be sympathetic, so the only choice was to say it and get it over with. "One night, last November,

I was in a bar, and I saw two women start a fight with you, and one of them got a cut beneath her eye. The bartender called the police, and you asked for a witness to the fact that you didn't start the fracas. I was ashamed to let my friends know I was hanging out in that bar. And I didn't help you, though I knew you were innocent. I'm telling you, because I'm asking you to forgive me."

If she had noticed Jada's narrowed eyes and pursed lips or the pulse beating rapidly at the side of her head, she might have prepared herself for the woman's explosive response.

"You bitch!!! You sit there like a saint and ask me to forgive you? Get outta my face! I spend ten days and nights in Ellicott City's jail for something I didn't do, plus I paid a thousand-dollar fine for disorderly conduct, and all because you and a lot of other cowards didn't have the guts to step up and tell the truth. For nothing but minding my own business, I got a criminal record. Me forgive you? Hold your breath." She got up, braced her knuckles on her hip bones, and added, "You ain't heard the last of me." With head high, shoulders back, and hips swinging, Jada pranced to the door.

" 'Scuse me, miss," a man sitting near the

door called to Jada. "I sure am enjoying the view, but I feel obliged to tell you your skirt's sliding down." Jada looked down, grabbed her skirt, and backed against the door.

It was one more thing she'd have to ask forgiveness for, but so be it. Petra laid her head back and howled. How sweet it was!

Chapter Three

Petra made some progress in ridding herself of the guilt with which she'd saddled herself, but more than once her absolution came at the expense of those to whom she went for forgiveness. Until he received Petra's call and met with her as she requested, Goodman Prout had thought himself a happy man. However, as he drove his silver-gray Lexus into his two-car garage, he had a feeling that a lot of time would pass before he regained his sense of well-being.

After supper — a meal that he didn't usually enjoy, because in seventeen years, his wife, Carla, hadn't learned how to cook — he told Carla and his sons that he wanted to talk with them.

"Can't it wait, Daddy? I want to watch *Grey's Anatomy.*"

"Tape it," he said.

With his family looking at him, expecting the kind of information he usually provided at family conferences — that he had X number of new students, had hired another teacher, planned to buy a new car, or something else indicative of progress — a yoke fell on his neck.

He rested his forearms on his thighs, knew that he wouldn't win unless he looked them in the eye, and made himself straighten up and lean back with an air of authority. "First, I want to tell you that I learned about this yesterday. It began almost twenty years ago, but I was not made aware of it. A woman I dated for about a year phoned me and told me she had an eighteen-year-old daughter of whom I am the father." He ignored their gasps.

"Her name is Krista, and this afternoon, she came to see me. I —"

"Get a DNA test," Paul, his younger son, advised.

"There's no point in that. I knew she was mine the minute I looked at her. The Prout genes don't lie. As I was saying, I knew nothing of her existence until yesterday, and she didn't know anything about me. I don't know why her mother chose to tell her now, but she did, and I have to deal with it."

"If she's eighteen, you have no responsibility for her," Carla said, "so there's no problem."

He looked at his wife, and a cloud of sadness enveloped him. He didn't want to hurt her, but he realized now that he would. "I'm her father, and the fact that her mother elected not to tell me at a time when I would have assumed responsibility for both of them is not Krista's fault. She's innocent in this. She's my child, and I plan to step up to the plate. If she needs me, I'm here for her. I'm going to give her piano lessons. Incidentally, she has a lovely mezzo soprano voice."

"Where does that leave us?" Peter, his older son, asked.

"I don't love you less than I ever did."

"Am I supposed to embrace her?" Carla asked.

"That's up to you. I'm not going to force her on you; indeed, I doubt she would allow me to do that. She wears her pride the way a peacock advertises his plumes. I admired her." Although he knew it would seem to them as if he lowered the boom, he had to say what came next; if he didn't, none of them would get the real message.

"Peter and Paul, I want you to get to know your sister, and I want her to get to know you. I want you to learn to care about each other." Neither said a word, but both looked at their mother.

"What are you expecting from me?" she asked him. "You drop this on me and expect me to start dancing?"

He told himself not to let them rattle him. "If she were the product of a former marriage, how would you react? You would accept her without question. I didn't ask for this, but I have three children, and I intend to behave as if I have three." He got up to leave, turned and looked at his wife. "I'm not guilty of anything that's wrong. If it isn't pleasant here, it'll be pleasant somewhere else. By the way, Carla, if Petra had told me she was pregnant, I would have married her, and I'm sure that I would still be married to her. She's a beautiful and gracious woman. Of course, my life wouldn't be one-third what it is today."

He needed her support, and he hoped she understood that he worked his fanny off days and many evenings not for himself alone, but to give his family the best. He'd bet she was uptight because he'd told her many times how much he'd love to have a daughter, but she'd said she finished child-bearing when she had Paul. Petra Fields gave him a daughter, and he meant to make her a part of his life.

Petra had begun to conclude that the

preacher's counsel wasn't good for all concerned, and, at times, she doubted if it was good for any of those involved, including her. Yet, she didn't feel sufficiently confident about her growing judgment of the matter to reject his advice, so she continued her efforts to atone for her wrongdoings. However, when she came to the item on her list for which she had to confess to immoral behavior, she balked.

"All or nothing," the old evangelist said when she begged to skip that deed, "and this is my last word on the subject."

She arose early one Saturday morning, summoned her courage, and went to her backyard, where she knew she would find her neighbor and friend — a woman fifteen years her senior — gardening in the cool of the morning.

"Ethel, I didn't want to tell you this, but —"

"You up early, girl," Ethel said, interrupting as she often did. "Come on over and get a cup of coffee. I need to rest a minute. I made some good old buttermilk biscuits, and Fred brought some Smithfield ham home yesterday."

"I don't think I'd better, Ethel. I have something awful to tell you."

Ethel stared at her. "Spit it out, then. It

couldn't be that bad."

"Yes, it is. I slept with Fred once. It was a stupid thing, and I'm sorry. Can you forgive me?"

The hoe landed on Ethel Archer's foot and, with her hands on her hips and her eyes nearly twice their size, she screamed, "You did what? Now, you ain't standing there telling me you been alley catting with my husband." She picked up the hoe. "Forgive you? I'll forgive you all right, just as soon as I chop your ass up with this hoe." She started toward Petra, who dashed into her house, slammed the door, and locked it.

"Well, I asked her to forgive me," Petra said to herself, gasping for breath. "I did my part." Feeling safer away from the back of the house, she walked to the living room and stood near the picture window looking at nothing in particular, still nervous. Suddenly, she rushed closer to the window and pressed her face to the pane.

What she saw was not a mirage, but Fred Archer running down the brick walk from his house barefoot and wearing only his jockey shorts. Ethel Archer was on the war path. In the twelve years that she'd lived in the house, she had never closed the blinds at her picture window, only the curtains. She closed the blinds, and with the picture of Fred charging down the walk holding up the jockey shorts that he hadn't had time to fasten vivid in her mind's eye, she laughed until she cried.

Later that morning, she got her shopping cart and prepared to do her weekly grocery shopping. Recently, she had developed the habit of marketing early in the day to avoid being waylaid by neighbors. Since learning of her imminent transition, as she thought of it, her capacity for small talk had greatly diminished.

About three blocks from her home, she saw Old Joe Cephus — as the man was known around the neighborhood — leaning against the fence around someone's yard. Old Joe Cephus wore his long rain coat every day of the year, regardless of the weather. With his face blackened by his eighty years and his affinity for being outdoors, the white hair visible from the edge of his black suede hat seemed whiter than it was. The man seemed to have only his walking cane for a companion, and he talked to it almost constantly.

Petra had disliked the man without reason since she was nine or ten years old. Her steps slowed as she neared him, and when she came abreast of him, she stopped. His apparent alarm didn't surprise her, because she had always ignored him and avoided him whenever she could. He was on her list, and she figured she might not get another opportunity, so she smiled. Both of his eyebrows arched, and his eyes seemed ready to jump at her.

She reached out in an attempt to put him at ease, but he stepped back. "It's all right, Mr. Cephus," she said, unaware that the man's real name was *Ceptuss* and that, over the years, people in the community had accepted someone's bastardization of it. His narrowed eyes failed to stop her.

"I . . . uh . . . never liked you, Mr. Cephus, and over the years I've said some nasty things about you. I'm sorry, sir, and I'm asking you to forgive me."

He looked in the opposite direction and spit out the juice from his tobacco, sending it a considerable distance. "Ain't that dandy! I don't mind a bit, 'cause I guess I've said worse things about you than you could even think up. No, siree, I don't mind a tall. I'm way ahead o' ya." He moved away from the fence and walked down the street whistling, his steps sprier than she'd ever witnessed.

Petra forced herself to move on. Not even when she fell flat on her face while trying to shoot a basket from center court and win the game for her high school basketball team had she felt so foolish. She looked neither right nor left from then until she finished her marketing and was back in her house. The good preacher could say whatever he liked. She was going to tear up that list, and from now on, if she sinned against anybody, she'd ask the Lord for forgiveness. She wasn't giving anybody else an opportunity to act superior to her. Old Joe Cephus was the last straw.

While Petra dealt with her list, Goodman and Krista faced the changes in their lives. Goodman sat in his office waiting for Krista to keep her first appointment with him. She'd been given Mondays off, and although Monday was one of his busiest days, nonetheless he agreed to give her lessons on that day. He looked at his watch, saw that it was precisely five-fifteen, and experienced mild annoyance. To his relief the door buzzer sounded, and she walked in.

"Hi. I ran all the way from the bus stop, because I didn't want to be late."

"You're right on time." He handed her three books. "These two are your piano books, and this is for your music theory. They're equally important. Come with me."

She sat at the piano, looked at him, and

smiled. "This is wonderful."

He pulled up a chair beside her, his head full of pictures of the first time he sat at a piano with a teacher beside him. He put her right thumb on middle C, and the lesson began. He'd planned to spend one hour with her each session, but when he looked at his watch, two hours had passed, and nobody had to tell him that, at that moment, fury raged in Carla Prout.

"I should be home by now, Krista. You're such an interesting student that I didn't notice the time. You have an aptitude for this. I'll see you same time next Monday."

"I hope you won't get into trouble when you get home," she said.

His left eyebrow arched sharply. "I'm not going to school, Krista. I'm going home . . . after I drop you off." He noticed that this time she didn't protest. "Let's go."

His office phone rang and, for a few seconds, he debated whether to answer it. "Hello."

"Goodman Prout? I'm Marsha Long. We're looking for a piano player and director to lead a community choir of thirty-six voices. You may have heard of us, The Oella Choral Ensemble and Orchestra. We've recently had six new applicants," the woman said, "but we don't want to accept them until we get our new director."

He sat down. The woman was asking him to direct one of the best group of singers in the city. "When do you practice?"

"Wednesday evenings from seven to nine."

"Thank you for the invitation, Ms. Long. Tell me where you meet, and I'll sit in Wednesday, and then we'll see what's what."

"May I say you're interested?"

He didn't like being pressured, but the woman was dangling a plum in front of him. "You may say that. Yes." He allowed her to give him the address, though he knew it well. "Thank you. I'll see you Wednesday."

"What was that about?" Krista asked him, and it pleased him that she felt she had the right to ask.

During the drive to her house, he explained the call. "It's a great opportunity for me. Before this time next year, I'll be a fixture in the community, as well known as the conductor of an orchestra."

"Will you still have time for me?" Krista's voice carried a note of fear.

"I will always have time for my children, all three of them."

"What did they say when you told them about me?"

"What could they say? I explained it to them as precisely as Petra explained it to me. It's natural for them to wonder if anything that would have been theirs now goes to you. They're good kids, and if nobody turns their heads, they'll come through this fine."

"Nobody meaning their mother?"

His head snapped around. Krista had a sharp mind, and he'd have to remember that. "You must understand, Krista, that my family has always been very tightly knit. There's a slight crack now but, in due course, it will repair itself. Does your mother know you're with me?"

"Only if you told her."

"So you're still feuding with her?" She indicated that she was. "I don't appreciate that. It's childish. She doesn't deserve it."

"Surely you're not still in love with her."

"No, I definitely am not. I love my wife." He parked in front of Petra's house. "Give your mother my regards. I'll see you next Monday."

"Yes, sir," she held the music books close to her breasts. " 'Nite."

"What a tragedy," he said to himself as he drove off. "If I had started her lessons when she was four years old, she could have been a fine classical pianist. What she learned in one hour, some students can't learn in a week."

■ ■ ■ ■

Goodman enjoyed a developing relationship with his daughter, but, with each passing day, Krista moved farther from her mother. Petra sat at the kitchen table waiting for Krista to come home and eat supper with her. At a quarter of eight, she got up and began heating the food. Where was it written that in order to be a good mother, you had to be a martyr? She only had a few days left, and enjoying them seemed to her the least she could do for herself.

"Nobody can walk on you unless you make yourself a door mat," her grandfather liked to say, and she didn't plan to forget that again. She served herself stewed chicken, dumplings, and string beans, poured ice tea from the pitcher on the table, bowed her head, and said grace. Seconds after she said "amen," she heard Krista's key in the lock. *She has a cell phone, and she could have used it to call me.*

"Hi, Mom."

"Hi. How did it go at work?"

"Fine. Piece of cake. It's so simple that it's almost boring. But compared to what I could be doing, it's great. Any mail?"

"You got a letter from Howard."

"Great." She started to her room, paused, and headed for the kitchen instead. "No. I'm gonna eat first, in case there's bad news." She ate her supper, took the dishes to the kitchen, and cleaned up, then went to her room and closed the door.

An hour later, Petra acknowledged that Krista didn't intend to tell her where she'd been since she left work or to share with her the content of the letter from Howard University. "I'm tired," she said to herself. "Except for that and these occasional headaches, I feel the same as I ever did."

She went into her room, sat on the edge of her bed, and let out a long breath. *Maybe that's what's happening; I don't remember being tired like this. Oh, heck. Anybody who went through what I did today would be tired. Not one thing I attempted in the office worked out; I walked five blocks out of my way in order to avoid running into Reverend Collins; I came home, cooked a nice supper, and had to wait almost two hours before I could eat it. On top of all that, Krista is acting out, and making my life as miserable as she can. She won't even tell me whether she's in contact with her father.*

"Oh, gosh. I promised Mama I'd call her." She dialed her mother's number, something she didn't do often, because her mother was holier than the Reverend Collins. She could take just so much of her mother's philosophy about life, best described as a flirtation with hellfire and brimstone. Lena Fields had never forgiven her only daughter for getting pregnant without the blessing of marriage, and she ascribed every problem and every adverse circumstance, however slight or ephemeral, to Petra's having had sex outside the bonds of holy matrimony.

"Hello. This is Lena."

Petra took a deep breath. "Hi, Mama. I think I need a vacation. I know Krista is eighteen, but I don't want to leave her alone in this house. Could she stay with you, or would you prefer to stay with her over here? Ever since I told her about Goodman, she goes and comes as she pleases, doesn't tell me anything she's doing. She did say she got a job selling linens at the department store, but she got a letter from Howard University today and hasn't bothered to tell me what's in it, though I'm expected to pay her tuition. This is getting to me."

"If she was mine, and she acted like that, I'd whack her behind. 'Course you know my views on that. If she'd had a daddy to raise her, she'd be more respectful. I'll stay with her. Just let me know when."

"I had a father to raise me," Petra said to

herself, "and he almost turned me against men." To her mother, she said, "Yes, ma'am. I'll let you know when I'm leaving."

It was well that her mother tamed Krista — and she would certainly do that — before they were both too grieved to accomplish that. It didn't seem that Krista planned to develop a relationship with her father, and what a pity that was, for she would need him.

The next day, Tuesday, was one that Petra would never forget. "I need a few weeks leave, Jack. Everything is pressing on me."

He pitched his calendar across the room and glared at her. "You just had a vacation. Ever since I promoted you and gave you a raise, you've been acting weird. I need you, babe, but you sure as hell are not indispensable. Anybody who's willing to sit still seven hours a day can do your job. I wish to hell I hadn't fired Gail."

"You said she was incompetent."

"Don't tell me what I said. I fired her because she was screwing Sally."

"That was no skin off your teeth, Jack. She's not your type."

"How do you know what my type is?" he roared. Suddenly he stood up and shook his right index finger at her. "I ought to fire you, and I just might. You can have the leave, but without pay. I'm not a gold mine."

She had what she wanted, time to see a few things she had always wanted to see. She surprised herself when she hugged Jack and kissed him on his left cheek.

"Hey, what the hell! Is that some kind of test? You know damned well I'm not gay."

"What? I wanted you to know that I appreciate your kindness."

"Yeah? Well, keep it between the lines. How'd I know what you meant? It wasn't the kiss I felt. You women forget about those soft things sticking out in front of you. Be sure and let me know where you'll be in case I need to ask you a question, so take your cell phone with you."

She wasn't going to do any such thing. After making certain that she left nothing pending on her desk, she removed all her personal things and, at four o'clock that afternoon, walked out and didn't look back.

On her way home, she stopped by Dwill's department store, and went to the linen shop. She couldn't have been more proud as she watched Krista at work. Somehow, her daughter had developed poise and gracious manners; if need be, she could take care of herself. She didn't want to leave without her daughter's forgiveness, so she would try one more time.

"Krista, I'm going to take a few weeks leave from the office. I'm tired, and I think I'll go out West and see a few things I've always wanted to see. Your grandmother will stay with you while I'm gone." She was careful not to say, "till I get back," because she didn't know whether she would. "I don't want to leave here knowing that you haven't forgiven me, Krista. I'm not offering excuses. Goodman doesn't hold it against me, but you do. Can you forgive me?"

"Where on the West Coast are you going?"

"I don't know. Wherever I get an urge to go."

"Are you kidding?"

She looked at Krista, so self-assured and confident. "I'm serious. Are you going to tell me whether you forgive me?"

Krista lifted her shoulders in a careless shrug. "You did what you had to do, so I don't hold it against you. When are you leaving?"

"Soon as I can pack and Mama can arrange to stay with you. Maybe day after tomorrow."

"Where you going first?"

"Probably the Grand Canyon or Mount Rushmore. I haven't decided yet."

"I wish I knew what had come over you. You wouldn't spend a dime to go to the circus, and now you're planning to run all over the country. Well, I hope you have a good time. Stay in touch. I gotta get back to work." She brushed Petra's cheek with her lips. "Behave yourself now, Mom."

Petra went home and called her mother. "Mama, I'd like to leave day after tomorrow. Do you think you can come over tomorrow?"

"I'll be over there about six. I'm on the seven to three shift, and unless some of the RNs call in sick, I'll be on this shift for at least the next month. I thought you just had a vacation. Anything wrong with you?"

She wasn't in the habit of lying to her mother, and she wouldn't do it now. "This scene is getting to me, Mama, and I feel like I'll cave in if I don't get some relief from it. I hope you can get Krista off her high horse."

"Of course I will. She'd better not act out with me. I don't understand it. She was always such a sweet and obedient child. Well, I guess the chickens coming home to roost. What goes around comes around. See you tomorrow."

Petra hung up and expelled a long, cleansing breath. "God forbid I should ever be as sanctimonious as my mother." If Krista didn't hold it against her, did that mean she forgave her? She'd probably never know.

Two days later, Petra took the commuter train to the Baltimore/Washington International Airport and boarded a flight to Rapid City, South Dakota. She'd never been so far from home or so far out of the reach of anyone she knew, but nonetheless, she experienced complete confidence.

"What's a good hotel?" she asked a woman at the information desk in the airport. The woman looked into a drawer and handed Petra a card.

"Either of these two will be good and not too expensive. You can get a little bus out front that goes to both of them. I'd call first. Lots of tourists in town right now."

Petra chose the bed and breakfast and was given a room that faced the Black Hills. After unpacking, she raced down to the woman who seemed to own the hotel and asked directions to Mount Rushmore.

"Better wait till tomorrow morning. Mr. Robinson will be going then. It might be more interesting to go with someone who's already been there. He's one of our roomers. A nice gentleman."

She didn't want to meet Mr. Robinson or any other nice gentleman. She had learned that one person's nice could be somebody else's nasty. However, when she entered the dining room for supper that evening, she saw only one other person, a blond man of about fifty. "Why don't you sit over there with Mr. Robinson?" the waiter said. "You're the last two, and anyway, Mr. Robinson loves to have company."

When she hesitated, the waiter said, "Come on, miss," took her place setting, and urged her to accompany him to the table at which the man sat.

"Mr. Robinson, this is Ms. Fields. She's from Maryland." Robinson stood and extended his hand. "Thank you for agreeing to join me, Ms. Fields. I'm always alone, and there's nothing I hate more."

She sat down, wondered about his accent, and decided that an appropriate question about it would serve to start the conversation. "How do you do, Mr. Robinson? I'm trying to place your accent. Is it Italian?"

She liked his smile, warm and friendly. "No, my dear, I'm from Scotland in northern Europe. I've always wanted to see Mount Rushmore, and when I learned that my sight is failing, I dropped everything and decided to see it while I could."

Shock reverberated throughout her system. She hadn't expected to meet a kindred soul. Compassion welled up in her. Imagine a man who hated being alone having to live in darkness. "I'm so sorry, Mr. Robinson. Have you seen it yet?"

"Oh, yes. I've been over there at least a dozen times, and I can tell you the trip here was worth it. I wouldn't have missed it for the world. What do you do in Maryland?"

"I'm office manager in a real estate office, or I was. I don't know about the future."

"That's something you should never worry about," he said, " 'cause you can't count on it." They went to the lounge and talked until the lights dimmed at midnight. "Will I meet any Native Americans while I'm here?" she asked him. His smile reminded her of her grandfather's patient and slow smile. "I don't see how you can avoid it unless you close your eyes. The Sioux are all over the place."

After breakfast the next morning, Petra left the hotel with Mr. Robinson. Walking along the Avenue of Flags, the sixty-foot-high carvings of the four presidents' faces loomed before her, and she stopped, awed. "Mr. Robinson, this is unbelievable. It's awesome."

"I know," he said, taking her hand. "I can't get enough of this view. For me, it's one of the great wonders of the world."

She squeezed his fingers, empathizing, for she understood well how he felt. For the next three days, they visited the "Shrine of Democracy," as the great memorial is known, and many of the surrounding areas. She delighted in their strolls along Presidential Trail and visits to the museums, and once they enjoyed a picnic beneath a tree that seemed to reach to the heavens.

She watched the man, marveling at his apparent contentment in the face of his coming tragic ordeal. He chewed slowly on a hotdog, savoring it as if he had all the time he could want. She reached for his hand and held it. "I'm glad I met you. You're thankful for what you have while you have it, and that's a lesson I appreciate."

"Thanks, Petra. I was wishing I had met you fifteen or twenty years ago, when I would still have had years and years to enjoy your beauty and your radiant personality, but I'm grateful for having met you at all and for these days we're spending together."

"It's time I left here," she said to herself on the fourth day of her visit, "before I get into trouble. Worse still, I could cause trouble. I shouldn't let a stray cat fall for me." When they returned to the hotel, she booked a flight to Las Vegas, Nevada.

She told him good-bye at breakfast the

next morning, but as she walked away, she stopped, turned, and looked back at one of the sweetest men she had ever met. Maybe . . . No, she couldn't. Her soul was in enough trouble as it was.

"What you gon' do in Vegas?" her seatmate, a middle-aged black woman clothed from head to foot in imitation Kente cloth, asked Petra. "Y'all work your tail off for a few pennies and give it all right back to The Man. Won't catch me doing it." The woman patted the back of her head wrap and settled confidently into her seat.

"Do you live in Las Vegas?" Petra asked the woman.

"I live in Alabama. This is my vacation. I followed the same route every year for the last twenty-three. After I see Mount Rushmore and pay tribute to our great presidents, especially Mr. Jefferson, I visit Old Faithful in Yellowstone Park. I tell you, those geysers are really something. Then, I always stop by Vegas on the way back home just to play the slot machines."

Petra turned fully to face the woman. "Are you saying that's not gambling?"

"Of course it isn't," the woman said, her tone upbraiding Petra for her ignorance. "Poker is gambling. I'd never stoop to that."

"Poor ignorant me," Petra said beneath her breath. "I always thought betting and gambling were the same."

"If you've never been to Vegas, be careful," the woman advised. "You're young, and if you get into those gambling joints, those men will have your clothes off you in a minute. You won't catch me playing poker and having to take off my clothes in front of a bunch of men. I have too much pride for that."

And enough ignorance and misinformation to match it. Petra found an aspirin in her pocketbook, asked the steward for a glass of water, took the medicine to ease her headache, and slept. However, she soon awakened when a male voice inquired whether she wanted coffee or another drink. "Ginger ale, please," she said to the steward.

"I'll have a gin and tonic," her seatmate said. "May as well get in the mood for Vegas."

"That'll be five dollars," the man said.

"Humph. One finger of gin ain't never been worth no five dollars. I'll pay you five for two of those tiny little bottles."

"Uh . . . sorry, ma'am, but the price is fixed."

"Y'all got a lot to learn about Vegas," the woman said to the steward as she accepted the drink and parted with a five-dollar bill. "A little gin makes a woman relax; two of 'em makes her very cooperative." She handed the steward her business card, and when he let it drop to the floor, Petra picked it up and read: "Sister Annie. Fulfilling all your needs for spiritual counsel, etc."

"Pardon me, sir. I think she meant for you to have this." Petra tapped the steward on the arm and handed him the card.

The man glared at her. "You're not serious."

What a woman! Maybe Mama isn't so bad, Petra thought, at least when compared to this woman. She'd begun to wonder why she chose to spend some of her last precious days in Las Vegas when she had several other places she wanted to go. By that doctor's count, time was at a premium. Except for her headaches and an occasional lack of energy, she still couldn't complain.

She checked into her hotel room, went to the window, and gazed down on the famous Strip. What the devil was she doing in Las Vegas? After unpacking, she wandered down to the game room and walked around.

"Like some company?" a tall man, who looked as if he'd never worked, asked her. Her gaze clung to his hair, slick, straight, and shiny. No black man in Ellicott City,

Maryland, would walk around with hair looking like that. His black suit, black shirt, and red tie complemented his hair style, and that, along with his diamond left ear stud marked him as a man on the make and the take. She wanted company badly, but if she'd been only ten years old, she would have known to avoid guys such as that one. Feeling clever, she smiled and said, "I'm neither giving nor selling. What about you?"

After quickly erasing a frown, the man said, "Me neither. Business is lousy. Let's take the escalator down to the next level and get a milk shake or something. That's about all I can afford."

"Did you gamble your money away?" she asked, falling into step with him.

"Naah. I'm not stupid enough to do that; I throw it away on another habit."

"Alcohol and drugs?"

"I've just given up drugs, but I'm in debt up to here." He sliced the air above his head. "I quit because my mother asked me with practically her last breath, and I promised her I would. If you owe these guys and you don't pay, somebody will find you lying in a vacant lot. What's got you? Something weighing you down?"

"This is the first time I've been away from home," she said, "and I guess it shows." She didn't intend to show the world a suffering face. The knowledge of it hurt more than whatever ailment she had.

"Oh, I could see that you're different." He ordered two raspberry milk shakes, and they sat on high stools at the milk bar and talked for several hours.

"I know this town," he told her after they had talked for a while, "and I think you should leave here. You don't know me from beans, and you've been with me for over two hours. By now, some dudes would have had your jewelry, credit cards, ID, and your cash, and you wouldn't even suspect them.

"Go back to Maryland, Petra, while you can. If you don't, you'll be beholden to some guy who'll steal all you have, then befriend you, obligate you to him, and put you on the street. You can't imagine how many women in this town fell into that trap. All this glitter is great when you're loaded with money, but when you're down and out, it's a snake pit. I know what I'm talking about."

"Thanks, Bill. I'll be careful." She put fifteen dollars on the table. "The shakes are on me." The man was pleasant enough, but she was not going to hang out with a loser.

Wishing that she had spent at least a day at Yellowstone Park in Wyoming, she walked through the elegant shops in the hotel's promenade until tired and then went back to her room. She hadn't left home looking for a good time or even to enjoy herself; she'd merely wanted to see some of the things she had always wanted to experience in person. So far, she didn't regret her decision. She ordered her dinner there, enjoyed it, watched an old Ethel Waters movie, *The Member of the Wedding,* and went to bed.

"I wish something would happen. I'm getting so tired of waiting."

The next morning, she took a bus tour of the city, then checked out of the hotel and took a train to Arizona. Sedona was supposed to be the most beautiful city in the United States, and people said the Grand Canyon was the most spectacular place. "You taking the train all the way to the Grand Canyon?" a woman asked her as they sat in the station waiting to board. "You must have a lot of time on your hands."

"On the contrary," Petra said. "Time is what I don't have, but clouds are all I can see from a plane. I won't be coming this way again, so I want to see what this part of the country is like."

"Red dirt. I'd be happy if I never saw it again."

Since beginning her journey, Petra had

learned that if you didn't agree with a person, a smile sufficed. If she'd learned that earlier, she might have had a smoother relationship with her mother. Instead, she had caused friction by expressing her opinions and insisting that she was right. So she smiled at the woman who hated red dirt, went to the newsstand for a paper, and changed her seat.

By the time she boarded the train, she was too tired to care who sat beside her, but relief swept over when a young woman, apparently in her late twenties, with very little luggage sat next to her. She noticed at once the woman's makeup-free skin, so tender and flawless that it seemed about to burst.

"I'm Greta," the woman said. "I hope you're going to the Grand Canyon and that you'll let me share the experience with you."

Alerted by the woman's precise speech and gentle manners, Petra asked her, "Are you going there for a special reason?"

"Oh, yes. I want to see all the things I've always wanted to see and do the things I've missed, so that I'll be content when I take the next step. I believe I'm doing what I'm called to do, but when I leave all this behind, I don't want to think what if. . . . Not ever."

"Are you getting married?" Petra asked

her. After all, some religions restricted a woman's movements after she married.

What a beautiful smile! "Oh, in a way. I'm entering a convent. My father doesn't approve, and he said I should see the world and be sure. I know he has a point, so I decided to take this trip. Are you on vacation?"

Petra thought for a few seconds. She was at the point in her life where lying didn't make sense. "Not really," she said. "I'm completing . . . or rather, I'm finishing up things. I'd hoped to see Sedona, but I don't know how far it is from the Grand Canyon."

"According to my guidebook, it's one hundred and ten miles," Greta said. "You can easily do that."

"I want to stand on that hill among those big red rocks and watch the sunrise just one time," Petra said. "I think I'll buy my breakfast, take it up that hill, sit on one of those rocks, and eat while the sun rises."

"Oh, that's very romantic, but I'm not sure I'd do that. Arizona has more rattlesnakes per square mile than any state in the country."

Petra swallowed hard. "There goes that idea. Maybe I'll get a taxi to take me up there, eat my breakfast, and watch the sunrise while I sit in the cab." A thought occurred to her.

"Greta, have you ever had a boyfriend?"

"Oh, yes. I've had a full life, Petra. I've loved deeply."

"What happened? You can tell me, because we'll never see each other again after we leave Arizona."

"He didn't want to live a Christian life, and I couldn't marry any other kind of man. For some reason, he didn't tell me until after we lived together for over a year."

Petra released a sharp whistle. "Miserable bastard! And I'll bet anything you were a virgin."

Greta's lips tightened perceptibly. "And according to him, the only one he ever had. He didn't deserve me."

"Have you forgiven him?" She asked the question, because she needed another view on the necessity of forgiveness in order to get into Heaven.

"I'm trying."

Petra sat up straight, turned, and looked hard at Greta. "How long have you been trying?"

Greta blew out a long breath and her shoulders sagged. "Three long years, and I still get angry whenever I think of what he did."

"I've had some experience with this,

Greta. Think of it as what you allowed him to do, and you'll find it easier to forgive the SOB."

"First call for dinner," the waiter walked through the train calling. "Next call will be at eight forty-five."

"Let's go," Greta and Petra said in unison. Laughter poured out of them as they got up and made their way to the dining room.

After their main course, they went to the observation lounge to have dessert and coffee. A verbose woman sitting beside Greta in a lounge chair put her hand to the side of her mouth and asked Greta, "Do you think that man over there" — she pointed to the man — "is an Indian? He looks like one, but he isn't wearing any feathers."

An expression of surprise flitted across Greta's face. "I can't tell by looking. You'll have to ask him."

Petra's lower lip dropped when the woman got up, walked over to the man, and, loudly enough for everyone in the car to hear, said, "You big chief pow wow?"

"No," the man said. "I'm a Native American, and you're an idiot."

"I may have seen redder faces," Greta said of the woman, "but I don't remember it."

When the train arrived in Flagstaff at seven the next morning, Petra asked Greta where she had a reservation. She remembered their having discussed hotels earlier, but couldn't recall the name of Greta's hotel.

"I was hoping to get one after I arrived," she said.

"Then why don't you come with me? I'm staying at a bed and breakfast hotel, and if the room has two beds, you may stay with me. I'll be here three days."

"I think you're a blessing to me," Greta said, "because you're the only person I've been able to talk to about my abortive affair."

At the hotel, Petra received permission for Greta to stay with her, and as they settled in, she told Greta, "I'd better warn you; in my entire life, I've never shared a room with anyone."

"You're either fibbing, or you're an only child and you're a virgin."

Petra gave the woman a withering look. "I'm an only child."

Chapter Four

Petra went to bed that night wondering whether to tell Greta about her predicament. Greta was, after all, almost a nun, a person with spiritual insight. Besides, hadn't Greta shared her problems? She wasn't sure. The last thing she wanted was a female Reverend Collins traveling with her, sharing a room and meals with her, and nagging her constantly about her soul. She decided to play it by ear and went to sleep.

After breakfast the next morning, they boarded one of the free shuttle buses and headed for the South Rim of the Grand Canyon. "Petra is an unusual name for an African American," Greta said at the beginning of their journey. "It's Scandinavian and German, isn't it?"

Petra had wanted to ask Greta about her background. The white people she knew back home didn't seek the company of African Americans if they had a choice, and

Greta had other options. "Apparently, it's Swedish," she told her. "I heard my father tell my mother, in a fit of rage, that he named me Petra to commemorate his affair with a Swedish woman shortly after he and my mother married. They were at loggerheads all the time. You didn't want to grow up in that house, Greta."

"My goodness. I'm sorry, Petra. Are they still living together?"

Petra sucked her teeth in disgust. "Definitely not. At a party at our house one night, Daddy met Mama's best friend, went home with her, and never came back."

"What a pity," Greta said, but Petra sensed that she was deep in very personal thoughts, thoughts triggered by Petra's story of her father's infidelity.

Yeah. What a pity!

"What's your background?" she asked Greta. "Were your folks born in this country?"

"My mother was, but my father was born in Frankfurt, Germany. He came here to work at the United Nations, married my mother, and stayed. They live in New York. I'm an only child, and if I go into a convent, they won't have any grandchildren. That infuriates my dad."

The driver of the shuttle bus announced,

"We'll be there in a minute. Don't wander away from trails and don't go off alone. Come right here for a bus back to Flagstaff. Have a good time."

"I'm going to the lookout," Greta said.

Chills plowed through Petra. "Lord, I can't go out there. I'm scared to death of heights. I get the urge to jump." She stopped walking. *What did she have to fear? Certainly, she didn't fear for her life.* She ran and caught Greta. "I always wanted to see this place. I can't wait." Emboldened by she couldn't imagine what magic, she followed the group to the lookout, but couldn't make herself go to the edge where people stood, protected from the mile-deep drop only by a metal fence.

"Come on," Greta said, "isn't this why we came?"

Petra walked to the edge, braced her hands against the fence, and gazed down at the abyss below. Instead of fear, she knew a strange calm, an inexplicable peacefulness. And as if they shared her wonder and awe, none in the small group uttered a word.

They remained there for more than half an hour, and as they headed toward the Tusayan Museum, Greta said, "I'll remember that view for as long as I live, even if I live to be a hundred."

"There's no likelihood that I'll forget it. I wouldn't have missed it for anything. These are the Tusayan Ruins," Petra said, reading from her guidebook. "The Pueblo Indians lived here more than eight hundred years ago." She gazed at the holes in the side of the great red hill, a community hulled out of a mountain side.

"They must have had a hard life. Considering how we live today, we have plenty to be thankful for," Greta said.

"Yeah, even when you look back on a ruptured romance, if the guy knew how to put it down, you're still luckier than a woman who never had a romance."

"You don't regret it?" Greta asked.

"No way. That's one of the few things I don't regret." She couldn't understand why breathing suddenly seemed difficult and why she was so tired. Maybe the time had come. "I think I'll go back to the hotel, Greta. You go ahead and enjoy the view. I'm awfully tired." For the first time since she left home, she wished for her cell phone, but she hadn't wanted contact with her office or her family, had wanted the complete freedom she had never experienced. "I'll . . . uh . . . see you later, Greta."

"I'm not surprised that you're out of breath," Greta said. "The guidebook warns about respiratory problems at this altitude."

Petra let her gaze scan the great canyon for a minute. "See you later," she said, turned, and started down the hill to the bus stop.

By the time the shuttle bus on which she was riding reached Flagstaff, Petra felt like her old self. "I'm getting fed up with this," she said aloud as she walked into her room. If she promised a client that the Watkins agents would sell a house within six months, that client would go at once to another real estate agency. But that stuffed turkey she had for a doctor practiced medicine by guesswork. "You may be pregnant," he'd once said after she'd just told him she hadn't been near a man in three years. She sucked her teeth. Did he think women conceived by osmosis? She'd often thought that, in his case, MD meant Moron Doctor. She went to him because he was the only black doctor near her, and she believed in patronizing her own.

Still, tests didn't lie, so she wrote the name, addresses, and telephone numbers of her mother and daughter on a sheet of paper, marked it "In case of emergency," and put the information in her pocketbook. When Greta returned much later that day, she gave Petra a small white Bible.

"You're serious about going to a convent, aren't you?" Petra asked her.

"After what I saw today, I know I've made the right decision." She sat on the edge of Petra's bed. "I met a really nice man. He was seeing all the places that he's always wanted to see and doing things he's wanted to do before —"

Petra sat up and put her hands over her ears. "Don't tell me. I don't need to know."

"Why not? He committed an armed robbery about ten years ago, and he's been on the lam ever since. He can't develop close relationships or get married and have a family or keep a good job, so he is going to turn himself in and take his medicine. Ten years from now, he'll only be thirty-eight, and he can start over."

"You spent a lot of time with that stranger."

"He needed to talk, I guess. He said his name was Richie, and that once he made up his mind to go back and face the authorities, he stopped being afraid." She grasped Petra's hand and held it. "What are you escaping, Petra? I know there's something going on with you."

"I . . . You're asking a lot. I haven't even told my family about this."

"That's what strangers are for, you said,

and you were right. They give us an opportunity to tell the truth, and we don't worry about what they'll think of us and who they'll tell. Do you think I've told anyone but you about the affair I've had such a hard time getting over?"

"I don't want people to feel sorry for me, so I've been keeping it to myself. Two months ago, my doctor told me I had six months to live."

"Wh . . . what?" Greta stammered. She jumped up, folded her arms beneath her breasts, and then sat down. "And you haven't told your family?"

"I didn't want to worry them."

"Great. And you think a shock would be more merciful?"

Petra shrugged. "How do I know? My mother gets along fine with shocks. When my father left home with her best friend, all Mama said to me was 'Good riddance to both of them.' And when I got pregnant, she said, 'I told you about wearing those miniskirts all the way up to your behind.' " Petra didn't see anything amusing about that, but apparently Greta did, for it took her a few minutes to straighten out her face.

"Sometimes, I think I'll wake up and discover that I've been dreaming," Petra said, "but I know it's true." She looked at

Greta, but her thoughts were elsewhere. "All things considered, it hasn't been so bad, but if I'm going to see Sedona and California, oh yes, and Martin Luther King's tomb, I'd better get moving." She checked the train schedule, phoned a hotel in Sedona and made a reservation. Then she packed.

"This room is paid up through tomorrow, Greta. I'm glad I met you. Have a great life."

Greta hugged her. "I guess you're doing what you have to do. Bless you."

Petra checked into the hotel in Sedona a few minutes after midnight, went to her room, and fell across the bed. Hours later, she awakened, undressed, crawled into bed, and went back to sleep. She awakened again at three o'clock in the afternoon, dressed, and went to the front desk for information.

"If you're leaving day after tomorrow, I suggest you take a sight-seeing bus. You can't see Sedona in one day."

"I overslept."

"It's the healthy air."

Petra could hardly believe that what she saw was not a mirage as the bus wound its way past the great red rocks, each a different shape and shade of red, and she gasped aloud at the breathtaking Oak Creek Canyon. She had never seen such beauty. "And to think that I might never have seen this."

She didn't want to leave the city or the area, but something inside of her said, "Move on." *I should phone Greta, see if she's still at the hotel, and tell her not to miss this.*

Petra phoned the hotel, identified herself, asked for Greta Muster, and was informed that no one by that name had been registered at the hotel. "But she checked in with me three days ago."

"Sorry, Ms. Fields, but you must be mistaken."

"I don't believe this. I must be going out of my mind." She hung up. "Oh, for goodness sake. The room was in my name, not Greta's, and I don't remember the room number. I must be losing it. Maybe I ought to call Mama or Krista and get my feet on the ground, as Grandpa used to say."

Right then, Krista was having a difficult time getting her feet on the ground, for she struggled against her grandmother's discipline. And as one means of escape, she spent as much time as possible with her father, who was less certain of his authority with her.

Goodman leaned back in his desk chair and scrutinized his daughter and oldest child, already aware in the short time he'd known her that she would push him to the limit if he permitted it. "Krista, I do not like spending evenings away from my family. You're to come here on time and keep your end of our bargain. I'll give you your lesson from five-fifteen to six-fifteen on Mondays, after which I'll have dinner at home. At eight o'clock, I rehearse The Oella Choral Ensemble. I told you that, so there's no point in sulking. I can't change my program just because you want to gauge your importance to me. That's childish, and I won't stand for it."

"Maybe I'll go with you to the choral ensemble."

"As an observer, yes. I'm not the sole arbiter of that group's membership. If you want to sing with them, you have to try out."

"You said I had a good voice."

"Yes, you do. How do you plan to spend the time between six-fifteen and eight?"

"You mean I can't go home with you? The only time I see you is here at the studio."

He got up, walked over to his piano, and ran the middle finger of his right hand over the white keys. "You're asking me to upset my wife, Krista, and I am not prepared to do that. At a convenient time, I'll introduce you to your brothers, and after you get to know them, I'll introduce you to my wife, though I expect the boys will manage that more easily than I."

"Are you scared of her?" she asked him.

"What a question! You don't understand male-female relations, do you? Can't you put yourself in her place? You will remind her that I once loved another woman, and that I loved that woman enough to give her a child. Why should I fear my wife? The answer to your question is that I love her, and I don't want to hurt her."

"Oh. Grandma never has anything good to say about my grandfather. She doesn't know where he is, and said she doesn't care. My mom's taking a vacation. She didn't say where she was going. I just . . . I think I'll go home. Maybe I'll go with you to the singing group next week." She looked at him with eyes wide and, in them, an expression of expectancy.

I'd better be careful with her. She's more vulnerable than I had thought. He enjoyed the choral group more than he'd expected. No conductor could resist thirty-six beautiful voices. He'd love to add Krista's mezzo soprano to the group, but he didn't want to be accused of nepotism. He drove her home, ate supper with his family, and rushed to the choral group's weekly rehearsal.

As he entered the room where they practiced, he noticed a new face, a lovely face, and waited to see where she would sit. However, she didn't sit with the altos or the sopranos; she walked up to the piano, looked him up and down, and said, "I like to sing alto, but if you want me to sing soprano, I can do that, too."

He raised an eyebrow, taken aback by her frank cockiness and — might as well admit it — blatant sexiness. To show her who was boss, he said, "Sing the first two lines of the National Anthem. What key?"

A half smile flittered at the corner of her mouth. "G is good."

He liked her rich tone, but he figured he'd better not tell her that. "Did Mrs. Long give you permission to join the group?"

"She said that's up to you."

"Sit with the altos."

"Thanks." She put her hands on her hips and looked at him from beneath lowered eyelids. "I sure hope you're not married, but if you aren't, the women around here would have to be crazy."

He didn't think he'd ever had a more direct pass. She might be reckless, but he couldn't afford to be. "By your definition, at least one woman is sane," he said. "Have a seat."

"She's a looker, all right," he said to

himself, observing her rich brown skin, slumberous, long-lashed eyes, and pouting lips about a mouth that invited a man to plunge into it. Hot, and she knew it. A smart man would avoid her as if she were the plague.

For the two hours that they practiced, the woman worked at him. Every time he glanced her way, she smiled or winked, and every such gesture amounted to an invitation. After two of the longest hours he'd ever spent, she sidled up to the piano.

"You wouldn't be going my way, would you?" she asked. "I could use a lift."

"What's your name?"

"Jada. Jada Hankins." She gave him her address.

His mind told him not to do it, that he was stepping into a hole and might not be able to get out of it. He ignored that inner voice that had served him so well throughout his adult life. "I'll drop you off, but don't expect this to become a habit."

"It won't. That is, not unless that's what you want," she said, letting him know that it was up to him, because she had no qualms about an involvement with a married man. If Krista joined the group, Jada wouldn't have a choice but to leave him alone.

■ ■ ■ ■

However, Jada had other plans for Goodman. When she went for a man, she got him. She meant to lure Goodman Prout into a relationship and get herself a cooperative apartment. In her view, a young and beautiful woman shouldn't have to get what she wanted by the sweat of her brow. That was what men were for.

"I'm gonna see what he's made of, and soon," she promised herself. "He's used to getting what he wants, but so am I."

"Does your wife work?" Jada asked Goodman.

"She owns a restaurant, a very nice one."

"Really? Which one?"

He had no intention of telling her where she could find his wife. He took his gaze from the traffic long enough to glance at her. "It may have been foolish of me to give you a ride this evening, but stupidity is not something that any thinking person would associate with me. Don't forget that."

"Not to worry," she said airily. "I'm a quick study. She doesn't interest me; you do."

He stopped at her house, aligned the car

with the curb, put it in park, and slid his arm along the back of her seat. "You're a reckless woman, and you're after something. There are nine men in that ensemble. Why'd you pick me? And you did. You made up your mind the minute I walked into that room."

"I liked what I saw. From head to foot, you're a man. Isn't that reason enough?"

"Not really. Be careful you don't find yourself on the left side of a bell-shaped curve."

Jada fanned herself. "Whew! Get outta *here*! Imagine me sliding my butt up anything." She leaned toward him. "Kiss me, and go on home."

He stared down at her slightly-parted, beautifully shaped mouth, and frissons of heat surged through him. An open invitation to trouble. He put his right hand behind her head and his left one on her breast and singed her mouth with his lips. When she attempted to suck him into her, he broke the kiss. "Do you have a man in there?"

"I woulda thought you were smarter than that," she said. "Why would I sit out here and kiss you where he could see me? No, I don't."

"I'd better be going. Good night."

She opened the door, looked back at him, and said, "I live alone. Good night."

Goodman drove off with less speed and deliberation than usually characterized his driving. What had he started and why? That woman was not the type to back off. He thought of Carla and how they related to each other. He was happy, wasn't he? True, Carla nagged him to join her in the restaurant with the view to opening at least two more, but he didn't know the restaurant business and wanted nothing to do with food other than to eat it. The smell of frying grease always made him think of blisters.

He looked at his long slender fingers as he clutched the wheel of his Lexus and laughed. An emery board was the most dangerous thing to which he expected to expose his fingers, fingers that were meant to caress piano keys and pick guitar and violin strings. No knives, fire, and scalding hot water near his hands. Music was his world, but Carla didn't seem to understand that. Never had. To her mind, he should have music as a hobby, something to distract him, but the restaurant was something he could pass on to his children. He meant to expose his children — all three of them — to the better things in life: music, art, travel, literature, sports, and humanitarian pursuits, and let them make their own choice.

He walked into his house, greeted Paul, his younger son, who lounged in the family room watching *Law & Order* on television. "Where are Peter and your mother?"

"Mom took Peter to a cooking demonstration."

"Did she now?"

A few minutes later, the other members of his family arrived. Carla hugged Paul, and Peter rushed to greet him, after which Carla said, "I think I'll turn in, hon."

Goodman glanced at his sons, hoping they would leave the room. When they didn't, he said to her, "Stay and have a drink with me. I . . . uh . . . I need to unwind."

"Thanks, but not tonight," she said, and he understood that that "no" covered any other suggestion he might make.

Frustrated and suddenly angry, he looked at his older son. "Remember that an ounce of prevention is worth a pound of cure." He heard her steps falter in the midst of her rush up the stairs and knew she got his message. He was also aware that she hadn't learned how to reverse herself.

In that respect, Carla and Petra were alike. "I'm getting tired," Petra acknowledged to herself, "but I'm not going back till I see everything I want to see. Except for being tired and a headache now and then, I feel fine." As tired as she was, Petra had an urge to keep moving. "How far am I from Phoenix?" she asked the porter in the bed and breakfast hotel in which she stayed near Sedona's midtown.

"Two or three hours by train. Less, if you catch an express. I'd leave here on the six A.M. express, if I were you, miss. You can see the sunrise along the way. It's like a changing painting. You never saw anything so spectacular. This time of year, it's not as great as it is midwinter, but it's still a sight." She took his advice, and when the train sped toward Phoenix, she sat aboard it, gazing out of the window at the breaking day and the rising sun. However, as beautiful as it was, the miracle of it escaped her.

"Spectacular, isn't it?" a waiter said as he walked through the car offering coffee.

"I guess you could say that," she replied. "I've seen so much recently that it's hard for me to enthuse about anything."

"Lady, this view would make a wild horse stop running."

She took a good look at the man, accepted the coffee, tipped him, and turned her face to the window. *Damned if I'm going to argue with a man whose four top front teeth are gold, two front bottom ones are missing, and who smiles as happily as if he had thirty-two perfect white teeth.*

"They've got some nice bridle paths in Phoenix, miss, and some of the sweetest mares" (the word came out like a whistle, Petra noticed) "you ever saw. Enjoy your stay." She thanked him, though she only spared him a glance, lest she give in to the laughter that bubbled up in her.

She'd never ridden a horse. To her mind, they were handsome creatures, with especially beautiful eyes, but they were big, and as much as she liked them, she feared them. However, as she entered the tourist office in Phoenix, she recalled her joy and excitement gazing down from the South Rim of the Grand Canyon in spite of her fear of heights.

I'm supposed to be having new experiences, seeing and doing things I've always wanted to do. Maybe I can ride a horse? What can I lose? I've only got another couple of months, anyway.

"Good morning, sir," she said to the clerk in the tourist office. "I've heard you have wonderful horses here, and I'd like to try riding one. What can you recommend?"

"Do you ride?"

"I'm embarrassed to tell you that I've

never been on a horse."

"Then I know just the place."

Armed with the address, she made her way to Phoenix Stables. "I don't know how to ride, but I want to try," she told a groom.

"Yes, ma'am. We have gentle mares that are very patient with neophytes. If you'll wait about ten minutes, I'll get someone to ride with you. It's much better than riding alone. I'll be back in a few minutes."

He returned with a man who appeared to be a cowboy, although admittedly, movies and television had formed her opinion of what constituted a real cowboy. "Are you a genuine cowboy?" she asked the man.

Except for his Stetson, boots, and stirrups, he could have been a New Yorker, and a mesmerizing one at that. Clean shaven and with an aura of elegance, the man stood out like a sore thumb. She didn't trip over men, but . . . She told herself to remember why she was in Arizona.

His voice seemed to come from someplace deep inside of him. "Do I work on a ranch? When I'm not on vacation, yes."

She put her hand up to shade her eyes from the sun. "How long have you been on vacation? I mean how temporary is this vacation?"

His laughter reminded her of a growl.

"You're a clever one. Since I own the ranch, I vacation when and for as long as I please." The mischievous twinkle in his eyes gave her some confidence that he was a good guy, but she didn't like being laughed at.

"Put your left foot in there," he said, motioning to the stirrup, "and swing your right leg over the horse." She did as he told her, gazed down at him from the back of the animal, and grinned. He tipped his Stetson, half bowed, and got on his own horse. "Good girl!"

"How do I make this animal stop walking?"

He cocked an eyebrow, and a grin creased his face. "Tell her to stop?"

"You mean it's a her?"

"This is your first time on a horse. Do you think anybody in Phoenix would be stupid enough to put you on a stallion?"

"But I wanted one, because —"

He didn't wait to hear the rest. "You mean to tell me you couldn't tell the difference?"

"How was I supposed to know?"

"What's your name, miss?" She told him. "Ms. Fields, you distinguish a mare from a stallion the same way you tell the difference between a baby girl and a baby boy. You got that?"

She took a deep breath and blew it out.

"Very clever." She could do without his grin, but he insisted on covering his face with it. "I grew up in the city."

"You mean they don't have babies in the city you grew up in? Gosh, what kind of city is that? What do you easterners do for recreation?"

He was laughing at her, and it was beginning to irritate her. "We don't insult visitors for the sport of it," she said between clenched teeth.

"Aw, come on. Where's your sense of humor? I was only being friendly." The horse looked back at her, and he immediately said, "Whoa." Both horses stopped.

"Why did they stop?" she asked him.

"Because I told them to. I think we've gone far enough. This is your first ride, and if you're at it too long, you'll be sore tomorrow morning. Let's go back now."

"I was enjoying it, but I'm sure you know best. How far is your ranch from here?"

"Not far. Six and a half miles. Ever been on a ranch?"

"No, and I'd like to visit one. I've seen a lot of them in the movies, and I really want to go to Tombstone to see the O.K. Corral. I'll never see Arizona again, so it's now or never."

"That story's had the guts dramatized out

of it, Ms. Fields. The Wyatt Earp/Doc Holliday battle against the Clantons and McLaurys in the infamous gunfight at the O.K. Corral didn't take place there but in a vacant lot behind it. Nothing there now but a wall and a sign, but if you want to go, I could fly you down there in about forty minutes. You'd be back here in Phoenix within two hours."

She was about to thank him when a thought flashed through her mind, and she voiced it. "If you own a ranch, why would you rent a horse to ride on a bridle path in the middle of the city?"

"I didn't rent a horse. That's my riding stable. When Jones, the groom, said you hadn't ridden before, I decided to go along with you."

"You're serious, aren't you?"

"Absolutely."

Rich, good-looking, and probably married. She didn't mind a fling; in fact, she'd enjoy one so long as the person didn't get serious, but not with a married man. "Thanks for the offer, but, no thanks."

"Why?" he asked. "There are no strings. If you're nervous about my company, I'll ask my dad to join us."

Somehow, that didn't add to her sense of security about a jaunt with him. "How old is your dad?"

The man laughed outright. "Seventy-one."

"That's not too old to be stupid. If you'd said he was ninety-one, I'd say, let's go."

His laughter seemed to take possession of him, changing his entire demeanor. After he calmed himself, he said, "My dad is so circumspect that what you're suggesting would make everyone who knows him laugh. He barely bends to pray."

Now it was she who laughed. "You shouldn't speak that way of your father."

His shoulder flexed in a shrug. "Why not? It's true."

"When can we leave? No. . . . Wait a minute. What's your name?"

"Preston McKay, and we can leave in forty-five minutes."

"Are you going to pilot the plane?"

His teeth showed in a wide grin. "Unless Dad wants to do it."

They returned to the riding stable and, because she wanted to verify McKay's story before she went anywhere with him, she paid careful attention to his interaction with the groom.

"I hope you enjoyed your ride, miss," the groom said to Petra, then looked up at her companion. "How'd it go, Mr. McKay?"

"She did extremely well for a first-time

rider. Would you get my car, please?"

McKay took out his cell phone, dialed, and waited. "Dad, I'm going to take a lady down to Tombstone, and I'd like you to join us. Fine. Tell Cullen to get the Cessna ready. I'll be there in twenty minutes."

Twenty minutes later, Preston McKay drove through an iron gate and onto his property. "Now you can say you've been on a ranch," he said. "My father's waiting for us at the plane, and I'll be your pilot." He drove up to the plane, stopped, parked, and got out.

"Dad, this is Petra Fields. She's seeing the Wild West. Ms. Fields, this is David McKay, my father."

"I see the resemblance," she said. "I'm happy to meet you, Mr. McKay." As they boarded the plane, she remembered that riding in any plane smaller than a jumbo jet petrified her. "At least it would be quick and painless," she said to herself, settled in, fastened her seat belt, and looked forward to the next crazy episode in her life.

About thirty-five minutes later, McKay set the plane down in the small Tombstone airport. "I'd say that was as smooth a job as you've ever done," David McKay said to his son.

"I had to be at my best," Preston said. "I

didn't want to frighten her."

"And you didn't," she said. "I enjoyed it, and I was only nervous when I looked straight down."

After a short drive into town, referring to the noonday meal, Preston said, "It's dinner time, so I suggest we stop for something to eat." He chose a steak house, and Petra got an example of how the average western man eats: Preston's platter bore a steak, pork chops, grilled sausage, a baked potato, turnip greens, and an ear of corn, and his father tackled a meal nearly as hearty. She had a small steak, French fries, and string beans.

"How tall are you?" she asked Preston.

"I'm six-five, but that has nothing to do with this; I love to eat."

"Are you married?" she blurted out, causing David McKay's head to snap up.

"No, but I'm open to suggestions," Preston said.

She frowned, and tried to erase whatever impact the frown may have had by saying, "Would you get upset if I said I think you're nuts?"

"It's possible, though I doubt it. Where are you headed after you leave here?"

The words "I don't know" were on the tip of her tongue when she stopped herself.

Saying that would require an explanation. She told Greta, but she didn't plan to tell any other person. Why dump that on anyone else? Listening to the woes of Tom, Dick, Harry, and Jane would soon be Greta's life, so she wasn't sorry to have burdened her friend with her tragedy. But not these folks!

"I'm going to drive down the Pacific Coast," she told him and was rewarded with his look of apparent skepticism.

They left the restaurant, crossed the street, walked down the block, and stopped at a wall beside the Fly Photography Gallery. "This was once the entrance to the O.K. Corral," David said. "Earp and Holliday killed Clanton and his pals right over there." He pointed to a spot. "Or so the legend goes."

"I didn't expect such a modern place. Was Holliday really a doctor?"

David shrugged. "Who knows? Back then, anybody could use that title and peddle snake oil and boiled herbs. Would you like a tour of the town? You can see everything of importance in less than an hour."

"Thanks," she said. "As long as I don't have to walk. I get tired in this dry climate." In less than an hour, she saw the town and was back at the airport.

"I told you we'd be back in Phoenix in

two hours, and I aim to keep my word," Preston said as he taxied for the takeoff.

When they were back in Phoenix, Preston drove Petra to the hotel at which she stayed, parked, got out, and walked around to the front passenger's door to open it. "Do you have to leave tomorrow morning?" He slouched against the car.

She hadn't expected that question, because he hadn't shown a personal interest in her. "I . . . Yes. I have a few more places to go before I . . . before this trip is over." His facial expression was such that she knew better than to joke.

"Before you do what?"

"Preston, you don't want to know. Before you ask, I am neither married, engaged, nor spoken for otherwise, but I may as well be."

He knocked his Stetson to the back of his head. "What the dickens do you mean by that?"

"If I was in a position to start anything, I certainly wouldn't pass you up. Thanks for far more than you could ever imagine," she said, reached up, kissed his cheek, and turned to run into the hotel.

But Preston McKay moved faster, gripped her arm, and spun her around. "You've got some explaining to do, miss. What kind of double talk is that? And I don't for a minute believe that a good-looking, intelligent woman like you would ordinarily traipse around with strange men she doesn't know anything about. You got into my car with me as comfortable as you please and rode with me to my ranch not knowing where the hell I was taking you. You let me fly you to Tombstone, a place you'd never been, and I could've been taking you to Mexico, for all you knew. Don't you know what a risk you took? I could be Preston the Ripper. Now, you're suddenly playing it safe. You're hiding something."

"I didn't risk much, Preston. In fact, I risked nothing. You're a great guy, and I . . . I'm glad I met you, but I'd better go now. Good-bye."

Petra ran into the hotel but his words, "Your mother or somebody should whack your fanny. You should go home," rang in her ears. She knew she had perplexed him and that he deserved more than she could give, but she couldn't let that worry her. He was a kind, gentle man, and she wished she could go back to him, but to do so would be dishonorable and unfair. Besides, there was no reason; the man was as rich as he was handsome and well-mannered, but she was not attracted to him, so she didn't even have that as an excuse for spending the night with him. She walked into her room, locked the door behind her, and started packing.

He'd said, "Your mother or somebody should whack your fanny," and as she packed, the words haunted her. Was her mother worried because she hadn't heard from her? No one knew her whereabouts, and if the end came, who would tell her mother and Krista? She hadn't previously thought about that. She remembered having put their names, addresses, and relationship to her on a paper that she kept in her bag, but that knowledge failed to assuage her guilt.

She rolled the pantyhose, put them in a plastic bag and dropped herself on the bed, suddenly exhausted. "Oh, well, I haven't had a headache recently, so maybe I'm tired because this air is so dry, or maybe because I did a lot today," she told herself. However, she didn't believe it. *Maybe I ought to call Mama and tell her where I am and how much fun I'm having.* Fun. She hadn't thought of that word in months.

I'd better call Mama in case she's worried. She hated to use the hotel phone, because of the cost, so she went down to the lobby and used the public phone. "Hi, Mama, I thought I'd call and let you know where I am. I'm in Phoenix, Arizona."

"It's time you called. When you coming home? Your boss called here a couple of times. He was like a madman when I said I didn't know where you were. I told him to drink an herbal tea like chamomile to calm his nerves, and I thought he was going to have a stroke. I wanted to tell him to pray for peace of mind, but I was scared that if I did, he'd come here and start a fight. How can you work with that man?"

"He's not bad, Mama. But Jack thinks he's calm, and when you suggested that he wasn't absolutely serene, it was like pouring gasoline on a wildfire."

"It's too late now. I told him not to be a nervous Nellie. You know men who boil over before the temperature gets to a hundred always did get on my last nerve. You come on home now. You hear?"

"Mama, how's Krista doing? Does she still have that job?"

"Yeah, she still working, and she's joined some kind of singing group, though she don't talk about it much. But long as she stays out of trouble and keeps her dress down, I won't complain. You come on home now. You hear?" Petra hung up, and although she hated to admit it, she felt better for having spoken with her mother. Maybe she should go home. No. She wanted to see San Francisco, Monterey, San Quentin, and the Golden Gate Bridge. She'd just have to hurry. Two months could fly by.

Lord, I wish it was over. I wish somebody would've invented something to prevent my thinking about anything depressing. This is getting to me.

What Lena Fields hadn't told her daughter, because she didn't know, was that Krista had begun to spend as much time as possible in her father's company and that she had mean little ways of punishing him.

"Why is that woman always hanging around you?" she asked her father after she joined the choir and attended the rehearsals a second time. "What's she after?"

"I think you're old enough to know the answer to that question."

"You really think all she wants is you? That chick's bargain hunting." Goodman's scowl didn't seem to bother Krista, for she continued as if she didn't know she had displeased him.

"You don't have to say everything you think, Krista."

"Why not? That way, you'll know where you stand with me. Daddy, that woman is after something, and what she gives you in return won't be worth spit."

She could be right, but he didn't want to hear it from his own daughter. He didn't like to think that he was more susceptible to Jada than she was to him, and a man needed a woman's undivided attention sometime, especially when he didn't get it at home.

"She's just a friend, Krista. The problem is that she enjoys flirting."

"Would you like me to have the kind of relationship with a married man that she's trying to have with you?"

"Of course not," he said, wearying of the topic, "but she's twice your age, single, and probably getting desperate."

"Humph," Krista snorted. "Twice my age and nowhere near half as smart."

After practice, Goodman drove Krista home. "Since I didn't grow up with you," Krista said, "and I don't have a brother, I don't know what makes men tick. Why would you take a chance with that woman, Daddy? To me, she's ordinary looking. Suppose Carla finds out."

He parked and turned to Krista, hoping to find the appropriate words. Well, she was grown, so he'd say what he thought and felt. "I always thought I had a happy, loving family. Maybe I thought so because I yearned for that. When I told them about you, I realized that Carla and my older son are concerned with themselves. Another thing, my wife knows that music is everything to me, but she thinks I should treat it as a hobby, give up my studio, and help her run her restaurant. She doesn't take pride in what I do and in who I am. At least twice a week, she tells me that if I worked with her we could open another restaurant and, within two years, we'd be multimillionaires. I don't need more than I have."

Krista had been silent, and he hadn't wondered about that until she said, "If she owns a restaurant, why do you have dinner at home every night? That's weird."

"Because it is *I*, and not my wife, who provides for my family. And I want my children to grow up like normal kids with chores to do, not with waiters serving them. Believe me, I had to fight hard for it."

"I see. So you're going to fool around, 'cause you don't get TLC at home. That's awful, Daddy. Real gross. Gotta go." She leaned forward and kissed his cheek, stunning him with the first gesture of affection he received from his daughter.

He waited until she was inside the house, circled back, and met Jada a block from the rehearsal hall. "What took you so long?"

she asked. "I don't hang around waiting for no man. You want me, you gotta act like I'm special."

"As soon as I get you home, I'll show you how special you are. I'm starved, and I don't mean for food."

She leaned back in the soft leather bucket seat of Goodman's silver-gray Lexus and smiled the satisfied smile of a conqueror. "Man after my own heart."

Two hours later, Goodman sat on the side of Jada's bed tying his shoes. "I need to get some gas. Lend me twenty till I see you next Monday night." A little later he pocketed the twenty-dollar bill, got into his car, and drove straight home. Krista was right. If Jada Hankins wasn't counting on getting something from him, she wouldn't have parted with her money so easily. She would learn one thing: he had no intention of adding her to his list of dependents.

Jada pulled the sheet over her nude body, flung her arms wide, and purred like a satisfied feline. "I put it down solid tonight, and I'm gonna get my condo sure as my name is Jada Hankins."

Chapter Five

Petra sat in Phoenix Sky Harbor International Airport with her feet resting on her small bag and watched the people hurrying around her, some at a dizzying pace. She didn't want to take the strong pill for her headache, because she needed to be alert in case she received a call for a standby seat on a flight to San Francisco.

"Can you spare a dollar, lady?"

No, she couldn't, because ever since leaving home, she had spent cash as if it rained down from the heavens. "What do you want it for?" she asked him.

The man sat down beside her. "You mind if I rest here a minute?" She told him she didn't. "I'm just trying to live from one day to the next, lady," he said, stretched out his long legs, and made himself comfortable.

She didn't want to open her purse while he was so close, because he could be a fast sprinter. "Have you tried working?" she asked, figuring that a man of around twenty-five years ought to work. He was handsome, too, provided you liked dreadlocks, and she didn't.

"Yeah. I tried it, but I figured Bill Gates didn't get where he is today by doing dirty work, so I quit."

Mildly curious, she asked him, "What kind of job did you have?"

"Sitting in a chair behind a stupid desk, seducing people into buying real estate they couldn't afford. Dumbest job ever invented. What's funny?" he asked when she laughed aloud.

He called that dirty work? She rolled her eyes skyward. "I was just about to give you a dollar, but since I earned it doing exactly what you consider dumb, I decided to keep it. Don't worry, you'll live."

She held her pocketbook tighter when the man stood and stared down at her. Unnerved by his rapt attention, she watched him put his hand into his pocket, pull out a roll of bills, and drop a dollar into her lap. "Wake up, lady. Since I left that chicken-shit job seven months ago, I made enough right here in this airport to buy me a real nice house in a cool neighborhood, and I don't drive no little Toyota neither. Have a good life."

"Wait a minute," she said, as he started off. "I don't need any money. In fact, I don't need anything except a seat on a flight to San Francisco."

He took a business card out of his wallet and handed it to her. "Go to Gate B3. My sister's on duty there. Give her this card, and she'll see that you get a seat. You hang in there, doll, and don't do no more chicken-shit work. Later."

She was about to drop the card into the waste basket, but remembered the wad of bills in his hand, took her bag, and went to the gate. When she saw that the attendant resembled the handsome panhandler, she handed the woman his card.

"Hi. Your brother said you'd help me get on a flight to San Francisco."

The woman observed her carefully, and Petra wondered if she'd made a fool of herself. "Where did you see him? Is he in the airport?"

"He was a minute ago."

"Have a seat. I'll have something for you in a minute."

She sat down, and as she let herself relax, she recalled her grandfather's words: "Treat every person you meet as if that person is more important than you are, and you'll always make friends. Never enemies."

An hour later, Petra boarded a flight to San Francisco. "I wanted to take a train in order to see the countryside," she said to her seatmate, "but it's an overnight trip, and I don't have much time."

"Anyway," the woman replied as she repeatedly pushed strands of hair from her face, "these days, everybody who is anybody flies."

Annoyed at the put-down, Petra said, "I never dreamed that it was the poor who made Pullman car porters rich with their heavy tips. And I thought people who fly economy class did so because they couldn't afford either the time or the money to do otherwise." She got a blanket from the overhead compartment, wrapped herself in it, and went to sleep.

She awakened half an hour before landing, brushed her teeth, and drank the tasteless coffee that the attendants served along with their smiles. She had managed to get a room in a hotel that was walking distance from Fisherman's Wharf, a luxurious one compared to the modest places in which she had stayed since leaving Ellicott City. As soon as she checked in and unpacked, she headed for the famous site.

"They're so noisy," a boy of about five said of the seals and to no one in particular.

"They're ugly, too," commented a girl who she assumed was his older sister.

Before turning her attention to the seals, she gazed at the children for a long time. *To be that age again with a whole life before you . . .* She shook off the encroaching melancholy. *I told myself I wasn't going to be a crybaby about this, and I'm not. I'm going to enjoy the rest of the ride right to the hilt.*

She strolled along the wharf, window shopping and watching tourists. At a women's boutique on the corner, a red cocktail dress caught her eye, and after staring at it for nearly twenty minutes, she went inside, tried it on, and bought it. *I'll never wear it, but I've always wanted to own something like this. Maybe I'll pack it and send it home to Krista. It's perfect for her clear complexion.*

Later that day, on a tour bus across the Golden Gate Bridge, a stunning structure that spanned the San Francisco Bay, she sat beside an old man who seemed to have more energy than she did despite his age. "Isn't it wonderful," he said, as they looked across the bay at Alcatraz — more like a resort than a prison in the rays of the dying sun, though it was indeed the prison of which she'd heard so much and seen in so many old movies. "When I was young, I didn't have sense enough to enjoy all this. I raced through life looking at everything but seeing nothing, feeling nothing, and believing in nothing. In the time I have left, I'm using my eyes and ears to enjoy life."

"Do you regret having skated through life without leaving an imprint?" she asked him.

His smile came slowly. "What's the point in regretting anything? It's more important to make the best of what's left, and I'm doing that. I went to Paris when I was twenty-two, but I only saw the French women. I went back in May, sixty years later, and I could see what I missed — the Louvre; the Musée de Rodin; Les Halles at four o'clock in the morning when the venders hawk what the Parisians will eat that day; Montmartre; people-watching at Place de l'Opera. This time I enjoyed Paris, lolling in the sidewalk cafes, strolling in the Place de la Concorde. I mean, I finally *saw* Paris, though I didn't look twice at one female, unless she was serving food or selling tickets." The old man laughed. "Ignoring the French women this last trip wasn't difficult; I had a lot of help from Mother Nature. I don't expect I'll see Europe again. Walking around all day is no fun when you're old."

"I've never been to Europe, and as things stand, I don't expect to get there. I'm fortunate to have gotten here. I always wanted to see San Francisco, and especially the Golden Gate Bridge and Alcatraz, and at least I got the chance."

"They're a sight, all right. But you're still young, and you'll get to Europe."

They talked until the bus driver returned to the bus, flashed his lights, counted the passengers, and headed back to San Francisco. "Well, if we don't run into each other again, I wish you all good things. Thanks for the company," the old man said. "Not many pretty young women would be satisfied to spend the day with an old man. Good-bye."

I probably wouldn't have either, six months ago.

Back in the hotel, she soaked her feet in hot water, showered, and decided to put on a dress. She hadn't expected such cool weather in July, but she had one long-sleeved, silk jersey wrap dress, and decided to wear it to dinner. The rose color flattered her, and when she saw her healthy and relaxed complexion in the mirror, she hardly believed her eyes. She put on a pair of silver hoops, combed out her hair, and went down to the hotel's dining room. She hated eating alone in restaurants, but in hotels, patrons were seen to have little choice if they were traveling alone.

She ordered a glass of wine, mainly to have something to sip while she waited for the first course. The waiter poured the wine, and she reached for the glass, but nearly spilled it when her gaze landed on a man who sat alone at a table across from her and who smiled when she looked at him.

She lowered her gaze, but the rapid flutters of her heart and her accelerated breathing continued, the least worrisome evidence of what was happening to her. The hand with which she held the glass shook so badly that she had to place her left hand on it in order to still it. In spite of her alarm at her reaction to the man, she couldn't prevent herself from looking at him again, for she could feel his gaze on her, unwavering. He smiled and raised his glass a little in a gentle salute and, in spite of her good judgment, which said ignore him, she smiled.

He wrote on something that he took from his wallet, called a waiter, and sent it to her. She looked at it, knowing that he'd locked his gaze on her.

"I am enchanted with you," she read. "Please allow me to share a meal with you."

She could almost hear her heartbeat. "You shouldn't start anything with this man, because you can only offer him pain," her niggling conscience warned. But she glanced up, saw his hopefulness, the eager expectation mirrored on his face, and ignored her conscience. When she smiled, he stood immediately, lifted his glass of wine, and walked over to her table.

"May I join you?"

"If you like." It sounded silly and unsophisticated to her, but she couldn't manage more.

"I'm Winston Fleet," he said and extended his hand. She took it, and jerked her hand away when electric sparks shocked her. They stared at each other, stunned by the charge emanating from their touch, and then they laughed. She liked his voice, his laughter, and the lights that sparkled in his dark eyes.

"Who are you?" he asked her. "Lord, I hope you're not married."

"I'm Petra Fields, and I'm not married."

He reached across the table for her hand and held it. "I have to tell you that something happened to me the minute I saw you headed this way. I live in Oakland, but I work over here. I'm staying over tonight and tomorrow night because I have breakfast meetings. Where do you come from, Petra, and how long will you be here?"

"I'm from Ellicott City, a little town in Maryland, and I'm on vacation. I always wanted to see California and the Wild West."

He squeezed her fingers. "I hope you haven't been disappointed. I came to California as a tourist and just couldn't leave. It's great out here. I was born and raised in Philadelphia. What do you do? What do you like? Tell me. I need to know that you're real, that you're not an apparition."

"I'm real, all right," she said and bit back the words, *but I don't know for how long.*

"What have you seen since you've been here?" She told him. "Ah, so you haven't been to San Simeon, Coit Tower, Alamo Square or . . . Have you been on one of the cable cars?"

"I haven't done any of that. Should I?"

He leaned forward, his face animated with what seemed to her an inner joy. "Yes, you should, and with me. I'm free tomorrow after one-thirty. Let me show you around."

She wanted to back off, to slow him down, but in his eyes there shone everything she had dreamed of in a man, everything she'd missed. At least once, couldn't she know what most adult women experienced throughout their adult lives? And could she have it without hurting him?

"Will you?" he urged.

"What can I say?" she replied, thinking aloud. "Fate's dancing her crazy little jig again."

"Absolutely," he said, solemn for the first time, "and I want to dance along with her. Don't you?"

The choice had been taken from her. She wanted to be with him for as long as she could. *I could love this man as I've never loved anyone. I know I'll only have a couple of days with him, but that little bit is more than I dreamed possible. What I'm doing isn't right but . . . Is it? For him, I could be only a passing summer shower, so what could be wrong with a loving exchange?* The waiter brought the crab quiche that she ordered for a first course, and her thoughts shifted to the food.

She noticed that he hadn't begun to eat and looked at him inquiringly. "What is it?"

"Will you meet me at the registration desk at one-thirty tomorrow? I don't want to lose you, Petra."

"Yes, I will. Now, eat your soup."

They sat there talking long after they'd finished the meal, talked until the waiter asked for the third time if they wanted anything else. Petra looked around, saw that she and Winston were the only patrons in the dining room, and said, "I think they want to close."

Winston looked at his watch. "Good grief, it's eleven o'clock. We've been talking for three and a half hours." He stood, walked around to assist her, and when she felt his hand on her back through the thin fabric of her dress, gentle but firm, as if it belonged there, she wanted to lean into him.

"I'm not ready to leave you," he said. "There's a nightclub next door, but we can enter it through that hall behind the elevators. Want to go there for a while?" She nodded, her emotions so near the surface that she couldn't speak. He reached for her hand, and she joined hers with his.

"What do you want to drink?" he asked her after they seated themselves.

The doctor had warned her about drinking alcoholic beverages. "I don't need any more wine. Do you think they'll serve me ginger ale?"

"Of course. I think I'll have the same."

Her eyebrows shot up. "If you'd rather have something stronger," she said. "It's all right with me. I'm from a small town, and we don't drink much. At least I don't."

"Ginger ale is fine. I have to make a presentation tomorrow morning at eight, and I also don't want demon alcohol to becloud my senses in regard to you."

"What do you do, Winston?"

"I design furniture and home furnishings, but I'm happiest creating furniture."

"That's interesting. I work for a real estate

agency . . . or did. My boss has probably fired me by now."

"He can't do that, can he?"

"He told me to bring my cell phone on vacation so he could call me whenever he needed to, but I deliberately left it home. He'd call me every half hour, and I didn't want that."

"Why should he do that? A vacation is just that, time away from the everyday stress of the office."

"Ladies and gentlemen," the master of ceremonies said, "give it up for the great Jackie Barrow, the number one comedian of our time."

The applause died down, and Jackie strode onstage decked out in a canary-yellow suit, yellow lizard-skin shoes, white shirt, and yellow tie.

"Don't I look good?" he began. Petra tuned him out. The only voice she wanted to hear belonged to the man beside her.

"Want to dance?" Winston asked her.

She hadn't realized that Jackie what's-his-name had left the stage and the band had replaced him. "Winston, this is moving so fast."

"I know, but don't be afraid of me, Petra. I will never do anything to hurt you." He stood and held out his hand to her, and she took it, knowing that her body would follow her heart.

"I'm not afraid of you, Winston, just scared to death of what is happening to me with a man I met a few hours ago."

Holding her hand, he walked with her the few feet to the dance floor. "I'm as vulnerable as you are and just as scared."

He opened his arms, and when she moved into them, she thought her heart skidded to the pit of her belly. Her breasts pressed against his chest, hardening her nipples, and she stepped back, too embarrassed to look into his eyes. His fingers stroked her back as if with the intent to soothe her, and the swinging of his hips along with the drummer's seductive rhythm nearly reduced her to putty. Her hand wound its way to his nape, and she tucked her head beneath his chin while she swung her body to his rhythm. Had she danced with him all her life? It seemed that way.

"The music stopped, sweetheart," he said after hugging her. "Would you rather sit down or wait for the next one?"

She was about to say she'd like to wait for the next dance, but her head suddenly began to pain her. "I guess I'd better sit," she said. "My head has decided to hurt." She neglected to tell him about her slight dizziness.

Walking back to the table, he asked her, "Does it hurt often?"

"It depends. They're something like migraines."

"Perhaps you're tired after so much sightseeing today. I've kept you too long. Would you like to leave now?"

"I think so, although I'm enjoying being with you."

He walked with her to her room. "I'm not going to ask you if I can come in, but I . . . I want to kiss you. Does that surprise you?"

She smiled because she wanted him to know how she felt about him. "No, it doesn't surprise me." She reached up and stroked the side of his face with the back of her hand while he stared at her, his expression fierce and his eyes stormy.

She closed her eyes, and his lips touched hers, not with the powerful and explosive passion that she expected, but with a soft, gentle loving that sent shivers throughout her body. He flicked his tongue across the seam of her lips, and she opened to him, sucked him into her, and felt him tremble a second before he put her away from him.

"Do you have anything for that headache?" She nodded. "Take it, and try to sleep," he said. "I'll see you tomorrow at one-thirty."

She pressed a quick kiss on his lips and said, "You're wonderful," opened her door, went inside, and left him standing there. She didn't remember having done many things that demanded so much self-discipline as not asking him to come in. More than anything he'd said or done, his kiss told her the kind of man he was, and as much as she wanted to invite him to spend the night with her, she didn't dare.

If only she had met Winston Fleet years ago, or if she had more time now! Maybe she shouldn't pity herself, but give thanks that she'd met him at all. "I promised myself I wouldn't wallow in self-pity, and I won't," she said to herself, but it didn't escape her that she had to remind herself of that promise with increasing frequency.

"At least, I'll see him tomorrow." She slept fitfully, anxious for one-thirty and the moment she would see him again.

After a breakfast of tomato juice, sausage, scrambled eggs, biscuits, and coffee, Petra strolled around the corner from the hotel to the shops she saw the previous day and bought a pair of white pants and some white sneakers. Her feet had taken a beating since she left Ellicott City. Winston hadn't suggested that they eat lunch together, so she bought a hamburger, a bottle of ginger ale, and a box of stationery, went back to her room, and ate lunch.

She wrote letters to her mother and to Krista, asking their forgiveness for not having told them of her illness and its prognosis, and penned a note to Goodman Prout that read:

Dear Goodman,

Mama and Krista don't know how sick I am, and when I'm gone, they'll be shocked. Please support them in every way that you can. I know Krista must have gotten close to you by now, and you must have learned that she can be difficult, but she's really a good child. Learning about you shocked her, and she's been acting out ever since. She hasn't forgiven me, but she will. Please take good care of her but, in doing so, don't neglect your wife and other children.

Yours, Petra

With a sigh of resignation, she addressed the letters, put them in the envelopes, sealed them, and stored them in her pocketbook. Someone would find them there and deliver them. After changing into her white pants, yellow and white-striped shirt, yellow jacket, and white sneakers, she left the hotel and window-shopped near it, trying to make the time pass. At twenty-five minutes after one, she headed back to the hotel.

She saw him standing beside the registration desk and told herself not to run. She hadn't previously known a man like Winston; indeed she hadn't developed close relationships with many men, and never had she reacted to one as she did to him. Nor had she been as secure with a man — not even Goodman — as she was with Winston Fleet. Maybe that was because she had nothing to lose. She'd known taller and more handsome men, but at about six feet and maybe an inch or two, a slim figure, smooth brown skin and large, beautiful, dark eyes, he'd taken her breath away.

He rushed to meet her and handed her a red rose. As if she'd done it all of her life, she kissed the side of his mouth. "Thank you. I love flowers, and I shall cherish this rose for as long as I live."

He slid an arm around her shoulder. "It will crumble long before you make your exit," he said. "I have my car in the garage. Want to see the Hearst Castle in San Simeon?"

"I want to go wherever you take me, but first I want to put my rose in some water. Be right back." When she returned a few minutes later, he said, "You moved so fast, you didn't give me a chance to tell you how nice you look."

"Thanks. You look nice, too," she said of his tan suit. It occurred to her that he left his business associates and came directly to the hotel to meet her. "Have you had lunch, Winston? I'm not hungry, because I ate a hamburger about an hour ago."

"Thanks for thinking about me," he said, "but I had coffee and a scone a little after eleven. We can grab a bite along the way somewhere."

Being with him seemed so natural. He explained the sights as they drove along, and, as he talked, she thought she heard a voice say, "He's falling for you. What you're doing's not right." When she turned around, she expected to see her grandfather sitting in the back seat.

I won't give him up. I can't. I need him! Just one more thing to tell the Reverend Collins, provided she saw him again.

Winston drove carefully, well within the speed limit, and, after about an hour, stopped at a roadside restaurant. "Hey, Winston," a young boy who proved to be the busboy said, "where've you been? We haven't seen you in months."

"I know," he said. "I've been inundated with work. How's Alma?"

"Mama's fine. She and Papa went to buy a new computer. What can I get you?"

"Petra, this is Jake." He patted the boy's shoulder. Jake was an eager teenager of about fifteen. "I want a bacon, lettuce, and tomato wrap with a big pickle and a cup of coffee with milk. What do you want, Petra?"

She didn't have to worry about gaining weight, so she was going to eat all the fattening food she wanted. "Two scoops of pecan praline ice cream. If it's real good, I'll have another scoop."

"You must have perfect metabolism," Winston said. "Girl after my own heart." A smile roamed over his face. "And in more ways than one."

She gasped at the sight of the Hearst Castle. "This brochure says it has one hundred and sixty-five rooms. What would one family do with that much space?"

"Entertain friends. I imagine all the world's bigwigs slept there during Hearst's day."

"He sure was lucky he came along before television, when people still read morning, afternoon, and evening editions of newspapers. If he was starting now, he might be as poor as the next guy trying to make people read."

"I don't know about that," Winston said. "A creative man — and Hearst was, if anything, very creative — is always a man of his time. He might have had thirty cable TV stations."

After they explored as much of the castle as their energy would allow, he drove down to the ocean, found a boulder on the beach, and sat there with her. "I know we're going to separate, because you'll return to Maryland, but I don't want this to end. I can't let it end. However strange it may seem, you're locked in my heart, and you were before you sat down at that table last night. One look as you walked toward me, and you alone were important to me. I've heard that a person could affect you this way but, until now, I didn't believe it."

With his confession, guilt weighed more heavily upon her. She knew he waited to know what she felt for him, and she had promised herself that she wouldn't lie about anything again.

She took a deep breath, squared her shoulders, and looked at him. "Winston, nothing so powerful as this ever happens to one person. I'm thirty-six years old, and I have an eighteen-year-old daughter, but I have never before felt for anyone what I feel for you. Never."

He stared at her as if he knew what would come next, and that he wouldn't accept it. "But?"

"But it has to end. I told myself to take what you were willing to give, because I need it so badly, but I care so much for you. I can't do it."

He pressed his hands to her knees as he faced her. "Have you committed a crime? I mean, are you on the lam?"

"In a way I am, although I haven't committed a crime."

"I don't understand. Talk to me, baby."

I won't go to pieces. I won't let him see me crack up.

He grasped her shoulders, leaned toward her, and kissed her eyes and her lips. "No matter what you tell me, you'll always be in my heart."

She shook her head from side to side, pushing back the truth, denying it, wishing she'd had the strength to tell him he couldn't join her for dinner at her table.

"Tell me, sweetheart," he urged.

"I . . . I'm ill, and I . . . I have less than two months to live."

He stared at her with quivering lips and

wide eyes, an expression of horror on his face. "Don't tell me that. It isn't true. It can't be."

"But it is, Winston. I shouldn't have let you come to my table last night, but when I looked at you sitting there, it was too late. I wanted desperately to be with you. Can't we . . . have today and tonight together? Tomorrow, I'll leave you."

"Are you sure of the diagnosis?"

"I have a brain tumor, and that's what causes the headaches."

"I see. For once in my life, I've found the woman I needed, and now this. . . ."

"Oh, Winston. I'm so sorry."

"It isn't your fault. My problem is that I want so badly to help you, but I can't even read an X-ray."

"Don't worry. I had so many tests that the doctors can't possibly have overlooked one."

"How can you be so cheerful?"

"I'm not cheerful, but I've accepted it, and if you do too, our remaining time together can be wonderful. Let's go out tonight and have a good time."

"I'm not good at fooling myself, Petra. I've never been so miserable in my life."

She slid to her knees, unmindful of what the sand could do to her white pants, reached up, and pressed her hands to his cheeks. "I'd change it if I could, and as much for you as for me. Let's envision ourselves together in the next life, and —"

"Doing what?" he interrupted. "Skipping through Heaven wearing white wings?"

She kissed the tip of his nose. "You'd rather shovel coal?"

He laughed, and she put her arms around him. "At least we have each other now. My grandfather said, 'Know when you're happy, because happiness is a temporary thing.' "

"He had a point there. Suppose we go back to San Francisco. I'll take you through Alamo Square, show you the 'postcard row' Victorian houses, and we can see Nob Hill before we go back to the hotel. If you brought any dressy clothes, we could —"

"I have a really fancy dress that I've never worn."

"Great. I'll call for you at about seven, and we'll go to a good restaurant and then come back to the hotel's night club. Would you like that? Or we could —"

"I'd love it. I don't really care what we do. I just want to be with you."

He stood, lifted her, and folded her in his arms. "If I dared to kiss you, I'd risk indictment for unseemly behavior. I need desperately to be alone with you." He shook his head as if in wonder. "How is it possible that I love you?"

"I've asked myself the same question," she said.

They walked arm-in-arm up the long slope to his car, and as he began the drive, the sound of Ray Charles singing and playing "What'd I Say" came over the radio. Winston sang some passages with Ray, looked at her, and grinned, and she wanted to shout for joy. Their first crisis took its toll, but it had passed. She leaned back and let her mind wander to Krista and how her daughter would fare without her.

Petra would have been surprised and pleased to know that Krista had begun to develop a relationship with her father. Although Krista frequently attempted to behave as if she and her father were adult equals, Goodman always refused to accept that, and she had begun to settle into the role of respectful daughter.

"You need to practice more," Goodman told her that Monday at the end of her piano lesson. "You seem to have a knack for piano playing, but you have to practice nonetheless."

"I would if I had a piano. I love it. When Mama comes back, I'm going to ask her to get me a piano. Daddy, do you think I can be a good singer? Shouldn't I study voice?"

"You're too young to study voice. Your voice hasn't matured. Right now, you're somewhere between a soprano and a mezzo. A voice teacher may decide to train you to be a soprano, but next year, you could be a contralto. Let's wait a couple of years. Learn music, and when you're ready for singing, it'll come in handy."

"Does Jada have a mezzo or a contralto?"

"Why do you spend so much time thinking about Jada Hankins?" Goodman asked her. "She's not important."

Krista put a piece of chewing gum into her mouth, although she knew he detested gum chewing. "Tell you what, Daddy. You don't tell me no lies, and I won't tell you any. Jada struts her stuff at rehearsal, and she wants everybody there to know that she's getting it on with you. If I was stupid, you'd be ashamed of me, wouldn't you?"

He loved her, but she could be a pill. "Krista, if you push a person into a corner, that person will come out fighting. Always allow a person an opportunity to save face. You'd make a lousy diplomat."

"I know. Has Carla decided to meet me yet?"

"My wife is not pleased with me these days. She wants our sons to go to a private school, and since there isn't an appropriate one here, that means they'd have to go to a boarding school. I do not want my fifteen- and sixteen-year-old sons living with a bunch of unsupervised kids in an avant-garde boarding school smoking pot and sniffing coke. They're staying right here until they leave for college. She says I'm old-fashioned. Fine. My kids are staying here with their parents until they are of legal age. Period."

"Can't you two get together and work these things out? I bet you could, if you weren't —"

"Krista," he warned, "don't push too hard. I am your father, and you are to remember that."

"Yes, sir. I'm saving my salary for school, and I need a laptop. Do you . . . I mean, can you give me the money for a laptop? It's kind of expensive."

"How expensive?"

"At least seven or eight hundred bucks."

A friend who dealt in electronics would give him a big discount on one. "Tell me which one you want, and I'll get it for you."

Her eyes widened. "You will?"

"Yes, but get me information on the precise model."

"Oh, yes." She flung her arms around him,

kissed his cheek, and then moved away from him with her head bowed. "I hate it that I didn't grow up with you."

For the first time, he had the feeling that she truly related to him as a daughter did to her father. He fought back tears as he sensed that what he'd missed in her growing up was an unrecoverable loss to both of them.

"Your mother did a wonderful job with you, Krista. I don't know that I could have done better."

"Thanks. I haven't been so nice to her recently. Maybe that's why she decided to take this crazy vacation."

That didn't sound right to him. The Petra he'd once known never did anything impulsively. "What do you mean by that?" he asked her.

"Nobody knows where she went, not even her boss, and he's driving Grandma and me crazy with questions about where she is and when she's coming back. She told Grandma she was going to see the West. She didn't have an itinerary."

"That's strange."

"It sure is, considering how careful Mama's always been with money. I hope she hurries and comes back."

"You haven't heard from her?"

"She called Grandma once from someplace in Arizona, I think. At least she was all right." She leaned against the piano and fidgeted with her fingers, a sure sign, he had learned, that she was about to test his patience, or thought she was. She didn't disappoint him. "Daddy, who did you love the most, Carla or my mama?"

What a question! "I've never compared the experiences, Krista. I was younger when I knew your mother, and it's possible that my feelings were — consequently — more shallow than when I was more mature."

She narrowed one eye and looked hard at him. "That's a cop-out, Daddy. I'm only two years older than Peter, so you went straight from Mama to Carla. I don't think you're crazy about Carla. If you were, you wouldn't play around with Jada."

"Why are you always on Jada's case?"

"Because I don't think she's worth the trouble she's going to cause you, and besides, I can't stand her."

How could she have so much of his personality and disposition? "Krista, try not to be so hard on people. Someday, you'll need compassion, so be sure you deserve it. And when your mother comes home, tell her that you're seeing me, that I'm giving you piano lessons, and that you've joined the choral ensemble that I direct. You've no right to keep these things from her."

"Uh . . . All right." She had her back to him when she said it, and he wondered about the prospects of peace and genuine love between mother and daughter.

Petra gazed at the calm waters of the Pacific Ocean as Winston maneuvered his Acura 230 across the Golden Gate Bridge. Goodman hadn't backed away from his responsibility for Krista, and had quickly agreed to get to know her. He'd always been a responsible man, and she knew he'd take care of Krista given the chance. She had tried to correct her mistakes as best she could. *The rest is up to Providence. Nobody is perfect, and I've been far from it. But I'm paying my dues and, at this point in my life, I refuse to sweat about anything.* Her body seemed lighter, as if a weight had fallen from it.

"What are you thinking?" Winston asked, and she realized that he had switched off the radio.

"I'm thinking how much I love fried catfish and hush puppies. I bet you don't even know what hush puppies are."

He glanced at her. "Sure I do. They're quiet little furry animals that wag their tails."

"Not so," she said. "They're noisy, barking little furry animals that wag their tails and have to be told to shut up. Do they have catfish out here in California?"

"Yep, and it's the same Mississippi catfish that you eat back in Ellicott City. We'll stop at the next seafood restaurant and see if they have any. I doubt they'll serve those little doggies you mentioned." She liked his sense of humor and told him as much. "Winston, is there anything about you that I won't like?"

She liked so much about him, his clean-cut appearance, strong chin, even white teeth that sparkled whenever he smiled, and his voice. And because he made her feel that he had always been a part of her life, and that he cared deeply for her, she could be free with him, free to care for him and to be herself. He reduced the speed, glanced at her, and appeared to be amused. "If I knew I had habits you wouldn't like, I doubt I'd volunteer the information. There's a place not far from here that we can try."

Holding hands, they entered Bob and Betty's Home Cooked, and Winston stopped at the cashier's desk. "Do you serve fried catfish? I don't dare ask if you have hush puppies."

"I'm from North Carolina," the woman

said, "and when I fry fish, I deep fry some hush puppies to go with 'em. Y'all have a seat."

"This is the best food I've had since I left home," Petra said as she ate, savoring the catfish, hush puppies, and stewed collards. "Do you like it?"

His wink would have sufficed for an answer, and his smile had the effect of a punctuation mark. "When I'm eating, smiling, and quiet, you know I'm in my element."

She put her fork on the side of her plate as a thought occurred to her. "Did you go to college, Winston? I finished high school, but I got pregnant that summer, and my mother said I was on my own. Not going to college is one of my few genuine regrets."

"I went to Penn State," he said and, as if sensing her need to know all about him, he added, "I did rather well academically and as a tight end on the football team. I loved playing basketball and was pretty good at it, but at six feet, one and a half inches tall, I couldn't make the team. I was best at shooting the bull with buddies over a mug of beer."

"I'll bet you had a lot of girlfriends. Girls like fellows who are gentle and considerate."

"Thanks for the compliment, but I wouldn't feel comfortable wearing a halo, Petra. I try to do what I think is right, but I've made mistakes. I made one of my college classmates pregnant, something that would never have happened if I hadn't guzzled too many beers. I would have married her, much as I hated the thought, but she decided to terminate the pregnancy. I still think about that, and I haven't been that careless since. You said you got pregnant the summer you finished high school. Do you mind telling me the circumstances?"

She gave him the details of that fateful spring and summer, including her decision to withhold information about her pregnancy from Goodman. "It was wrong of me to do that, Winston. I should have let him make the choice. When I told him about his daughter a few months back, he didn't get mad. He said that if I'd told him, he probably wouldn't be the man he is today. I'm still sorry I didn't tell him. My daughter is angry that I deprived her of her father's nurturing, but it's too late to change that."

"Does it weigh on you?"

"It did. But I asked them both to forgive me, and I've forgiven myself. I'm trying not to let it burden me."

Later, as they headed to San Francisco,

she told him about Goodman and Krista and the ways in which she had tried to make amends for that and what she regarded as her other transgressions. "Don't feel guilty about anything," he told her. "I've met a lot of people, known a number of nice women — wealthy ones, poor ones, educated ones, and some with only a few years of schooling. You don't have a single thing to be ashamed of." He sucked his teeth. "Tomorrow, you'll leave me." Turning into a parking lot near Coit Tower, he said, "This is one of those times when life's a friggin' bastard."

She grasped his arm, stopping him as he was about to get out of the car. "We have today and tonight, Winston."

"Yes. And let's use every second."

Chapter Six

"Gee, what a lovely stream," Petra said, when Winston detoured from the highway and drove along a two-lane road. "It's idyllic along here."

"I love this drive, and when I have time, I like to drive through here. I wanted to see it with you, and I'm glad you're enjoying it."

She looked up at the ponderosa pine trees on either side of the road, some blocking the sun and others filtering the sunlight so that their shadows created intricate patterns across the road. Such phenomena were not strange to her, for Ellicott City was a town of trees and lovely landscapes, yet the beauty of the scenery and the peace that it communicated to her seemed very special. She closed her eyes and let the vision of it soothe her. Why hadn't she enjoyed all that life offered while she could, before the diagnosis, the headaches, and, recently, the occasional problem with her memory? Was she one of those women who came alive only when they loved a man?

"We're not too far from my grandmother's house. Would you mind if I stop by to see her for a few minutes?"

"No, indeed. I'd love to meet your grandmother. I would have thought your family was back East since you're from Philadelphia."

"Most of them are. After my grandfather died, I relocated my grandmother out here where I can look after her. I'm her only grandchild. My mother's a widow, and I think it's enough for her to take care of herself. When she retires, I hope she'll agree to come out here, too."

"They're fortunate to have you in their lives, Winston."

"I'm lucky to have them, Petra. They've always been there for me. I take care of my own." He drove off onto a side road. "Would you like to sit by this brook, river, or whatever it is?" He didn't wait for her answer, but walked around to open the door.

When she stepped out of the car and into his arms, he hugged her so tightly that she wondered at the strength with which he held her. "What is it, Winston? What's the matter?"

He slackened his hold and stared down at her with eyes that reflected such pain that it seemed to stab her heart. "How can you ask?" Holding her hand, he led her to a grassy area. "Let's sit here for a few minutes."

Petra sat down, and he lay on his back with his head in her lap and looked up at her. Suddenly, as if propelled by a powerful emotion, he wrapped his arms around her, squeezed her to him and, with a groan, buried his face against her belly and kissed her. She bent over, kissed his face, his ears, his hair. He braced his left hand on the grass beside them, raised himself up, and kissed her lips. "I think we'd better go," he said. "If I'm not up to snuff, my grandmother will detect it in a second, and she'll stay at me to tell her whatever it is that ails me. I always thought I was tough, but —"

"You *are* strong," she said. "I feel it when you hold me, sensed it when I first saw you. I hear it in your voice and in the words you choose when you speak to me. This isn't an ordinary situation, so don't judge yourself harshly."

Why couldn't I have met this man when I . . . Lord, if I start thinking like that, I'll go to pieces. But why couldn't I have this? It's so right . . . so . . . She reached into her pocketbook, got a tissue, and blew her nose as hard as she could. Doing that had always warded off her sneezes and her tears.

"You okay?" Winston asked her.

Her vigorous nod must have been the biggest lie she'd ever told. "How old is your grandmother?"

A smile flashed over his face, and she thought, "This man loves his grandmother."

He swung their hands as they walked to the car. "She says she's eighty, but I wonder. She looks and acts more like sixty."

When Winston parked in front of a moderate-sized, attractive yellow ranch house, Petra asked him, "Did you buy this house for your grandmother?"

He looked at her before he answered, and she figured he wanted to determine her reason for asking the question. What he saw must have pleased him, for he grinned and said, "Absolutely, and I'm more proud of this than of anything else I've managed. She enjoys her garden and the pool behind it. I asked whether she'd prefer three bedrooms or two bedrooms and a pool. She preferred the pool, and she swims every day. Boy, does she love this place!"

Winston held Petra's hand as they strolled up the walk to the house. She wondered at the absence of nerves, but only for a moment, before she reflected that her absence of concern sprang from her prognosis for the future. The woman's reaction to her would have no influence upon her well-being. As the doorknob turned, she felt Winston's arm ease around her waist.

A tall woman, who might have been his mother rather than his grandmother, opened the door, and her face lit up as if the sun had suddenly shone on her.

"Winston! Oh, son, what a wonderful surprise!" She opened her arms, and embraced him. Petra waited, short of breath, until the woman's gaze captured her.

"Well. You've brought this lovely lady to see me." Without hesitating, the woman opened her arms to Petra. "How nice of you to come," she said.

"Grandmother, this is Petra Fields. Petra, this is my paternal grandmother, LeAnn Fleet."

Still basking in the warmth of the woman's welcome, Petra couldn't help grinning, for the loving greeting had lifted her out of her near-moroseness of minutes earlier. "I'm so glad to meet you, Mrs. Fleet," she said and meant it. She never knew her grandmothers, but she would have given much to have a mother as warm as the woman who had just hugged her.

"Come in and make yourselves comfortable," LeAnn Fleet said. She looked at her grandson, her pride in him stamped on her every gesture. "Do you have time for a bite to eat, son? I have fried chicken and buttermilk biscuits."

He draped an arm around his grandmother's shoulder. "We just ate. If I'd planned to stop here, we wouldn't have. Why don't you put some in a bag."

They chatted for a while about nothing in particular, before Winston kissed his grandmother, promised to see her again soon, and said, "We have to leave now."

LeAnn took Petra's hand. "Next time you're out here, be sure and come to see me often. I've enjoyed meeting you."

What did she say to that? She'd stopped lying, so she said, "I doubt I'll get back here, but it's been wonderful meeting you."

"You'll be back, and you come to see me," LeAnn said, just before she hugged Petra.

Shivers shot through Petra, and she needed all of her strength in order to steady herself. As they walked back to the car, she couldn't help thinking that the inevitable encroached. *Maybe I shouldn't go out with Winston tonight. But I need to be with him. It's all I'll ever have of this man.* He opened the car door for her and stopped, as his lower lip dropped and an expression of deep and pensive thought settled on his face.

"Did you forget something?" she asked him

"Hmmm. No. It's . . . Never mind." Although pleasant enough, he seemed pre-occupied as he drove back to San Francisco, and she couldn't shake the feeling that something important pressed him. After parking in the hotel's garage, he said, "I'll pick you up at your room at seven o'clock." He thought for a minute. "Tell you what. I'll phone you ten minutes before I leave my room. Okay?"

"Fine. You're scared I'll go to sleep, but that's wasted worry. I'm too excited to sleep."

Petra waited with him at the hotel's elevator, feeling as if her nerves had unraveled. The time was rapidly approaching when she would leave him and never see him again. She didn't think she could bear to tell him good-bye.

As if sensing her change of mood, he pinched her nose. "Behave yourself. We're playing by your rules, and you said we're going to be happy for the time we have, although as much as you've learned about me, you can't think that I'm letting you walk out of my life for good."

"But I told you —"

He held up both hands, palms out. "I know what you told me, but if it's true and if you don't have but one hour, I intend to spend every second of that hour with you. Do you hear me?"

When the elevator opened on the ninth floor, the one on which she had a room, he attempted to follow her, but she kissed him on the cheek, and said, "Don't make it hard for me. See you at seven."

Inside her room, she kicked off her shoes, laid out what she would need that evening and the next morning, packed everything else, and put her bags in the closet. She turned on the radio so that she could hear it while she took a bubble bath and did her best to empty out her mind. After applying her favorite body lotion liberally all over her body, she walked around nude until the excess lotion evaporated, put on the white terrycloth robe that the hotel supplied, got a sheet of hotel stationery, and wrote a short note to Winston.

Dearest Winston,

Always know that you have given me true happiness and that you have made these last days memorable. If I ruled this world, I would never leave you. You are the only love my life has known.

Petra

Petra put the note into an envelope, placed the envelope in her evening bag, and switched on the television in hopes of finding a tennis match or something else distracting that didn't involve interpersonal relations.

She thought of calling her mother, but would the day be a happier one if she didn't? She gazed around her hotel room. "This place looks as if it's unoccupied," she said to herself, "but that's too bad. I hope Winston doesn't become suspicious when he walks in here and looks around." To lessen the chance of that, she hurried to finish dressing before he arrived.

"Why didn't I ever wear anything like this before?" she asked herself aloud when she scrutinized herself in the red chiffon dress, silver hoops, slippers, and beaded bag. "I look like a different person." She lifted her right shoulder in a quick shrug. "Oh, well. My looks aren't the only things I've squandered." She dabbed perfume in strategic places, and spun around toward the television when she heard Luther's voice begin the song, "Here and Now," only to remember that she'd turned on the radio.

"Oops!" She grabbed the cabinet door to steady herself when a wave of dizziness hit her. "You stay away from me," she said, shaking her fist toward the ceiling. "At least let me have tonight."

The moment passed, and she sang "Just My Imagination," the Temptations' hit song of the 1960s that her father loved and her mother hated. She hadn't finished the first verse when she heard the knock on her room door.

His eyebrows shot up, and his eyes widened when he looked at her. "You're so beautiful." His words came out on a slow breath, as if he breathed rather than said them. "Can I . . . Can I hug you?"

She opened her arms and knew again the strength and sweetness of his caress. He handed her a tiny package. "Put that in your purse and open it in the morning. It's meant to commemorate this special evening."

Petra tried to smile, but she wasn't certain as to what her expression communicated to him, for he hugged her again and said, "I'm only going to think about the good things." Her next thought questioned what those *good* things might be. She noticed that he didn't leave his key at the front desk as he'd done previously, but she didn't question him. He asked the doorman for a taxi.

"Madam is lovely tonight," the doorman, who appeared to be about sixty said, "and it's a fine evening to enjoy a lady's company." The comment drew a five-dollar thank you from Winston, and she smothered a laugh. She was learning that proper care of the male ego was tantamount to building bridges.

"My goodness," she said to herself, "a restaurant with a canopy and a uniformed doorman, and we're not even in New York." As they walked to their seats, she counted the long-stemmed glasses at each place setting. Five. She hoped they served something other than wine or spirits, because she didn't want Winston to think her a wimp. She saw the waterfall and the huge chandelier in the center of the room and caught her breath. He wanted to make the evening memorable; how could she forget it?

"This place is beautiful and so elegant," she said to him after they seated themselves. "You've gone out of your way to make this a special evening. It's wonderful."

They refused cocktails and began their meal with lobster bisque. To Petra's surprise she had no difficulty consuming the seven courses that ended with Floating Island and expresso coffee. "If anyone had told me that food could be so wonderful," she said, sipping her coffee, "I would have named them liar. This was a feast."

"I enjoyed it, too," Winston said, "and I'm happy that you did. I won't have an aperitif now. Perhaps later. What about you?"

She declined. "I wish I had a picture of that waterfall."

Winston called the maître d' and asked if he could borrow a Polaroid camera. "Yes, of course, sir. Where would you like the pictures taken?"

"By the waterfall." She stood with him beside the waterfall, and the maître d' took several pictures of them.

"Would you like one set or two?" the man asked Winston who, without looking at her replied, "two please. Thank you."

"May I have my set, please?" she asked Winston when they were in a taxi on the way back to the hotel. "I'll put them in my purse." She didn't want to forget them and, considering her nervous anxiety, she figured she was capable of forgetting her name.

They entered the nightclub that adjoined the hotel, and a waiter rushed to greet them. "Ah, my friend from last night," the man said. "Would you like your same table? Come with me."

They walked behind the waiter to the table they shared the night they met. "I'd appreciate his welcome," she said to Winston in an aside, "if I didn't think it was prompted by the size of the tip you gave him."

"No doubt, but we tip for service, and he serves for tips. I haven't previously thought about it but, in a sense, we're both dishonest. I tip when I'm not pleased, and he'll smile when he knows the tip is inadequate. I thought he was a good waiter, though."

"Is madam having ginger ale tonight?" the waiter asked.

"I think I'll have a margarita," she said.

"Ah, so it is a special night. Madam looks lovely for it."

"Thank you," Winston said. "I'll have the same."

"Back where I come from, a man probably wouldn't take kindly to his date's receiving compliments from other men," she said to Winston after the waiter left the table.

"These guys are Latin, and they court women even when they don't open their mouths. After I got used to it, I realized it's nice, so long as they keep it between the lines. Makes a woman feel good."

She didn't want to sit across a table from Winston, but to snuggle close to him in the curve of his arm. The waiter brought the drinks, and Winston hooked his arm through the curve of hers, and they gazed into each other's eyes as they sipped their drinks. Suddenly, he rested his glass on the table. "This is . . . It's hell," he said under his breath, but she heard him and, at that moment, she cursed fate. The band members finished tuning their instruments, and the alto saxophonist blew the first notes of the Beatles' "Let It Be."

"Dance with me."

She stood and went into his arms. They danced as one and, when it ended, they stood there smiling into each other's eyes. Then, the band began a slow rendition of an old Fats Waller number from the Depression years, "Two Sleepy People." Winston stopped the pretense, folded her close, and danced a slow one-step, barely moving his feet. When she rested her head on his shoulder, he asked her, "Do you want to finish that drink?"

"No."

"Will you go with me?"

"Yes."

He went back to the table, signaled for the waiter, paid the bill, and said, "Thanks for everything."

"Thank you very much, sir," the waiter said. "Please look for me when you come back." Winston didn't answer, and she could see that he had to force the smile. He took her hand. "Let's go."

They stepped on the elevator, and she pushed the button for the seventeenth floor, taking from him the option of going to her room. At the question in his eyes, she said, "You said 'Will you go with me?' so I figured you wanted us to go to your room. What's the matter? Are you sloppy?"

"Actually, I'm neat. I also wanted you to come with me." His eyes darkened. "Are you really leaving me tomorrow?"

"Please let's not be sad, Winston. If I could, I'd stay with you always."

"I believe that." He walked into his room holding her in his arms. "I've waited all my life to feel this way." He kicked the door closed, let it support his back, and wrapped her to him. At last, she had his tongue deep in her mouth and his fingers loving her flesh as his hands roamed over her back and hips. She wanted to experience everything with him, because she knew it could only happen this once.

"Do you want me?" he whispered.

"Yes. Oh, yes. It's all I want."

He unzipped her dress, let it fall to the floor, and gasped when her firm and erect breasts stood bare before him. Like a child alone in a candy store, his eyes sparkled as his fingers brushed across her hardened nipples. "Mine. All mine," he said, and sucked one into his mouth; he suckled her while heat plowed through her, tormenting her until the liquid of her passion dripped down her leg. When she undulated against him, he picked her up and put her in his bed.

He stood beside the bed, shedding his clothes and gazing into her eyes, then kicked off his shoes, bent over and slid his finger into her bikini panties. "May I remove these?" he asked her and was already ridding her of them. She opened her arms to him, and when he covered her with his body, she thought she'd die of happiness.

He stared down into her face, "I'm deeply in love with you, Petra. If you love me, trust me to make this work for us."

"Surely you know that I love you, and I trust you."

With his eyes, his lips, and his hands, he played her body the way a gifted lyrist plays a lyre. She tried to control her wild response until he whispered, "I'm trying to drive you crazy. Don't fight it; let it have its way."

"Why don't you get into me?" she begged. "Now. I want to feel you in me." He spread her legs, raised her knees, and went into her. Joy suffused her when he began moving in and out of her. Then he dispensed with the gentle strokes and started displaying his strength with powerful thrusts, thundering toward his goal until she screamed and capitulated, threw wide her arms, and yelled, "Take it. Take whatever you want, anyway you want it." He accelerated his movements and thrust more vigorously.

"Oh, Lord. Help me. Help me," she screamed and erupted into orgasm. His grip on her tightened and, as if shrouded in ecstasy, he splintered in her arms. She hadn't known that a man could regroup so quickly, but within less than half an hour, he claimed her again, loving her until she exploded, imprisoning him within the fiery walls of her vagina. When he fell over on his back, she thought him enervated, leaned over to kiss him, and he pulled her on top of him and held her there.

Hours later, exhausted and spent from the many times they'd loved each other, he folded her in his arms, and his tears bathed her lips as he kissed her, murmuring over and over, "I love you. I can't let you leave me." Eventually, he fell asleep with his left hand between her legs. As soon as she could do so without awakening him, she moved it gently to his side.

For a long time, she gazed at Winston, asleep, his face relaxed and peaceful. Fighting back the tears, she leaned over, grazed his forehead with her lips carefully to avoid awakening him, and slid out of bed. She stood beside the sleeping man, watching to see whether he would awaken, and when he seemed to sink into deeper sleep, she began to dress as, at last, tears soaked her clothes. She finished dressing and pinned the note she wrote earlier to the pillow on which her head had rested.

Legs of lead propelled her to the door and, when she opened it, her hand seemed to glue itself to the doorknob. Finally, without looking back, she forced herself to walk out of the door and close it. Once outside the room, her presence of mind returned, and she sped down the corridor to the elevator. Minutes later, bags in hand, she checked out of the hotel, got into the taxi, and headed for the car rental office.

Only an hour had passed since she kissed him good-bye, but it seemed like forever when she ignited the engine of the rental car, and drove away from San Francisco and Winston Fleet. In the early morning darkness, she drove slowly, unfamiliar with the route she wanted to take and uneasy about the precarious status of her mind. Could she drive safely in eighty-mile-an-hour traffic? She didn't care for herself, but for other drivers on the road. And could she handle the feeling that she stood at a precipice, about to scale a great divide, to cross an abyss of unknown depth? Maybe this was it. If only she'd brought her cell phone, she could call Krista and her mother.

About eighty miles south of San Francisco, feeling the pangs of hunger, she saw a sign pointing to Santa Cruz and took the next exit off Highway 101. She had envisioned Santa Cruz as a place where people drove flashy cars and lived in skimpy bathing suits, but as she drove through the town, she saw people dressed in business clothes dashing along at a dizzying pace, as if they wouldn't have a second chance at whatever they sought. And nobody greeted anyone. By comparison, Ellicott City seemed dull and tame. She didn't think she'd like to live in such a place. But it didn't matter. She walked into a restaurant and took a table, looked down at the pants and shirt she'd worn repeatedly since leaving home, and grimaced at their worn appearance.

"What can I get you this morning?" the waitress asked her.

"I'd like some grits, scrambled eggs, and sausage, please."

"Grits? I don't know as we've got any grits, but I'll ask." She took out what appeared to be a walkie-talkie and punched a button. "Jimmy, we got any grits back there?"

"Not one ever-loving grain. Try buttermilk biscuits."

"I'll take the biscuits instead," Petra said, "and coffee with milk." She didn't order orange juice, but the waitress brought it, explaining that the price of the meal was the same, juice or not.

"You're not from 'round here, are you?"

"No. I'm from Maryland. Is there a hotel near the beach that's not too expensive?"

"Girl, everything in this town costs an arm and a leg. Try the Breakers. Three blocks in the direction of the traffic, turn left, drive four blocks, and if it doesn't get out of your way, you'll drive straight into it."

Petra's lower jaw dropped, and the waitress laughed. "Local joke. These drivers don't give way for anything or anybody. Some of 'em drive like they expect the Pacific Ocean to get out of the way, and the fire department has pulled more than one car out of it. Take care."

Petra found the Breakers easily. She hoped for a day room, a place to rest and freshen up after sightseeing, but after comparing the reasonable cost of a room to the opulence of the lobby, she took an option on staying longer with full service. She collected tourist brochures and fliers from the hotel's concierge and looked them over. It seemed that swimming was the most popular pastime, but she didn't know how to swim, because the water frightened her. And although she had yearned from childhood to ride the Ferris wheel, her fear of heights had always stood in the way. She went down to a shop in the hotel, bought a bathing suit and a pair of blue, cropped pants, and went back to her room.

Minutes later she headed down to the hotel's pool and asked the lifeguard for swimming lessons. If she was going to do and see things she always desired to do and see, she should swim at least once. *And you should ride that Ferris wheel,* her mind nagged.

"You'll need a few lessons," the guard said. "Nobody ever learned to swim on the first try. Besides, I have to teach you when I'm not working, which means before ten or after six." She made an appointment to meet him at the pool at nine the next morning. "Don't eat first," he called after her as she left the pool room. She went to the hotel registration desk and booked the room for three nights. If she didn't learn by the time she had to leave, so be it.

"Where is that recreation place with the Ferris wheel?" she asked the registration clerk. He told her and added, "But that's old hat. Try that thing that looks like an elevator." She said she would, but she meant to ride that Ferris wheel as well as a roller coaster at least once. She hadn't been scared standing at the edge of the Grand Canyon's South Rim, though she knew her lack of fear was psychological, springing from the knowledge that she had a terminal illness and not much life to lose.

She thanked the man, followed his instructions to the beach, bought tickets, fastened herself into the roller coaster seat, closed her eyes, and held her stomach with both hands. As the roller coaster made a figure eight, she laughed, screamed, clutched the man in the seat beside her, and at times thought she'd swallowed her heart. When it finally came to a stop, the man took her arm, helped her out of her chair and had to grab her when she nearly collapsed from a wave of dizziness.

"Sure you're all right?" he asked, steadying her.

"Thanks so much," she said. "I'm fine. I've never been on one of those things before. It wasn't nearly as bad as I thought it would be."

"I guess I can be thankful for that," he said, drawing her attention to the shirt sleeve on his left arm that had been ripped to threads.

She gaped at him. "You mean I . . ."

"Pay it no mind," he said. "In less time than it took you to do that, I blew three thousand on blackjack. Have a good life." He winked at her and walked off.

She ran after him. "I wasn't scared. Do you hear me? I wasn't scared. I enjoyed every minute of that ride. I wasn't scared."

"Good. I'm happy for you," the man said. "But don't press your luck." He walked on, but she headed for the Ferris wheel, which she considered far less frightening than the roller coaster.

"I'm not afraid of heights anymore," she repeated over and over. "I'm not scared."

She gave the uniformed man her ticket, took a seat, and waited for the chills of fear to settle over her. "My goodness," she said to herself at the end of the short experience, "that was less unsettling than being on a horse. What else have I missed because I didn't have the guts to try it?" Petra passed an ATM, stopped, and debited her savings account for five hundred dollars. Credit cards were handy, but you couldn't use them at a drink or candy dispensing machine.

Exulting from her triumphs over herself and bursting with a need to share her victory with someone — anyone — who knew of her reticence to embrace new experiences, she dashed back to her hotel room and telephoned her friend, Twylah.

"Hello. Sorry I got no time to talk. I got to get to work, and I'm running late," Twylah said.

"Hi, Twylah. This is Petra. I forgot about the time difference. I'll —"

"*Petra!* Girl, where in hell are you? Nobody's heard a word from you since . . . Girl, where are you?"

"Oh, calm down, Twylah. I'm in Santa Cruz, and I called to tell you I just rode on a roller coaster that made a figure eight, got off, and took a ride on the Ferris wheel."

"Huh?"

"And tomorrow I'm going to take swimming lessons."

"Do Jesus! You sure you all right?"

"Don't I sound all right?" she asked to avoid lying.

"You call your mama. She said you won't have no job when you get back. Your boss has practically hung himself. I gotta go. Call your mama." Twylah hung up, and Petra wished she hadn't called. The exchange hadn't satisfied her. Winston would have rejoiced with her. Winston! *If I let myself think of him, I'll go to pieces.* She had to call her mother, but with the three-hour time difference, that would have to wait until evening.

She ate a modest dinner, hamburger, French fries, and ice tea, in her room, and at precisely seven o'clock, she telephoned her mother. "Hi, Mama. This is Petra."

"Like I don't know my own daughter's voice. I sure am glad you called. Your boss is threatening to fire you. Do you know any reason why Reverend Collins called here three times to find out how you are?"

"Oh, he was working on me just before I came on vacation," she said, as casually as she could. "I ought to be home in about a week. It's so nice out here, Mama. I wish you could live in a place like this."

"Well, honey, don't worry 'bout it. If you poor one place, you'll be poor everywhere you go. I'm always going to be a licensed practical nurse, and nobody's ever going to pay me as much as they pay registered nurses. Besides, it gets hot there just like it gets hot here."

In just three short weeks, how could she

have forgotten how negative her mother could be? "How's Krista doing?"

"Fine, I guess. I hardly ever see her. She comes home from work, eats her supper, and goes to her room. Here lately, she's joined a singing group, and she goes to that on Monday evenings. Otherwise, nothing's changed far as I can see. Oh, yes, she said something about trying to get into college, but you know these young people don't stick with anything long."

"Krista's dogged and determined, Mama. If she sets her mind to something, she goes after it. I wish you'd encourage her to go to college."

"I would, if I could back it up with money."

Petra didn't pursue it, but the conversation saddened her; her child would need her, and she wouldn't be there for her.

In spite of Petra's fears for her daughter, Providence appeared to provide for her. Goodman walked out of Price's Electronics with a brand new Compaq laptop computer, and an Epson color printer-scanner-copier. He took it to his office and waited impatiently for five-fifteen when Krista would arrive. To his chagrin, he opened the door and looked at Jada, wearing a skirt that was much too tight and a T-shirt from which her voluptuous bosom threatened to escape.

"I told you not to come here unless we arranged it ahead of time," he said, not bothering to hide his irritation. "Suppose my wife or one of my children was here."

"Sorry, I needed to see you. Besides, I figured it was time you got some attention."

"Look, Jada. I have duties at home, and I'm not nineteen."

"You couldn't prove that last part by me."

He leaned back in his chair, looking at her, trying to figure out what she wanted, since he was certain she was faking her attraction to him. The buzzer rang. "Oh, shit!" he said. "Now you've done it."

"Oh, for Heaven's sake, don't get bent out of shape. Use your head. I'm one of your music students."

He got up, started for the door, paused, and said, "You couldn't prove that by anybody in my family. They're all musicians."

"I need about fifty bucks," she said. So that was her game.

"Oh, hell. I was just going to ask you for twenty-five," he said, opened the door, saw Krista, and relaxed.

"You two know each other," he said, refusing to introduce them.

Krista strolled in, sat down, crossed her knees, and said, "Maybe she knows me, but I don't know her."

He looked straight at Jada. "Krista is my daughter, the oldest of my three children."

Jada seemed taken aback, and he meant to take good advantage of her misunderstanding. He stood. "Jada was just leaving, Krista." To Jada, he said, "I'll see you to the door."

"Aren't you going to kiss me?" Jada asked when they were alone.

"The way you screwed things up? Are you going to give me the twenty-five dollars? You'll get it back Monday night."

She gave him the money. "Is your daughter going to tell your wife?"

He shrugged. "She's a female. How the hell do I know what she'll do? See you Monday."

"What did she want?" Krista asked him when he returned to his office. "Suppose I had been Carla? What would you have done?"

"Good question. I have your laptop and your printer. I'll take them home for you. Do you want me to hook them up?" Krista swung her crossed leg carelessly as if she didn't have a care, but he noticed that she didn't look at him.

"Well?" he said, agitated. After all, hadn't he told her a minute earlier that he'd bought her both a computer and a printer? Didn't she know what they cost?

"How do you and my grandmother get along? Is she gonna be mad if you come to the house?"

He stared at his daughter. She didn't grow up with him, and he didn't believe genes contributed that much to the socialization of a person, but she was so much like him that it made him nervous. She had the guts to say whatever she felt and thought. He'd also been that way, but the years had taught him the efficacy of bridling his tongue.

"I haven't seen her since before you were born, and from what I remember of her, she probably holds me responsible for your having been born out of wedlock."

"What'll you do if she gets on your case?"

"If ignoring her doesn't work, I'll tell her who's really responsible. I'll be there tomorrow at five-fifteen." In the short time he'd known Krista, he'd learned that in order to handle her, he had to take control.

"Okay. I'll be there. Thanks for my stuff. I still can't believe I'm going to own a computer, not to speak of a printer. I mean, you're really four square, Daddy." She jumped up and kissed his cheek. "I missed a lot not growing up with you."

"Because I could give you things?" He didn't want that kind of relationship with her; he wanted her to see him as her loving and supportive father.

"Oh, Daddy, for goodness sake. How could you think that? It's . . . Daddies are different from mothers is what I meant."

"That's the least they should be," he said, understanding what she wanted to say but couldn't articulate.

He stooped to pick up the boxes and grimaced. "I can carry one of them, Daddy. The laptop can't be too heavy." She lifted it and headed for the door. "It's fine. Come on."

He reached the door where she stood with her hand on the knob and handed her a key. "Put that box on top of this one, and lock the door behind us."

Sons were easier to understand, and probably also to raise, than daughters, and he'd defy anyone to disagree. His appreciation for Petra mounted each time he was with Krista. As they left the building together, it occurred to him that Petra's behavior didn't make sense. After more than eighteen years of silence, she asked to see him and told him he had a daughter nearing her eighteenth birthday and, shortly thereafter, took off on a vacation to nowhere in particular, just wherever her mind led her. He wasn't a psychiatrist, but he had sense enough to know that Petra had either experienced an epiphany or she was in some kind of trouble.

Goodman placed the boxes in the trunk of his car, closed it, and asked Krista, "Has your mother ever done anything like this before? I mean like suddenly announcing that she's going on a vacation without leaving plans, an itinerary of addresses where she may be reached?"

"Nope. And Mama isn't stingy, Daddy, but she handles money like it was an egg, and for her, a vacation is like . . . like staying home two days from work. Once, she went to Virginia Beach, but since she can't swim and she's scared to death of water, that was a flop."

"Is she sick?"

"Mama? Sick? Not since I knew her. Mama's strong as a horse."

He opened the front passenger door for Krista, seated himself, and ignited the engine. "Looks as if she got tired of being regimented," he said, but he didn't believe it. Something was amiss, and Petra had not shared it with her family.

CHAPTER SEVEN

Petra stood at the window in her room looking out at the vast expanse of the Pacific Ocean. *I'm just beginning to live, to understand what life is about, and I have to leave all this. Well, I'm going to do my damnedest to enjoy what's left. My insurance policy will take care of Krista until she can fend for herself, and Mama would work as long as she can stand up even if she got a windfall.*

She took the soiled clothing from her suitcase, and her gaze landed on the little evening purse that she carried the previous evening. Her heartbeat accelerated when she remembered that it contained the little package that Winston gave her. She opened the little box, sat down on the edge of the bed, and stared at the gold band. Dumbfounded. After a minute, she looked at the inscription inside: the date they met and the word LOVE. She slipped it on the third finger of her left hand, and a feeling of contentment washed over her.

Feeling upbeat and almost happy, she washed the soiled clothing, hung it over the bathtub, and went down to the lobby. "Do you have a brochure specifically on the Boardwalk?" she asked the concierge.

"We do, indeed, ma'am." He gave her several pamphlets. "Please let me know if I can help." Petra got a cup of cappuccino at the coffee bar and sat down in the lounge to enjoy it and study the brochures.

"Miss, will you keep an eye on the baby while I run over there to the ladies' room? I'll be back in a minute."

Petra glanced up to see a baby carriage in front of her, and, before she could respond, the woman ran off, obviously in a hurry to get to the women's room. After perusing the tourist leaflets, Petra decided to browse the shops and then take a nap, for she wanted to go to the theatre and then see the midnight fireworks on the Boardwalk. Intending to ask the concierge for theatre tickets, she stood, noticed that the baby carriage was still there, and remembered the woman who was supposed to have made an urgent trip to the women's room. She peered into the carriage, saw a newborn baby, and knew at once that the woman had abandoned the child.

She went to the concierge and told him what she suspected. "I'm sorry, ma'am, but you'll have to remain right here while I report this to the police," the man said, and in a tone less friendly than when he previously spoke to her.

"Why should I wait?" she asked him, provoked because she envisaged a problem that was not of her making.

"Madam, how do we know it isn't your child?"

Petra took a deep breath and let it out slowly. "That's the dumbest thing I ever heard of. Anybody can see that it's not my baby. That child is white."

"I've seen a lot of people who said they were black, but who were as white as I am," the man said, and tapped a bell. Within seconds, a uniformed and armed guard appeared. "This woman is to wait here until the police arrive," the concierge told the guard. He left and returned with the baby carriage.

Two policemen arrived at about the time the baby began to cry. "Would you at least feed the child?" the concierge asked Petra.

"With what? You have as much milk as I do. You feed it," she said and had the pleasure of seeing his face turn to crimson.

"You have to come with us, ma'am," one

of the policemen said. "Child abandonment is a serious matter."

"Yes, it is, and I hope you find that woman." She would never forget her embarrassment at leaving the hotel with a policeman on each side of her.

She walked into the station house and looked around at the men and women likely to leave there in handcuffs. "Officer," she said to the desk sergeant, "I happened to be at the wrong place." She described the woman who asked her to keep an eye on the child. "Now, I'm a victim."

"If that isn't your child, there's no problem. We have to fingerprint you and ask you some questions."

"I understand that, sir," she said, "but you could settle the whole thing by getting a gynecologist to examine me. That baby can't be more than four days old."

"How do you know that?" the officer asked.

"Because I have an eighteen-year-old daughter, and I know a newborn when I see one. So, could we please go to the nearest hospital? I want to see the head of the GYN service. Otherwise I'll miss my plane, and all my connections."

"Where're you headed?" the officer asked her.

"Ellicott City, Maryland, with a stop off in Atlanta."

"Okay. This won't take long. Have a seat."

Hours later, the police had determined that her fingerprints matched none of those on the baby carriage or the baby's bottle, and a physician, called at Petra's insistence, determined that her breasts were not those of a woman who had recently given birth.

"Can you draw well enough to sketch a picture of the woman who left that baby with you?" one officer asked Petra.

"I can try." She did the best she could and decided that she'd given them a fair enough likeness. "I'd like to go back to the hotel now, Officer," she said to the one who brought her there, "but I've never been in Santa Cruz before, so I don't know how to get back there."

"If you'll wait about ten minutes, I can drop you off at the Breakers, Ms. Fields."

"Are you on vacation?" he asked as he drove to the hotel. "Maryland is a long way from Santa Cruz."

"I know it is, but there are so many things I haven't done and so many places I haven't been, so I just bought a ticket and headed for South Dakota. For the last few weeks, I've been seeing this part of the country. Believe me, it's been an eye opener."

He glanced at her from the corner of his eye. "You're young. You're not on the lam, are you? Why did you feel the need to do this now? It isn't like you had one foot in the grave and the other on a banana peel, so to speak."

His words sent chills throughout her body. "You couldn't have put it more perfectly or more succinctly."

"What?" He slowed down, drove to the curb, and parked. "What did you say? I mean, were you serious?"

"Unfortunately, I was. From what the doctor said, I figure I've got a few months at the most, and you guys made me throw away almost four hours of it sitting in a police station." She tried to lighten the mood when she said, "Not that it wasn't a pleasure to be in the company of so many great-looking guys; it was, but I'd rather it had been under different circumstances."

He leaned back and closed his eyes. "You mean you're terminally ill?"

"Yes, but at least I know it, and I'm having a ball with what's left of my life. So don't be gloomy."

"You've accepted this?" he asked in a tone of wonder.

"What was I supposed to do, shake my fist at God and say no way?"

"Look, this is . . . This thing put a knot in the pit of my gut. For the last four and a half hours, you've had your hooks in me, and now this." Suddenly, he opened the car door, jumped out, and lost what she assumed was his lunch. After a few minutes, he got back into the car, reached into the glove compartment for a hand sanitizer package, opened it, and washed his face and hands. "I've never had anything like this happen to me," he said. "I'm sorry. Look, will you at least have dinner with me?"

"I'd love to, but you shouldn't waste your time on me, because it can't lead to anything good. Besides, I was planning to go to the theatre and after that to the midnight fireworks."

"May I do that with you? After dinner, of course. I don't expect more than your company. It just seems a shame not to have at least an evening with you. Is . . . this something that could happen any minute, or will you get a warning?"

"I don't know. I have an inoperable brain tumor, and the only symptoms I've had so far are sporadic headaches."

"You're a brave woman, Petra. I've never imagined there was a woman like you." He ignited the engine, moved away from the curb, and headed to the hotel. "Let's see.

It's three-thirty. I'm going home to change, and I'll be back at five-thirty."

She should tell him not to come, that she had nothing to offer him, but the day's aggravations had chipped away some of her courage, and left her lonely for her family and lonely for Winston.

"All right?" he asked, his voice and demeanor hopeful.

"I'll look forward to seeing you at five-thirty," she told him, and immediately her spirits lifted.

She walked over to the concierge, intent on getting some of her own, and said, "Remember me? I thought you should know the police are still looking for the mother of that baby, and they don't have me in mind."

She enjoyed watching the man's face take on a red hue. "I'm sorry, ma'am, but I had to do my job. It took me long enough to get this one, and I can't afford to lose it."

"No problem, but you can imagine how I felt walking out of this crowded lobby between two policemen." She went to her room, drew a bath, dropped pink crystals into the warm water, stripped, and got in the tub of pink bubbles. She stayed in it until the water cooled, dried off, and, after setting her alarm clock for one hour, crawled into bed and fell asleep. She woke up on time and answered her phone at five twenty-five.

"Petra? Hi. This is Bob Elroy. I'm downstairs at the registration desk."

Gosh, she hadn't even asked him his name. "I'll be right down." She put on a sleeveless, red linen dress and its three-quarter sleeve jacket, a pair of black mid-heel shoes, the only decent-looking ones she brought with her, checked her hair and the silver earrings, got her little black straw bag, and hurried down to meet Officer Robert Elroy. *I sure hope he's a gentleman; that uniform doesn't guarantee it.*

She hardly recognized the man in the beige suit who waited at the bank of elevators. "Hi, Bob. You look ten years younger without that uniform."

"I'm thirty-six," he said, "so don't let the absence of gray hairs fool you. You're so beautiful, Petra. I'm glad I can legally carry a gun."

Her eyebrows shot up. "You've got a gun with you tonight?"

"I'm required by law to carry it at all times. I hope you don't mind."

"Not a bit." She grinned. "As long as I don't see it or hear it."

"At least you have a sense of humor about it. Knowing I have it frightens some women.

There's a real nice Italian restaurant that I like — by the way, if you like Italian food and can't go to Italy, Santa Cruz is the place to be. Want to go there? It's right on the ocean, and since we'll be early, we can get a table by the window and see the sunset. It's spectacular."

"I'm in your hands."

"And I'll take good care of you," he said. "I hope you got some rest, because the fireworks don't start till midnight, but there's plenty to do on the Boardwalk. What do you do in Ellicott City, Petra?"

"I'm office manager at a real estate agency. Or I was. I suspect I've been fired by now. I was granted leave, but not nearly as much as I've taken, and I didn't bring my cell phone as the boss told me to do."

"Does he know your con . . . er . . . situation?"

"Good heavens, no. Jack has about as much feeling for people as a flea. I didn't even tell my family, because I don't want people to feel sorry for me."

"But if people love you, is it fair to deprive them of their right to care for you and to make your days as pleasant as possible?"

"Bob, I could never expect that of my mother. She would find a dozen reasons why I'm responsible. Oh, she dearly loves me, but negative is her middle name."

He was right about the restaurant's reputation. "I doubt I've ever had such great Italian food. It's wonderful," she told him.

"In this town, it would have to be. We have a large Italian population, and Italians care about what they eat."

"I've heard that."

"We have plenty of time to get to the theatre," he said. "I got tickets for a production of *Flashback.* It received wonderful reviews. I hope you'll like it."

She didn't tell him that she would enjoy most anything that absorbed her so completely that she didn't think of Winston Fleet and how she longed to be with him. They walked along the Boardwalk to the theatre, and a human figure dressed in a white sheet with a black rope around his waist stopped them.

"Give me your hand," he said to Petra, "and I'll tell you your future."

"You'd be wasting your time and mine," she answered, "but thanks for the offer." She noticed that Bob handed the man a dollar bill.

"I've heard that he's a rather good seer, but I imagine you've already heard more about the future than you wanted to know." He looked at his watch. "We have some time. Let's check in here for a few minutes."

They entered the duck-shooting booth, and he won a beautiful doll for her. "Thanks. I'll cherish this doll. I had one doll when I was very little, but one of my playmates took it, and my mother wouldn't buy another one. She was strict about my taking care of my books, toys, clothes, you name it. She bought me some 3-D puzzles instead. I give my daughter plenty of room to grow and make mistakes."

"Who's taking care of her?"

"She'll be eighteen in a couple of months, but my mother is staying with her while I'm away. I can't believe she's old enough to enter college."

She didn't want to ask Bob personal questions, because to do that would increase the intimacy between them, but she didn't want him to think that he was so lacking in importance to her that she had no interest in him as a person. She asked him a simple question.

"How did you happen to join the police force, Bob?"

"I'm a fourth generation policeman. My father and grandfather expected it of me, and I did it. It pays well, but I may someday walk away from it. I have all these ideas in my head that are raring to come out."

"You want to write or to invent things?"

"Invent. I'm studying physics in the evenings at the university." They reached the theatre, and as they walked in together, he said, "I'm going to name something a 'Petran' after you." She restrained herself, but the impulse to kiss his cheek nearly overpowered her. He wanted by that act to give her a measure of immortality. "Be sure it's sharp and won't rust," she said in an effort to bring levity to the conversation.

"I'm serious. If I name it for you, make no mistake, it will last for centuries." The curtain rose as they took their seats, and she was saved the necessity of answering him. She enjoyed the play, but she would have thought it spectacular if it hadn't contained a lot of Ebonics. "The acting was superb, but those elegantly dressed women speaking Ebonics bothered me," she said to Bob after the show. "I couldn't believe a word I heard. That director must be off his rocker."

"My sentiments precisely," he said. "That so-called black talk makes me squirm every time I hear it. It's not cultural, it's the language of the uneducated. Let's go down to the docks and get a ride out to that big cruiser sitting offshore. We can dance, play the slots, take in a comedy show, or just stroll around and people watch. Want to? The boats come back every fifteen minutes. If you like, we can see the fireworks from there."

She didn't recall playing the slot machines, hadn't even considered it, but why not, just this once? Her purpose in California was to experience all that she could, wasn't it? "Sounds good to me. I think I'd like to take a turn at playing slots before . . . Uh, let's go."

He stared down at her for a few seconds, frowning.

She grabbed his hand. "Come on, Bob. It's like a bad cold. Eventually, it happens to everybody." That kind of pretense was nothing short of lying, something she'd said she wouldn't do again. Putting on a face to make others feel good was the very reason why she hadn't told her family and friends about her prognosis.

"Don't work so hard at making me comfortable, Petra. I am not going to be happy no matter what you say or do, but I promise to enjoy your company . . . That is, if you'll let me."

"I'm sorry, Bob. I know it's best to be honest. Come on. I'm anxious to see the inside of a cruise ship."

A small motorboat took them out to the

big ship, which was anchored offshore to allow gambling. The boat hooked on to an elevator that took them up to the ship's deck. Almost immediately they heard the first notes of the Village People's monster hit, "Y.M.C.A."

"Do you line dance?" he asked her.

"I can do the Electric Slide, and maybe Cotton Eye Joe." He took her hand, headed toward the sound of music, and within minutes she was mentally back in high school doing the Electric Slide, a dance she hadn't thought of since she reached her eighteenth birthday.

"I forgot this could be so much fun," she said. "I wouldn't have missed this for anything." A few minutes later, "Jackson," a song that Johnny Cash and his wife made famous, came over the loud speaker, and a young crowd took to the floor.

"Can I have this dance, miss?" a tall man with a southern accent asked her.

"Thanks, but I don't know how to clog," she said.

"Oh sure, you do, and if you don't, I'll show you."

"No, thanks. I'm with this gentleman, and I don't care to leave him." She didn't look at Bob, because she didn't want him to enter the conversation.

"He doesn't mind, do you, buddy?"

"Please excuse me, mister. I'm sure I would enjoy the dance, but I don't want to leave my friend." She didn't know what else she could do or say to get the man to leave them. He'd had much too much to drink, and she didn't want to aggravate him unduly. Moreover, she couldn't forget that Bob had that gun.

"What's a pretty girl like you doing with this bum?" the man asked her. She sensed the tension in Bob, and her nerves seemed to riot throughout her body.

Suddenly, Bob's hand gripped her arm like a steel band, and he stepped in front of her. "Be careful, mister," she said, "my friend is chief of police in Santa Cruz. You'll get in trouble if you bother with him."

"I don't believe you," the man said. "Let me see your badge, buddy." Bob unbuttoned his coat, exposing both his badge and his gun. The man saluted Bob, and nearly stumbled as he did so. "I owe you one, lady. The last thing I want to do is tangle with one of these California cops."

"What did you think I was going to do to him?" Bob asked her after the man weaved his way through the several onlookers.

"I didn't know. My only thought was that you'd gotten mad, and you had that gun."

An odd expression flashed across Bob's face, then he expelled something akin to a snarl. "I wouldn't use the gun on him; I had other ways of bringing him down. Still, you never know. Thanks for getting rid of him."

"I wish I knew why alcohol makes men think they're stronger, bigger, better looking, and better everything else than they are?"

"Good question. It makes an ass out of some people, women as well as men. A lot of people would still be alive if they hadn't drunk too much liquor."

"I imagine so," she said. "Do they have cones of ice cream on this ship? I'd like to walk along the deck eating ice cream from a cone, not a cup."

"We can do that, but first, you have to try your hand at the slots. I don't gamble. I'll give you a ten-dollar bill. If you win ten dollars, you give me back my ten. As soon as you've played back all your winnings, you stop. Deal?"

"Deal."

He bought a card for forty chances and led her to a twenty-five cent slot machine. "Have fun." She inserted the card, pulled the lever, and discovered how easily one could lose a quarter. Twenty minutes later, she had pulled the lever forty times and discovered why the machine was often referred to as a one-armed bandit.

"I ought to give you back your ten dollars," she said. "I have a feeling that if I hadn't promised, I'd be sitting at that machine now, throwing away my money."

Just then a pain shot through her head, stabbing as if someone were plunging a dagger through her skull. She squeezed her eyes tight and pressed her hand to her forehead.

"What is it?" he asked her. "What's the matter?" His voice carried alarm and urgency as he grabbed her arm. "Is it . . . What's wrong?"

"My head. It's never been this bad before. Please. Just give me a minute, and maybe it will be all right."

With an arm around her, he edged their way slowly out of the crowded hall and onto the deck. "Shouldn't I call for the doctor?"

"No. Please don't. He can't tell me what I don't already know. It usually passes after a few minutes . . . unless . . ." Shudders passed through her, and she knew he felt them. "Bob, I shouldn't have come with you."

He wrapped her in his arms and held her close to his body. "Yes, you should have," he whispered. "I needed this time with you. Is it any better?" he asked, stroking her back.

She should move, because she had nothing to offer him, but right then she needed his strength. For the first time since Barnes gave her that awful news, she'd nearly panicked. Fear plowed through her. Eviscerating. Nearly sending her to her knees. She gulped air. *I'm not as brave as I thought I was.*

Bob's arms tightened around her, and when his breathing quickened, she kissed his cheek, and moved away from him.

"It's so tempting to take advantage of your protectiveness, Bob, but you know how it is with me. As much as I need it this minute, I can't encourage it."

"I feel so helpless, and it's a feeling I'm not used to. Is it any better?"

"A little."

He reached toward her, hesitated, and then embraced her. "I know you're trying to protect me," he said, "but I have to take what I can get when I can get it. How is it now?"

"It's eased a lot," she told him though, in truth, there'd been only moderate improvement. "Maybe we can get that ice cream now. Raspberry and vanilla for me."

He hesitated, obviously skeptical. "All right, if you think so, but it's getting windy out here. Maybe we ought to stay inside."

She didn't want to be cloistered inside with a couple hundred people. "The fireworks should start soon, and this is a great vantage point for watching them," she said. "Besides, even though it's a little windy, it's still nice out here." She considered that the fresh air might have relieved her headache.

"I'll get the ice cream," he said. "You stay right here."

She leaned against the edge of the door and let the wall take her weight. The pain in her head had disappeared, but she had a weak, lethargic feeling. If she were only at home in her own bed in Ellicott City! *I must have been out of my mind taking off by myself like this.*

Her gaze skipped over the ocean, past the dark horizon, and lingered on the sky where not one star could be seen, although a blanket of them had covered the sky when she and Bob got on the boat. The clouds, dark and ominous, hung low, and she thought the wind would knock her down. A sharp flash of lightning lit the sky a second before a crack of thunder roared so loudly that, in fear, she turned her face to the wall. She longed to run inside, but if she did, would Bob find her? When a squall nearly drenched the deck, she ran inside and nearly knocked the cones of ice cream from Bob's hands.

"Rain is coming down in sheets," she told him. "If I had stayed there longer, I would have been drenched."

He handed her a cone of ice cream. "I do everything I can to keep my promises," he said and his eyes twinkled. "But if nature intervenes, or if I don't feel up to climbing a ninety-degree hill, I do what comes naturally. I see you operate on the same principle. Anyway, rain's good. Once, when I was tramping through Africa and had sweated out the Nigerian heat, an afternoon downpour cooled the air. I stripped, went outside in the back garden, raised my hands to the sky, and knew what happiness was."

Visions of him standing naked in the rain with his arms toward the heavens struck her as funny, and laughter poured out of her, momentarily cleansing her of the fear and tension that had gripped her. "That's a riot. I'd have given anything to have seen that."

Bob's left eyebrow shot up. "It was funny to me, too, till I looked up and saw the people I stayed with — the man, his wife, and his four kids — staring at me through the window. You could have bought me for a green papaya." Her amusement at that quickly vanished when she leaned toward him and everything seemed to tilt along with her.

He put out his hand and barely managed to steady her. "It's not you," he assured her. "It's the ship. The water has gotten terribly rough. We'd better go over there and sit down."

After a few minutes, the captain's voice was heard over the loudspeaker. "We'll settle down in a minute. You are advised not to go on deck until further notice. Unfortunately, that means we'll miss the fireworks tonight, but safety comes first."

An hour later, they took the first boat back to shore. She hated having missed the fireworks, but the earlier part of the evening more than compensated for it. She'd never seen a big display of fireworks, but she consoled herself with the thought that she'd missed many other things of greater importance.

She wondered at her lack of dread at telling Bob good-bye. He stood with her at the elevator. "Good-bye, sweetheart. I don't like leaving you like this, but I always try to keep my promises." His smile didn't fool her, and when he gathered her to him in a steel-like grip and pressed his lips to hers, she hugged him, but what she felt was pain, and she didn't part her lips. To have done so would have been misleading.

"Tell me why you're wearing that ring, Petra."

"It isn't a wedding band, Bob. It's a memento for something that can never be. I'm not married."

He gazed at her for a long time. "I could really love you."

"I know, and I wish it could have been different. Take good care of yourself, and . . ." The elevator door opened. "Bye," she whispered and fled into the elevator just as the doors closed. She slumped against the wall, not in despair but in relief that Bob hadn't tested her integrity, and she hadn't been tempted to make love with him only because she felt guilty about his feelings for her.

She went down to the hotel's breakfast room the next morning thinking it best that she head to Atlanta and get back home as soon as possible. She took a seat near the window so that she could see the ocean.

"I'll have grits, sausage, scrambled eggs, biscuits, and coffee," she told the waitress.

"I'll be happy to get you all that except the grits," the waitress said, and soon returned with the order. Petra ate breakfast, hardly tasting it; her mind had traveled back to the years when she struggled to raise

Krista, worked hard, and had no social life. She sipped the coffee long after it had become cold.

"You're not from out this way, are you?" the waitress asked.

"No, ma'am. I'm from Maryland. Ellicott City."

"Back East, huh? I thought so. You can always tell a Southerner; they have good manners, and they love their grits. Can I top off your coffee?" She added hot coffee to Petra's cup. "You look kinda lost. Can I help?"

"Thanks, but I don't think you can." The waitress didn't move from the booth.

Petra took a good look at the woman who stood there smiling, tall, around sixty years old, and still very beautiful, her face etched with experience. "I'm thirty-six years old," Petra said, "and for nearly all of my adult life, men have been content to ignore me. But in the past month, two men have fallen in love with me, and two others might have if I'd hung around. I don't get it."

The waitress leaned against the edge of the booth. "That's because there's something different about you, something that attracts men. You're good-looking, that's for sure, but I see something sad in you, a kind of vulnerability, and men are drawn to vulnerable women. You're probably much less independent and self-sufficient now than you normally are. I'm sure you know what I'm talking about. Did you fall in love with either of those men?"

Petra gazed beyond the waitress and into the past. "Oh, yes. Head over heels."

"I'm sorry." She patted Petra's shoulder. "It'll be all right. In the long run, life just goes on, and we tolerate whatever it dishes out."

"Yes. Especially when we don't have an alternative," Petra said after the waitress walked away. She put a one-dollar bill on the table, paid the cashier, and, on her way out, she waved at the waitress.

Back in her hotel room once more, Petra leafed through her brochures. She had a date with the lifeguard for her first swimming lesson, but what would she do after that? She tried to plan the day, but couldn't concentrate on it, for the memory of those minutes the evening before when she thought the end had come loomed large in her thoughts. Each time the pain was more unbearable, and each time it lasted longer. She reached for the telephone and dialed her mother's number.

"Hi, Mama. I thought I'd call to see how you and Krista are getting on."

"We'd be fine if we weren't worried about you. This is not one bit like you, Petra. You got some explaining to do. Where's all this money you spending coming from? Jack practically took my head off yesterday telling me what he thought of you. When you coming home, child?"

"I want to go to Atlanta to see Martin Luther King, Jr.'s tomb and museum. That'll take a day, and then I'll fly home from Atlanta. So it won't be but about four days, I guess."

"You come on home, now. I don't need to worry my head about no almost forty-year-old woman. Why Reverend Collins always asking about you? I sure hope you didn't confess nothing bad to him. I never was sure about Reverend Collins. Lord forgive me, but if you can't trust a man around women . . . Never mind. The Lord don't want me to judge Reverend Collins. He'll do that."

When her mother got on her sanctimonious horse, there was no stopping her. With her mind on the cost of the phone call, Petra hastened to get Lena off the subject of Jasper Collins. "I'll call him when I get back, Mama. You don't know how I appreciate your looking after Krista while I'm away."

"Of course I know. You take care and

hurry back. I got to get to work now."

"Mama, let me speak with Krista."

"Krista's at work. Before that she was out jogging. That's something else she started here lately. Every morning, she's running over there in the park. I'll tell her you called. You got that cell phone, and you should've taken it with you. Then, your family could keep in touch with you. I declare! Well, you stay safe now, and come on home."

"I will, Mama. Bye."

Was everybody else's mother a trial? She had needed some solace, a little nurturing, but even when Lena tried to be motherly, her effort had the quality of a sermon. Still, her mother was a good woman who worked hard and who did her best for her only child. She opened the window and inhaled deeply of the fresh ocean breeze. Strangely revived with a burst of energy, she skipped over to the television, turned it on, and saw there the competition for national swimming champion.

"That's for me," she said aloud as visions of herself skimming over the ocean floated through her mind.

Chapter Eight

Petra put on her bathing suit and the hotel's white terrycloth robe and took the elevator down to the hotel's Olympic-size pool. Blue was not her favorite color, and the blue tiles covering the walls around the pool and the hallway approaching it reminded her of a painting she once saw hanging in the foyer of an otherwise dull-looking hospital room.

She looked at the water, blue-green from infusions of chlorine intended to neutralize the assorted germs it received from human bodies. Did she want to get into *that*?

Oh, heck! I've always wanted to swim, and my fears wouldn't let me. What have I got to lose now? Nothing but a few weeks, and that's not much. This is hardly the time to protect myself from adventure. Do it, girl. She jerked around at the sound of footsteps coming behind her, and saw the young lifeguard approaching.

"Hey," he said. "I should have told you

not to be in here alone. It's not a clever thing for a woman to do."

She stared at his six foot height, washboard middle, rock-like biceps, beautiful legs, and handsome face. "What a sin," she said to herself. "He can't be a day older than eighteen, if he's that. Thank God, I'm not stupid."

"You're a great ad for bathing suits," he said and, as if his comment was nothing personal, he added, "Let's go around there to the exercise room. I want to show you some important strokes." For about twenty minutes, he had her practicing the crawl and breaststrokes while she stood facing him. "All right. Let's get into the water."

An hour later, Petra left the pool feeling that she could conquer Mount Everest. "You're a quick study, Petra," he said. "Not an iota of fear. See you same time tomorrow morning."

As the day progressed, Petra decided to skip the next swimming lesson and leave Santa Cruz the next morning. She went back to the pool late that afternoon and, though she didn't see a lifeguard, waded into the children's end. She managed to stay afloat with the breaststroke and was soon swimming in deeper water. She got out of the pool an hour later, buoyant with the knowledge that she had actually stayed afloat and that she hadn't been scared. She left payment for the lifeguard at the registration desk, went to her room, and packed. Time was passing, and she had two more important stops to make. In the end, she wanted to be at home with people who loved her. As she packed, she worked at banishing the hollow that had opened up inside of her. If only she had gotten Winston's address, she could have written him a note asking his forgiveness for having left him the way she did. She stiffened her back. What was done was done. The next morning, she got into the rented car and headed for Highway 1 and Monterey.

A few minutes out of Santa Cruz, Petra stopped for gasoline and did something that, a month earlier, she had never attempted, possibly because she had never owned a car, although she was an experienced driver. She put the fuel in the car, checked its tires, and then washed the windshield. She drove off, feeling chipper; she later supposed that her success with the fuel pump must certainly have accounted for her frivolous mood, for she passed a man who thumbed for a ride, stopped, and waited for him. She turned and watched as he approached the front passenger's door, told herself that nothing could happen that wasn't going to happen anyway, and opened the door for him.

"Hi. Thanks for stopping. How far you going?"

"Haven't decided. I'm Petra, and I'm headed for Monterey, but I've a mind to see Malibu. Where're you headed?"

"Los Angeles. My dad's not doing too well."

"Gosh, I'm sorry. I hope he improves."

"Not much chance of that. Say, it's not a good idea for you to pick up strange men. It never occurred to me that you'd stop. I've been out here for a while, so I decided to thumb everything that passed. You better be more careful."

"Not to worry. My days are numbered. I don't expect that anything you or any other man can do to me will be worse than what I'll face in a few days or weeks."

He turned so as to see her better and asked, "You serious?"

"I sure am."

"Well, look here, babe. If you're expecting me to do your dirty work, you can just forget it. I'm a law-abiding citizen. I wouldn't even steal a package of gumballs. Besides, I love women, and when I put my hands on one, I do it to give her pleasure.

What's wrong with you? You look the picture of health to me."

"As my grandfather used to say, 'Don't let looks fool you.' The doctor said I had six months maximum, and a big part of that time have passed. I'm getting tired of waiting; I want it to be over with."

"Yeah? Where you from?"

She told him.

"Well, what're you doing out here on the other side of the country?"

"I'd never been out of Ellicott City, except to go to Baltimore a few times, and I wanted to see the places I'd dreamed of visiting, and do some of the things I'd dreamed of doing, so I declared myself on vacation and bought a ticket to Rapid City, South Dakota, 'cause I wanted to see Mount Rushmore. I've been vagabonding it ever since."

"I hope you've been staying out of trouble," he joshed. He pulled out a bag of potato chips and offered her some. "I can't imagine a woman doing what you say you've done."

"I'll bet you never met a woman going through what I'm going through," she said, biting into a large, crispy potato chip. "I try not to dwell on it, but sometimes it drops down on me real hard, and then I just . . . just want to be done with it."

"I'm sorry. I guess that's the way my dad feels, but he's seventy-one with a full life behind him and you're what? . . . Thirty?"

"I'm thirty-six. You know, the funny thing is that I have enjoyed life more in the past couple months than in the rest of my life combined. I even fell in love back there in San Francisco."

"You're joking! If that's the case, how come you're out here by yourself?"

She wiped the moisture from beneath her left eye. "This is no joke, friend. I love that man. I've been thinking about him every minute when I'm awake. My feelings for him are haunting me. The problem is that I don't have anything to offer him, not even a date for Christmas. I know he feels rotten now, because he loves me, too, but I couldn't dump all this misery on him, and I couldn't bring myself to say good-bye, so I sneaked out while he was asleep. The awful thing is that I left him there after the only time he made love to me."

The stranger let out a sharp whistle. "I feel you, babe, but you sure gave it to him where it hurts. A guy gets it on with his woman, wakes and finds out she gone, and he has no idea where or why. Babe, you definitely didn't help his ego."

"I hadn't thought of it that way. I loved

him too much to let him sweat through this with me." She released a long sigh. "But let me tell you it hurts like hell. Every nerve of my body and all the pores of my skin miss that man."

He offered her a sip from his half bottle of ginger ale, and she accepted it gladly, figuring that most ordinary germs needed more time than she had to do their damage.

"I think you ought to go back to him," he said.

"I wish I could, but I can't. He was so kind, so gentle, and so loving. I never felt with a man what I felt with him. I knew him only a very short time, but I felt as if I'd always known him. I was completely comfortable and at ease with him. Funny thing is that we made no demands on each other. I told him about my prognosis, but he didn't want to accept that, and I knew he'd either detain me in San Francisco, or follow me. So, like a coward, I ran away. Why am I telling you all this?"

"A good psychologist will tell you that the best therapist is a stranger who you know you will never see again. You're not worrying about what I think of you. You don't even care. Strangers give us the opportunity to have a genuine catharsis."

She turned on the windshield washer, realized that her tears caused the blur before her, and turned them off. "Oh, well. At least I won't have long to hurt. You know, I always wanted to swim in the ocean. I took a swimming lesson in Santa Cruz, learned the breaststroke, and I'm going to swim in the ocean. I know you're in a hurry, but it would be great if you'd stop off with me for a couple of hours. I can see Monterey by car, get a swim, and we could head on to Malibu."

"Works for me, but I still think you ought to go back to that guy. If he fell in love with you, he's going through hell. You ought to let him measure out his own poison. If he's much of a man, he can take it."

"He's a whole lot of man. Let me tell you. But in these last few weeks, I've become less self-centered. I don't want to hurt anybody, or do anything to cause other people unhappiness."

"You wanna be sure you get into those Pearly Gates, huh?"

"I guess so. My pastor told me to confess to all the people I've wronged and ask forgiveness, and I have."

"Humph. How did that go?"

"Most didn't take it so well."

"Of course they didn't. What you did was unload your guilt at the expense of individuals who are left to deal with your transgressions. As far as I'm concerned, that sucks."

"Maybe, but I'd rather go through those Pearly Gates than to hell, wouldn't you?"

"I never thought much about it," he said, appearing pensive. "Let's get off this serious topic. It's enough I have to worry about my dad."

They rode on to Monterey in silence. Once there, he guided her to the places she wanted to see and the areas that tourists found most attractive. She asked if he needed money for lunch, but he didn't. "Then why were you hitchhiking?" she asked him.

"I'm a graduate student. Oh, I know I'm as old as some of my professors, but I dropped out of college, realized how stupid I'd been, and went back. I'm paying my own way, and that means not spending what I don't have to spend." They ate a lunch of hamburgers and French fries, then changed into bathing suits in rented cabanas.

"I thought you said you had only one swimming lesson," he said, "but you're not acting like it. Get too cocky, and you could drown in a minute."

"Might as well go happily," she said, grabbing his hand. Her gaze swept over his hard, masculine body. He exuded power and virility. Then she said to herself, "Don't even think it."

"You lose interest rather fast," he said in a mocking tone.

"Not really. In these last days, I've become very honest. God made many lovely things, and when I see one that's pretty near perfect, I happily genuflect in reverence. But my heart's still back in San Francisco." She spun away, plunged into a small wave and, because she didn't think to hold her breath, came out of the wave gasping. Alarmed, he carried her to shore and signaled for a lifeguard.

"I don't need that," she protested, still gasping, when the lifeguard began giving her artificial respiration.

"Maybe you don't, but I need this job, and you are definitely not conking out here on my watch, lady," the lifeguard said. "If you can't swim, stay out of the ocean, especially if you're not wearing a life jacket. Experienced swimmers have drowned right out there."

"Thanks," she said. "I wouldn't want to get you into trouble." She declined the lifeguard's offer of medical assistance, saying that she didn't need it.

She and the stranger walked back to the cabanas that they had rented, dressed, got into the rented car, and headed for Malibu. "I have to tell you, that after that stunt you pulled in the ocean, I don't feel comfortable riding with you," he told her. "But I'm scared that if I leave you, you'll do something really dumb. Petra, if you do anything else that foolish, I'll try getting a ride with somebody else. You scared the bejeebers out of me."

"But I told you I had only one swimming lesson and that was in a pool."

"Yeah. You did. I should have stuck closer to you. Where're you going after Malibu?"

"If I'm still all right, I'll go to Atlanta. I want to see the Martin Luther King, Jr. Historic Site. I feel like paying homage to the man who did so much for people like me."

"What's the matter?" he asked, when she slowed down, his voice low and urgent.

"I had such a sharp pain in my head, the worst I've had yet."

"Pull over to the shoulder," he said, and she did. "Is it still painful?"

Petra shook her head. "No. But it's as if a dagger went through my brain."

"Look, Petra, be sensible. Let's go back to Bakersfield, turn the car in, and you skip Malibu and get a flight or a train to Atlanta."

"But you'll be that much farther from Los

Angeles."

"Not to worry about me. I'll get a ride. If push comes to shove, I can always take a train. Turn around, please. I can't leave you here on the road."

Admitting to herself, that he was, for the moment at least, wiser than she, she headed back to Monterey. There, she turned in the car and, to her amazement, he insisted on going with her to the train station and staying with her until she boarded the train, five hours later.

"You're a great gal," he said. "If you get there before I do, say a word for me." His embrace, fierce and sincere, left her nearly breathless. He stared down at her, kissed her on the mouth, and walked off.

She watched his long strides until he was out of sight. *Good grief! She hadn't asked his name.* The conductor yelled, "Board. All aboard." She knew the stranger had not fallen for her, but he cared about her well-being, and she was sorry for that and sorry that he would always be for her an anonymous face on a beautiful male physique. The train wasn't half-full, so she had two seats to herself, put a pillow beneath her head, and was soon asleep. The next day, she changed trains in Amarillo, Texas, and, on a stormy Saturday morning around seven o'clock, arrived at last in Atlanta.

At the airport, she booked a hotel, checked in, and crashed into bed. "I've never been so tired in my life," she said aloud, forced herself to sit up and used the hotel phone to call her house. Krista answered the phone.

"Fields residence, this is Krista."

"Honey, how are you? This is Mom."

"Mom?" Krista shrieked. "Where are you? You've got everybody going crazy. Are you all right?"

"I'm in Atlanta, and I'm fine, except for a headache now and then. How's Mama?"

"Mama's okay, but I wish you'd hurry back, because she stays on my case. I'm working full time, and I only go out anywhere on Monday nights, but she still finds things to nag me about. She's on duty today, and that means I get some peace."

"I thought you'd be working at the store on a Saturday."

"I usually do, but I put in twenty hours overtime this week, so they made me take today off. When you coming home? Nobody would be surprised if I did something like this, but you're always so . . . so sensible."

"I . . . uh . . . I'll be back in a few days. You'll be surprised at what I have to tell you."

She imagined that Krista rolled her eyes to the ceiling when she said, "Mom, from here on, nothing you say or do will surprise me. I'm still in shock from this."

"I imagine you are. Do you go to see your father?"

"Yeah. He's cool. Tell you about it when you get back."

"All right. Give my love to Mama. Bye."

She hadn't expected such warmth from her daughter, but she was glad for it. Maybe in the time she had left, they could recover their loving relationship. With that thought, she dozed off to sleep. She awakened at five o'clock that afternoon, dressed, and went down to the lobby in search of a sandwich. Finding none, she bought a copy of the *Atlanta Constitution* and sat down to read until the restaurant opened for dinner, but couldn't concentrate.

Winston Fleet filled her thoughts, and in her mind's eye, she saw every breath he took, every blink of his eyes, and every crease of his face as he made wild and passionate love to her. She folded the newspaper, rested her head on the back of the lounge chair, and fought back the tears. In her peripheral vision, she became aware that a man had sat down opposite her, remembered that she sat in a public lounge, got up, and went into the bar.

"What'll it be?"

For reasons she didn't question, she ordered a margarita, the drink she shared with Winston. She had sipped most of it before she realized that she was the only woman sitting at the bar. The realization gave her an uneasy feeling; she hadn't previously been in a bar alone. When an older man took the stool next to her, she marveled at his resemblance to her grandfather.

"You not from round here," the man said in what was a statement rather than a question, and she sensed censorship in his tone.

"No, I'm from Ellicott City, Maryland. Actually, I'm trying to see as many of the things I've always wanted to see, and do things I've missed."

"Another one?" the bartender asked her.

"I think I will." She savored the drink. "According to my doctor, I don't have much longer to live." She took another sip. "So I've decided to live while I'm living."

"Hogwash!" She stared at him, suddenly frightened. "You look the picture of good health. Nothing's wrong with you; you're just looking for an excuse for your sluttish ways."

"What?" She could almost feel herself shrivel up. Not only did the man resemble

her late grandfather, but his words — especially the expression, "sluttish ways" — and his tone were those of her grandfather. Shaking with fear, she handed the bartender a twenty-dollar bill, fled the bar, and ate supper in her room. To her mind, she hadn't done anything immoral. Besides, she tried to treat people right, and she paid her debts. Maybe Atlanta women didn't go to bars, but how would she know? She decided that as soon as she saw the King Historic Site, she would take a plane to Baltimore and go home to Ellicott City.

Thinking back on the past couple months, it seemed to her that she had taken selfishness to the limit. She had to tell her mother, Krista, and her friends about her condition, and she should train someone to take her job. *I'm going home tomorrow night, no matter what.*

The next morning, she had a breakfast of grits, scrambled eggs, country-sage sausage, and coffee and headed for the corner of Auburn Avenue and Jackson Street, North East. She stood before Dr. King's tomb for a long while, thinking that no matter how great we are and how many wonderful deeds we do, in the end, we are all equal. She didn't feel power or the awesome reverence one experiences when beholding a mighty man, as she'd thought she would. And there certainly lay before her the remains of such a man. She released a sharp expletive, and cursed the soul of James Earl Ray. Elegant though it was, the memorial didn't communicate what she had expected. Instead of a sense of great sorrow and loss, a strange peace enveloped her. She couldn't understand it.

She didn't feel troubled or sad as she should have, for she revered Dr. King. Indeed, a feeling of contentment, of acceptance of life pervaded her while she walked back to the bus stop. Suddenly, she became aware of the hot sun bearing down on her and had to resist the urge to unbutton her blouse. "Why do I feel so lightheaded?" She rushed to get to the bench at the bus stop, so that she could sit down and regroup. When her self-awareness returned, she lay in a hospital bed gazing up at one sweet-looking brother.

"Where am I, and how did I get here?" she asked the man who she took to be a doctor. "What happened? What am I doing here?" She gazed around her and verified that she was lying in bed in a hospital.

"I'll get the doctor," the man said and turned to leave.

"Is somebody going to give me something

for this splitting headache?"

The man turned, walked back to her, and stroked her forehead so gently that she hardly felt his touch. "Feeling better?" he asked in the deepest, sexiest voice she'd ever heard.

"If I'm going to die," she said, "I want to go right here and right now."

The man left the room and returned a few minutes later with an authoritative, Denzel Washington-looking man who wore a white coat. "I'm Dr. Hayes. How're you feeling?" He removed his stethoscope from the pocket of his white coat and began to examine her chest.

"How'd I get here?" she asked him.

"I'm told that you passed out on the street near the King Historic Site. Someone called an ambulance, and the ambulance brought you to us."

"Don't waste your time on me, Doctor. I already know that I only have about six weeks left, and I don't want anybody performing heroic measures in order to keep me here."

Hayes stopped examining her and frowned. "Where'd you get that idea? We've done numerous tests, and the MRI and CAT scan show a small tumor that's operable." As if that settled the matter, he said,

"I need to ask you a few questions. How old are you?"

She told him. "Ever had surgery?" She hadn't.

"Wonderful. You have to sign this form giving permission for the surgery. Afterward, take proper care of yourself, and you should live a long and productive life."

"Sure, and King Kong was a real live ape that climbed to the top of the Empire State Building," she said, because she didn't believe that an operation would preserve her life. "But, what the heck! I'll sign it." He handed her the form, and she signed it without reading it.

"Surgery is tomorrow morning at seven," Hayes said, ignoring her belittlement not only of his advice but of his skills as well.

"Who's he?" she asked Hayes, pointing to the man who was with her when she awakened.

"Connor. He's your nurse."

Her eyes widened, and her lower lip dropped. "You're joking. Now this is what I call hell. I have a good-looking man all to myself, and what does he do but wash my face, blow my nose, and change my soiled gown. There is no justice on this earth."

A grin transformed the doctor's face. "If that's payment for your sins, I'd say you got lucky. See you in the morning."

After the doctor left, Connor began taking her temperature and pulse. "Nobody jokes with Hayes. He's the head honcho here, and you're lucky. He's the best brain surgeon anywhere around. When you get back home, you ought to sue that chicken shit doctor of yours, and get another one."

"I'm not counting on getting back there, at least not yet. But if I do, his name is Mudd."

"The thing for you to do now," Connor said, "is think pleasant thoughts. You want to call anyone?"

She thought for a minute. "I never told my folks I was sick, or what the prognosis was, so I'll just let it go. My ID is in my purse. If I come out of this, fine."

"Your purse is in a safe. You want to read, watch TV?"

"Just give me an aspirin or something, and I'll go to sleep."

Unaware of the drama taking place in Petra's life, Winston Fleet struggled to get his life back on track. He understood why she had left while he slept, but it hurt that he didn't know where she went, how she was, or even if she was still alive. That Sunday morning, he teed off after his buddy and golfing partner and, for the first time in his life, he hit a hole in one.

"Man, what's wrong with you?" his friend, Ron Bailey, asked him. "You just hit a hole in one. Are you all right? I mean, you're not sick are you?"

"In a way, I guess you'd say I am. Yeah. Finish your round. I've had it."

"Who is she?"

"Petra Fields, and I don't know where the hell she is."

"That's tough, man. Maybe your grandmother can help."

"Maybe she could, but I don't want any bad news. I'd rather not know. Would you believe I don't have Petra's address or phone number?"

"She must have given you a double whammy, man. You're usually more meticulous than that. We may as well go. A man who doesn't dance after he makes a hole in one is in no shape to play golf," Ron said. "If you think over your conversations with her, you'll find that she gave you a clue as to how you can reach her. Search your brain, friend."

Winston spent the evening doing precisely that, but the effect of three bottles of Pilsner beer was a befuddled mind, and he went to sleep mentally exhausted and with a heavy heart.

In the meantime, unaware of Petra's upcoming surgery, Goodman tried to give their daughter the support she needed. He put the boxes containing the computer and printer on the floor and rang the front doorbell. When the door opened, Lena Fields's pursed lips and dark frown greeted him.

"What do you want? I thought you'd gotten lost years ago."

"Proves you shouldn't waste your time thinking," he said, caught himself and smiled the smile that usually got him out of jams. "How are you, ma'am? I want to set up this computer and printer for Krista."

"She's not home. She said she was going to some kind of choir rehearsal. Whether that's true, I can't say."

"That's where she was tonight," he said, remembering Petra's frequent complaints about her grandmother's constant negativity. "She's sitting in the car talking on her cell phone."

"She shouldn't have a cell phone. Who knows who she's calling? I'll be glad when Petra comes back here. Krista's my grandchild, but I don't enjoy being responsible for her. She's just as uppity as she can be."

He ignored that. "Where's her room?"

He set up the printer and the laptop docking station, showed Krista how to operate both and, as soon as he finished, prepared to leave. A little of Lena Fields could last him indefinitely. He had avoided her when he and Petra courted. He suspected that if she hadn't been so mean and judgmental, he and Petra would have had more privacy, and he probably wouldn't have slipped up and impregnated her.

"I'd better be going, Krista. Your grandmother is not one of my fans."

"Oh, she's not so bad. You just have to ignore her when she starts preaching. I'll see you next Monday."

She jumped up from her perch on the bed, hugged him, and kissed his cheek. "You're the best dad I ever had," she said, grinning. "You're super."

He supposed he preened. Maybe that was the difference between daughters and sons. His sons gave him a sense of male pride, but Krista made him feel as if he were king of the world. He hugged her, and it surprised him that she seemed genuinely touched by it.

"See you next Monday," he said again and loped down the walk to his car. He dialed

Carla to let her know that he was on his way home.

"I should be there in about twenty minutes," he told his wife. "Where're the boys?"

"I suppose you forgot that they have French tutoring tonight, so stop off somewhere and get your dinner. We ate."

And didn't save dinner for me? he thought but didn't say. "I'll do that," he said, his tone sharp and unfriendly. He hung up and dialed Jada's number.

"This is Goodman. Have you eaten dinner?"

"Yeah, but if you're real nice and come straight here, I can give you some fried chicken, stewed collards, candied sweets, and baked cornbread."

"Woman after my own heart. I'm on my way." The only other person who fixed him a meal like that one was his mother, and she'd moved from Ellicott City to Shreveport, Louisiana. He knew, however, that Carla's thoughtlessness did not justify his philandering. The first time he did it, his conscience hammered at him, and he felt guilty for days, but each time he betrayed his own principles, doing so became easier. Krista suspected that he was unfaithful to his wife, and he hated that, because he wanted her to see him in a different light.

He parked around the corner from the building in which Jada lived and, within little more than an hour and a half, he filled his belly, emptied the seed of his loins, and headed home.

She'd asked him for money she needed to eke out her rent, but he knew she had enough for that and more. "Babe, you know I'd give it to you if I had it, and I'd have that and plenty more if the students would pay up. I was going to hit you for a few bucks." She gave him thirty dollars, and he didn't even pretend that it was a loan. If she'd get the message that he was not going to give her money, he'd stop hitting her for money he didn't need. As he put his key into the lock of his front door, he had a niggling, unpleasant feeling that, if he didn't change course, he'd lose his self-respect.

At that very moment, Petra regained consciousness in the intensive care unit of one of Atlanta's largest and most reputable hospitals. "How do you feel?" Connor asked her.

"Tell me you're not an angel," she said.

"Why should I tell you that?" he teased. "A lot of women will attest to the fact that I am." He took her temperature. "Good. You're on your way, sweetheart."

She thought she felt a sharp prick in her hip. "Did you stick something in me?" she asked him.

"Mind your mouth, lady. All I did was give you a pain killer."

Leaving Winston would be the most difficult thing she'd ever had to do. Soft brown eyes seemed to follow her. Now, those eyes had long legs, and a group of them sat on a big boulder by the Pacific Ocean and beckoned to her. She tried to run to them, but her feet did not obey her. Suddenly, it began to rain millions of brown, long-lashed eyes that dropped around her like snowflakes.

"Wake up. You're having a nightmare," the voice said. "Come on. Think pleasant thoughts. You're getting well, and you'll soon be going home." A hand stroked her arm and the back of her hand. "Come out of it, Petra. Now. Talk to me."

She'd never been so thirsty. Looking around, she saw that the sun cast a ray across the foot of her bed. Her hand went up to her head where a strange, tight feeling warned her of bandages. She looked at her left arm, but she wore no watch, only a yellow plastic tag that read Petra Fields and a long number. Water. She wanted water.

As she looked around for a way to call a nurse, a doctor walked in, smiled, and said,

"Do you remember me?"

"Yes. You're Denzel Washington. . . . I mean, excuse me . . . I mean Dr. Hayes. May I please have some water?"

He poured a glass of water from the pitcher on her nightstand and handed it to her. "Your tumor was benign, the operation was clean, and you'll be as good as new in a couple of weeks. Be sure and tell that doctor of yours that I said you can expect another sixty years."

"You're serious, aren't you," she said, becoming more alert by the minute.

"Absolutely. I suggest that whenever you get a serious medical diagnosis, especially one of this consequence, you should seek a second opinion."

"Yes, sir. Thank you for everything, Doctor. I sure am glad I passed out near the King Historic Site. If it had happened somewhere else, I might have been taken to a different hospital."

"Relax and don't strain your eyes too much," he said. "By the way," he went on, as if what he was about to say was not important, "why did you say I was Denzel Washington?"

"The first time I saw you, you reminded me of Denzel, and . . . Oh, well, it was really a compliment. Where's Connor?"

"Oh, I'm not complaining about that. I just have to know that your brain is functioning properly. Connor probably hasn't come on duty yet. Who is Winston?"

"Someone I fell in love with a few weeks ago back in San Francisco. Head over heels. Reckless. I did a lot of dumb things during those months when I thought I could die any minute. I leaned over the rail at the South Rim of the Grand Canyon, even though I'm petrified of heights."

Hayes sat in the chair beside her bed. "Really?"

"I really did. I also took a swimming lesson, and I swam in the Pacific Ocean. Would you believe I'm scared to death of the water? I set out to do all the things I'd wanted to do and either hadn't had a chance or was too scared to attempt. I rode my first horse, first Ferris wheel, and first roller coaster, and I wasn't even scared. How do you account for that?"

"It isn't difficult, Petra. To your mind, you had everything to gain and nothing to lose. I suspect you also wanted to cut down on the waiting time. Fortunately, you weren't successful." She tried to sit up, so he raised the mattress enough to give her relief from lying flat.

"You won't believe the mess I made," she

said, "not only of my life, but of other people's. Until that doctor told me I had less than six months to live, I had been as circumspect as the bishop. The epitome of conservatism. To tell you how foolish I got, Dr. Hayes, I actually picked up a hitchhiker, a man, while I was driving along the highway out of San Francisco. Luckily, he was a law-abiding graduate student."

"What about your family, Ms. Fields? Did you have Connor call and tell them that you were having an operation, and that I expected you to come through it as good as new?"

She couldn't force herself to look at him. "No, sir. They don't know about my prognosis."

"What? Were you off your rocker? Suppose you had expired someplace all alone!"

"If I'd told them, they wouldn't have let me take this vacation. It wasn't a vacation, actually. I bought a ticket to Rapid City, South Dakota, and, from there, I went where my mind took me. I'd do it again if I had the money, but I wouldn't take those awful chances."

He stood and moved toward the door. "I'm satisfied that your brain is functioning perfectly. You'll be just fine. I'll tell the nurse to bring you some breakfast."

Well, what do you know? He was examining me, and I thought he was sitting there because he cared. She shrugged, having taught herself in the past few months not to care about little things, and pulled the sheet up to her neck to ward off the chill from the air conditioner. *At least he knew what he was doing when he was digging around in my brain. Lord, if I had believed that I would be all right, I'd have been scared crazy about that man cutting my head open.*

"How's my favorite patient today?"

She looked around to see a nurse's aide bringing a tray. "Boy, am I glad to see you. I feel as if I've never eaten in my whole life."

"Trust me, this won't stuff you, but you can have some more in about two hours. You can't have any heavy food right now."

Petra eyed the tray. The Jell-O, soup, and yogurt looked like steak and lobster to her. "If it fills me up, I don't care what it is."

Two weeks and four days later, Petra opened the front door of her house with her key, walked in, and dropped her bag by the door. She had her life back, but would she ever be the same? "Anybody home?"

Chapter Nine

Petra walked through the front door of her house and began reacquainting herself with each room. She hadn't previously noticed the frayed carpet in the dining room or the loose brick in the living room fireplace, nor had she recently appreciated the view from her dining room window. She stood by the wall-to-wall window gazing at the blooming crepe myrtle tree, the green pears that strained the limbs of their host, the roses beneath them, and the green grass that seemed to cradle the flowers and trees.

I've always taken this for granted the way I did my family and my friends, as if I were entitled to their love and to the beauty of nature. I realize now that I'm not entitled to anything. And I had no business going off as I did without saying why or where.

She opened her suitcase, removed the soiled clothing, and took the remaining things upstairs to her room. Tired from the trip, she had to resist lying down and going to sleep. She dialed Lurlene's number at work.

"Jim's Electronics meeting your every need. Lurlene Bruce speaking."

"Hi, Lurlene. This is Petra."

"Petra? Girl, where you been? You got some talking to do. Your mama said Jack fired you. I meet him on Long Street the other day, and he practically assaults me. Like I knew where you were. My friend Josie said you were probably off somewhere having an abortion, but I told her she was crazy. She was, wasn't she?"

"Girl, don't joke like that. It had been years since I was even near a man. You see a brother around here that you'd let impregnate you? Well, neither do I, and it's not even funny. How's Twylah?"

"Still overweight. She lost three pounds, and she was so happy I thought she was going to have it announced on the radio. It's not a joke. The doctor told her last week that if she didn't lose eighty pounds, she was going to be a sick woman. The next day, we went shopping, and she bought a case of beer and a bag of Oh Henry! bars. You going to be home tonight?"

I'm not going to do what other people want me to do. Life is too precious to spend it that way, and I'm not going to lie. "I'll be home, Lurlene, but I'm tired, and Mama and Krista will want me to tell them what I've done and where I've been, so let's get together another night."

"Uh . . . Well, all right. I'll ask Twylah if she'd like for us to play pinochle one night. Girl, I bet you got a whole lot to tell, and I can't wait to hear it. See you soon."

She did have a lot that she could tell, but they'd never know all of it; she couldn't bear their jokes and questions about Winston Fleet. She heard the front door open, got up and started downstairs, slowly as the doctor warned her to do.

"Lord have mercy if it ain't my child," Lena Fields screamed and raced up the stairs at a pace that belied her age. She stopped short before she reached Petra. "What happened to you, child? You been in an accident? That's what you get for running all over the country. How'd it happen?"

Petra turned and walked back up the stairs. What had she expected? Her mother's delight in seeing her had been short-lived, and she immediately became the preacher and accuser. Petra walked into her room and sat down on the edge of the bed.

"I'll tell you all about it, Mama, but I'll wait till Krista gets home so I won't have to tell it twice."

"All right, but as soon as she gets here, I'm going home. I need to see about my place."

"Mama, I thank you for staying here with Krista. I know she can be wayward and troublesome, and I hope she didn't give you any problems. She's a good girl, but she's strong-minded, and she was so mad at me about Goodman. I never should have told her that lie, that he was dead, I mean."

"You shouldn't ever lie about anything, 'cause it sure will catch up with you. Besides, if you're gon' lie, you have to have a perfect memory, and that alone ought to make you tell the truth. Is your head going to be all right? Just tell me that much."

"It's going to be as good as new."

Lena sat down and patted her thighs. "Well, I may as well tell you that you ain't got no job. Jack Watkins called here two or three days ago and screamed at me like he was paying *me,* telling me he'd fired you. Made me mad as the devil. I put my hips up on my shoulder and told him you wasn't likely to starve."

Petra released a long breath, thinking she'd give anything to stop listening and just lie down in a quiet place. "He was real nice, Mama, if he waited till three days ago to fire me. I figured he'd do that. Too bad. I worked hard for that job, and I loved the work."

Lena's eyes narrowed, and Petra could see a sermon coming. "Then why in Heaven's name did you go off like that?"

"Mama, I told you that I'll explain it when Krista gets home. Right now, I want to rest. I'm exhausted."

"Mom! Mom, wake up. I didn't know you were coming home today, or I would have come straight home from work. I went to my singing group this evening."

Petra sat up, rubbing her eyes and yawning. "How are you, honey? Sit down here and let me look at you."

"What's the matter with your head? Grandma said you got into something, but she didn't know what. Is it going to be all right?"

"It's going to be fine. Is there anything to eat?"

"I made chili last night, and Grandma just cooked rice. You feel like going downstairs?"

Petra rolled to the side of the bed, sat up, slipped her feet into her house slippers, and stood, hoping that she wouldn't be groggy. "I could eat a gallon of chili. All they serve you on the plane is some kind of liquid, and

I hardly ate any breakfast." She took a few seconds to steady herself.

"What happened to you, Mom? You're not quite straight." Trust Krista to cut to the chase.

"I'm OK, and I'll explain it in a minute."

She ate the dinner that Krista and Lena prepared and, though she hadn't asked the surgeon whether she could have coffee, she took a cupful to sip while she talked with them. They sat together facing her, as if prepared to measure her every word. She began with the day her physician, Reginald Barnes, told her that she had an inoperable brain tumor and from four to six months to live.

They gasped in shock, but she raised both hands, palms out. "I've hardly begun. Relax. You see I'm still here." An hour later, she finished her story, including her attitudes and the changes in them, omitting only her affair with Winston Fleet. She didn't intend to give her mother an opportunity to trash that and make it seem common and ugly.

"You mean if you hadn't gone to the King Historic Site, you'd have passed out somewhere else, and you might have gotten a doctor as stupid as Dr. Barnes?" Krista asked.

"Let's just say I was blessed, and I'm asking you not to breathe this to anybody. Barnes could sue you. All he knew was what the radiologist told him. I'm just thankful I'm going to be all right."

"Whew!" Krista said. "As I get it, you were going off to die someplace all by yourself and not tell us."

Petra's back stiffened. "You tell me that if you got some news like that, your first and only thought would be of your grandmother and me, and I'll tell you you're lying. You'll think of yourself and why such a thing should happen to you. It isn't a time when you become saintly. I went to see Reverend Collins, and he dropped a guilt trip on me. I wish I hadn't listened to him."

"Well, I don't," Krista said. "If he hadn't I would still think my dad was dead."

"I'm just gon' give thanks," Lena said. "We've all been given another chance to love each other. Let's use it. I'm going home and see if my apartment is still there. Krista, honey, do you feel like cleaning the kitchen?"

"Yes, ma'am. I'll do it."

Petra didn't fool herself; the more her mother thought about Petra's illness and her "vacation," the sharper the tongue-lashing she would eventually perfect. She telephoned her friend, Twylah.

"I sure am glad you're back here in one piece, girl. Lurlene call me at work, and she's got all kinds of speculations about what you were doing and where you went. If you weren't in jail, I'm satisfied."

Petra couldn't help laughing. "I wasn't in jail, at least not the kind you're thinking about."

"Hey now, you can't say a thing like that and not explain."

"In due course, friend. When are we meeting?"

"Sunday over at Lurlene's place. That OK with you?"

"Yes. See you then."

She looked through her sewing materials, found a piece of white piqué large enough for a turban, and put it aside with the intent of making the turban the next morning. Friends would wonder about her new style headdress, but they would speculate more about the bandage on her head and the patch of missing hair.

Goodman Prout answered his cell phone with not a little annoyance. He detested calls when teaching. "Prout speaking. I'll return your call as soon as I'm free."

"Sorry, Dad, but I have to tell you something."

Every nerve in his body seemed suddenly on edge. Krista had telephoned him only once, and that was for the purpose of introducing herself and telling him that she wanted to meet him.

"Excuse me for a minute, Alonzo," he said to his piano student. "I'll only be a minute."

"What is it, Krista?"

"When I got home from work, Mom was there and —"

He interrupted her. "And what? Anything wrong?"

"I . . . Mom's head is bandaged. She said she had an operation for a brain tumor. She said Doctor Barnes misdiagnosed it, said it was malignant and inoperable and gave her six months at the most to live. That's why she took off like that." She told him the remainder of the story. "Mom made me promise not to mention it. Do you think a person can live after that kind of operation?"

He leaned against the wall feeling like a balloon into which someone had just rammed a nail. So that was it. "Was it malignant?"

"No. The doctor said it was benign."

"Is she walking?"

"Yes, sir. And tonight she ate enough chili for two people."

"Then don't worry. She'll be fine. I'm glad you called me. If you need me for anything, I'll be here."

"Thanks, Dad. Bye."

He went back to his student, but almost at once, the door opened and in walked Jada. He imagined the pleasure of strangling her. "Haven't I told you not to bother me when I'm teaching? This student has to concentrate. Please leave."

"Well 'scuse me. Next time you itch, find somebody else to scratch you."

"Excuse me, Alonzo. I'm sorry for these interruptions. I'll give you an extra half hour."

"You'd better hurry, sir. She's mad as a bull in a swarm of bees."

He caught up with her in front of the building. "Look, Jada, I'm sorry if I was rude, but I don't allow anybody to come into my studio when I'm teaching, and that includes the members of my family."

"What are you going to do to make it up to me?"

He nearly bit his tongue, but he calmed himself, because he suspected that she could be reckless. "I was just about to ask you how you were going to make it up to me. I'm the one who's been wronged. By now, my student is steaming. He's paying by the hour."

"You want to come by tonight?"

"I'd love to, but I have an engagement tonight." He patted his back trouser pocket. "Damn, I forgot I had to get my vest out of the cleaners. I need ten dollars. I have to wear that vest tonight."

As he'd known she would, she opened her purse and handed him two five-dollar bills. "I'd love to see you in one of those fancy suits. Maybe we can go away for a weekend someplace, and we can get dolled up."

"I can't kiss you on the street," he said, ignoring her suggestion. "I owe you one."

"Sure you do. And, baby, I plan to collect big time."

He went back to his studio deep in thought, almost certain that with Jada, he'd made the biggest mistake of his life.

Petra got out of bed early the next morning, feeling almost like her old self, and went down to the kitchen to prepare breakfast. "I thought I'd fix breakfast," she said to Krista.

"You don't need to. I had juice, toast, and coffee."

"Any coffee left?"

"Uh, maybe half a cup. I have to go. Bye."

Petra grabbed Krista's arm. "What is this?

Are you still feuding with me?"

Krista jerked her arm out of her mother's grasp. "Who's feuding? I have to get to work."

So nothing had changed. *She cared enough to be concerned when she didn't hear from me, but that was all. Oh. Well. I've got to look for a job.* But first, she had to call Jack, apologize, and give him a chance to vent.

And vent, he did. "Yeah, I fired you. The best worker I ever had. You knew more about the business than I did, and you went off and left me in a rut. I called you every name in the book. What happened to your cell phone? Did you lose it?"

"I didn't take it with me, Jack. I thought I was terribly ill, but it was a misdiagnosis. Will you give me a reference? I need a job."

He waited so long that perspiration dampened her blouse. "What the hell! Yeah. I'll put it in the mail today."

Petra didn't want to go to an employment agency, so she decided to buy a copy of *The Woodmore Times* and check the want ads. As she entered the drugstore, she bumped into the Reverend Collins.

"Haven't seen much of you lately, my child, and you haven't been to church. You can't afford these lapses. Have you straightened things out with all the people you've wronged?"

The idea of walking away without saying a word appealed to her, but she considered his great age and didn't do it. "I'm fine, Reverend, but I'm not sure I did a lot of good by unloading my guilt on other people."

"Now, now, sister! You feel that way now, but they'll one day thank you."

"If you say so. My daughter is still feuding with me because I corrected a lie I told her. It was the right thing to do, but she's feeling a lot of pain."

The reverend patted her shoulder, and his old eyes darkened. "It never hurts to do the right thing, sister. You come to church, now."

"Yes, sir."

For the next hour, she sat on her back porch checking the ads in the paper, but didn't see a single prospect. "My life was fine till that two-bit doctor misled me. How on earth could he make a mistake that big?" she said aloud. Josh Martin had benefited from her misdeed, and he gladly forgave her transgression. But he was the only one.

She answered the phone. "This is Sally. Could you come by and get your severance pay, or do you want me to mail it?"

"Hi, Sally. I'd appreciate if you'd mail it. Thanks."

"Don't thank me. I'm doing what Jack told me to do. If it was left to me, you wouldn't get air."

"I told you I was sorry, Sally. I forgot how homophobic Jack is. Otherwise, I wouldn't have told him."

"But it wasn't your business. Anyway, what's the use of wasting my breath on you? You got yours, and you won't be switching around here lording it over the rest of us like you owned the place. I don't want to see your shadow, much less you. Gail walked out on me, and it's your fault. You caused me to get demoted and lose a third of my salary, and I don't make enough to take care of her."

"Sally, I never . . . I'm sorry. I . . . Oh, what the hell." She hung up. *Reverend Collins does not want to give me any more dribble about forgiveness. I've had enough of it for now. I do not even want to see his face.*

Nonetheless, the following Sunday morning, Petra dragged herself to church, although she didn't want to go. Her mama insisted that she attend and give thanks that the surgeon hadn't taken her life. She sat on the aisle in the last bench and, with a lot of effort, made herself stay awake. She wasted no time leaving as soon as the preacher said the benediction. Her decision to go directly home and not stop at the corner coffee shop to gossip with friends as she usually did had consequences that she would gladly have avoided.

As she opened her gate, Ethel, her next-door neighbor stepped out of the house. “Hi, Ethel,” Petra said and paused for a talk, temporarily forgetting that Ethel probably hated her. “How’s Fred?”

Ethel stopped, pressed her knuckles to her hips, and glared at Petra. “How is Fred you asked me? How is my husband? He’s off with some other lowlife woman doing what he did with you. I kicked him out of my bed, and the bastard is out of my life. My husband of thirty-two years, the father of my grown children, the man you fornicated with right under my nose does not live here anymore. *Don’t speak to me!*”

“I’m sorry, Ethel. I thought I was doing the right thing in telling you. It only happened once. I wish you could forgive me.”

Tears streamed down Ethel’s cheeks. “I would rather not have known. I was happy till you told me, and now I got no husband and no friend.” She raised her head, laid back her shoulders, and walked on.

“I’m beginning not to respect Jasper Collins’s opinions,” Petra said to herself. She entered her house with a heavy heart. If only she hadn't come back! Oh, she loved Krista and her mother, but she longed to shed the concerns that had weighed on her since she returned. And she longed for Winston. Why hadn't she gotten his address or at least given him hers? She stooped down, picked up a handful of mail and went to the kitchen to get a cold drink, which she would sip while she read her mail.

She browsed through the mail, tossed most of it into the waste basket, and went to her room to look at the pile of letters that arrived during her absence and the day before. "Good grief!" she said, jumping up and dropping the half-full glass of ginger ale. "When did I spend all this money?" She opened a bill from another credit card company and gasped. With those bills, she would have been better off if the prognosis that Barnes gave her had been correct. She had paid full fare for each flight, taken train trips in sleeper cars, failed to seek low-budget lodging, and done a lot of other foolish things. As if her travel expenses weren't enough, all of her regular living expenses faced her. *I must have been out of my mind.*

Krista came home from work that afternoon bringing a smoked ham. "I won this at work," she said. "I also received a hundred bucks in cash and a bottle of Dior perfume. I'm employee of the month, and I can choose a complete outfit for up to six hundred dollars. What do you think of that?"

"I think I'm proud of you."

"I'd rather have had the whole thing in cash to put toward my tuition."

"Did you get accepted?"

"Not yet. I received a letter inquiring about my financial situation. When they do that, they usually admit you."

"Well, these credit card bills are telling me it was the wrong time for me to chase around the Southwest. It'll take me ages to pay this off, especially since I don't have a job."

"Oh, you'll find a job. Till then I'll make sure we eat."

"I appreciate that, Krista, but I'd be much happier if I thought you'd forgiven me for telling you that lie."

"I forgave you, Mom. It just eats at me sometimes."

"I'm going over to Lurlene's tonight. We're playing pinochle with Twylah."

"Then don't worry about me. Mom, you and Ms. Lurlene ought to encourage Ms. Twylah to get rid of some of that blubber she carries around. It's unhealthy."

Petra stifled a laugh. "That's true, but don't talk that way. She'd be hurt if she knew you said that."

"By the way, Mom, tonight's my night to attend choral rehearsal. I'll be home around ten."

"I gather you're going to tell me how you became involved with these singers."

"Sure. No problem." Krista eyed Petra with what seemed to be misgivings. "You're not too happy about my growing up, are you?"

"I wouldn't say that, but I'm not happy about you acting as if you're eighteen with the rights and privileges of an eighteen-year-old when you're still seventeen."

"Jeez. That's deep, Mom." She kissed Petra's cheek, something she hadn't done since she learned about her father. "See you later."

Her phone rang, and Krista rushed to answer it. "Yes, this is Krista. You mean . . . Okay, I'll tell her."

"That was miss Lurlene. She said she has a headache and doesn't feel like playing pinochle tonight. She'll call you."

Petra phoned Twylah. "What's the matter, Twylah, y'all don't feel like playing cards tonight? Since when did a headache stop Lurlene from doing anything she wanted to do?"

"You asking me? When Lurlene called me

and said she was going to bed, I figured she was mad with either you or me, and if it wasn't that, she met a man. If she'd met a man, she'd be shouting it from the steeple on top of City Hall. I guess she's hot because you didn't feel like giving her the gossip the minute you got back in town. 'Course, I ain't exactly pleased with you about that, but I guess you were tired. What's all this about you having your head bandaged up? If you don't tell people what's happening, they make up their own version."

"You feel like coming over? I can give you some ham and hash browns."

"Don't mind if I do."

Petra hung up. On top of everything else, her two closest friends were displeased with her. She'd bet anything that her mother told Twylah and Lurlene about her operation. Nothing had changed, and she wondered why she had thought anything would.

Goodman sat at his desk in his studio waiting for Krista. He planned for the two of them to eat something together after he gave her her piano lesson, and then they would go to rehearsal in his car. Five minutes before he expected Krista to arrive, Jada sauntered in.

"You don't teach this evening," she said, defending her presence there.

"You're wrong. My daughter gets her piano lesson, and she'll be here in two or three minutes."

"Well, she's already seen me here. Did she tell her mother?" So Jada thought his wife was Krista's mother. It was well to leave her in ignorance.

"How do I know? The man hasn't been born who can figure out a woman. What do you want? You have to leave in a minute."

"I'm having trouble on my job. I'm up for a promotion, and I'd be dealing with sensitive material. I need somebody to speak for me. A couple of years back, I was accused of starting a brawl in a bar. I didn't. Honest! But I spent ten days in jail for it. About five months ago, Petra Fields told me she was in that bar, and saw the whole thing, and —"

"Who? Did you say uh . . . Etta Fields?"

"No. I said Petra Fields."

"Uh . . . I thought you said Etta. Go on." He knew she said Petra, but he was not about to involve himself in any deeper entanglement with Jada. He'd already gone too far with her.

"Anyway. That woman didn't want anybody to know she'd been to a bar, so she didn't witness for me, and I spent ten days in the Ellicott City jail for something I didn't do."

He thought for a minute. "I don't see what I can do about that, Jada."

"Maybe you know a judge or somebody high up who'll sign something. Otherwise, I won't get that raise, and I'll always be stuck in that cubicle I'm in now."

He sat on the edge of his desk and swung his right foot. "It doesn't work like that, Jada. If I approached a judge on your behalf, I'd be interfering with the law. I can't do that, especially since you were convicted. I think it's best that you try for a job that isn't . . . well, sensitive."

"I'd like to put Petra Fields out of commission."

He didn't like the sound of that, because he was almost certain that, underneath, Jada had a rough texture. "Why? She didn't do anything to you," he said, careful to keep the anxiety out of his voice and facial expression. He looked at his watch. "I'll see you at rehearsal."

She stood and looked at him for a long minute without the sexiness that she usually tried to affect. "I've been thinking. If a woman's got a man who's making it, and he never gives her one dime, he's either stingy as hell or she ain't worth much in the sack." She walked toward the door, but without her usual arrogance. "I put it down every time, so you must be stingy." She walked out and closed the door.

Goodman didn't have time to think about that for, a minute later, Krista walked in. He didn't ask her whether she encountered Jada, because he knew that if she had, she'd volunteer the information. "Hi, Daddy." She kissed his cheek. "I hadn't been accepted to any college, and today I got acceptances to three."

"Which three?"

"Howard University, Ohio State, and Brown. Brown is the bomb, Daddy."

"I suppose that means you think it's top quality."

"It is, but it costs a lot of money. I saved all I made this summer, but that won't get me in the front door."

"We'll deal with that later. Do your finger exercises.

"You did well today," he told Krista an hour later at the end of the session, "but you'd be much farther along if you practiced more. Come on, we're about to be late to rehearsal."

"OK, I'm ready, Daddy," she began, skipping backward as they walked to his car.

"When are you going to introduce me to my brothers? You're not ashamed of me, are you?"

He stopped walking and grasped her arm. "Of course not. I've told them about you, so they know you're here and that they will eventually have to reckon with you. But seeing you in person will be, for them, like receiving a court summons when up to that time, they could still hope that someone else would be accused. Once they see you, they'll have to deal with your existence."

"So why procrastinate about it? The longer you take, the more you'll dread it."

"I know, but I'm not ready to deal with the turmoil."

Goodman knew he did it, but efficient and capable Petra wouldn't have thought herself guilty of procrastination. Yet, instead of dealing with her enormous credit card debt and looking for a job, she took the bus to Maryland Avenue, crossed the railroad tracks at the station, and walked down to the Patapsco River's edge. Immediately, her thoughts roamed back to the day the doctor gave her the dreadful news that she would die within six months. Thoughts of that rainy and chilly day, a bleak day when she had been numb with her fear of the future, brought tears to her eyes.

Perhaps she had behaved foolishly in what she now realized was not only an attempt to cram a lifetime into the few months that she thought remained, but also an effort to escape, to avoid dealing sensibly with the problem. She sat there until twilight encroached, and then found her way back to the bus stop. Now, however, a different kind of blues weighed upon her, and heavily, too. Her grief over Winston Fleet poured out of her eyes, grief for the pain she had surely inflicted upon him when she ran away, taking a course that made things easier for her but surely not for him. And grief for a love lost.

Petra dried her eyes and boarded the bus. She paid the fare, found a seat, and told herself, "If I could face dying, I can face never seeing Winston again. I'll move on. Somebody will hire me." The next morning, she phoned the credit card company to which she was most indebted and worked out a payment plan, then took half of the money that remained in her checking account and paid off the other credit card bill.

"Lord, I hope I find a job soon," she said to her mother, who came to Petra's house late that afternoon with a bowl of stewed collards, a pan of baked cornbread, and half a dozen seasoned and breaded catfish.

"While I stayed here with Krista, I got out of the habit of eating by myself," Lena explained. "We can heat this up, and I'll fry the catfish soon as Krista gets here. You got any coffee? I could sure use a cup."

Well, here we go again, Petra thought. *When Mama and coffee get together, reasoning flies out of the picture; she just talks.*

Petra handed her mother a cup of freshly brewed coffee, sat down at the kitchen table opposite her, and told herself to be patient.

Lena didn't make her wait long. She sipped her coffee, leaned back in the chair, and said, "You know, I'm glad I got here before Krista came home. It doesn't pay to let your child know everything that goes on with you. Krista's smart aleck enough as it is." She took another sip of coffee, savored it, and narrowed her left eye.

Here it comes, Petra thought.

"You tell me there's nothing to this awful gossip going on about you. One of the women at church, a good friend of mine, too, asked me if you went off to get rid of a baby."

Petra could feel the heat of the anger that began to furl up in her. "I would certainly like to know your answer to that, Mama. I can imagine who that was."

"Well, did you?"

"I told you why I went away. Have you forgotten?"

"Now, don't get your back up, and don't give me no sass," Lena said. "I have a right to know what goes on in my family. Somebody else told me you slept with Docia Holmes's husband and her son, too. 'Course, I didn't believe the part about Docia's son. Jimmy's so full of pimples, a woman couldn't get near him. That is, not unless she wore dark glasses and was desperate. But surely you didn't sleep with Chuck Holmes. Docia's been a real friend to me, and I wouldn't stand for you mistreating her." She sipped more of her coffee. "Docia's real down."

Petra looked at her mother with sad eyes, acknowledging that her mother loved smut and gossip as much as her friends did and was a principle carrier of tales, as many untrue as true.

Well, she'd give her something to talk about. "Mama, I wouldn't consider sleeping with either of those Holmes men. If there's anything I can't stand, it's the smell of beer on someone's breath, and Amstel beer could make a profit just off Chuck and Jimmy Holmes alone. Fred, my neighbor, is the only married man I ever slept with, and that only happened once. Tell the gossips they have the wrong man."

Lena gagged on the coffee she'd been about to swallow and jumped up from her chair. "What in the name of the Lord have you been doing? You telling me you went to bed with Ethel's Fred? He's been staying with Armena for the past few weeks. How many women has that man had? I never would have thought it of him. Why, the man's a deacon, and a front row deacon at that. Well, I declare! I never." A key turned in the front door.

"That's Krista," Lena said. "Let me get this pan hot and warm up these collards and this cornbread. Lord, what my ears have heard here today!"

It did not escape Petra that her mother hadn't commented on her lapse of morals, but had instead focused on what would be fodder for gossip. She wished she'd kept the matter to herself.

"Hi, Mom. Hi, Grandma. Mom, one of my coworkers said her mother is retiring as a court reporter. Didn't you say you could speed write or stenotype? I got the information for you in case you want to check it out tomorrow."

"Sure I can stenotype. I may need a couple of days to brush up on it. I couldn't get a stenotyping job here, because the court only hires three. I'll be down at court tomorrow morning at eight-thirty."

Lena fried the catfish and served the meal. "This is the bomb, Grandma." Krista looked at Petra. "Grandma cooked some first-class soul food while you were away, Mom. I was wondering what kind of people you met. Like you didn't always travel and go sightseeing by yourself, did you?"

Petra had promised herself not to tell anymore lies, so she decided to remember selectively the people she'd met. "Honey, you have a high school education, so please don't start every sentence with the word 'like.' It sounds awful. Now, as I recall, I met some remarkable people, but I doubt I would have gotten to know some of them if I hadn't thought my days were numbered. On the other hand, if I hadn't been so certain that I wouldn't live long, I would have let myself know some of them better."

"Really?" Krista said. "Does that include any men?" Trust her daughter to release a bombshell. She had no intention of telling a seventeen-year-old girl that she would have developed a liaison with a strange man, and certainly not that she picked up a hitchhiker on an interstate highway. As her grandfather always said, "Never lie, but use the truth selectively." In dealing with Krista, that was a very good principle.

"There were some who wanted to be friendly, but my motto is that if you want to avoid making stupid mistakes, never do anything away from home that you wouldn't do at home."

Krista rolled her eyes. "The gospel according to my great grandfather. I'll clean up, Mom," she said, and Petra realized that Krista wanted peace between them, but without apologizing for the times she'd behaved rudely.

I don't care. As long as she returns to her loving, generous self and remains that way, I'll be happy and grateful.

The next morning, Petra dressed in her pink linen suit, white shoes, bag, and hat and walked into the personnel office at the city courthouse precisely at eight-thirty. "Well," the clerk said, when told that Petra was a stenotypist, "we thought we'd probably have to go out of Howard County to find a stenotypist, maybe even to Baltimore. Good ones are rare."

Petra handed the woman the curriculum vitae that she'd put together the night before and held her breath. "This looks good. I need a reference from a local employer, a health certificate and your birth or naturalization certificate. We don't hire anyone who isn't a citizen. The job will be available two weeks from today. I'll call you in a few days, so be prepared to take a stenotyping test."

"I'll look forward to that," Petra said and left with the feeling that the woman liked her and would give her the job if she met the criteria. At home, Petra phoned Jack and asked him to send the woman a reference.

"Sure, babe. I'll send the messenger over with it today, and I hope you get the job."

She thanked him, turned on the television to watch the Judge Mathis show and familiarize herself with legal language, brought out her stenotype machine, and got busy brushing up her skills. Four days later, she had the job as court reporter at a higher salary and with better working conditions than she'd ever had. After receiving the call, she took a minute to thank the Lord, then jumped up and screamed. "I got it. I got the job." But almost immediately, moroseness enveloped her. *If only she could talk with Winston, see him, touch his flesh, and feel his strength.*

"Get a hold of yourself, girl. That's over and done with!"

Chapter Ten

A week after Petra began her job as a court reporter, exhilarated because she knew she would be able to pay her bills and help Krista attend college, she received a telephone call from Dr. Barnes's office.

"This is Petra Fields," she said, wondering who would call her at her new job.

"Ms. Fields, Dr. Barnes wants you to come in and see him as soon as you can."

She had no desire to see the man whose misjudgment caused her to turn her life around. True, she had gained much from her trek out West and, especially, her time in San Francisco, but as a result, she was heavily in debt for the first time in her life and hopelessly in love with a man she would never see again.

"I'm very busy," she said. "How did you get my number here?"

"From your mother, of course," the woman said.

"I'll call you back," Petra said, her half hour break having expired. But she didn't call back, because each time she considered doing it, her anger almost suffocated her. Moreover, she considered that Barnes probably was after some self-aggrandizement, and if not that, she'd bet he wanted her to contribute her body to science. Wouldn't he be surprised!

"Did you get a call from Dr. Barnes's office?" her mother asked when they spoke by phone that evening.

"Yes, I did, and I don't have one thing to say to that charlatan."

"Now. Now," Lena began. "Dr. Barnes does a lot of good, so don't you go scandalizing his name. He told you you had a tumor, and you did. You call him. He may have something important to tell you."

"All right, I will."

She waited a week before calling him. *According to his diagnosis, I should have wings by now.* "This is Petra Fields, when can Dr. Barnes see me?" she asked the doctor's receptionist. They agreed that she would visit the doctor that day during her lunch hour.

Petra didn't trust herself to say anything to the doctor, and it surprised her that she greeted him civilly. "What did you want to see me about, Dr. Barnes?"

He sat in a chair opposite her, took her right hand, and adopted his best bedside manners. "You'll be happy to know that the radiologist misread your tests and gave me an incorrect evaluation. You do have tumors, but they are not malignant."

"I already know that, Dr. Barnes." She pulled her hair away from the area on which the surgeon operated so that he could see the evidence of it. "While I was in Atlanta, I passed out. The surgeon who removed the tumor told me it was benign. You said it was inoperable." Not nice, maybe, but probably the only revenge she would get. To soften it, she added, "If you want his name and phone number, I'll be glad to send it to you."

Barnes shook his head, clearly perplexed. "I can't see how he did it. He must have taken some pictures, and I'd like to see them. It's too bad we don't have a second diagnostic service here. The hospital has a rather good one, but I'd thought these specialists would do a superior job."

"I remember that the surgeon's name was Dr. Hayes, and my nurse said he was a neurosurgeon and head honcho at that hospital. I'll send you his number."

"Don't bother. I can find him. He's well-known, and you were very fortunate. Let's be glad it turned out for you as it did, but there's going to be some reckoning. Be sure of that."

She supposed that a tarnished reputation would upset any person and particularly a doctor whose prestige depended on the word of his patients. She bought a hot dog and a pint of milk at a corner deli and headed back to the courthouse.

And what about me? My daughter has been on the outs with me; my mother has one more excuse to preach to me and to berate me. Worst of all, my finances are a mess. Some of the reckless things I did — thinking I was going to die anyway — could have killed me. Reckless doesn't nearly describe the stupidity of picking up a hitchhiker on a highway with a forty-mile stretch between rest stops.

"And I've got a few things to say to Reverend Collins, too," she promised herself. "If it was necessary for me to get forgiveness from every person I thought I'd wronged, shouldn't I also tell people that I have a grudge against them about something? That way, I won't have to grin at them if I don't feel like it."

As it happened, she met Reverend Collins in the post office, where she went to buy some stamps on her way home that afternoon. "You haven't stopped by to tell me how you are, sister," he said. "You look well. Are you sure Dr. Barnes didn't make a mistake?"

He'll probably blab it from the pulpit Sunday morning, but I may as well tell him. She told him about the misdiagnosis and her operation. Then she added, "Reverend, I think it was a mistake to dump my guilt on people. I caused a lot of trouble. My neighbor and her husband separated after twenty-five years of marriage, and a lot of people are still furious with me. I dropped a few bombs."

He ran his fingers through his thick hair and smiled as one does with a cute, but naughty child. "You let them worry about their salvation; you did the right thing, and if your neighbor doesn't speak to you, go over and invite her to come to church with you Sunday morning."

She stared at the man until he backed away from her. "Yes, sir," she finally managed, but she knew that if she said one word to Ethel about church, the woman would probably throw something at her. "Nice to see you, Reverend," she said and got away from him as quickly as she could. Her daughter knew the truth about her father, and that was the only good thing to come from the ill-conceived confessions. Jada Hankins's temper had almost raged out of control. Anyone with such a temper was capable of violence, and she hoped not to encounter Jada again.

"I can't be angry with anybody, not even Dr. Barnes and Reverend Collins. What I shared with Winston Fleet more than compensates for any worry, pain, or inconvenience I experienced. And I have a better job than I've ever had. I hate bills, but I'll get them paid." A frown creased her face. "How on earth did I spend eighteen thousand dollars in such a short time? Oh, well. If I could see Winston again, I guess I wouldn't care about the bills or any of these other problems."

Petra couldn't know that Winston longed for her as much as she yearned for him. It disgusted him that he hadn't heeded his thoughts and gotten Petra's address or, at least, her telephone number. But it hadn't occurred to him that she would leave him while he slept rather than face the end with him. As he drove to his grandmother's house along the same road he'd traveled with Petra, he wondered if she were still alive. And who could he ask? Visions of her suffering alone brought tears from his eyes.

"I can't bear it," he said to himself. As he drove up the lane leading to his grandmother's house, the sun shone through the leaves, making intricate, lacy patterns that seemed too delicate for the wheels of his Acura. The delicate beauty of the scene reminded him of Petra and the way he felt when he held her in his arms.

He parked in the circle before his grandmother's house, got out of the car, and walked around to the back of the house where he knew he'd find LeAnn setting the supper table for the two of them. He leaned down, draped his arm across her shoulder, and kissed her cheek.

"It's such a beautiful day, Granny. I wish I'd brought along my bathing suit."

Her eyes twinkled in that way that he found so familiar and comforting. "It'll take me about twenty minutes to fry the chicken, and that ought to be time enough for you to skinny-dip. Look in the linen closet and get a beach towel." Wasn't it always that way with her? From his early childhood, he had been able to count on her finding a way to make him happy. His hug was intended to let her know what she meant to him, but it must have communicated something else, for she gazed at him with a quizzical facial expression.

"Something's eating you. What are you planning to do about Petra? She's never going out of your heart, you know."

"Granny, I don't know whether she's living or dead, and I don't have her phone number or her address. I'm on my way out of my mind. She said she had a couple of months to live." He repeated the remainder of Petra's story. "Somehow, I don't have the feeling that she's dead."

"Go ahead and swim. We'll talk about it afterward when you're relaxed."

He raised an eyebrow at that. "Yes, ma'am."

After she went into the kitchen, he got a beach towel, undressed, and dived into the pool's cool, shimmering waters. He told himself to get Petra off his mind, but he knew she would be forever in his system. After punishing himself, swimming as fast as he could until he was nearly out of breath, he climbed out, wrapped himself in the towel, dried off, and dressed.

"Feel better now?" LeAnn asked as she came outside with a platter of fried chicken and a plate of biscuits. "I've got some string beans in there to go with this," she told him.

"You sit down. I'll get it. Anything else?"

"Lemon meringue pie for dessert, and there's a pitcher of lemonade in the refrigerator." He got the string beans and lemonade and sat down to eat, but he wasn't in the mood.

LeAnn patted his hand. "Stop worrying, son. When Petra was here with you, she was certain she wouldn't be back, but I told her she would be. Don't you remember?"

He thought for a minute. "I knew there was something about that visit that I needed to remember. Yes, you said that. Do you . . . Can you figure out anything about her?"

LeAnn picked up a crisp drumstick, leaned back in her chair, bit into the chicken, and chewed for a while. Then she smiled. "She had a tumor, and it may still be there, but I don't see it now. These things I see come and go."

His heart skipped a few beats and, bracing his hands on the table, he leaned toward her. "What else? Is there anything else? Granny, tell me. Is she married?"

"She's not married, and I see you around her. I mean, she's very sad about you. I can't see anything else."

"So you think she's still alive?"

"I have yet to see anyone who's passed on. But, there's always a first time. Did she tell you where she's from?"

"Yes, ma'am. She's from Ellicott City, Maryland."

"It couldn't be so big. I never heard of it. Did you?" He shook his head, but he focused all of his energy on his grandmother. "Well, if she lives in a small town or city, you should be able to find people with her last name. If she's for you, you'll find her."

"I think she said that around sixty thousand people live there. It isn't far from Baltimore."

Would LeAnn Fleet encourage him if she didn't know that he could find Petra? He believed in his grandmother's psychic powers, and it was one of the reasons he had gone to visit her that day. He suspected she knew that and could direct him to Petra if she cared to, but she obviously wanted him to be certain of his motives.

"I'm going to try and find her, Granny. I can't go on this way, unable to focus on my work or anything else. As soon as I fill an order for a dining room set I'm working on, I'm going back East and look for Petra. I'll visit Mama, too."

"Good. How long before you can fulfill that contract?"

"A month maybe. It's a very ambitious design." He jerked forward. "Why? Is she . . . Is it urgent?"

"Not to my knowledge, but there may be a lot that I don't know."

■ ■ ■ ■

Petra had just begun to realize how much and how drastically her life had changed. For years, she'd played pinochle with Lurlene and Twylah at her house on Thursday evenings, and nothing, not a fractured wrist or any other ailment prevented Lurlene from playing pinochle, her favorite form of entertainment. Petra usually made a coconut cake to serve with their coffee. On that evening, Lurlene pleaded a headache and didn't join her and Twylah. And Twylah refused the cake, claiming that she was dieting. In addition, Petra's mother had gotten into the habit of bringing her supper over to Petra's house and eating it there. Her tolerance for Lena's pettiness and gossip shortened with each of her mother's visits. For the first time in her adult life, apart from her mortgage, Petra was not debt free. But, more important, she had developed a yearning to go to college. She loved her job, but she disliked being invisible, the person who sat silently taking notes, and who few people spoke to or seemed to be aware of.

Some of these trial lawyers don't use their heads, or maybe they don't care; they get paid anyway. I could have won that case, but that lawyer is incompetent, and the poor old woman is in trouble. Maybe if she increased her savings and went to college evenings, she could get a degree in four years. But after paying the credit card company the amount she'd agreed to send each month and taking care of her other bills, Petra saw that she had barely enough for two weeks' groceries. As much as she hated to do it, she would have to talk with Krista about their finances. Perhaps, if they gave up cable television and their cell phones, she could cut expenses by about three hundred dollars a month. She had to do something about her life.

Goodman leaned back in his swivel chair and looked around his office, which he had recently redecorated. The beige-colored walls, and the good reproductions of Doris Price, Van Gogh, and Cezanne paintings made the place look classy. He'd spent more than he wanted to on his executive desk and matching walnut chair, and on the Persian carpet and other furnishings, but the effect was worth the cost. With as many students as he could handle and good name recognition, he'd done well since opening his studio eleven years earlier. He'd been pleased with his life then, so pleased that he hadn't noticed how it had changed, how he and Carla related to each other only superficially. Without realizing it, his studio had become more like home than office, because it was the only place where he had peace of mind. Recently, his philandering with Jada threatened to shatter that peace, and his family didn't even notice the obvious changes in him and in his formerly clocklike behavior.

He had started the affair with Jada as a response to their first genuine family crisis, a foolish and childish thing to do. When had he and Carla lost their passion? Long before he knew about Krista, they had fallen into a habit of relating to their sons rather than to each other. He rethought that: they dealt with each other *through* their children. If he didn't end his ridiculous affair, he'd lose his family; already, he had a hard time respecting himself.

On an impulse, he dialed Carla's cell phone number. "Hi, babe." The minute he said it, he realized that it had been weeks, maybe months since he called her "babe," his once favorite name for her. "Why don't we all meet at Guido's for supper?"

"Hi. Uh . . . Well, Peter has a college entrance exam tomorrow, so —"

He was having none if it. Did she think he

wasn't aware that she used the children as a means of getting around him, of avoiding her responsibilities to him and to their marriage? He interrupted her in sharp tones. "Then Peter can stay home and study. I'll be at Guido's at seven. Bring Paul with you."

When she sputtered for a moment and then said, "Uh . . . OK. We'll be there," it occurred to him that whatever problem they had could be his fault. He was the head of his family, but if he relaxed in that role the least bit, Carla went her own way. He hung up and busied himself revising his arrangement of a gospel anthem for his choral group.

The door opened, and he looked up. "Damn! I thought I told you to call before coming here."

Jada smiled triumphantly. "So you could tell me you're busy or that you have company. You've been scarce recently, but let me tell you, darling, no man drops Jada Hankins."

His heart thudded so rapidly that it frightened him. Best to get it out, for if she thought she had the upper hand, she'd be unbearable.

"What do you want from me, Jada? Lay it all out now."

Jada's gaze fastened on his crotch, but he refused to be taken in by her brazen suggestion. "You have to ask?" she said, confirming her unspoken answer.

"Yeah. Don't tell me it's sex. You can get that anywhere, just as you probably always did. And if it's money, forget it. I have three children, and I plan to send all three of them to the best universities. That rules out supporting a mistress. So what is it?"

He had crushed her spirit, and he hated doing it, but he didn't intend to let this woman or any other one ruin his life. "I didn't expect you to act like this." She fluttered her eyes and looked at him from beneath lowered lids. "You could help me get that promotion."

"Jada, what you asked me to do could land me in jail. I'm sorry."

"Come home with me."

He blew out a long breath, and it barely indicated the extent of his frustration. "I'm meeting my wife and my younger son for dinner."

She walked over to the window and looked down on the street. "Has she figured out that you're fooling around? Or did your daughter tell her?"

"That isn't your business, Jada."

She pulled her tight skirt, shifting the side

seam back into its place, and then pushed it down as if to make it longer. He had noticed that her clothes usually fit too snugly, and he suspected that she bought them that way purposely. Her face bore a sad expression when she looked at him. "I need to get a little place to stay, and you could help me if you wanted to. Just a small, one-bedroom condo would be security for my old age."

He nearly swallowed his tongue. "Let me get this straight. You're asking me to buy you a condo? Are you out of your mind? Woman, you should've picked a man with money. Hell, I can barely pay the mortgage on my own house. Jada, you're wasting your time on me. You could do better. Much better."

"I know. My main problem is that jail rap I got. If I could get my hands on that Petra Fields, I'd wring her neck. She could have saved me from this trouble if she hadn't been such a coward."

He draped his right ankle over his left knee, wondering where the conversation was headed. At least she was no longer strident. "She's not responsible," he said, "so don't get yourself into real trouble, and you will if you assault her." He had to get her off the subject of Petra, but how? Petra was not his problem, but she was the mother of his child, and because of that he felt some responsibility for her well-being. "Tell you what, Jada. I'll write you a reference as a member of the choral group, stating that you're punctual, well-mannered, and decorous. Will that do?"

She hung her head and kicked at his precious Persian carpet. "It's more than I expected, and it should help."

He believed in grabbing opportunities when he saw them. "And you and I are going to end this farce," he said. "It doesn't suit either of us." He took out his wallet and counted eighty dollars. "This is what I borrowed from you."

Jada looked at the money. "You kept a record?" He nodded. "You're not going to see me anymore?"

"Jada, you're old enough to realize that you have no future with a married man, and especially with one who has never expressed any feelings for you. You ought to have more self-respect than to be content with a man who can't even walk the street with you."

Her face seemed to swell with her anger. "I was thinking only of what I could get."

"Same here," he countered, "and I'm ashamed of myself." He typed out the recommendation on his business stationery, signed it, and gave it to her. "This squares it with us. You're welcome to continue with the choral group, but I'm through cheating on my wife."

She read the note, put it in the envelope he gave her, and slipped it into her pocketbook. "Is this the first time you did it?"

"Yeah, and I'm surprised at how easy it was."

She surprised him when she walked over, leaned down, and kissed his cheek. "I ought to be mad at you, Goodman, but I started it. Your wife better work on that marriage, 'cause right now, it's about as strong as smoke in a hurricane wind. See you at rehearsal." His lack of relief when the door closed behind her didn't surprise him; he wouldn't lay five cents on what Jada Hankins would do next.

A few minutes before seven, he left the studio and walked the three blocks to Guido's restaurant. Unless Carla had experienced a mind-blowing epiphany, she would surely arrive late; his wife didn't understand the meaning of punctuality. He took a table near a window overlooking the park and waited. Among the trees, waterfall, and shrubs, lovers strolled in the twilight of the late-August evening, holding hands or stopping for a kiss. Could he enjoy that with Carla again, and how could he get them back to that point?

She arrived at sixteen minutes past seven, tall and elegant in a navy-blue linen suit, pink blouse, and pink hat. With Carla, he had long realized, everything had to harmonize. "She wants everything and everybody around her to be in sync, except herself," he muttered beneath his breath as he rose to greet her. He took a few steps toward her as she approached with their son, Paul, just behind her. He hardly recognized his own child, a boy now six feet tall, dressed as he was in a navy-blue suit, pale blue shirt, and red tie. When had his boy grown to six feet in height, only a few inches shorter than he? Goodman realized that his attention hadn't been on his family, but on his job, on making money and a name for himself.

He kissed Carla's cheek and patted Paul's shoulder, though he had an urge to hug the boy and, in that way, perhaps recapture some of the time lost. "You two make a man look good and feel great," he said and meant it. "Was Peter upset because he couldn't come with you?"

Paul shrugged first one shoulder and then the other, in what Goodman surmised was the latest teenagers' expression of boredom. "Dad, you know nothing stresses Peter. I think he was glad for us to get out of the house and let him study undisturbed."

He gazed at his son with not a little pride. "You're a fine-looking young man, Paul. I don't know when I've seen you out of torn jeans and a baggy T-shirt. I'm impressed."

Paul's grin reminded him of Krista. "Thank you, sir. I . . . Sometimes I clean up pretty good. Uh . . . gee . . . thanks."

Whatever he had expected, it wasn't that diffidence. *Here I go again, communicating with one of the children and ignoring Carla.* He smiled at her. "You look great. I think I should have suggested that we eat at Grayson's."

"Good Lord, no," Paul said, oblivious to his mother's evident pride in her husband's compliment. "If you'd said Grayson's, Mom would probably have made me put on a tux." The three of them laughed and, at that moment, he decided to get his house in order.

After finishing his pecan praline ice cream, his favorite dessert, Paul cleared his throat a few times and looked first at one parent and then at the other one. "What is it?" Goodman asked him, unaware that the boy would raise the issue that his father had avoided for months.

"I . . . Look! I want to meet my sister. Peter doesn't, because it will mean he's no longer the oldest, but can't you just take me to meet her? I'd like to have a big sister."

Momentarily stunned, Goodman's lower jaw sagged, but he quickly seized the moment. He'd needed that opening. "You're right, son, and I should probably have brought her to meet my family as soon as I learned about her. But although she was born before I met your mother, Carla still has some rights, too, and I've been waiting for her signal. Krista has been badgering me about meeting her brothers and her stepmother, and I've told her what I just told you."

"When do you see her?" Carla asked him.

"She has a beautiful mezzo soprano voice, so I had her join the choral group, and I give her piano lessons every Monday afternoon. We go from the studio to rehearsal, after which I drive her home."

"I see. Do you like her?" Carla asked him.

"Of course I do. She's my child."

"When have you seen her mother?" Paul searched the faces of his parents.

"I haven't seen her since the day, almost three months ago, when she told me about Krista."

"Well, if Mom doesn't want to . . . I mean . . . Why can't I go to the studio when she's there taking a lesson, or maybe she and I can go to a movie or something."

"Tell you what," Goodman began, "I'll bring her here for dinner, and —"

"That won't work," Carla said. "Not in a public place. What about Sunday? We can have a barbecue, and everybody will be relaxed."

"Wonderful," he said, feeling truly connected with his wife for the first time in many months. At home, later that night, he made love with her and realized that years had passed since he'd gotten more out of their lovemaking than physical relief. He delighted in every centimeter of her body that he could reach, mastering her, playing her like a lyrist plays a lyre. Yes, he had enjoyed his wife, possessing her, shattering her composure. He knew she had questions because of it, but he also knew she wouldn't ask them for she, too, was culpable. He went to sleep holding Carla in his arms.

The next morning, he telephoned Krista. "Can you come to my home Sunday afternoon to meet the rest of my family?"

"You serious? What brought this on? Sure I can," Krista said.

"Good. I'll pick you up at about two-thirty. Dress for a barbecue, but don't overdo it."

"Gotcha. I'll wear a skirt . . . maybe."

Now, if Jada would only leave him alone.

Petra shifted around in her mind ways of broaching to Krista the need for them to reduce expenses. "There's no way to do it except to do it," she said to herself, and when Krista got home from work that afternoon, Petra said, "Sit down, honey. We have to talk."

"OK," Krista said, "but I was just going to ask you if I could have a piano."

Certain that her lower jaw sagged, Petra shrieked, "What? If you can have a *what*?"

"A piano. Daddy's giving me piano lessons, and he said I need to practice more."

Petra braced the heels of her open palms against the dining room table and pushed her chair from the table. "Taking lessons from him? How long has this been going on?"

When Krista didn't look at her, she knew the girl was about to drop a bomb. "Since before you went on your vacation. I see him every Monday, first for my piano lessons and then we go together to rehearsal." She paused, looking at her feet. "While you were out West, Daddy gave me a computer and printer and set them up for me. I . . . uh . . . I like him. A lot, Mom."

"I'm glad you do," Petra managed to say.

"He's your father. Have you met his family?"

"Not yet. He's taking me to meet them this coming Sunday, and I'm a little bit nervous about it."

"No need to be nervous. They're the ones who'll be worried about whether you'll get something that would normally go to them."

"I'm prepared to like my brothers, but I don't know about their mother. She may not want me around."

"Remember that she's your stepmother, and be respectful."

"Yes, ma'am. I'll remember it every time *she* remembers it."

Petra stared at Krista. In six weeks, her daughter would be eighteen years old, and she was already prepared to take the measure of a woman old enough to be her mother. "Be careful, honey. Don't forget that you must always respect your elders."

"Yes, ma'am. But if she's not nice to me . . ." She let it hang, but Petra knew her daughter, and she didn't have to guess what Krista left unsaid. "Uh, Mom, guess what."

"What?"

"I think Daddy's been getting it on with somebody. And why he'd pick that woman beats me."

Petra's eyes widened. "You know her?"

"She's in the chorus, and she came to his studio once when I was there. He didn't like it, either. I saw her leaving another time when I was arriving, but she didn't see me. Mama, that woman is common."

"Don't be so harsh, Krista. Maybe she's poor and not well-educated."

"Humph. Jada Hankins has no morals, Mom, and Daddy ought to leave her alone. I told him he shouldn't fool around with her, and if he doesn't stop it, I'll tell Carla."

Petra jumped up from her chair and grabbed Krista by the shoulders. "Jada Hankins? Good Lord! What's he doing with *her*?"

Petra told Krista how she knew Jada. "That woman is capable of violence."

At the end of her first shift the next day, Petra left the courtroom and headed to her office to type out her text. Keeping her attention off the handsome witness hadn't been easy, not so much because he attracted her, he didn't, but because she either attracted him, or he enjoyed flirting. Before she reached her office door, the witness for the defendant, whose testimony she'd just recorded, stopped her.

"I was hoping I'd catch you before you disappeared," he said in his deep, mellifluous voice. "Lady, you were messing up my head while I was trying to answer that prosecuting attorney's questions."

"Your head's easily messed up, mister. Excuse me."

"Wait a minute, will you? I want to get to know you. May I call you? Will you give me your phone number?"

"Sorry. I can't even talk to you before the judge says this case is closed. Excuse me, please." She liked his looks and his self-assuredness. Six months earlier, she might have given him her phone number, but she loved Winston Fleet, and no other man existed. The law forbade her to be in the man's company and, as she no longer faced imminent death, tempting fate — with the possibility of losing her job — no longer appealed to her.

"But we can talk by phone. What's the harm in that?"

She attempted to pass him, but he blocked her way. "None for you, maybe, but I like my job. Come back after the case is closed. I'll be here. Now, let me pass."

She opened the door, stepped inside, and would have closed it had the man not prevented it with his foot. Petra whirled around and ducked past him, back into the corridor.

Hmm, so the brother liked to live dangerously. "Do you want me to call the court officer?"

"Sorry," he said and rushed off.

"First time a man wanted me for my notes rather than for my sex appeal," she said under her breath, went into her office, and locked the door. "I must be losing it, and I'm not even forty."

Instead of transcribing her notes, she stared out of the window, despondent. How could she ask Krista to help with the bills, when it was she and not her daughter who had created the financial crisis. Besides, Krista worked to save money for college.

"I'll find a way," she vowed. "I have to."

Goodman fretted over Krista's first visit to his home. He dressed in a pair of beige Dockers, a green and beige plaid shirt, and sneakers, got into his car, and drove to Petra's house. When Petra opened the door, he realized that he hadn't expected to see her.

"Hi," he said. "I . . . hope you don't mind if I take Krista to my house for a cookout with my family. I thought it high time she met her brothers. I'll . . . uh . . . bring her back home before it's too late." He hated that he fumbled for words, nervous and unsure of himself.

"Come on in, Goodman," Petra said. "Of course, I don't mind. Krista told me about it, and I think it's a good thing. She should know her brothers."

"Hi, Daddy."

He looked up and saw Krista skipping down the stairs and felt a catch in his throat. Young, beautiful, and so vulnerable. How had Petra managed alone to raise such a charming girl? He walked a few steps to meet her.

"You look perfect," he said of her white pants, green and white striped T-shirt, white sneakers, and green socks. When she reached up to kiss his cheek, he bent down to facilitate it, glad that his daughter felt free to kiss him in front of Petra. *Points for Petra,* he thought.

"Thanks for the compliment, Daddy. I tried not to overdo it. I know I said I'd wear a skirt, but I changed my mind, and since I work in a department store, I just collected what I wanted and got my nice fat discount. Say, you look good, too." She kissed her mother's cheek. "See you later, Mom."

He felt strange walking out of Petra's house with Krista, almost as if he were deserting her. But what did he say, or do? It didn't seem proper to kiss her good-bye.

Petra solved it when she said, "You two have a good time," and walked toward the back of the house. As he drove home, it occurred to him that he didn't know how he felt about Petra, and that he ought to sort it out. At times, he wondered why, after eighteen years, she decided to tell him about Krista. Something was behind it, and he'd better find out what it was.

He parked in front of his house, a two-story brown brick that sat well back from the street at the end of a tree-lined, upper-middle-class cul-de-sac.

"Gee, Daddy. Do you live here?" she asked as she searched for the car door handle.

"Sit right there," he said. "I want you to learn to let a man open the door for you."

"I know, but I'd be out of the car before you could get around here to open the door. Gee, it's so quiet."

"It isn't noisy where you live," he said, taking her arm. He had hoped that Carla would walk out to meet them, but he supposed that was too much to expect.

At that moment, Paul emerged from the side of the house, a smile shining on his face. "So I'm meeting you at last, Krista," he said. "I'm Paul, your younger brother." He stopped and gazed at her. "Gosh! You look just like Peter and me."

To Goodman's amazement, Paul caught Krista in a bear hug before she could speak and swung her around. "I've been dying to meet my big sister," he said and kissed her cheek. "Thank goodness, you're not a little runt."

Krista's face bloomed into a smile. "I've been scared to death all morning, Paul, and I'm gonna love you for being so nice. I've been after Daddy to let me meet you and Peter." She frowned. "Is Peter going to like me?"

Paul shrugged. "Peter was the oldest, but now, you're the oldest." He spread his hands. "What can I say?"

It seemed to Goodman that Krista became uncharacteristically pensive. Her face darkened. "I'll make him like me. After all, he's my big brother."

"Yeah," Paul said. "Lay that on him, and he'll cave right in."

Goodman stood alone, dumbfounded, as Paul took Krista's hand and walked with her to the back of the house where he knew Peter and Carla waited. Paul and Krista seemed to have forgotten his presence. Well, that was one he didn't have to worry about. However, Carla was like a black walnut, hard to crack, and Peter was very much like her, except that his ego responded well to buttering; Carla's did not.

CHAPTER ELEVEN

Goodman leaned against the side of the house watching as Paul led Krista not to his brother but to Carla. Carla laid a pair of tongs on the vast, chrome outdoor grill, wiped her hands on her apron, and shook hands with Krista. "Mom, this is Krista. Krista, this is my mom."

"We've been looking forward to meeting you, Krista."

As if Carla's greeting was about as cool as she had expected, Krista didn't smile. "Me, too. And I'm glad to know who you all are," she said, then turned and looked at Peter, who rose slowly from his perch on the edge of the deck. "I've been especially anxious to meet my big brother. Hi, Peter. Can't I have a hug?" She started toward him with her arms open.

Goodman realized that Peter had planned to be withdrawn, but when a smile formed around his lips and slowly worked itself over the rest of his face, he knew that Krista had won the battle of wills and captivated Peter, who hugged her and then kissed her cheek.

"Gee, you're pretty, Krista," Peter said, as he stepped back and stared at her. "This is weird; you look just like Paul and me."

"That's because you're my brothers."

"Where do you go to school?" Peter asked her, but Goodman didn't hear her response, for at that moment, Paul moved close to him and said, "What a relief! Peter intends to be friendly. She's nice, real nice, Dad."

"I didn't plan this, son, but this is the way it is, and I want the three of you to love and care for each other."

"Shouldn't cause any sweat," Paul said, "especially not if Mom gets her hips off her shoulder."

Goodman stepped back, staring at his youngest child. *"What? What did you say?"*

Paul lifted his right shoulder in a quick shrug. "You can't clean the house by shoving dirt under the rug, Dad. The dirt's still there. Mom will have to get used to the fact that, before you met her, you loved somebody else. I don't see the problem, but I don't understand females, either."

Out of the mouths of babes! "I hope we can at least enjoy each other when we're together," Goodman said, in a tone more prayerful than hopeful.

Petra did not begrudge Krista her new family; indeed, knowing that her daughter would have a father's love gave her not only satisfaction but a sense of redemption. She sat in her living room facing the television and staring at *As Time Goes By,* the British comedy in which she always found delight and escape, but on that occasion, she couldn't concentrate on it. Her thoughts revolved around Winston. Maybe if she went back to Oakland, where he lived, and searched for him. . . . She dismissed the idea as wishful thinking. She didn't even have the price of a plane ticket. Besides, he had probably grieved for her for a few days and then moved on.

She looked at her watch and slumped down in the big old chair. She had other worries, including how Krista was getting on with Goodman's family. She hoped none of them provoked a dose of truth from Krista's sharp tongue. At about nine o'clock, the front door opened, and Petra scampered across the room to the hallway. "How'd it go?" she asked Krista, sounding as if she were out of breath.

Krista brushed a kiss on her mother's cheek and breezed on past her. "Paul's a dream. Real super. Peter's older, and he was a little standoffish at first, but I kept telling him how nice it's gonna be having a big brother and, just like Paul said, Peter shaped up. I like both of them. Carla was OK, but no more than she had to be.

"Paul wants me to go bowling with him, so I said OK, but I'd have to ask you. Can I?"

"Sure, and I think it would be better if you said Miss Carla. You understand?"

"Yes, ma'am, but no way am I sucking up to that lady. I'll be as nice to her as she is to me."

"You catch more flies with honey than with vinegar, Krista."

Krista let out a long breath. "Another one of Grandpa's sayings? Well, I guess you can, that is, if you're interested in catching flies."

The next afternoon, Monday, Petra got home after an unusually stressful day at court — mostly because the same witness ogled her incessantly — and found two letters in her mailbox. She opened the one bearing Dr. Mark Hayes's return address first, and her fingers trembled so badly that she failed in repeated efforts to unfold the paper. *Please God, don't let him have any bad news, no more misdiagnoses, for me.*

She dropped the letter to the table, sat down, closed her eyes, and tried to relax. After about half an hour, she went to the dining room table and flattened out the sheet of paper.

"Dear Ms. Fields," she read. "By now, you should have healed completely. However, as your surgeon, it is my responsibility to be certain. Please call my office for an appointment as soon as possible. Yours, Mark Hayes, MD."

Petra breathed deeply, as if she hadn't done it for a while, folded the letter, and returned it to its envelope. She would telephone him, but as for going to Atlanta, she figured she'd get back there about as soon as she'd find herself in Oakland, California.

The second letter came from Dr. Reginald Barnes. She considered not opening it, surmising that it probably contained the bill for his services. She did not need any more bills.

"Open it, Mom," Krista chided. "Even if it's a bill, you gotta pay it." Petra opened the letter and stared at the words written there in black and white. Suddenly, she jumped up, hitting her knee cap on the corner of the table, although she barely felt it.

"What is it, Mom?"

"I can't believe it. Dr. Barnes is suing the laboratory that misread my tests, and his lawyer says I should join the suit."

"What are you going to do?" She heard the anxiety, or was it hope, in Krista's voice. "If you got some money out of it, Mom, maybe you wouldn't have to work so hard."

"I love my work, honey, but at least I'd be able to pay my bills. You know, that trip I took sank me into the worst financial hole I've ever been in. Right now, I can't see my way out of it. You want to go to school, and so do I. So, if anything comes of this, maybe it'll be the answer for both of us."

"Yeah, but if I were you, Mom, I'd get my own lawyer. Dr. Barnes is not exactly squeaky clean in this."

"You're right, and before I answer Barnes, I'm going to talk to one. I see lots of lawyers at court every day."

The next morning, she walked into the courthouse an hour before her shift began, intent upon finding the lawyer who'd won a large judgment in a suit settled the previous week. She located him as he was rushing out of the building.

"I'm in a bit of a hurry just now, Ms. Fields. Call me in a couple of days."

"I have to make a decision today, Mr.

Lyons. I've been working here as a court stenographer long enough to know I have a case."

His left eyebrow rose just enough to let her know that he questioned her temerity. "Sum it up in two minutes."

She did. "Barnes wants me to join him in a suit. Should I do that or get my own lawyer?"

"Absolutely do not join him. He's got a smart lawyer. If you join Barnes in the suit, you can't sue him, and you damned well should."

Her hands shook so badly that she put them behind her where he couldn't see them. He represented people of status and wealth; maybe he'd be insulted if she asked him to take her case.

"I was . . ." she began. He looked at his watch. "Would you . . . er . . . take my case?"

He studied her for a minute. "Yes. All right. Be here tomorrow morning at about a quarter of eight, and we'll discuss it."

She didn't want to sue Reginald Barnes. Although she knew he was not a struggling brother, she didn't believe he was a wealthy man; she told the lawyer as much. "Then you restrict the suit to the lab," Lyons told her, "and let's not get sentimental about this. A brain tumor can cause a lot of problems, including blindness, and you were told that it was inoperable."

He pulled his glasses up off the tip of his nose and sucked his teeth. "You really ought to sue the bastard. He says he's a doctor, so he should know his stuff. This is a clear-cut case. This lab company's incompetence caused you a lot of heartache, fear, distress, and financial loss, and if you hadn't encountered a doctor with sense, you could have died. Barnes may want you to witness for him if he has to go to court, but avoid that unless you get a subpoena. I'll be in touch."

"What are we asking for?"

"Plenty. Every dime they've got. It will take a while, but you ought to clear a few hundred thousand. I will need an affidavit from your surgeon."

She had hoped for thirty or forty thousand, enough to pay her bills and get Krista started in college. "I'll call him today," she said, shaken by the prospect of paying off her mortgage and sending both herself and Krista to college.

"Don't count on it, yet," he warned. "These things take time, so it may be a year or more before we settle."

She thanked him for taking the case and went to her office where she picked up an envelope that someone had pushed beneath the door. "What's this?" She didn't recognize the handwriting.

"I'm sorry if I irritated you yesterday," she read, "but I don't remember ever having been so strongly attracted to a woman. Can't we talk for just a few minutes? I'll wait for you at the donut shop at the corner of Court and Park when you leave work this evening. Please!" She ran back to the lounge and breathed deeply in relief when she saw that the lawyer remained where she left him.

When he saw her, he didn't move his pen from the paper on which he'd been writing. "Did we forget something?" he asked.

She handed him the note. "That man is a witness in a case I recorded yesterday. He followed me to my office and left only when I threatened to call a court officer."

Lyons took the note, read it, and looked her in the eye, scrutinizing her. "Did you tell him it was illegal for you to speak with a witness during the trial?" She told him that she had. "Do you know his name and the case in question?" She wrote it on the back of the letter. "I'll see that he gets a warning and that you get a ride home each evening," he said. "Doesn't look wholesome to me." Nor to her, and she feared she might have to leave the best job she'd ever had.

▪ ▪ ▪ ▪

Later, at home, Petra changed into a pair of jeans and a sweatshirt and went out to her back garden. She hadn't worked there much since returning from her vacation, and neither Krista nor her mother paid the garden any attention during her absence. Her mother wanted nothing to do with gardening; Lena claimed that she had worked enough in the fields for less than minimum wage before she moved from Alabama to Maryland, and that she couldn't eat a strawberry without remembering the times she picked them for three cents a quart while crawling on her knees in the hot sun.

Petra expelled a long breath. Her mama didn't have pleasant memories about many things or, if she did, she kept them to herself. A few drops of rain splattered her back, as she tugged at a deeply-rooted milkweed that choked a rose bush. She pulled harder, fell backward, and wiped the rain from her face. As she pulled herself up, she noticed Ethel, her neighbor, sitting on her steps. Why would Ethel sit outside in the rain unless she couldn't get inside?

She walked to the fence and called her

neighbor. "Ethel, what's wrong? Can't you get in the house? It's pouring rain out here."

Petra stared as the woman began to cry. "Ethel, for goodness sake. What's the matter?"

"You have to ask? I can't find my keys, and if you had been the neighbor you claimed to be, I could have gone over to your house."

"For goodness sake, Ethel, you don't have to talk to me. Come on over and get dry. You'll catch your death of cold sitting out here in the rain."

"I'm not going in your house, Petra. Not after you screwed my husband."

Nearly soaked and experiencing a renewed bout of guilt, Petra stamped her foot and didn't bother controlling her temper. "Oh crap, Ethel. You been over here dozens of times since I did that. Besides, I didn't screw Fred; it was the other way around. He'd been telling me for months what he wanted to do to me and how good it would be. Heck, I'd never felt anything like he was offering, and I just laid down, opened my legs, and let him do it. It wasn't worth the time it took me to lie down, and especially not worth the case of guilt it gave me. Come on over here out of the rain."

She opened the gate at the back of her

property and waited. Ethel took her time getting there, as if she wanted Petra to get a thorough soaking.

"I'm still mad at ya, Petra," Ethel said. "It's bad enough to lose your husband, but if your best friend's the cause of it, that's really rough."

Petra opened the kitchen door and waited until Ethel entered it. "Sit down in the kitchen somewhere, Ethel, while I find you one of my caftans."

"That's right. Rub it in. I know I can't get into your clothes. Mind if I turn on the oven and stand in front of it? These wet clothes feel awful."

Petra handed Ethel a dark blue caftan, took her wet clothes, and put them in the dryer. "I'm hoping we can get past this, Ethel," she said. "I know you said you'd rather not have known." She related to Ethel the reasons why she told her about her one sexual encounter with Fred. "But Reverend Collins insisted that I'd go to hell if I didn't ask forgiveness of everybody I'd ever wronged."

Ethel stared at Petra with her mouth agape. "In that case, I suppose he's planning to ask Fred's forgiveness. A bigger hypocrite never put on shoes. Don't look at me like that; you're not the only one who can be seduced. Rev has a great line and, unlike Fred, he can back it up."

Well. Well. Who would have thought it? Petra made a pot of tea, toasted some biscuits, and put that on the table along with butter and raspberry jam. "That misdiagnosis really fouled up my life, Ethel. Imagine me running around the country spending money like I was the United States Treasury Department. I got debt up to the ceiling. I tell you, I don't know what got into me."

"I expect if I thought I was facing death, I'd'a acted the fool, too." They settled into their former habit of gossiping over tea or coffee. "How's Krista's job at Dwill's Department Store? I saw her working in the linen department a few days ago."

"She's head of the section now, and they recently gave her a raise. Krista's smart, and I want her to go to college."

"Yeah? You always was highfalutin. I'm glad to see our people getting ahead. I hope she makes it."

They talked until Petra said, "I guess I'd better get supper together. When Krista comes, she can crawl through that little window on your back porch and open the door for you. You can eat with us." She gave Ethel her clothing, which she had tumble-dried in her dryer.

"I sure do thank you, Petra. This has meant everything to me."

Ethel's smile didn't quite reach her eyes, so Petra didn't fool herself into believing that her relationship with Ethel would be as warm and sisterly as it had once been. Ethel may have been unfaithful to Fred, Petra reasoned, but she loved him and, considering his lack of skill in bed, it was hard to blame Ethel for finding relief elsewhere. Still, she didn't feel comfortable with Ethel knowing that the woman hadn't been able to forgive her.

Petra set about preparing supper for Krista, Ethel, and herself, nervous because thunder and lightning had joined the rain. She closed the kitchen window a second before a flash of lightning nearly unnerved her.

"I'm sorry, Ethel, but I have to go in the living room and sit down. These electric storms scare me to death."

"Don't worry, Petra," Ethel said, "I have one of those bodies that repels lightning. So nothing can happen to you long as I'm with you, and that's the Lord's honest truth."

She walked over to Ethel, who sat hunched in a low-back kitchen chair. "Ethel, I guess you're a better woman than I am. If you'd done to me what I did to you, I'm not sure I'd be as nice about it."

Ethel glanced up at Petra. "Don't lay no halo on my head, Petra. I done my share of dirt before I was saved, and after, too. When I was young, single, and good-looking with my breasts standing out high and my stomach flat, I thought nothing of walking off with another woman's man and doing whatever I pleased with him. I broke up Fred's first marriage. He was hot stuff back then, but he's fooled around so much that nowadays he ain't worth the time it takes you to pull off your clothes. All the same, I'm used to him."

Petra didn't want to discuss Fred with Ethel, and she welcomed the sound of Krista's key in the lock of the front door. "Hi, Mom. Hi, Miss Ethel. Mom, can I invite Paul to have supper with us one night?"

"Of course. But you should invite Peter, too. You don't want him to dislike you. And honey, would you please crawl through Ethel's window and unlock her back door. She locked herself out. You can do that after we eat supper."

"Yes, ma'am. Don't worry about Peter and me. He won't dislike me, but he probably isn't going to love me, either."

"How're you getting on with Carla?"

"I've only seen her that one time. Paul and I talk on our cell phones. Say, remind me to talk to you about Jada. It's too weird to tackle right now." The phone rang, and Krista rushed to answer it.

"Hello." She listened for a few seconds. "This isn't Petra. This is her daughter, and you watch your mouth, lady." She hung up.

"Who on earth was that?" Petra asked.

"I don't know, but she sure was angry. Said you ruined things for her with Gail Somebody or other. How do you know anybody with a mouth like hers, Mom? Pure filth."

"Jack fired her girlfriend because of something I said. I told her about it and asked her to forgive me, but she won't. I was trying to do the right thing, according to Reverend Collins."

"Yeah," Ethel said. "I don't want to hear the name of that hypocrite. Wait till I see that man again."

"I wish I could fix it, Ethel, but I know I can't. You're not the only one who wants to see Reverend Collins."

The storm subsided, and after their supper, Krista climbed through the window, unlocked Ethel's kitchen door and put her shoes back on. "My butt's getting too big for this window," she said to herself, checking to be certain that she hadn't ripped her jeans. "Gee, Miss Ethel, wouldn't it make sense for you to give my mom a key? If you got sick in here and I wasn't around to get through that little window, somebody would have to break down your door."

"I thank you for letting me in, Krista, and I'll sure think about what you said." She rubbed her hands up and down her sides. "Maybe Fred'll come back. I don't know."

Krista stared at Ethel. "You mean you'd take him back after he's been living over there with Miss Armena? If it was me, I'd kick his . . . behind."

"You think like that 'cause you still young and pretty. Ain't no man wants me at my age."

Krista's face creased into a frown. "You don't look that old to me. Gotta go. Bye." Maybe she should ignore Jada's fooling around with her father. Carla might leave him if she knew about it, and she didn't want to hurt her father. Still, Jada should leave him alone.

Krista's concerns about Jada were no less than Goodman's. Jada had the job she wanted, thanks to his recommendation, and he prayed that that would satisfy her. He had spared no words in telling her that he didn't intend to give any woman money, that he meant to use what he had to educate his three children. He planned to be more creative in making love to his wife in the hope that she would help him put some sparkle, some passion in their marriage. He realized from his sexual encounters with Jada that his wife was indeed a cool woman, not cold, but definitely not hot. Jada was hot, but he'd finished with her; he'd had to, and not because she was becoming overbearing; she had been on the verge of becoming an addiction.

Goodman looked at his watch for the tenth time in the last half hour. His studio door swung open, and his accountant swaggered in as if he didn't know he was thirty-seven minutes late.

"One of these days, you'll keep your appointments on time," Goodman said. "What do you have for me?"

"Sorry, Goodman. The traffic, you know. Now. Your daughter is a year and some months older than Peter, and that's the problem." They struggled with figures and options for nearly two hours and, in the end, Goodman had a plan that suited him.

Later, he called Krista. "Can you come to

my studio now? Get a taxi, and I'll meet you at the front of the building with the fare."

"Yes, sir. Should I dress up? I'm wearing jeans." He told her to come as she was, locked the studio, and went down to the building's front door to wait for Krista.

"What's so urgent, Daddy?" she asked after kissing his cheek.

"I have to make some plans, and I have to start with you." He unlocked the door to his studio, got two bottles from the refrigerator, lemonade for Krista and ginger ale for himself, and sat down. "You've been admitted to three universities. I can't afford Brown, so I hope you'll agree that's out. I was graduated from Howard with honors, and I'd be happy if you agreed to go there."

Krista jumped up, ran to his desk, and braced her hands on it. "Are you telling me you're going to send me to Howard? Huh? You're gonna pay for it?"

He leaned back in his chair and looked her in the eye. It seemed as if she still didn't understand. "Krista, I have three children, and I intend to send all three of them to a university. You're the oldest; you're ready to go, so I'm dealing with you first. If you're willing to go to Howard, bring me the papers, and I'll sign as the responsible parent. Your mother has had the responsibility alone for nearly eighteen years, but not any longer."

She ran around the desk and hugged him. He was used to her outbursts of affection, but this was the first time he'd seen her cry. "Now. Now. None of that. I'll take you home. If I'm late for supper again tonight, Carla will have a fit."

As if he'd administered shock therapy, her tears stopped abruptly, as if they had turned to ice. "Where were you last night, Daddy?"

"Baltimore. I went to a fraternity meeting." He meant for his frown to serve as a mild reprimand, but it evidently didn't register as such with his daughter.

"Were you with Jada?"

He placed a hand on each of her shoulders. "Get this straight, Krista. There is nothing between Jada and me."

She seemed downcast, and he sensed that she didn't believe him. She confirmed that when she said, "I have a feeling she wouldn't agree. Okay, let's go."

He parked in front of Petra's house and sat there until Krista asked him, "What is it, Daddy? Should I get out?"

"It has just occurred to me that I can't make plans for you without discussing things with your mother. I'm going in with you." He used his cell phone to telephone his home. "Paul, would you tell your mother that I have to speak with Petra about Krista, and I should be home in less than an hour. Thanks. She's here with me, but you two can talk later." He walked around to the front passenger's door and opened it. "I hope Petra will allow you to go to Howard. It's our best shot."

Petra's eyes widened when she saw Goodman enter with Krista, who rushed to her and hugged her with more fervor than usual, as if to assure her mother that she still loved her. "Mom, Daddy decided that he needed to talk with you. May I stay and listen?"

Petra looked at Goodman, every inch the epitome of a successful man. "It's all right with me if you agree. Have a seat. Krista, please get your father a glass of lemonade. The pitcher's in the refrigerator."

"She can sit with us," he said. "You've done a fine job with her, and I'm proud she's my daughter. Petra, I'm hoping to send all of my children to a university. Krista's the oldest of the three, and as things are now, I can send her to Howard, but I can't afford Brown. She's agreed to go to Howard, but I need your approval."

She shook her head in amazement. "I'm stunned. I would have expected anything but this. From what I hear, Howard's a fine school, and it has agreed to admit her. What a blessing! It's expensive, Goodman."

"I can manage it. By the way, do you have health insurance for her? If not, I can put her on my family plan until she's twenty-five. Maybe I'd better switch her over anyway, and that will be less expense for you."

"Goodman, I'm ashamed of myself. I should have contacted you about Krista long ago."

"Sometimes our errors are our salvation, Petra. Who knows how it would have been long ago?"

"You really have forgiven me?"

"Look at it this way. You freed me of the responsibility of a family, allowing me to lay the foundation for a good life, but you made the wrong decision for Krista and yourself, and I had no input in her upbringing." He stood and walked across the room to the fireplace. "Little girls make kings of their fathers, and I missed that. But that's passed, and I'm happy with Krista. We're developing a good father-daughter relationship, and that's what I want."

He paused and didn't look at Petra. "If

you hadn't gotten that bad news, would you ever have told me that I fathered this wonderful girl?"

She remembered her vow to tell the truth no matter what and fixed her gaze on him. "I don't know, but I have a feeling that I might have let the lie stand. It cost me a lot to tell Krista about you."

"I imagine it did." He walked over to where his daughter sat with an expression of bemusement. "Be sure and bring me those papers when you come for your lesson Monday." When he fingered his chin, Petra remembered that he always did that when he'd arrived at a decision about something. "Look, I'll stop by and get them around six tomorrow evening. The sooner we confirm that you're going, the better."

Goodman walked over to Petra and extended his hand. She stood and shook it. "Thanks for everything, Goodman. You know, if it hadn't been for that misdiagnosis, all this wouldn't have happened, I wouldn't have seen the Grand Canyon, and I still wouldn't be able to swim."

A frown replaced his smile. "You can swim?" Petra nodded. "Incredible! Well, I won't ask how *that* happened. Krista will need a lot of things for school. I'm here to help. Good night."

"What's the matter, Mom? You're so quiet," Krista said. "Seems to me you should be dancing, since you don't have to worry about me getting into college."

"Oh, I'm happy about that, but he was right about a lot of things. When you were two to five years old, you were so sweet, pretty, charming, and smart. I imagine you would have been the light of Goodman's world."

"No point in sweating it, Mom. Considering what he said; today he would probably have been working at McDonald's in the day and trying to play gigs in honky-tonk joints at night. He's got a palace over there, a real cool studio, and he's conductor of a big community chorus. He's rowing it right, Mom. Quit worrying."

"He says it's okay, and you say not to worry, but it isn't all right, and I can't undo it. I know you and your father care for each other, and you're getting along well, but lost time is never found again, as my grandfather would say. I can't help feeling as if I robbed both of you. I'm lucky Goodman's the man he is. Get those papers, honey, and fill out your part tonight. We have to let him know that we appreciate what he's doing."

Krista stared at her. "He's my father, Mom. He's doing his part like you're doing yours. I appreciate you both. By the way, Miss Lurlene called you. I got excited when Daddy called me to come to the studio, and I forgot to tell you."

"Really? Lurlene hasn't called me but once since I've been back. Thanks." She didn't associate Lurlene with remorse, so the woman wouldn't have called to apologize for her attitude about Petra's trip.

She dialed Lurlene's number. "Hi, Lurlene. This is Petra. Did you call me?"

"I sure did. How come you don't feel like playing pinochle these days?"

Remorse? Why had the word even come to her mind? She let out a big belly laugh. She couldn't help it. When she could control herself, she said, "Lurlene, bless your heart, I haven't had anybody to play pinochle with."

"Well, you could play with Twylah and me if you wanted to."

"Where?" she asked, because they usually played at her house.

"Over here. Now. Won't take you but three or four minutes to get here. Nobody's asking you to dress up."

"I haven't had dinner."

"I got food."

"All right. I'll be over there in twenty minutes." She went to the bottom of the stairs and called Krista. "Can you get yourself some supper? I'm going over to Lurlene's and play pinochle."

Krista skipped halfway down the stairs. "Sure. Have a good time. I thought they were pouting about something."

"Lurlene was for sure, but they want to play cutthroat, and they need me for that." She expelled a long breath. "You wouldn't believe how I messed up, spending all that money and —"

"Oh, come on, Mom. How much debt did you pile up?"

"Around eighteen thousand dollars. And there's more. I . . . I fell in love with someone, and —"

"You *what*?"

"He's a wonderful man, and I just walked off and left him, because I didn't want him to watch me die. He doesn't know where I am or how to reach me, and I only know he lives in Oakland."

"You sure had a busy month, Mom. Give me his name. If he really does live in Oakland, I can find him. No sweat. That's what computers are for."

"Thanks, but I slipped away without telling him I was leaving, so he's probably gotten over me by now."

"Mom, you should sue the . . . You should

sue Barnes and that lab." She put her hands on her hips. "What a mess! I'm sorry, Mom. Are you going to get over him?"

"Maybe. Who knows? I'll see you later."

"Come on in, girl," Lurlene said when Petra arrived. "I got some good old southern fried chicken just like you like it."

"I'll eat it, Lurlene, if you promise not to tell anybody else that I went out West to have an abortion."

"Oh, girl, people don't take things like that seriously. I told my boss this morning that I deserved a raise, and he just laughed."

"Yeah. If I'd been there when you said it, I'd'a laughed, too," Petra said and submitted to Lurlene's hug because she knew it sufficed for an apology.

"We're having some of this fried chicken, but Twylah's eating grilled chicken breast."

Petra sat across from Twylah. "Is that true?"

"It's that or kidney and blood pressure problems. Y'all eat. I don't mind a bit."

After they ate, Lurlene cleared the table and brought out the cards, soft drinks, and hot coffee. "Let's get started. Petra, you deal. Did you meet any interesting men in California?"

"I met some really fine men in South

Dakota, Arizona, and California. I'm speaking nice guys."

Twylah pulled air through her teeth. "Then how come you're here and they're there?"

"Possibly because I couldn't pick up a six-foot-four-inch, two hundred-pound man and carry him. The one who took me to Tombstone, Arizona, had to be taller than that. Bid, Lurlene."

Lurlene sucked her teeth. "If it had been me, you bet I'd'a tried."

"Did you make out with any of them?" Twylah asked. "Tell me, so I can be jealous."

"Girl, get your mind out of the gutter," Petra said. "Think about something other than sex."

"If I don't think about it, I'll forget what it's like," Twylah said.

Lurlene trumped Twylah's ace of hearts. "Don't worry. It's like swimming. No matter how long it's been since you swam, all you have to do is get back into the water."

"How would you know?" Twylah asked in a voice suggestive of annoyance.

Lurlene raised her chin and looked into the distance. " 'Cause I've been back in the water, and boy, did I swim!"

On the surface, their camaraderie appeared to be the same as always, but Petra listened with the ears of one with a sensitivity sharpened by the experience of making every minute of her life count for something important. That experience had also lessened her tolerance for tomfoolery, she realized somewhat sadly. How long had their chitchat been full of forced gaiety?

"You know, it has just occurred to me that I haven't been really happy in years," she said.

Lurlene regarded Petra with an expression of disdain. "What you need, Petra, is a good roll in the hay."

"Be serious," Twylah said. "Petra's gotten so prissy, she wouldn't even break a sweat. A good man would be wasted on her."

Petra tossed out the ace of clubs, topped Lurlene's king, and won the hand. "You all go right on and talk about me like I wasn't here. By the way, I didn't tell you that Krista's father is sending her to Howard University. She didn't even have to ask him. Close your mouth, Lurlene. That's what a father is supposed to do."

"I thought Krista's father was dead," Lurlene said.

"A case of mistaken identity," Petra said and remembered that she'd vowed never to lie again. "Goodman Prout is Krista's father."

"I don't know the man," Twylah said. "Why the devil did you tell us he was dead? A lot of men don't marry the mother of their children."

"He would have if I had told him I was pregnant, but I didn't tell him. And don't ask me why. I was seventeen, and you could argue about the extent of my maturity."

"You couldn't have been too stupid," Lurlene said, "or you wouldn't'a done such a good job of raising Krista. When did you tell her?"

"When the doctor said I had six months at the most to live."

"Well, I'll be danged if that don't beat all," Twylah said. "You ought to thank that doctor for misleading you. If you hadn't told them, you'd be shelling out your pennies to Howard University every month for the next four years."

"I have to get up early tomorrow morning. Judge Harper will be sitting, and you don't dare be late to his trials." She stood, and allowed herself a deep yawn. "Thanks for calling me, Lurlene. I sure enjoyed it. Next week at my house?"

"Of course," they said in unison.

Petra headed home walking at a fast clip.

She had indeed enjoyed playing cards. But although she still loved her two friends, for the first time, she was critical of them. She saw them as frivolous. Were they, or was it that her values had changed? *I don't want to judge my friends or anyone else. I only want to enjoy being alive.*

When she walked into her house, Krista said, "Mom, a Dr. Hayes called you from Atlanta. He said for you to call him tomorrow morning between nine and eleven o'clock. And he said don't worry; nothing's wrong."

"Thanks, hon. Looks as if I'll have to go to Atlanta for a checkup. I feel fine, but —"

"But he wants to be sure. If you don't have any money, I can give you some for your ticket."

"Krista, you can't know how proud I am that you could help me, but since Goodman's sending you to school, life will be easier for me."

After speaking with the doctor the next morning, Petra obtained a two-day leave of absence from work, got her mother to stay with Krista, and flew to Atlanta that evening. He'd said it was a routine exam, and she hoped he was right.

Chapter Twelve

Petra walked into Dr. Mark Hayes's office the next morning with her head high, feigning courage and nonchalance, but the touch of her fingers felt like ice on her skin, and she'd have sworn that both of her feet were wooden planks.

The doctor stood, extended his hand, and smiled. "You look wonderful, Ms. Fields. I don't have any news for you, good or bad, but I have to examine you before I release you. We'll take a lot of tests today, and I should have the results by tomorrow morning. If we don't find anything, you may go home."

"That's nice, Dr. Hayes, but I didn't book a hotel room for tonight, and my ticket is for a six o'clock plane back to Baltimore."

He fingered his chin, obviously searching for a solution. "Then I'll check you into the hospital. Give me your plane ticket. With a doctor's certificate, we can get that changed without cost, and if you want to telephone anyone back in Ellicott City, speak to my secretary. Go down to admissions, and then come back here. All right?"

"Yes, sir."

After getting admitted, she stopped at the newsstand, purchased papers, magazines, and a bag of miniature Snickers, and went back to the doctor's office.

Mark Hayes looked from Petra's small suitcase to her and back to the luggage. "You'd better leave that here until we get you a room. We'll get the MRI and CAT scan first; then we'll do some blood tests. Later, I'll check your equilibrium. Okay?"

Petra agreed. At the end of the day, with the tests behind her, exhaustion prevented her from reading, so she watched television for a few minutes and fell asleep. After breakfast the next morning, she dressed, packed her bag, and waited for Dr. Hayes. As promised, he walked into her room at nine o'clock.

"You're in great shape," he said, "and you shouldn't have any problems. It's a job I'm proud of. I understand Dr. Barnes is suing that laboratory. I sent him an affidavit."

"Oh, dear. I may need one, too."

"Your lawyer — Lyons, is it — has been in contact with me, and I'll send him a copy of my final report on this case. You're discharged."

"Thank you so much, Doctor. By the way, I haven't received a bill from you or from the hospital."

"Don't worry. It's taken care of." He shook hands with her. "Your case will be reported in a medical journal, but your identity will be protected. I hope you don't mind."

"No, indeed. Good-bye, Dr. Hayes, and thanks again."

Before Petra could get her keys out of her pocketbook, her mother opened the door. "Well, what happened? I don't see no reason why you had to go back there in such a hurry. You sure you went to see the doctor?"

Petra dropped her suitcase beside the door. Nothing ever changed with Lena Fields. "Hi, Mama. The doctor took a lot of tests, and he's satisfied that I healed up all right. He released me. I'm fine."

Lena picked up Petra's bag as if to take it upstairs, but dropped it and fastened her knuckles to her hips. "Who was that man that called here last night? And after midnight, too."

The hair on Petra's hair crackled as if

electrified. “How would I know, Mama? Did you get his name?”

“I didn’t need his name, waking me up after midnight, and I have to get up at six o’clock. ‘Is Miz Petra Fields there?’ ” She mimicked him, rolling her eyes toward the ceiling. “I told him I’m her mother, and don’t call here after midnight again.”

Petra picked up the suitcase and headed up the stairs to her room. Winston didn’t know how to find her, so she didn’t care who had called. She suspected the witness at the Hobart trial of having located her name and address with the intention of making a nuisance of himself. If he persisted, she would report him.

“I guess I can go on back home,” Petra’s mother called up to her. “I need to do my uniforms. Did I tell you that Reverend Collins wants you to call him? Lord bless him; he’s a good man. Thank goodness your head healed up all right. Hug Krista for me; she was real good. I’ll call you.”

The front door slammed, and Petra breathed deeply in relief. She loved her mother, and she had never doubted that Lena loved her, but she couldn’t understand why such a rigid perspective on right and wrong colored everything her mother did and said, even when it had to do with her own child. She learned fairness, honesty, and kindness from her mother, but few people who knew Lena would believe it. They saw Lena Fields as a rigid and judgmental woman.

She had wondered more than once if her mother's hard take on life came before or after Lena conceived her only child. Maybe Lena had become bitter when her husband deserted her for her best friend. She'd probably never know the answer.

Petra fried the catfish that her mother had stored in the refrigerator, baked cornbread, and steamed string beans. Krista arrived from work as she finished setting the table.

Krista ran to her. "Mom! You're back. You all right?"

"I'm fine," she told her excited daughter. "Dr. Hayes thinks he did a perfect job. I don't have to go back."

Krista hugged Petra and kissed her cheek. "Cool. I was scared. Feeling that real deep. Guess what, Mom."

"What?" Krista always began an important piece of news with "guess what."

"Miss Carla called me and invited me to Daddy's surprise birthday party Saturday evening. She's sending Peter — he's sixteen — to get me in her car, and she said I'm not to breathe a word of it to Daddy. I said yes, but she's gonna call and ask you if it's all right."

Petra nearly spilled a dish of string beans. "Are you making this up?"

"No, ma'am. She surprised me, too. I didn't mark her down as miss Warm and Friendly, but she was real nice on the phone."

"If there's anything I've learned in the past few months, it's not to judge people solely on the basis of what you can see. Remember that she's your stepmother."

"Yeah. You told me. It's funny having a stepmother. Some of my friends have them, but that's because their parents are divorced, and their dads remarried. Gee, this is weird."

About an hour after they finished supper, Petra answered the telephone and heard Carla Prout's voice for the first time. The woman repeated her invitation to Krista.

"This is a very nice gesture on your part, Mrs. Prout," Petra said, "and I appreciate it."

"It's the right thing to do. Goodman loves Krista, and all of his children should be with him on his birthday. Thank you for allowing her to come."

"It wouldn't occur to me to say no. I'm happy that they're developing a healthy, father-daughter relationship."

"So am I, Ms. Fields. My son, Peter, will be at your house around five-thirty Saturday."

"I presume it's a dressy affair?"

"Yes. Thank you for asking. I didn't know how to broach that to Krista."

Petra hung up and knocked on Krista's door. "That was Carla. She said it's a dressy affair. I'll meet you at Dwill's at five o'clock tomorrow, and we'll get you a nice dress — one that covers your behind — and some shoes. You need things for school anyway."

"Okay, Mom, but can we afford this?"

"Don't worry, honey. I'll get some money when that case is settled. It may not be much, but it will be enough to pay for your clothes."

Goodman parked in his garage at exactly seven o'clock that Saturday evening. "Where're you going?" he asked Paul. His younger son had insisted that he needed a saber jacket and mask for his fencing exhibition match the following Monday morning, and he'd taken him to Baltimore to get them.

"Nature calls, Dad," Paul said and dashed into the house.

Where was everybody? On an early evening in mid-September, his family could usually be found on the deck either roasting something or preparing to eat something that had been roasted. He removed Paul's fencing gear from the trunk of his Lexus, tried the kitchen door, saw that it was locked, and walked around to the front of his house.

"Some of the neighbors must be having guests," he said to himself when he noticed the extra automobiles parked throughout the block. "We used to have parties and friends in occasionally, but Carla isn't inclined to do that these days. Oh, well." He let out a deep breath and opened the front door.

"What the . . . Where's everybody? What's this I smell?"

Suddenly, a camera flashed, then the house came ablaze. "Happy birthday to you. Happy birthday to you," they sang and crowded around him.

"What on earth?" he exclaimed, blinking his eyes. And then his children, Peter, Krista, and Paul crowded around him, hugging him and telling him "happy birthday." He looked through the many faces that he recognized and saw Carla walking toward him. How had he been so foolish? What had possessed him to cheat on her? He'd made only a tiny effort to get their marriage back on track, and she had responded so eagerly. He didn't bother to wipe his tears. He didn't think he would ever forgive himself.

He took his wife into his arms and pressed his lips to her waiting mouth. "Thank you for . . . for everything, and especially for inviting Krista to celebrate with me along with her brothers. I had expected we'd have a cookout or something." He hugged her close to his body. "Does Paul really need that fencing gear?" he asked her with a wide grin.

"Not that I know of," Carla said. "We can return it next week. Have you noticed what a beautiful young woman Krista is? In that sexy green dress and those spike heels, and with her hair curling around her shoulders, I hardly recognized her."

"Peter and Paul aren't showing any slack," he said. "They look like gentlemen. Do I have to say something to our guests?"

"After I start it off, then you may say a few words, but not too many. Everyone's hungry."

Throughout the evening, making small talk with his family and friends, his mind didn't stray far from the colossal error he'd made with Jada Hankins and what it could one day cost him. Later, after thanking the guests for the surprise and bidding them good night, he prepared to take Krista home. But he discovered that he resented doing it, not because he considered it an inconvenience, but because his children belonged in *his* home.

"Don't even dream it," he warned himself. "I'll take you home," he said to Krista.

"Oh, not yet, Daddy. Paul, Peter, and I are going to straighten up the kitchen. You got an apron?"

"We are?" Peter asked, clearly aghast.

Krista put her hands on his shoulders and turned him toward the kitchen door. "Yes, we are, big brother. Come on, Paul. You, too. Your mama must be half dead already, so we're not going to dump this on her. Do you have a radio in this kitchen?"

"Yeah, right over there," Paul said, pointing to a place on a counter.

"Good," Krista said. "Music makes work a lot easier."

"I can clean up in the morning," Carla said.

"We'll do it," Krista told her. "You keep Daddy company."

Goodman leaned against the grand piano thinking about his blessings and vowed to stop taking them for granted. Carla joined him, took his hand, and said, "Let's go sit down. I thought I was something special because I had given my husband two sons and no daughters, but I see that daughters can be wonderful. Maybe the boys will consider helping in the kitchen sometimes."

He eased an arm around her waist and hugged her. "If I didn't already love you, I think I'd fall head-over-heels for you. Let's work hard at keeping what we've found again."

She nestled closer. "I want to, Goodman. I thought I was losing you. I don't know what brought you back to me, and that's not what's important, but I'm happy for it."

"I slipped," he heard himself tell her — as the words sent shock waves through him — "and I've deeply regretted it. You and I had a problem, and we treated each other as if that problem wasn't there. I faced the fact that the way I dealt with it was wrong, dishonorable. I walked away from it, because I have to respect myself."

"I know. Is it over?"

"Absolutely. It barely started. I realized that it wasn't my style and decided to try and rebuild our relationship."

Carla rested her head on his chest. "I didn't think I'd ever be this happy again. I helped create the problem, and I'll do what

I can to help solve it. We're going to be all right."

A second after he bent to her eager mouth, he heard Paul say in a voice tinged with mirth, "Hey, you two, break it up. I'm underage, and I'm not supposed to be looking at heavy duty stuff like that."

"Leave 'em alone," Peter said. "Let 'em have fun while they're still young."

"You guys are fresh," Krista said. "Ready when you are, Daddy."

He gazed down at Carla for a second, bent to her lips with what was more a promise than a kiss. "See you later," he whispered, feeling like a man released from jail and hearing the sound of prison gates slam behind him.

When she heard Krista's key in the front door lock, Petra raced to the door. She had spent the evening worrying about the treatment her daughter would receive at her father's birthday party, and whether Carla may have had an ulterior motive in inviting her.

"How did it go?" she asked.

"Great. I met some cool people. Miss Carla was real nice. I mean she was great, Mom. She introduced me as her stepdaughter. My brothers were super, too. Guess what?"

"What?" Petra asked as they walked to the living room. "I made Peter and Paul help me clean the kitchen after the guests left. They'd never done that before. After they eat, they go sit on their butts while Miss Carla cleans up the kitchen. I told them I'd rather have daughters than sons 'cause I always help my mom. We had a good time together while we were cleaning up. I'm going to teach Peter how to do the Electric Slide."

Petra released a long breath. "You can't even imagine how relieved I am. I didn't know what to expect."

"Not to worry, Mom. I can hold my own. Mom . . . I think Daddy ought to stop fooling with Jada. Why do men do things like that?"

"Are you saying he's having an affair with her?"

"I already told you about that. He says there's nothing between them, but she acts as if she has some special rights with him. I'm not stupid, and I'm going to tell him to stop it, or I'll tell Miss Carla. I have a good mind to tell her anyway."

Petra sprang from her seat on the sofa. "For Heaven's sake, don't do that, Krista.

Don't ever do a thing like that. You could cause the destruction of that marriage. I'll be back in a second."

She went to the kitchen and got a bottle of lemonade for Krista, a can of ginger ale for herself, and two glasses. "It isn't easy for me to tell you this, but I see that I have to." She poured the ginger ale into the glass and took a few sips, not so much because she would enjoy it as to procrastinate. She didn't relish telling her daughter what she'd done.

"You remember when I told you the truth about your father. Well, as you know, I did it because I thought I was dying. Reverend Collins told me I had to ask forgiveness of every person I had harmed, mistreated, or hurt in any way." She swallowed hard and told herself to go on.

"I'm ashamed to tell you that on one foolish occasion, almost a decade ago, I slept with . . . with Fred, Ethel's husband, and —"

"You *what*?"

Petra blew out a long breath. "I've already had to deal with enough drama about this, Krista, so let me get to the point, please."

Krista found something on the floor to look at. "I can't wait to hear it."

"Following old man Collins's advice, I

told Ethel about it and asked her to forgive me. Ethel nearly went berserk, poor Fred had to leave home in broad daylight practically nude and holding up his jockey shorts with one hand, and . . . Listen, Krista, if I'd thought it was funny, I wouldn't have told you."

"Mom, I've got this picture of Mr. Fred flying out of the house nude and barefooted, holding up his drawers, his belly hanging out over them, and Miss Ethel chasing him with a broom." She rested her head on the back of the chair and whooped.

"Krista, my point in telling you this is that if I hadn't told Ethel about that one time, they would still be together. Now, they're separated, and Ethel is miserable."

Krista looked toward the ceiling. "If I'd been married to him — Heaven forbid — I'd have been miserable from the moment I said, 'I do.' What could you have been thinking, Mom?"

"He was the biggest braggart you ever saw. I was twenty, and he must have been thirty-five. I hadn't been seeing anyone since Goodman and I broke up almost three years earlier, and Fred made me think he could spin the world backward. Turned out he had no idea what he was doing, and I was disgusted with myself. I kept it inside for years. Now, they're on the outs, and Ethel and I will never be the friends we once were."

Krista got up, collected what remained from their drinks, and took it to the kitchen. "Miss Ethel shouldn't feel too badly, Mom. I've seen at least two men over at her house when Mr. Fred was at work, and they usually stayed long enough to create a little mischief. Haven't seen that recently, though; actually not since I was about thirteen. Gotta go get some shut-eye. 'Nite."

"Wait, Krista. I told you that, because I don't want you to do or say anything that will break up Goodman and Carla. She'd be miserable if she knew that, and her pride would make her leave him, or more likely, she would ask him to leave her and their children."

She stood and grasped Krista's shoulders. "Please don't mention this to Carla. You can say anything to your father that he allows when the two of you are alone, but not in the presence of anyone else. And whatever you do, don't breathe it to his sons."

"Okay, I won't, but if I catch her sidling up to him again, I'm going to give both of them a piece of my mind."

"Be careful, Krista. Never overplay your hand. Love doesn't cover everything, and you never know when you've crossed the line until you get a shock."

Krista's face sagged, reminding Petra of three-year-old Krista's response when told that she couldn't have more candy, ice cream, or lemonade. "It's for the best, honey," Petra said.

"He acts like he loves Carla. How can he fool with Jada?"

"If he told you there's nothing between them, he's probably telling the truth. Perhaps there had been something, and he ended it. Some women are persistent in these matters. Be careful."

"Yes, ma'am. Growing up is not easy."

Petra could attest to that. At Krista's age, she'd gotten pregnant and had to face her religious, born-again mother. She would always remember it as one of the darkest days of her life.

Petra stepped out on her back porch and gazed at her garden, the young trees now bare of all but a few leaves, but eerily beautiful as the branches stood shrouded in the moonlight like ghostly creatures devoid of life. The rising wind caused her to shiver, and she folded her arms across her bosom for warmth. Not a light shone in Ethel's house. Was that Ethel sitting on the porch? She opened the screen door and stepped outside in order to get a better look. Seeing her friend in a listless pose, she walked to the fence and called her.

"Ethel. Is that you, Ethel? Anything wrong with your electricity?"

"Petra? I just don't feel like being in this big old house by myself."

She hadn't counted on that complication. "You want to come over here and sleep on my sofa?"

"Thanks, but I guess not. You feel responsible for me, but there's no need for that. I brought this on myself. It's been a good fifteen years since Fred and I slept in the same bed. I caught him cheating, and I told him he could stay, but he was never going to touch me again. Then, I cheated and with more men than Jasper Collins, too. Fred wants to come back, but in the time he's been gone, I got used to not hearing him snore. I just don't like living by myself."

"Well, whenever you think you could use some company, I'm here." Petra went back inside and got ready for bed. She'd never realized that life could change so drastically for so many people in a few short months, and she sensed that greater changes were yet to come. "Trust they'll be for the best," her mother said, when she mentioned to Lena her premonitions.

Krista came home Monday night after her piano lesson and choral rehearsal and flopped down in the dining room where Petra, Twylah, and Lurlene were playing pinochle. "I can't believe I'll be entering college in two weeks," Krista said, holding her admissions letter high for all to see. "Daddy assured me that with my 3.75 average, I wouldn't have a problem getting into college. I'm happy, but I hate to give up my piano lessons. I'm already playing simple hymns and other pieces. Daddy's a great teacher, Mom."

"I see Krista love her daddy," Lurlene said when Krista went up to her room.

"She does, and he loves her," Petra said, surprised by the pride in her voice. "I have to figure out how to get her a piano. She wants a grand, and that's almost like buying an automobile."

"You'll manage," Lurlene said. "That's what we women do; we manage."

"I hear Armena put Fred out. She said she wasn't putting up with no man who didn't know how to diddle," Twylah said. "Don't that beat all?"

Petra's cards fluttered to the floor. "When did you hear that, Twylah?"

"Yesterday morning after church service. I hadn't gotten halfway down the aisle before

Rosa told me. Maybe he'll go back to Ethel."

"Maybe. Let's call it a night. I want to speak with Krista before she goes to bed."

The next day on her lunch hour, Petra went back to see the credit card company representative again. "I have to lay out a considerable expenditure," she told the man, "and I'd also like to reduce my payments by twenty dollars a month. My daughter is entering college the first of the month, and I don't suppose I need to say more." She hadn't lied, and she didn't intend to. She left with a reduced payment plan, wondering if she would ever stop atoning for that month of freedom. Krista would get a discount at Dwill's, but Petra didn't want Krista to spend the money she'd saved for college on clothes and other necessities.

Still, feeling that her life would run more smoothly, at least for the near future, Petra hummed a favorite tune as she hurried up the courthouse's concrete steps in order to get back to her office before her lunch hour expired.

"Sorry. My dear, I wouldn't have hurt you for the world. Are you all right?"

Petra looked up from where she lay sprawled at the top of the courthouse steps and gazed into the eyes of the star witness at the Hobart trial. He reached down to help her up, but she knocked his hand aside.

"Leave me alone," she sneered. She limped to her office favoring a bruised leg and browsed through her notes to check the man's name. After finding it, she phoned the court officer and registered a complaint. "I don't know why he's pursuing me," she told the officer, "but I'm suspicious."

"Did you tell him that it's illegal for you to talk with him?"

"I sure did, and he suggested we see each other anyway."

"Avoid him. I'll put in your report."

She thanked the officer and set about transcribing the previous session's notes. The ring of her cell phone interrupted her. "Don't mention that I asked you for a date. It wouldn't be wise."

It took her a few seconds to close her mouth for she recognized the voice. She flipped on her recorder. "Are you threatening me?"

"No, my dear. I would never harm you. I'm so enchanted with you. Please don't deny me any longer." The voice suddenly became less obsequious. "And don't you dare report this conversation to anyone. You hear me?"

She hung up, as chills streaked through her. "He's testing your mettle," her lawyer said when she told him about it. "Don't worry. We're going to put an end to this." However, her lawyer didn't act quickly enough.

Petra arrived home around five-thirty that afternoon to find Krista, whose day off it was, cooking her special chili con carne for her brothers, Peter and Paul. The boys sat in the kitchen watching the process as Krista worked.

"Hi, Mom. Paul, this is my mom. Mom, you remember Peter. They like chili, and when I hinted that chili was my specialty, they invited themselves to check it out."

Petra greeted Paul, a tall, handsome boy much like his father and siblings, who embraced her with a hug. "I hope you don't mind Peter and me barging in on you, but chili is our favorite dish, and our mom has no idea how to make it."

"I'm delighted to have you here," she said. "You're welcome to come whenever you like and as often as you like. If you love chili, you're in for a treat. Krista's chili is hard to beat. I'll be down shortly. I want to change my clothes."

"Mom, don't bother cooking for Paul and me," she heard Peter say, evidently using his cell phone. "Krista's making a big pot of chili, so you know we'll be full when we get home."

After a meal of chili, rice, and broccoli, with vanilla and raspberry ice cream for dessert, Petra sat in the living room watching television while Krista and her brothers cleaned the kitchen. She heard the doorbell ring and rose to open the door.

"Stay right where you are," Peter said. "I'll get it."

"You want to speak with Mrs. Fields?" she heard him say.

"Who is it, Peter?" Krista called.

"A man who wants to speak with your mother."

Cold chills shot down Petra's spine when she glimpsed the man's reflection in the hall mirror. When she yelled, "I don't want to see that man," Paul rushed from the kitchen to the front door.

"What do you want with her?" Paul asked him, "and what's your name?"

"My name is not your business."

"The hell it's not," Paul said. "You come here asking for her, and you tell us it's not our business. She just said she doesn't want to see you."

"I'm not leaving here till I see her," the man said.

"You planning to walk through us?" Paul asked the man. "I wouldn't try it if I were you."

Petra gave silent thanks for the presence of Krista's brothers and shuddered as if expelling all the air from her lungs when, from the dining room window, she saw a police car pull up to the front of her house. Thank God, Krista had phoned for help.

Two policemen rushed up the walk. "What's the problem here?"

Petra joined the boys at the front door, explained to the policemen the man's insistence upon breaking the law, and that she had already reported him to the court officer.

"I doubt you'll have more trouble out of this man, ma'am," one of the officers said.

"I don't know what we would have done if you hadn't been here," Petra told Peter and Paul. "Both of you are bigger than that guy, but I wouldn't want to see you get into a fracas with anyone."

"I'm planning to study law," Peter said. "Do you think I could sit in on some of those cases? I could write a paper on it and use it for my senior project."

"I will ask permission tomorrow."

The next morning immediately after Petra got to work, the court officer knocked on her office door. "Judge Harper wants to see you."

She unlocked her desk, removed her tape recorder, and accompanied the officer to the judge's chambers. "Don't be nervous, Ms. Fields," the judge said when Petra folded and unfolded her arms and then locked her hands behind her in an effort to control them. "Have a seat. A police officer delivered this report to me a few minutes ago. Do you have any idea how this witness found your home address?"

"I'm listed in the phone book, Your Honor." She handed the judge her small recorder. "He warned me not to report him; it sounded to me like a threat. I happened to record that."

"Good. I commend you for not having allowed him to charm you into breaking the law."

"Thank you, sir. Your Honor, my daughter's half brother is a high school senior who's planning to study law, and he wants to sit in court and write a report on his observations for his senior civics paper. Is that possible?"

"Leave the information with my clerk, and he'll have a pass ready when you leave today."

She thanked the judge, stood to leave, and

had a second thought. "Your Honor, what if that man tries to get even with me?"

"He'd have to do it from jail. He attempted to bribe a juror and managed to date another one. In your case, he attempted to obstruct justice. By the time he gets out of jail, he won't remember what you look like."

Goodman had not expected Jada to contact him again, so her phone call both surprised and angered him. "I know you don't like interruptions," she said, "but I'm behind in my rent, and I was wondering if you could help me out." If his silence distressed her, he didn't much care. "I could meet you downstairs at the studio, or —"

"Or what, Jada?"

"Or I could come upstairs and wait till you can stop what you're doing and let me have a couple hundred dollars."

"Jada, I'm surprised that you're so transparent. I really thought you were more clever. You can't blackmail me, Jada, because I sat down with my wife last Saturday night and told her what went on between us, including your attempt to barter sex for a condominium apartment. So if you tell her, she won't be surprised. In fact, I'm going to tell her about this conversation." He began pounding his fist on his desk as if to reinforce his point. "When I told you it was over between us, I meant it. Don't come back to the Oella Community Chorus. We both know that was never your real interest. I'm sorry we couldn't have remained friends."

He didn't feel good about trouncing Jada, but what choice did he have? He had learned that if you gave the woman an inch, she took a mile. He'd served her well in bed, but she could forget about that; he'd finished with cheating.

When Petra got home that evening, she gave the court pass to Krista. "This is for Peter," she told her.

Although Carla had telephoned her once previously, it nonetheless surprised Petra to receive the woman's call. "I don't know how to thank you for getting that pass for Peter. He'll be ecstatic when he learns that he'll be able to sit in court."

"I was glad to do it, Carla. Children need encouragement. I thank you for allowing Krista to share your family's life. She's so happy to know her brothers. Tell me, is it true that you can't make chili?"

"Absolutely true."

"I could give you a good recipe."

"Oh, no," Carla said in a voice that carried a sound akin to terror. "Thank you, but I don't want to learn. As long as Krista's willing to make it, I'm satisfied just to eat it. She sent me some, and I'd never tasted any that good."

After Petra hung up, she called Lena. "Mama, I want to cut a deal with you. Krista needs a piano, and I don't have the money. It'll take what I have for the things she needs for college. You don't like living alone and, especially, eating by yourself. Why don't you buy Krista a piano, close your apartment, which you hate, and move in with Krista and me." She would have to learn to tune out her mother's constant negativism. Maybe if she didn't respond to the complaints, accusations, and put-downs, she'd hear fewer of them.

"Sounds good," Lena said. "I get tired of sitting here looking at these old walls. The place needs painting, but I can't get the landlord to lift a finger. If Krista's going to college, why does she need a piano here?"

"She'll be home on weekends, Mama, and Goodman said she's doing well, but she needs to practice more."

"Well, it's a bargain," Lena said. "I want her to have the opportunities that you and I didn't have — not that you couldn't have had 'em if you'd stayed away from Goodman Prout like I warned you. If Goodman's paying for her college, I can sure buy her a grand. May as well do something big for once." They talked for a few minutes, and Petra marveled at her mother's lack of stridency and attempts at joviality.

If only she could get her own life in order. "I wonder what would happen if I went to Oakland and searched for Winston." She pulled air through her front teeth, disgusted with the situation in which she found herself. Go to Oakland? Heck, she could hardly afford a taxi to the airport. Sitting on the edge of her bed, alone in the house because Krista had gone bowling with Paul, Petra wiped tears that she rarely allowed to flow.

Sometimes I miss him so much that I feel like I'm drowning in loneliness. She got up and washed her face. "I can't afford to think this way," she said to herself. "If I do, I'll be miserable for the rest of my life. At least I'm alive and well."

Several days later, Petra rearranged her living room and then watched as delivery men placed a Baldwin grand between the fireplace and the picture window.

"I can't wait till Krista sees it," Lena said, smiling more happily than Petra had ever witnessed. "When you gon' call Reverend Collins?" she asked immediately, as if she couldn't bear the camaraderie with her daughter. "He asked about you at prayer meeting, Wednesday night. 'Course nobody expects you to go to prayer meeting."

If she told her mother what she thought of Jasper Collins, Lena would preach and pray over her for a week, so she didn't comment. As it happened, she encountered the preacher when she stopped at the supermarket on her way home the next afternoon.

"I'm fine, Reverend Collins," she told him when he asked, "but some of the people I asked to forgive me aren't fine. Ethel and Fred separated, and she's miserable. Sally's girlfriend left her, and Sally hates me."

He looked as if a bomb dropped directly in front of him. "Ethel and Fred separated, you say?"

"Yes, they did. I told Ethel I once slept with Fred, and she kicked him out. I wasn't involved with Sally and Gail."

He seemed not to have heard what she said about Sally or that she had confessed to sleeping with Ethel's husband. Shaking his head slowly, he said, "Ethel and Fred, huh?"

"That's right, Reverend, and Ethel confessed to some hanky-panky of her own. You know, Reverend, my reputation has taken a beating. Those things I asked people to forgive me for weren't all that bad, except for sleeping with Fred, but add it up, and I seem like an awful person. People in this town talk, and while they're talking, they embellish. My best friends have heard stuff. They haven't said so, but I'm judging from the way they act.

"It wouldn't have mattered much if I had died, but I'm alive, and it hurts. I'd as soon wipe the Ellicott City dirt off my feet for good and never look back." She didn't wait for his response.

When she arrived at work the next morning, she saw the red light on her phone blinking. "This is Petra Fields. How may I help you?"

"Ms. Fields, this is Attorney Eric Lyons. Can we meet in my office at noon? We've settled the suit."

Chapter Thirteen

With the sun's rays caressing his body, Winston Fleet reclined in the hammock tied between two aged California walnut trees in the back of his grandmother's house, where he loved to lie after a brisk swim in the pool. He closed his eyes, though he wouldn't sleep, for his grandmother always seemed to think he needed food and a cold drink after swimming. He knew without hearing a sound that she'd come to sit on the stool a few feet away; somehow, he always felt her presence.

"I brought you some lemonade and a slice of chocolate cake," she said, "and I've got some nice hot buttermilk biscuits in there if you want some." He'd rather have the biscuits than the cake, but he didn't tell her because he didn't want her to get up, and he was too comfortable to contemplate moving.

"When are you leaving?" she asked him.

"Why are you so certain that I'm going anyplace?"

"You're tormented. That's why."

"Considering the time she said she had left, it's probably over," he said, truly acknowledging that possibility for the first time. He marveled that he and his grandmother discussed Petra without either of them mentioning her name.

"I don't see a thing dark around her. She's alive and among living beings. It's not all smooth, mind you, but I told you once, like I told her: she'll be back out here."

"I hadn't planned to look, but not knowing finally got the better of me. I found her address and phone number in Ellicott City, Maryland, but I didn't get much satisfaction from that call, because the woman who answered the phone said she wasn't there and hung up. That left me wondering about the kind of people she lives with."

"What time did you call and when?"

"Night before last, around midnight there. When I got the number, I was so excited that I couldn't wait to find out how she was and to talk with her. Boy, what a letdown!"

"You probably woke somebody up."

"I guess. Don't think I've given up. I haven't. At least the person didn't say that she doesn't live there. I'll find her, even if she's been laid to rest and even if I have to walk all the way from Oakland to Ellicott City, Maryland."

"She hasn't been laid to rest. Next time you call, be sure you do it at a reasonable hour. The ice is melting in this pitcher of lemonade."

He swung off the hammock, went over to her, and poured a glass full. "If it wasn't for you, I'd probably be off my rocker by now. Thanks for the encouragement. Sometimes it's seemed as if I'm staring into a vast nothingness." He leaned down and kissed her forehead.

"Men usually think they're sinking when they fall in love. You're no different."

A half laugh slipped out of him. "It happened so fast that there wasn't time to think about sinking or anything else. It's getting cloudy. I'll put these chairs in the garage for you. Then I have to go." He doubted that anyone would believe he discussed his personal affairs with his grandmother. He'd done it for as long as he'd known himself, and she had yet to censure him. He couldn't imagine what he'd do without her.

He drove slowly as he headed to Oakland. Whenever he drove along that two-lane road leading to the highway, it was as if Petra was there with him, for he relived the time when she went with him to his grandmother's house. If only he could be with her again and know if the Petra he remembered, the one he loved, was real. He got home shortly before five, went inside, and phoned his travel agent.

In Ellicott City, Krista's shrieks caused Petra nearly to fall down the stairs in her rush to know what ailed her daughter. Then she remembered the grand piano and walked down more carefully. She stood on the bottom step watching Krista run her hands over the wood, as if testing it or adoring it, she didn't know which.

"You like it?"

"Do I like it?" She jumped up with her arms toward the ceiling. "You asking me if I like it? I think I'm going to faint."

"Please don't do that. Mama bought it for you."

When Krista gasped, Petra said. "We have to talk. Mama's going to live with us now, so she said that since she won't have the upkeep of that apartment, she'd buy the piano."

"Gee. That's real deep. You won't be alone while I'm at school; I'll have a piano when I'm home weekends, and Grandma won't be by herself." A grin crawled over Krista's face. "And Grandma is a better cook than either you or me. I'd better practice. Won't Daddy be surprised!"

"I'll be at your department at Dwill's tomorrow at five. We have to start shopping for your college things."

The next morning, Petra sat in her lawyer's office. Speechless. "The laboratory made an offer of two hundred and sixty thousand," he said, "and I suggest you take it. If we turn it down, they'll ask for a jury trial, and you probably won't get as much. If the laboratory's error had caused you physical harm, you'd have gotten at least seven figures, but it didn't harm you, only frightened and inconvenienced you."

She was in no mood to tamper with a sure thing. After the lawyer took his forty percent, she'd still have one hundred and fifty-six thousand dollars. She would be able to pay her bills, wipe out her mortgage, and have some left for a nest egg. "All right," she said. "Let's settle."

"Good. I should be able to complete the transactions within a couple of days."

"I'm not throwing this money away," she said to herself, "but I'll be able to get a good little used car. Maybe I can get one at an auction of repossessed cars." She felt lighthearted and happier than she'd been in months, now that she had money in the bank once more.

She swished into her house several days later and stopped as if she'd been poleaxed. Goodman Prout sat at Krista's piano.

"Oh! Uh . . . hello," she said, seeing him for the second time since she told him he had a daughter named Krista Fields.

He got up, walked to meet her, and extended his hand. "How are you, Petra? I'm tuning the piano, and this one's a beauty," he told her. "Fortunately I know how. I hope you don't mind, but whenever you move one of these babies, it must be tuned. Even moving it three feet can affect the tone."

"I don't mind at all. In fact, I'm grateful. How is Krista progressing?"

"Beautifully. She takes to music the way a bird takes to the air. I'd say she has a natural gift for music. My sons are musical, too, but not nearly to the extent that Krista is. Thank you for giving me a chance to be a part of her life."

"I'm ashamed that I only did it under the threat of death. Her father should have had an opportunity to help nurture her."

"I've thought about that a lot, Petra, and I know I could have made a difference, but I'm not dwelling on it. We have a good relationship now, and that's more than many parents can say of their eighteen-year-old daughters. She's all set for Howard University, and I'm as excited as she is."

"So am I, and nervous. She'll be on her own for the first time, and I hope she remembers what she's been taught."

"It takes a smart one to get past Krista. She's got some strong principles, and she's very observant, so I'm not worried about her, and neither should you be. I'll drive her to school, and you're welcome to come with us. I hope we can agree on her restrictions. I wouldn't like to see her stay away from the dormitory any night except when she's here, that is, unless the university is responsible."

"I agree. She's planning to come home every weekend for her music lessons. I don't know how long that will last."

"If she wants to participate in something at school, she'll have to let us know in advance," he said, "and as long as we're together on this, she'll cooperate."

How good it would have been all those years to share the parenting with him. She hadn't been wise, but she hadn't made a good relationship between Goodman and Krista impossible. For that, she would always be grateful.

"What y'all doing with this door wide open? The devil's still busy you know. I brought some flow—" Lena's lower lip dropped, and she stared at Goodman, who stood only a few feet from Petra. "What you doing here? You a married man, for Heaven's sake. When you shoulda been here, you wasn't."

Petra grabbed her mother's arm. "Mama, we have to get this straight right now. If I had told Goodman about Krista, he would have been here for her then just as he is now."

Lena put the flowers on a chair. She narrowed her eyes. "Some people are like puppies: feed 'em once, and they always come back. Krista's grown now, and she don't need you."

"Calm down, Miss Lena. You're getting hot for nothing. Krista will be eighteen soon, and, from then on, what she does or with whom will be none of your business. Her mother and I are cooperating like civilized people, and you can do your share. This piano is out of tune; Krista asked me to tune it; and I am going to tune it. Period!"

"When did you learn how to tune a piano? All I ever saw you with was that good-for-nothing guitar."

Goodman turned to Petra with a shrug

that suggested the hopelessness of trying to talk with Lena. "You explain it to her," he said to Petra.

"Mama, Goodman owns and operates a music studio."

"Oh, I know he's teaching Krista the piano, but . . ." She threw up her hands. "I gotta put these flowers in some water." It wasn't often that Petra saw her mother capitulate, and it gave her a good feeling. Maybe she'd be less difficult to live with than formerly.

"I'm thinking of buying a little used car," she said to Goodman. "You know, one of those that the banks or rental car companies auction off."

He wrote something on the back of a card. "Call that number, and don't accept the first price. Bargain."

"Thanks. I'll leave you alone and get supper started. Krista's shopping this evening."

"I know," he said, and she realized that she knew nothing of Krista's relationship with her father. A little over an hour later, the sound of Mozart's Piano Concerto No. 23 floated through the house. She stumbled into the living room stunned by the elegance of his playing.

Lena joined her. "I never heard such playing. And that piano sounds fantastic."

"It's fine now," he said, ignoring the praise. "I have to get on home. Good seeing you both."

Petra walked to the door with him. "I'll see about getting leave from the office in January to go to Washington with you and Krista. Thank you for letting me join you."

"It's the right thing to do, Petra. You gave me a beautiful, well-mannered, charming, and intelligent daughter, and you deserve to share her every moment of glory. Call me when you know whether you can travel with us."

"I will, and please give my regards to Carla and the boys."

Give her regards to his wife and children? Goodman didn't know how to deal with that, for neither his wife nor his sons had confided to him that they knew or had had contact with Petra. He didn't want to join the two families, but he wanted their relations to be cordial. Carla opened the door for him, as she had recently begun to do, and stood on tiptoe for his kiss. He gazed down at her and couldn't help grinning. She wanted him, and hell, jolts of happiness shot through him. He slapped her on her buttocks, picked her up, and let her have his tongue as far into her mouth as she could pull it.

"With a welcome like this, I may quit work and just hang around here," he said when she finally released him. "By the way, I was over at Petra's house tuning Krista's new piano, and Petra asked me to send her regards to you and the boys. I didn't know she'd had any contact with you."

"We've talked twice," Carla said. "I like her, and the boys like her, too." He raised an eyebrow. "Don't you remember Krista cooked chili for them and sent us some."

"I remember about the chili, but I didn't realize they ate it at Petra's house."

Carla frowned. "Surely you don't mind."

"Of course not. I'm marveling at how things fell into place without my having to bother about it," he said.

"I suppose that was inevitable; Krista likes having brothers, and Peter and Paul like having a big sister, especially since they know she's so fond of them. They learn from her, too. Would you believe I was taking out the trash and Peter jumped up and said, 'I'll do that'? I'm still getting used to seeing them clean the kitchen after supper. She's good for them."

"Yes. Funny. I used to be glad we only had boys." He wanted to get off the subject of family and to keep Carla in the mood she was in when she opened the door. "Come on, woman," he said, "feed your hungry man." He didn't deserve to be so happy, and in the future, he meant to keep it between the lines.

"I hope you're not going to start something up with Goodman again," Lena said to Petra at dinner. "He had his chance and didn't do a thing about it." Petra heard Krista place her fork on the side of her plate, but she didn't glance in her daughter's direction.

"Mama, Goodman is married. We have a daughter in common, but that's all. I respect him, and he respects me, but I don't even feel sisterly toward him. He's good to Krista, and he's good for her. End of topic."

"Thank the Lord," Krista said. "That would be weird. Besides, you're in —"

"Krista, that's enough."

Lena looked at her granddaughter. "What were you going to say?"

"According to Mom, I've already said enough. We have banana pudding for dessert. Who wants some?"

Petra couldn't help laughing. Krista could change a conversation with such finality that you didn't dare return to the rejected topic.

"I'll have some," she said, "but not too much. My weight is exactly where it should be."

"Well, mine's not," Lena said, "but I'm sure going to have a healthy helping of that pudding."

After dinner, Lena watched the news on television and then went to her room, saying that she had to get up early. Krista practiced the piano. Suddenly, as if she'd been dropped into a well of loneliness, Petra had to fight tears, and the more she tried to stop their flow, the more difficult it became. On the way to her room, she saw the telephone book, picked it up, and found the Oakland, California, area code.

"I can't do it," she told herself, but she got Winston's number nonetheless and dialed it. As she listened to the ring, she thought her heart would bound out of her chest, but slowly, when he did not answer, futility and despair descended over her. She hung up and gave in to her feelings.

However, the faint sound of a knock on the back door rescued Petra from the torment that was about to conquer her. She rushed to the bathroom, splashed cold water on her face, and ran down the stairs. It didn't surprise her that Ethel stood at the back door, but Petra would not have dreamed that her friend would be dressed up and wearing makeup.

"Hi, Ethel," Petra said. "I almost didn't hear you."

"Sorry to bother you so late and all, but I was wondering if you had any chili peppers."

Petra imagined that her eyes doubled in size. "Did you say chili peppers?"

"Well, I stewed some collards for supper, and Fred loves them with real hot chilies, so —"

Petra interrupted her. "Fred? Fred's over at your place? Since when? Is he back to stay?"

Ethel fastened her gaze on the steps beneath her feet. "He say he is. He say Armena fuss at him all the time about where he put his shoes and his soiled laundry and things. He say she ain't ever quiet. Maybe all that's true, and maybe it ain't."

Petra swallowed hard, trying to find something to say. Finally, she managed. "I guess constant talk would get on anybody's nerves. Come on in and let me see if I have any peppers. Mama likes them, so she could have put some in the refrigerator." She found a bag of chilies in the vegetable crisper, wrapped a few, and gave them to Ethel.

"I'm glad Fred's back," she told Ethel.

"Now you won't be alone." And she'd feel less guilty.

"I don't know, Petra. Right now, he sitting at the table waiting for his friggin' supper, and I keep asking myself, who's this little old man who thinks I'm suppose to wait on him while he sits on his ass and don't even set the table." She looked into the distance. "Petra, I never used to think like that. Well, thanks a lot."

Petra watched Ethel drag herself home, as if she'd rather go anyplace but there. *If only I'd kept my mouth shut, Ethel never would have found out how dull, boring, and selfish Fred is.* Will I have to carry this guilt for the rest of my life?

She raced after Ethel. "All this is my fault. I'm so sorry. If only I hadn't —"

Ethel spun around and stared at Petra. "Your fault? How's it your fault? Fred ain't worth chicken poop and never has been, but I'd lived with him so long I got used to him. I thought I missed him while he was away, but he wasn't back here half an hour before I was sick of him. Thanks, again." Petra went back into her house, shaking her head in bemusement.

She left home the next morning prepared to walk at a fast clip and stopped short when she saw Fred rushing out of Ethel's house with a suitcase in his hand and his shoulders sagging as if he carried the weight of centuries.

"And this time, don't come back," Ethel yelled. Pretending not to see the unfolding drama, Petra walked on until a white garment whizzed past her head.

"Take your old drawers," Ethel screamed. "Ain't no man getting somethin' for nothin' here. And wash your dirty feet."

Petra looked toward the house where Ethel stood with her back to the door and her knuckles fastened to her hips. "You never was no bargain," she yelled after Fred, piling on another insult.

Alarmed, Petra rushed to Ethel. "You sure you're not taking this too far, Ethel? I mean . . . You'll be lonely by yourself."

Ethel sucked her teeth and rolled her eyes. "Armena kicked him out, and he's a liar if he says she didn't. He thought that after fornicating with her for months, he could move back in my house and half an hour later start jumping up and down on me. He never was no good at that anyway. Shucks, I'd rather watch TV and eat pretzels."

"Oh, Ethel. I'm sorry."

"Humph! Wasted sympathy. I made fresh coffee. You got time for a cup?"

She didn't have time for coffee, but she

went inside anyway, drank one cup, put the scones she was offered into her briefcase, and made it to work with less than five minutes to spare.

As soon as she'd finished transcribing her notes from the previous session, she telephoned Goodman. "Hi, this is Petra. If I'm going with you to take Krista to Howard, would you please tell Carla, and ask her to come along. I want to have good relations with her, and that means respecting her. She is, after all, my daughter's stepmother. And Goodman, please don't do anything that causes her to feel excluded."

"You're right on all counts, and I hadn't even thought about it. The boys told us you said they're free to come to your place whenever they like, and I thank you for that. Krista's showing them that obedience isn't a bad thing. Peter can be obstinate, and she's already taught him how to snow Carla and get what he wants by being a loving and helpful son rather than by confronting her."

"I'm so happy that it's working out, Goodman. What time do we leave Saturday morning?"

"I should be at your place around ten-thirty. See you then." She told him goodbye, hung up, and opened her mail. She gazed at a subpoena requiring her to witness for the prosecution against the man who stalked her with the intention, in her opinion, of influencing her recording of his testimony.

"Why is that case on the docket so early?" she asked the court clerk.

"It has to be decided whether he's guilty of jury tampering and of stalking you before the other case can go forward."

The following Monday morning, Petra — the happy mother of a Howard University freshman — took the stand as the prosecution's second witness against Marvin Powell. She let her gaze travel over the members of the jury, more out of daily habit than purpose, but it locked on one juror, a woman who she would have recognized anywhere. She had to do something, so she began to cough and continued coughing until the judge ordered a recess until after lunch.

When the clerk brought her a glass of water, she told him, "Tell the DA he has to get Gail Norris off that jury. She's going to vote against whoever my testimony supports."

The woman narrowed her eyes. "All right, I'll tell him, but if the judge finds out you faked that coughing fit —"

"I didn't fake it; I always react that way when I'm alarmed."

A few minutes later, the clerk returned. "The DA wants to see you in the judge's chambers."

"What is this about? It had better be good," the DA said.

She told them that she had previously worked at a real estate agency owned by Jack Watkins. "He appeared to have a crush on one of his employees, Gail Norris. Not remembering that he was excessively homophobic, I told him he was wasting his time chasing Gail because she was Sally Kendall's bird. He went berserk, fired Gail, and demoted Sally, who hates me. She didn't make enough money on her lowered salary to support Gail, and Gail left her."

A frown beclouded the judge's face. "I see. Since you're a key witness, this may affect the trial."

"I'd like to see her replaced," the DA said.

After lunch, the jury returned to the courtroom, and Petra breathed more deeply for she saw that a man had replaced Gail. She completed her testimony for the day, locked her office, and started down the carpeted corridor. A second later, she lay sprawled on the floor, a pain in her head, and the sound of familiar giggles ringing in her ears. She managed to sit up, but saw no one until, after a few seconds, a woman and a small boy emerged from the ladies' room facing her.

"You all right?" the woman asked her.

Petra nodded. "Did you see a woman wearing a red jacket and dark pants in the ladies' room?" Petra asked the woman.

"Yes, ma'am," the little boy said. "I saw her."

Petra thanked the boy, pulled herself up, and reached for the door as Gail was coming out of it. She blocked Gail's exit. "If you plan to be a criminal, Gail, you'll have to change that giggle of yours. I knew it was you who tripped me up, because I heard you laugh. I should report you to the court, but you're off the jury, and that's what counts. Mess with me again, and it will be my pleasure to have you prosecuted for it." She had the satisfaction of seeing Gail's bottom lip tremble and her gaze dart from place to place like someone cornered. "Have a nice day, Gail."

Petra closed Krista's piano and opened the windows to let the rain-refreshed air blow through the house. Goodman had warned her that dampness affected a piano's tone. Yellow, purple, and golden leaves covered her front lawn and her backyard, giving her the first inkling of what her life would be like without Krista, who enjoyed raking the autumn leaves.

"I need to get on with my life," she said to herself.

That laboratory's error, Barnes's bad judgment, and what happened during those long months when I thought I could die at any minute are still circumscribing my life, impacting practically all my thoughts and nearly everything I do. I can't wallow in that forever. A lot of good came out of it. I did have a tumor, and a doctor removed it. I had the most wonderful experiences out West, met a wonderful man and, for the first time in my life, I knew real love. To top it off, I'm a hundred thousand dollars richer, my daughter's father loves her and is paying for her university education, and she knows and loves her brothers. I said I was going to college, and I'm going to do exactly that.

Petra remembered Goodman's advice about getting a car, so she phoned a car rental agency and asked about cars for sale. "If you can wait about ten days," a man told her, "we'll be selling this year's models. They'll all be in top condition."

"Then why are you selling them?" she asked.

"Because we only rent current models. If you want a car that's been leased, that's a different proposition. We don't lease cars."

"I was told to go to a rental agency."

"Great. If you come to the office, I'll get a good one for you, but I can't promise a specific color."

"Just so it isn't red."

The man laughed. "We don't have red cars. That's the first thing a state trooper looks for."

She took his name and made an appointment to see him that afternoon. Then, she went to the local library and got half a dozen catalogs of schools offering degree programs for part-time students, and began examining them. With her notebook crammed with information on special degree programs, Petra headed to the car rental agency. When she left there, she had committed herself to the purchase of a comparatively new Ford Taurus.

So buoyed was she that she sat on the agency steps and telephoned Lurlene. "I know you're busy at work right now, but you and Twylah come over tonight, and let's play a few games of pinochle. I could use some relaxation. Mama's barbecuing some spareribs and that, with some rice, sweet potatoes, and turnip greens ought to do it."

"Works for me. I got half a caramel cake I made day before yesterday, and I'll bring that for dessert."

"You ate half a cake in two days?" Petra asked her.

Lurlene treated her to a lusty laugh. "I don't want poor Twylah to feel bad about that blubber she carries around, so I decided to gain a little weight."

"Lurlene, you shouldn't say such things about Twylah."

"She weighs almost three times as much as I do, and it never seems to bother her. I'm not only going to jab her till she loses some of that blubber, but I'm going to turn the knife."

"You expect her to pass up that caramel cake?"

"If she doesn't, it won't be no skin off my teeth. *I* only weigh a hundred and twenty-seven."

So much for consistency, Petra thought. After she hung up, she remembered the last time she'd played pinochle with her two friends and how dissatisfied she'd been with them and their attitudes and outlook. They hadn't been too happy with her, either. *Lord, I hope I haven't just made a mistake.*

She headed home, her spirits high in spite of her dread of the evening. "How are you,

Mama?" she called when she smelled the pork roasting in the oven. "Lurlene and Twylah are coming over tonight, and Lurlene's bringing what's left of her caramel cake."

"Yeah? Well, you call her right now and tell her I said don't gobble up half of what's left and come here with a sliver. She knows I love that cake."

"She said she had half a cake."

"If she come here with less, she's getting none of this barbecue."

Petra laughed. Her mama was in a good mood, and at such times, Petra enjoyed being with Lena. "Mama, would you believe that after all this time, I finally signed my name on the dotted line for a car? It's a used one, but it'll be in great condition."

Lena whirled around with the wooden kitchen spoon shaking like an admonishing finger in front of her. "You go 'way from here, child. Well, if we ain't finally gon' be big shots! Wonder what old Miss Laura'll say about that? Sure, she'll swear a man gave it to one of us.

"That old woman's been a jackass for years. When I got pregnant with you, she went to my father's house and asked him if I was 'in the family way' as she put it. My poor father ran her out of the house. Mama had to stop him from nearly jumping out the second-floor window." Lena sighed at the memory. "At least I wasn't the one who told him. She did me a favor though; two days later, your father and I got married."

She'd just given Petra a chance to ask a question that had puzzled her for years. "Since you went through that, why were you so hard on me?"

Lena put the spoon in the sink and sat down at the little kitchen table. "After your daddy ran off with Myrtle, I had a hard life raising you, with no help from anybody. I worked, paid a sitter, went to school, did all my cleaning, laundry, shopping, you name it. Sometimes I was so tired, I thought I'd fall apart. And we hardly ever had enough. I could see you going through the same thing, and the thought nearly killed me."

"Didn't Grandma help you?"

"She wanted to, but Papa wouldn't let her. He said I made my bed hard, and I should lie in it. That's why I did what I could to make your life easier than mine was. In those days, I'd never heard of a father paying child support. But it didn't matter, your daddy was woman and motorcycle mad. He loved that Harley more than he loved me — or Myrtle — and one day, after he left here with that strumpet, an eighteen-wheeler knocked him off it. You were barely a year old."

Petra went over to her mother and hugged her, something she rarely did, for Lena was not demonstrative. To her astonishment, Lena put both arms around her and held her close.

"I don't often say so," Lena whispered, "but you've always been precious to me. You . . . You remind me so much of him that even now sometimes, I can hardly bear it. He was everything to me. I still miss him."

Petra fought back the tears. Would she still love Winston Fleet thirty-six years from now, and would memories of him hurt her so much that she could hardly bear the pain? She patted Lena's shoulder and went out into the garden, but seeing Ethel's solitary figure in the ghostly twilight exacerbated her loneliness. If only she could see him, touch him. . . . She whirled around and went back inside. If only! A lot of good wishful thinking did.

Chapter Fourteen

Petra enjoyed dinner with Lurlene, Twylah, and her mother because there'd been no incident that might have marred it. If she hadn't been anxious throughout the meal that Lurlene would either comment about Twylah's weight and eating habits or make a caustic remark about Petra's five weeks' "vacation," she would have been able to pay proper homage to her mama's barbecued pork loin. She breathed deeply and let herself relax. She needed her friends, and the way in which their relationship had cooled almost to nonexistence following her return from vacation distressed her. Lurlene had displayed a viciousness of which she wouldn't have thought her friend capable, and only because Petra had refused to turn her guts inside out for Lurlene's perusal. She attempted to bring back some of the old, natural camaraderie.

"Imagine me, a nobody, with a daughter

in Howard University," she said and lifted a card table to begin unfolding it. "Not even in my day dreams did I conjure up that scenario."

"You must be doing something right, girl," Twylah said. "People always say Howard is 'the capstone of Negro education.' Not bad for a working mom."

"Miss Lena, let's you and me clean the kitchen while Petra and Twylah set up the game," Lurlene said.

Lurlene's cynicism had on more than one occasion brought a vile epithet from Petra's lips. She could understand only a word or two of what the younger of the two women said in the kitchen, and when her mother didn't answer, but began humming instead, Petra's antenna shot up. Lena did that to express annoyance.

When the two women returned to the dining room, Lena treated Petra to a withering look. "I would have thought that you had explained to your two *best* friends" — she emphasized the word "best" — "why you took a vacation, what you did while you were gone, and who you did it with. Good night, y'all."

Twylah looked at Lurlene. "Looks like you tore it real good."

Petra didn't try to stifle the gasp that

escaped her. *So Lurlene volunteered to help in the kitchen hoping for a chance to pick Mama's brain. I should have known better.* "If you want to know my business, Lurlene," Petra said. "Ask me. I don't share my private affairs with my mother." She ground her teeth, squeezed, opened, and squeezed her fists again. "Look. I don't really feel like playing cards tonight." Petra knew that if she didn't play with them, she was in effect ending the friendship, and that didn't appeal to her. She looked at Twylah, her favorite of the two. "Are you going to forgive me, if I don't play tonight?"

Twylah tempered the effect of her shrug with a wink. "You know me, girl. I'm with you sink or swim."

"I . . . uh . . . I'm sorry, Petra," Lurlene said. "I shouldn't have done that. I'm real sorry about it. Miss Lena's totally ticked off, and you're so mad you're sizzling. I don't have to know everything."

"You definitely don't," Twylah said. "Half the people we know are speculating about where Petra went and why, and you want to know so you can gossip. That's why I don't tell you my business."

"All right. We're not going to have a fight," Petra said. "Lurlene, deal the cards."

Later that night, alone in her room, she

admitted that they'd lost their confidence that each was important to the others and that each bore the other's sisterly love. *Who would have thought there could be so many drastic changes in my life in so short a time?*

The next morning, Sunday, Petra went to church with her mother. As they left the church, the Reverend Collins approached. "Good morning, ladies. It's a blessing to see the two of you here together. Sister Petra, you never did tell me whether you're still walking in the shadows, or whatever. You know the conditions for granting absolution."

She decided not to upbraid him in her mother's presence for violating a trust. "Reverend, I'm sure I'll need absolution till the day I die. How's the building fund coming along?"

"Slow but sure. People put their needs before the Lord's needs."

Petra handed him a twenty-dollar bill. "Good day, Reverend. I'll bet the building fund never sees that twenty dollars," she said to her mother. Petra took Lena's arm and headed home, a short, six-block walk.

"There you are. It wasn't enough to get Gail fired from her job, you had her kicked off the jury. You're lucky I don't tar your pretty face."

Petra looked at Sally Kendall's twisted face, narrowed eyes, and rapidly drawn breaths. "Did Gail tell you what she did to me in court, Friday? And did she say I didn't report her — yet?" Sally stared at Petra, obviously confused. "She tripped me up, and I fell flat on my face. I could have been seriously injured. I have a witness, too."

Crestfallen, Sally said, "She didn't tell me that."

"Are the two of you back together?" Petra asked her, hoping she'd say yes.

"She came back to me, but with Gail, you never know what will happen next."

"But at least she's back for now. Sally, this is my mother, Lena Fields."

"I'm glad to meet you, Ms. Fields," Sally said, extending her hand.

"Likewise," Lena said, and made the handshake a brief one.

"Someday, you'll tell me what that was about," Lena said as they walked home.

"Yes. I hope that's the end of it. Jack fired Gail when I told him that she and Sally were lovers."

"Why?" Lena wanted to know. "It wasn't no skin off his teeth."

"That's where you're wrong. He had the hots for Gail."

"Enough said!"

The encounter with Sally should have made her feel better, but Petra couldn't seem to lift herself out of the dumps.

Many of the problems that plagued Petra as recently as a few weeks earlier had been resolved or, for various reasons, had become less important, but a restlessness, a troubling discontent continued to envelop her. At times, the wretchedness amounted to unremitting pain. She knew its true source, but she was also aware that only time could diminish it, for nothing and no one other than Winston Fleet could heal it, and he was lost to her.

She sat in court that morning recording the proceedings mechanically, without much interest in her surroundings, and in the back of her mind there formed the decision to register for college the following semester. Happier than she'd been in weeks, thanks to her decision, she stopped herself as laughter almost spilled out of her.

Two loud, popping sounds alerted her to her surroundings, and she looked up as three men dived toward another who stood in the aisle with his hands in front of him holding a gun. She heard another popping sound and dashed behind the waist-high wall in front of the witness stand. Two guards led the armed man out of the courtroom.

"The trial will continue after a fifteen minute recess," the judge said, having first determined that the shots hadn't hit anyone.

"Who was that guy?" Petra asked a court officer.

"He's the brother of the man you testified against last week."

"Then he was shooting at me?"

"Don't get upset," the clerk said, "I don't think he was shooting at you. All the shots landed on the other side of the courtroom, near the judge."

Perspiration beaded on her forehead. "Why doesn't that make me feel more secure?"

"Don't worry about it," said the clerk, who resembled a heavyweight fighter in size and confidence. "That Joe will spend a long time either in an asylum or a jail." She thanked him, but when she left the courthouse that day, she would look over her shoulder, nonetheless.

Her cell phone rang as she sat in her office later that day. "Petra Fields speaking. You have? I can? Oh, my goodness! I'll be there about quarter past five. Thanks a million." She hung up and looked at the clock.

Eleven-twenty. In six hours, she'd have her car. When her workday finally ended, she all but ran from the courthouse and took a taxi to the car rental agency's used car showplace.

"Gee, it's beautiful," she told the salesman of the four-door, glistening white Mercury Montego. "I thought I was getting a Ford. This is a much better deal than the one you first offered, a better car for the same money."

"When it came in, I thought of you at once," the salesman said. She got in, drove the car around the block, and brought it back to the man.

"You have my down payment," she said and wrote a check for the remainder of the price. "I want to be able to say I don't owe anybody a red cent," she added with pride. Only a few weeks earlier, she'd been mired in debt and unable to see her way out of it. Never again; if she couldn't pay for it, she wouldn't buy it.

The brother showed her a perfect set of white teeth. "You won't catch me saying no to honest money. Enjoy it."

She got into the driver's seat, closed the door, hooked her seat belt, leaned back in her car, and grinned. She looked at the registration. It was hers all right. She headed past the B&O Railroad Station, the oldest railroad station in America, thinking that whoever planned Ellicott City didn't really have a city in mind and that its quaint beauty happened accidentally. She arrived at the Baltimore Center for Wellness after using twice the amount of gasoline that a straight route would have required. She waited in front of the building until she saw her mother emerge from the front door and honked the horn.

"Mama," she called, but Lena didn't look in her direction. After calling once more to no avail, she yelled, "Lena!" and opened the front door.

Lena approached with both hands on her hips. "Well, do tell! I thought you'd bought a little old secondhand car. This is brand new, and it's a big one, too. Well, I never!"

"It's a used one, Mama. I thought I'd give you a ride home."

"Cloudy as it's getting, I'm sure glad you did. Well, I do declare if we ain't got a car in the family. Can you beat this!"

"Now, I can drop you off at work."

"That'll save me a lot of bus fare. I was gon' stop by the market and get some sage sausage for supper, but —"

"We can drop by there," Petra said, aware that her mother hadn't nagged her about it as was her habit. "What else do we need?"

"Well, while we're there, we could get some wild catfish. It tastes a lot better than the fish they cultivate down in Mississippi. You probably can't park around there, so I'll get it," Lena said.

Petra sat in the car waiting for her mother and wondering what had happened to change the woman's attitude. Ever since . . . So *that* was it! The source of Lena's seeming contentment hit her suddenly, like a flash of lightning in a black sky. Being asked to live with her daughter and granddaughter had made her feel wanted.

"Did they have any sausage, Mama?" she asked when Lena returned with her parcels.

"Sure did, and they'd just made it. And these catfish looked as if they'd come out of the water, so I got some collards and sweet potatoes. We'll have a feast."

An hour later as Lena cooked and hummed in the kitchen, Petra set the table in the dining room, thinking how much happier they could have been together if she had understood her mother's emotional needs and personality. She answered the telephone.

"Hi, Mom. Guess what?"

"How are you, honey? Are you all right?"

"Everything's super. Peter and Paul are

coming over to see me this weekend, and Dad's going to take us on a tour of the city. Imagine me in the White House."

"That's wonderful. Give them all my regards. I want you to have a good time, but remember why you're there."

"Yes, ma'am. I'm planning to make the Dean's List. If I make good grades, I'll get into a lot of things, maybe even have a chance to spend a year abroad. It's real deep, Mom. Only a dork is stupid enough to flunk out of college. What's Grandma doing?"

She released a breath of pure contentment; Krista's head was still clear and straight. "Your grandmother is in the kitchen humming and cooking up a blue streak."

"Don't tell me. I can practically smell it. Gotta go. Bye."

"Was that Krista? How's she doing?" Lena called.

"That was Krista, Mama, and she's as level-headed as ever."

"Thank God. I wish I'd had half of her sense when I was her age. Be ready to eat in fifteen or twenty minutes."

Petra started up the stairs but turned back when the doorbell rang. Anxious for her safety in light of the incident at the courthouse that morning and also remembering the witness from whom Peter and Paul had protected her a few weeks earlier, she eased Krista's fencing foil from its holder and went to the door. When the bell rang again, she slipped on the chain and cracked open the door.

"Who is it?"

"Is Petra Fields here? I'm Winston Fleet."

The foil dropped from her left hand, barely missing her foot. *"Who . . . What did you say?"*

"Petra. Sweetheart, please open the door."

"Winston? Winston! Oh, my Lord! Winston!" she screamed.

Lena came running from the kitchen holding a plastic spatula in front of her. "What's the matter? Who is it?"

"Oh, my goodness!" Petra said as awareness returned and, with it, her common sense. She slipped off the chain, flung the door wide open, and gaped at Winston. There he stood. In person. She opened her mouth, but not a word escaped. She stared at him, trembling uncontrollably.

Then, he smiled, opened his arms, and she dived into them, living once more the magic, the wonder of being in his arms, arms as strong as she remembered, and his body as warm and as protective as it had been all those months ago.

He locked her to him. Fiercely. Possessively. His words, "I love you," soft and sweet were like fresh spring water in summer heat, giving her life.

"Me too. Me too," she said, and tears streamed from her eyes as she sobbed his name. "Winston. Oh, Winston."

He stared down into her face. "When I realized that you'd left me, I went half crazy. Don't you understand what love means? I'm here for you for whatever time you have left. Let me share these days with you? I *need* to be with you to the end."

She remembered then that he didn't know and gently pushed away from him. "Winston, I'm all right now. I'm well."

He stared at her until she could see doubt replacing compassion. "What are you saying? I thought —"

She put her right index finger to his lips. "I continued down the coast to Santa Cruz, and then I got an urge to go home. But I wanted to see the King Historic Site, so I went first to Atlanta to pay my respects to that great man. I passed out on the street in front of Dr. King's tomb and woke up in a hospital."

"And?" Winston said, his whole body seemingly primed for the news. He didn't breathe.

"The head neurological surgeon there didn't agree with my original diagnosis. He said the tumor was operable, and he removed it. It was benign, and I'm fine."

Like a man strung out, he slumped against her. Then, he straightened up to his full height and, with his eyelids squeezed tight, held her close. "Thank God. I prayed, but only to see you again. I didn't dare ask for this."

"Y'all acting like this right in the front door? Petra, for goodness sake, who is this man? Come inside here, mister. What the neighbors gon' think?"

Winston loosened his hold on Petra sufficiently to extend a hand to Lena. "I'm Winston Fleet, and I think you answered the phone when I called here one night about six weeks ago. I apologize if I woke you up."

Lena looked from Winston to her daughter. "Hmm. I wish you'd told me your name."

A grin crawled over his face. "I couldn't. You hung up."

"Well, come on inside," Lena said. "I hope you're hungry, 'cause we just fixin' to eat."

Winston gazed down into Petra's eyes, drawing her to him as a magnet draws a nail, telling her without words that food was not on his mind. And as if of its own volition, her left hand reached up, caressed his cheek, and then urged his face toward hers. His mouth touched her lips, shivers shot through her, and she didn't try to control her shattered emotions as she trembled in his arms. His hands roamed over her arms, back, and shoulders as if reacquainting themselves with her body.

Lena cleared her throat. "You'd better wash your hands and come to the table, Winston, before this gets out of hand and my supper gets cold."

"Yes, ma'am," he said. He walked over, kissed Lena's cheek, and grinned when her mouth became a gaping hole. "Where's the washroom?"

"Right around here," she told him and beckoned him to follow her.

Petra watched them as one would observe any unfolding drama or Broadway play, as an onlooker who had no role in the proceedings. So many times she had dreamed of being with Winston again and now, he was here. But was it real, or had she begun to hallucinate? She plodded toward the dining room and heard the water running in the bathroom. Yes, he was there in her house. How had she ever thought she could live without Winston Fleet?

Lena put the food on the table, and the three of them sat down. After she offered the grace, Winston grasped their hands. "Lord, I didn't dare ask for what you've given me, but I accept it with thanks, and I'll try to take good care of it."

"Help yourself," Lena said to Winston, "and then you two can tell me what's going on here."

Winston told Lena their story. "All I knew was that she lived in a place called Ellicott City, and that she could be suffering someplace without friends or family to care for her. You can't imagine how relieved I am."

Lena passed him a plate of hot buttered biscuits. "When she was telling me about her trip, she managed to skip everything about you. It's all right, though. I'm glad you found her. If it had been me, I'd'a gone looking for you soon as that doctor said I was out of danger."

"I wanted to," Petra said, "but considering the way I left him, I figured he'd gone on with his life. I did look up his number and call his house about a week ago, but no one answered, and I didn't leave a message."

"I'd already left home with you as my final destination. I meant to find you or someone who knew what had happened to you."

"What do you do for a living, Winston?" Lena asked him.

"I design modern furniture and home furnishings, ma'am."

"I see. Do you make a living at it? Here. Have another piece of this catfish."

"Thanks. My grandmother's the only other person I know who can cook like this. These biscuits are unbelievably good, and this fish . . . Well . . . This meal is wonderful. Oh." He stopped eating and looked directly at Lena. "Yes, ma'am. I make a very good living. I own my home, and I built a really nice home for my grandmother about ten miles from my place."

"Excuse me for a few minutes," Petra said, went to her room and returned wearing the gold ring that Winston gave her.

When he saw it, his eyes sparkled. "You still have it?"

"Of course." She handed Lena the picture taken of them in the restaurant beside the waterfall.

"You look nice together," Lena said. "Well, Winston, I can see you're a solid man, but I hate to think of my only child so far from me."

"Plan to retire in Oakland, ma'am. I'll see that you don't want for anything."

"I believe you." Lena went to the kitchen

and returned with a raspberry trifle topped with vanilla ice cream.

After supper, Winston cleared the table as if he'd done it there for years. "I'll put the dishes in the dishwasher while you two talk about me," he said with a wink.

"He's really something," Lena said. "Just imagine having a man like that one!"

"I know." What Petra was about to say wouldn't come out easily, for her mother was straight-laced, but she'd say it anyway. "Mama, if he's registered in a hotel, I'm going with him, and I'll see you tomorrow."

"I kind of expected that," Lena said. "Remember that when you give away everything, you got nothing left to bargain with."

At the moment, bargaining was not on Petra's mind; time enough for that when he offered something.

"Kitchen's clean, at least by my standards," Winston said when he joined them in the living room. He sat on the sofa beside Lena and took both of her hands in his. "This is probably improper, ma'am, but I do everything aboveboard. I'm registered at the Longacre, and I want to take Petra with me when I leave here."

Lena eyeballed him and, to Petra's delight, Winston didn't flinch. "That doesn't surprise me," she said, stood, and patted Winston's shoulder. "Y'all grown people. Come back to supper tomorrow. Good night."

Petra stared at her mother's departing back, her eyes wide and mouth agape. Lena Fields had just given Winston Fleet her blessings. He stood, spread his arms, and she didn't wait for a verbal invitation. Wrapped in his embrace, she knew she'd been right, that she loved him and belonged with him.

"This is weird," he said, and she could feel the tension in him. "My grandmother's psychic. She said you'd come back to California, and that I shouldn't give up."

"That's right. She also told me I'd be back there, but I didn't give it any credence. I need to call my daughter."

He handed her his cell phone, and she dialed Krista's number. "How are you, honey? How're things going?"

"Great, Mom. What about you and Grandma?"

"Top of the world, hon. Do you remember my telling you that I fell in love with someone in California? He found me. He's right here, and I'm so happy."

"What? Get outta here! You're kidding."

"I'm not. Winston, come say hello to Krista."

"Hello, Krista. I'm glad to have a chance

to speak with you."

"Me, too. You be good to my mom. She was broken up about you."

"Believe me, I was, too. Don't worry. She's precious to me, and I'll treat her that way."

Petra took the phone. "Are you concentrating on your studies?"

"Yes, ma'am. Would you believe I got a bid from the Deltas?"

"That's wonderful. Take it. We'll handle the cost."

"Thanks, Mom. Give Winston and Grandma a hug good night."

With his arm around Petra's waist, Winston asked her, "Will you spend the night with me?"

"I'll have to put a few things in a bag."

She wondered at his frown. "Do you want to go with me? Do you love me, Petra?"

His questions surprised her. "How can you ask? Yes, I love you, and yes, I want to be with you as much as you want to be with me." She turned to go up the stairs, paused and looked back, as if to see whether he was still there. Seeing him in her home continued to rattle her. She had to snap out of it. At the top of the stairs, she turned left, and knocked on her mother's bedroom door.

"Come in."

"Mama, I know this shocked you. I'm still stunned."

"He's a good man, and he loves you. I couldn't ask for more for you. That radiologist at the lab did you a favor."

She leaned over, hugged and kissed her mother, and couldn't remember when she'd last done that. "See you tomorrow afternoon."

As she walked into that hotel with Winston, her thoughts went to the night months earlier, the one time they made love. Suppose it wasn't as she remembered and that her mind had tricked her into months of longing for him.

"I never thought I'd be in your arms again. I'd given up on you," Petra said to Winston.

"I never gave up. I couldn't." He put the key card in the lock and looked steadily at her. "Has there been . . . I mean is there anyone else?"

"There were opportunities, but I was never once close to being tempted. You were always on my mind and in my heart."

He slid the key card through the lock, opened the door, pushed her bag inside it, and walked in with her in his arms. She wrapped her arms around him and knew at last the unbridled joy of being with him again, of feeling his strength and passion. He held her away from him, stared down at her and, when a harsh groan tore out of him, she knew he felt what she felt.

"Love me," he said. "You're everything to me."

"I do love you, Winston, and I always will love you."

A smile brightened his face as his eyes shone like stars. Then his gaze darkened, and the storm in his eyes sent excitement roaring through her body. He gripped her buttocks with one hand and, with the other, he imprisoned her head, and at last she had his tongue deep in her mouth, possessing her. Her hot blood raced to her loins, and she twisted against him, seeking any friction that she could get. Exasperated, she placed his hand on her breast and, as if he suddenly remembered, he pulled her sweater over her head, released her left breast and sucked her into his warm mouth.

"Take me to bed. I want to feel you inside of me."

He stripped away her remaining clothes, lifted her, and placed her on the bed. As he stood above her, gazing at her and slowly peeling off his clothes, she thought she'd go mad.

"No. Let me look at you. I thought this was beyond me, and I . . . Sweetheart . . ."

She opened her arms to him. "Come here to me."

He kicked off his shoes, dropped himself into her waiting arms and, with all the niceties and foreplay forgotten, they went at each other the way a long-starved person goes at food. When she screamed her completion, a volcano rupturing around him, he shouted his release, spilling into her like a hot waterfall, and collapsed upon her.

"I didn't believe it could be this wonderful again," he said, breathing heavily. "Did you?"

"I didn't imagine we'd have the chance. It was . . . It couldn't have been any better." She reached up, clasped his nape, and kissed him.

Hours later, he opened the bar, uncorked a bottle of champagne, filled two flutes with it, and put the glasses on the night table beside the bed. Kneeling at the bed where she lay propped up by one elbow, he said, "I love you, Petra. Will you marry me? I'll do my best for you and our children, and I'll be faithful to you until my last breath."

"Oh, yes. I love you. I want to be your wife."

Silently, they sipped the champagne, alternately smiling at each other and shaking their heads, amazed at the turn their lives had taken. "If we're going to have a family, we should start soon," he said.

"I agree, and that reminds me. If I'm moving to the West Coast, I have to talk with Krista's father. Mama will live in the house and look after Krista when she's home from college on weekends, but it's best that her father have a clear picture of his role."

"Absolutely. What do you say I invite him to dinner with us?"

"Good idea, but shouldn't we invite Carla, his wife, as well? She and Krista have a good relationship."

"Right. Call him and make a date for dinner at a first class restaurant. Can Krista come home Saturday? If you'd like, we can go to Washington and get her."

"I'll let you know after I speak with her father. He's sending her to Howard, and I don't know what he has planned. The best food is at the Crab Shanty, nicest ambiance is at Pinnetta's."

He closed one eye and half laughed. "Ambiance would be fine if I planned to propose, but I've already done that. Let's go for the food." He thought for a minute. "Scratch that. Ladies like to dress up. We'd better go to Pinnetta's."

Taken aback by Petra's call, Goodman paced the floor in his studio office, wondering at her true reason for inviting him and Carla to dinner. "Look, Petra, if there's anything behind this, I want to know it now."

That didn't sound friendly, and she could accuse him of being suspicious of her, but he couldn't help it. He had everything going his way these days, and he didn't want anybody to toss a monkey wrench at him.

"There is something, Goodman, but I didn't know how to broach it to you. I'm moving to Oakland, California, where I plan to get married. I want to talk with you and Carla about arrangements for Krista and to introduce you both to my fiancé."

He stopped pacing, stared at the phone, and then relaxed. "Really? Well, hell! This is great news. Congratulations. I was planning to bring Krista home Friday night, but she just called to say she wanted to attend some kind of sorority shindig. Don't worry, babe. We'll look after Krista."

He knew Carla would love a chance to get dressed up, so he didn't hesitate to commit them. His surprise at seeing Petra elegant and beautiful in a red chiffon dinner dress equaled his shock in learning that he was the father of a seventeen-year-old daughter. This Petra had come a long way from the practical, almost dowdy woman he'd known, and one look told him she'd chosen a brother who had class.

He shook hands with Winston. "I'm glad to meet you. Congratulations. Petra is as fine a woman as there is. I wish you both much happiness." And he meant every word of it. Turning, he put an arm around Carla and tucked her close to his side. "Winston, this is Carla, my wife."

During the dinner, they spoke mainly of Krista, although Goodman wanted to know how and where Petra met a man like Winston Fleet. But he didn't ask; Krista would tell him.

"Will you bring Krista home to her grandmother every weekend?" Winston asked him. "If not, I can arrange for it."

This brother meant business, a man who handled responsibility the way a great general handled his troops. Goodman shook his head. "I'll do it. It's important that she knows I'm responsible for her, and that she can always depend on my being there for her. When she's in Oakland with you, you look after her."

"Fair enough," Winston said. "It will be my pleasure."

"When are you leaving?" Carla asked Petra.

"The day after Krista's birthday. That's ten days from now."

Carla leaned forward, her eyes sparkling with delight and anticipation. "Let's plan a big party for her." To Goodman's amazement, they immediately began exchanging ideas. Occasionally, Winston offered a suggestion. The more he saw of the man, the more reassurance he gained that the man would be a good influence on his daughter.

He leaned back in his chair, and the conversation around him became a low hum as he considered his good fortune. He had the love of his wife, his sons, and his daughter and the respect of those who knew him. All this in spite of his momentary foolishness when he almost threw it all away on Jada Hankins. He knew she'd leave him alone now, because she had what she wanted and what she had hoped to squeeze out of him. A member of the community chorus showed him her invitation to Jada's housewarming party to celebrate her new condominium. "You know Ralph Hayes, don't you?" the singer asked him. "He flipped over Jada and bingo! Jada has a condo."

Yes, he said to himself. Another married man set a trap for himself. He wondered how long Jada would be happy alone there while Hayes found one more lie to tell his wife in order to spend an hour or forty-five minutes with her. He felt sorry for both of them.

Ten days later, having shipped Petra's car and personal belongings to his home in Oakland, Winston Fleet stood with Petra in the Baltimore/Washington airport. He kissed his future mother-in-law and stepdaughter good-bye, shook hands with Goodman Prout, and took Petra's hand as they walked through the airport to security.

"I know this isn't easy for you, sweetheart, but I'll do everything within my power to see that you never regret it."

"How can I regret it? I'm leaving my family in good hands, and I'll be with the man I love and who loves me.

"You paid for first class seats?" she asked him as they sat down in the plane.

"I promised to do my best for you, and I meant it." He kissed the tears of joy that spilled down her cheeks.

EPILOGUE

Four years later, Petra and Winston walked through the Baltimore/Washington airport with their one-year-old twins. He carried their son, and she carried their daughter. Goodman, Carla, and Lena met them at the airport, and they traveled in Goodman and Carla's cars to Washington to attend Krista's graduation from Howard University with *magna cum laude* honors. Krista along with Peter and Paul — junior and freshman, respectively, at Howard University — met them at the Willard Hotel where they would stay during the graduation proceedings.

After registering and getting a nanny for the children, the two families sat in the hotel's lounge having high tea. "I'm surprised Krista didn't major in music," Lena said, her pride in her granddaughter obvious from her radiant face. "She plays so beautifully."

"She's naturally gifted," Goodman said.

"If she wants a degree in piano, all she has to do is take an exam. She'll be a great lawyer."

"You've done your job, Goodman," Winston told him, "and you still have to educate Paul and Peter for who knows how long. I'll send Krista to law school."

Petra gave silent thanks for her blessings. Until her daughter married or established a place of her own, she would continue to divide her time between her parents and her two sets of siblings. Old man Collins's advice had caused a lot of problems but, in respect to Goodman and her daughter, his counsel had been a wise and wonderful thing.

ABOUT THE AUTHOR

Gwynne Forster is an award-winning, national bestselling author. She is also a demographer and former senior United Nations Officer, in which capacities she has traveled the world. She lives in New York City. Visit her website at GwynneForster.com.

The employees of Thorndike Press hope you have enjoyed this Large Print book. All our Thorndike, Wheeler, and Kennebec Large Print titles are designed for easy reading, and all our books are made to last. Other Thorndike Press Large Print books are available at your library, through selected bookstores, or directly from us.

For information about titles, please call:

(800) 223-1244

or visit our Web site at:

http://gale.cengage.com/thorndike

To share your comments, please write:

Publisher
Thorndike Press
10 Water St., Suite 310
Waterville, ME 04901